# STORM OF PASSION

"A man delights in his wife, Johanna," he said, feeling her resist the pressure of his hands. "He delights in her beauty, in her touch, in touching her."

His breath came warm and soft against her face, and his eyes were fairly ablaze with the light of his inner flame as he pressed one of her trembling hands against the coarse, curling hair on his chest. She felt the wild hammering of his heart beneath it. He gently cupped her breast. "And, if she but allows herself, a wife can find much delight with her husband." With his lips touching her hair, he implored, "Do not impede me, Johanna. Let me delight you."

# EYE OF THE WIND
## Donna Gilmer

LEISURE BOOKS ∞ NEW YORK CITY

To my husband,
Jim,
and our children,
Traci, Aaron, Barry, Garrett and Nathan,
who encouraged me to pursue my dream
and bore with me while I did,
and to Mom,
who never doubted that I would succeed—
with all my love and gratitude.

A LEISURE BOOK

Published by

Dorchester Publishing Co., Inc.
6 East 39th Street
New York, NY 10016

Printed in the United States of America

# EYE OF THE WIND

# PART I

APRIL 1770 - AUGUST 1771

# 1

There would never be another day like this one. Not ever. Not in all her life. This day only came once to a girl—a woman. Unless, of course, she was unlucky. Or maybe lucky. Jane supposed it all depended on one's point of view. But however one chose to look at it, it only happened for the first time once. And it wasn't supposed to happen like this!

" 'Bout finished are ye, Jane?"

"Aye, Mam. Just done."

"Hold it up, then, so's I can have a look." Gently, Jane lifted the fragile wreath of wildflowers from the marred, petal-strewn kitchen table and displayed it on upturned palms. "Aw, that's pretty. Real pretty. Let's see it on."

Self-consciously, Jane laid the wreath on her head.

"Loose yer hair."

But when, freed from its thick plait, Jane's hair lay in crimped, sun-gold waves halfway down her back, Meg McPhee frowned and shook her head. Wiping floury hands on her much-mended apron, she crossed the room.

"Nay, gal. 'Twill be like so," she said, combing Jane's hair with her fingers and spreading it over the girl's shoulders. "There, now." She stepped back to better

judge the results. "Why, with yer hair like so and wearin'
that lacy bit of a shawl fastened with yer grandmam's
cameo . . . Oh, I vow, Jane, ye'll be the fairest bride ever
seen here'bouts! Ye'll set good Mr. Seymour's heart to
poundin' some, too. For a fact, ye will!"

Jane smiled weakly. She wasn't at all sure she wanted
to set Mr. Seymour's heart to pounding. She had seen
him only once; that more than a year ago and from afar.
She could recollect nothing more about him than that he
was a youngish man, tall, broad-shouldered and deep-
chested, with hair the color of chestnuts. And that he
carried himself proudly.

She remembered that proudness well enough! It had
shown in the way he walked and stood: easy-like but not
relaxed, with his head high and his back straight. He had
made Pap and her oldest brother Jacob look like the
poor relations they were, though they had worn their
best jerkins and breeches for the occasion of the gentleman's visit. She remembered thinking at the time that
even if he'd been dressed in simple clothes, Mr. Seymour would have looked grand. It was all in the way he
carried himself.

She had felt queer inside, watching him, seeing Pap
humbled and doffing his tricorn to a man. She had never
known Pap to take off his hat to anyone but ladies and
the Lord. And that last had been rare enough, seeing as
he hadn't been a churchgoer despite the parson's
efforts to persuade him to become otherwise. Parson
Dye used to come by the farm often—until the day Pap,
in his burring, Scottish brogue, had hotly quoted
Scripture at him. Since then, the parson hadn't been by
but twice.

Today would make the third time. Today he was
coming to do the marrying.

Jane tried not to think about that as she cleared away
the cluttered leaves and twigs remaining from the
construction of her bridal wreath. But she could only

wish that Parson Dye was coming for somebody else's wedding. And that Mr. Seymour had never come at all.

"Is he a good man, Mam? And kind, d'ye think?" she asked, needing to hear again the reassurances.

" 'Course he is, gal. A fine gentleman, indeed. He'll make ye a husband to be proud of!" Meg added more flour to her bread dough. "And he's kin to ye, too, don't forget: yer grandmam's sister's daughter's boy. That makes him yer second cousin. Or is it third?"

"But I don't know him, Mam!"

"Ye'll come to know him soon enough." She smiled encouragingly over a strong shoulder. "Be a good wife and he'll be a good husband. Be a cheery companion, submit yer will to his as it pleases the Lord ye should do, and ye'll bring happiness to the two of ye. And mind yer temper. Ye've more o' that than a man finds pleasin' in a wife." Meg's eyes suddenly swam with tears. "But ye're a good lass, Jane, and I'm loathe to see ye go."

"So'm I, Mam!" Throwing her arms about Meg's thick waist, Jane pressed herself hard against the full breasts which still nurtured the last of the McPhees' nine surviving children.

"There, now. There," Meg soothed. "I hadn't meant to say that. I've known this day was comin' and in my mind I'm ready for it. 'Tis my heart that's givin' the trouble." Holding the girl away from her, she raised Jane's tear-streaked face to her own. "Now, don't take on so. And don't be frettin' over us. We'll be gettin' on just fine. Why, Jacob and John are doin' a grand job of runnin' the place, and Julia and Jenny are of an age to be of help to me. We'll get on just fine!" Raising her eyes, Meg seemed to peer through the rough-hewn timbers of the ceilingless room and far into the Virginia sky. "What must yer Pap be thinkin' of us, gal? Here we be, weepin', while he's up there, smilin' down, happy that ye're to be so finely wed."

Jane forced a smile. "Aye. 'Twas all Polly could

speak of yesterday; how I'll be gentry after today."

"And so ye will be, too," Meg said, giving Jane a quick kiss on the cheek. "Here, now." She straightened the wreath, which had been knocked askew by their embrace. "Best put that by in the springhouse; won't do if it's wilted. And so long as ye'll be down there, fetch back the cream we've been puttin' by and call to one o' the boys to bring the ham in from the smokehouse. If I know anythin' I know yer weddin' guests are expectin' a feed!"

Jane knew that, too. What Meg pleased to call wedding guests were, in fact, a handful of neighbors who had endured as hard and hungry a winter as the McPhees. There had been no summer the previous year. Not one to speak of. Livestock hadn't bred well. Crops had been poor. Nothing had gone right. The farmers had scratched their heads in puzzlement, all the while they rubbed their empty bellies, trying to figure out what had gone wrong and what to do about it. They had never answered either question.

But 1770 looked to be better. Spring had come early and the menfolk had a good start on their plowing. Even though it was only mid-April, some of the neighbors had finished already and were lending her brothers a hand in clearing the new land Pap had bought before he died. Considering that, Jane supposed she ought not begrudge them a healthy meal. Truth be told, if this was anyone else's wedding day, she would be looking forward to the wedding feast herself!

Walking briskly back toward the house with the jug of cream hugged to her chest, Jane wondered if Mr. Seymour knew what it was to suffer hardship. Did he know how it felt to go to bed with his stomach so empty it hurt, or what it was like to have a supper of cornmeal mush and skimmed milk because the hunting was poor and the last ham in the smokehouse, like the precious cream, had to be saved for a wedding feast? By all accounts, he didn't. By all accounts, Mr. Seymour didn't want for much of anything.

Never considering that Mr. Seymour's good fortune would soon be hers, Jane deposited the jug on the kitchen table and set about kneading the bread.

"Mayhap he's not comin', Mam," Jane said quietly, her eyes on the empty, rutted cart track which passed for a road. " 'Tis past time for him to be here."

Meg stroked the cheek of the baby suckling at her breast. " 'Tis a long way to come, from Williamsburg. He can be excused his tardiness." A merry whoop followed by a burst of laughter reached them from the parlor below. Meg chuckled. "Seems as we're the only ones missin' him. The festivities sound to be gettin' cheerier since Jacob broke out the hard cider."

"But I'll be shamed if he doesn't come, Mam. Shamed! And in front of our friends!"

"Hush, Jane, the babe's sleepin'. Stop frettin'. He'll come."

Jane turned back to the window. As a reluctant but nonetheless anxious bride, she had it flung wide open to afford an unobstructed view of the countryside. "But if he doesn't, if he spurns me, I'll never be able to hold my head high again. I'll be a laughin' stock, Mam! Everybody'll say I wasn't good enough for the likes of . . ." But she left the sentence hanging and craned her neck for another glimpse of the something that had caught her eye across a newly furrowed field.

Breathlessly, she watched a rider appear over the crest of a hill and gallop full tilt across the knoll; not on the road but across country. With a grace she could not have imagined, horse and rider cleared the far fence of the cow pasture, gathered themselves, then flew over the near one. They disappeared briefly behind the out-buildings and when they reappeared it was at a leisurely trot, neither looking the least bit winded for all their impressive leaping about.

"Do ye see him, then?"

"Aye," came the breathy, awestruck reply, "I've never seen the like of it, Mam! He took the pasture fences. Flew over 'em like a leaf on the wind!" She turned wonder-filled eyes on the woman.

"I'd expect a breeder of horses could ride one." Laying the baby across her knees, Meg began to refasten her bodice.

Her attention back on the yard, Jane found that the marvelous pair had covered the considerable distance between barn and house in astonishing time. Mr. Seymour dismounted, flipped his horse's reins around the rim of a cartwheel in lieu of a hitching post, pulled off his gloves, and began dusting off his forest-green velvet coat.

Stunned by the richness of his costume, Jane watched him flounce the lace frill at his breast and the ruffles peeking from his coat sleeves. His breeches were of white satin and fitted him well, leaving no doubt of his manhood, and he dusted them off, too. Then, tugging a cloth from inside his coat, he braced each foot on the wheel hub in turn and bent to buff up the sheen on his high, black boots. Straightening, he stuffed both cloth and gloves under the pommel of his saddle, gave his coat and the gold brocade waistcoat under it a downward tug, then, with no hint of motion to forewarn her, he turned and stared straight up into Jane's admiring eyes. Before she could react, he touched a lean finger to the brim of his cockaded hat and disappeared under the eaves.

Jane's knees turned to water. Seen at close quarters, he was a most splendidly handsome man. And his eyes . . . Surely, it had been a trick of the light. No one had eyes that color!

"Mind Jeremiah for me whilst I greet yer bridegroom," Meg said, laying the drowsy infant on the straw pallet which would no longer serve Jane as a bed.

"Aye, Mam," Jane said numbly, not moving from the window.

She was still standing there, staring blindly down into the yard, when nineteen-year-old Jacob, the man of the family, brusquely announced from the doorway, " 'Tis time, Jane. D'ye hear? I said, 'tis time."

"Aye."

"Come along, then. And . . . see ye don't shame us, Jane."

Willing her feet to move, Jane crossed the room, scooped up the sleeping baby, and apprehensively followed Jacob downstairs.

No one noticed her standing uncertainly at the base of the stairs. All eyes were on the man across the room who stood, with his back to the rest of them, quietly conversing with Meg McPhee and Parson Dye. Following the stares, Jane thought that Jacob had delivered his warning to the wrong party. It was the elegantly garbed, majestically sized, regally deported Mr. Seymour who, by his very presence, seemed to shame them all.

"Why was I not informed?" Seymour demanded in a tone laced with surprise.

The parson looked uncomfortable and nervously ruffled the pages of the prayer book in his hand. It was the woman who answered. Jane strained to hear her mother's words to no avail. But whatever she had said apparently satisfied Mr. Seymour; he nodded slowly several times and said something in a low, gentle voice. Then, again without warning, he looked at Jane.

No cursory glance, this. From the bridal wreath on her head, his gaze slid slowly downward, taking in the sheen of her hair, the clarity of her wide-set blue eyes, and the rosiness of her complexion, all of which were certain signs of good health. Then he appraised the gentle swell of her bosom beneath the age-yellowed lace shawl with its cameo clasp before his eyes stopped short, riveted on the baby in her arms.

Over the spellbound hush filling the room, he said, "I
trust, miss, that is not yours."

Jane looked quickly down at the bundle which fitted
so comfortably into the crook of her arm that she had
forgotten she held it. Indignantly, but with a blush
heightening the color in her cheeks, she said, "Nay, sir!
'Tis my brother, if ye please."

Seymour smiled, and his teeth flashed white in his
shadowed face. "Oh, I am pleased, indeed. It gives me
great pleasure to know that I am expected to take on
but the one of you."

A nervous titter went up from the small assemblage,
and Jane flushed hotter. Julia, prompted by a neighbor
woman, rushed to relieve her sister of her embarrassing
burden.

Flustered to find that now she was the focus of
attention, Julia roughly snatched the child from Jane and
turned to hurry back to anonymity—all but colliding with
the towering Mr. Seymour. He was crossing the room,
intent on presenting himself to his bride. They played a
brief game of duck and dodge, each trying to sidestep
the other, until Mr. Seymour stood his ground; a benign
smile quirking the corners of his generous mouth as he
looked down his fine, straight nose at the girl. To the
accompaniment of the startled infant's bawling and the
good-natured laughter of the company, the mortified
girl finally made her escape.

With the obstacle between them removed, Jane
found herself staring dead center, at her betrothed's
broad chest. Tilting her head up at a sharp angle, she
defiantly met his eyes. But her boldness slipped away in
a sickening rush. It had been no trick of the light: His
eyes were golden. Amber. The color of oak leaves in
autumn.

"Damon Seymour, your servant," he said with a nod
and a bow. Then, with fingers far softer than her own, he

youngest, and accepted the strangely subdued farewells of her neighbors.

Then Parson Dye handed her an inked quill and pointed to two blank lines on a page otherwise filled with writing. "Sign here. Christian name; maiden surname. And here. Christian name; married surname." When he turned and offered his back for a table, Jane dully did as she was bidden, her mind on the painful farewell yet to come.

It came and went too quickly.

"I'll miss ye so, Mam!"

"Be happy, lass. God bless ye," Meg said, ending the brief embrace.

Jane was blinded by tears when Mr. Seymour handed her into the carriage and settled her on the front-facing seat. He took his place on the opposite one and, as soon as the driver was up behind him, wasted not a moment in saying, "Go, Eb!"

The landau, with Mr. Seymour's horse tied behind, made a wide arc in the farmyard, raising a powdery cloud of dust and setting the hounds in the kennel to baying. Jane wiped her eyes dry on a sleeve and turned to wave a last farewell.

"Don't look back!" The stridently voiced command snapped Jane's head around. "Look to me," Seymour said more quietly but no less firmly. "Look ahead."

The farther eastward they traveled, the cooler and cloudier the afternoon became. Somewhere toward the middle of it, when rain threatened and they had been jolting over the rugged, rutted road for hours, Mr. Seymour called to the driver to stop. Giving his wife a hand down, he instructed that the carriage be enclosed. Then he turned to the girl who stood staring miserably down at her shoes.

"Shall we walk?"

Taking that for another of his commands, Jane dutifully fell in step—two of hers to one of his—beside him. Without warning, he snatched the wilted, bedraggled-looking wreath from her head. Jane gasped and made a grab for it, but it had already left his hand and was sailing with the rising wind toward a clump of bushes.

"Why'd ye do that?" she demanded, glaring at him angrily.

"You've no more need of toadflax and buttercups. It will be roses and the fragrance of lilies for you from now on."

Tugging his hat securely down against the wind, he made his way toward a thicket close beside the road. Uncertain if he meant for her to follow or stay, Jane hesitated, then hastened to catch him up.

"If you please, a moment's privacy," he said, tossing her a smile over one broad, velvet-coated shoulder. "It will be several hours before we stop again. Might I suggest that you avail yourself of some handy shrub?" Then he disappeared into the privy of his choice.

Jane flushed scarlet and, out of an sudden urge to be contrary just for the sake of it, decided to ignore his advice. But, realizing that this humiliation was preferable to that of having to ask him to stop later, she stomped off into the bushes at the other side of the road.

When she emerged, Seymour was standing beside the now enclosed carriage, talking with two plainly clad horsemen. At her approach, the younger of the men straightened in his saddle and stared at her openly. The other indicated her with a lift of his chin, at which Mr. Seymour tossed her a glance, then dismissed the men with a wave of his hand.

"Outriders," he explained as the horsemen cantered off. "Highwaymen are not unknown in these parts."

Without further ado, he handed her into the carriage's now dusky interior. Almost before they had taken their seats, Ebenezer sent them on their bone-jarring way again.

"Did I hear you called 'Jane' this morning?"

She looked at him sharply. As he had not spoken to her before, she was surprised that he did now. "Aye, sir."

Little more than the combined span of their knees separated them but, close as he was, Jane had to strain to make out his face in the gloaming. She thought he was scowling.

"Your given name is Johanna, is it not?" He pronounced the name distinctly, not slurring over the "h" as most people did, but giving it an important sound.

"Aye, sir."

"Why do you not go by it?"

"I don't know, sir. I've always been Jane."

"I prefer Johanna. 'Tis less common. Although, it might be amusing to call you Jane Seymour." He seemed to smile, but she couldn't be sure in the fading light. "You know who Jane Seymour was, do you not?"

"Nay, sir."

"She was mother to Edward the Sixth; wife to Henry the Eighth. It is said she was the great love of his life."

"She was a queen?" He nodded. "Are ye—Are ye kin to her?" she asked, her heart in her throat. She didn't think she wanted to be kin to royalty. Not even distant kin. It was frightening enough that she had married a gentleman!

Seymour chuckled. "Perhaps. It was a much-argued question in my great, great, etcetera, grandmother's day. You see, she claimed that Queen Jane's brother, Sir Thomas, fathered her son—on the wrong side of the blanket. Sir Thomas's paternity was never proven, but neither did he contest it when she christened the boy a Seymour." He paused. "Can you read, Johanna?"

"Oh, ah, aye, sir."

"And write? More than just your name, mind."

"Aye, sir."

"And cipher?"

"Some."

He hummed appreciatively. "Do you play?"

"Not much. I mostly haven't time for anythin' but workin', sir."

He laughed. "I meant, do you play music?"

"Nay," she said flatly, angry that he had laughed at her.

This time his hum was thoughtful. "I presume, from what you said this morning, that you know something of dancing."

"Not enough to please ye, I'm sure, sir."

Seymour ignored her sarcasm and said, "My name is Damon. If you would please me, use it when we are alone together. At other times, when we are in company, Mr. Seymour will do. What do you know of parlor entertainments?"

Having no idea what "parlor entertainments" were, Jane correctly assumed she knew nothing about them and said so—adding a defiant "sir."

"Mine is a simple enough name, Johanna. Cannot you say it?"

"I cannot use yer Christian name when ye're all but a stranger to me."

"As my wife," he began, sounding annoyed, "you will shortly come to know me exceedingly well. A Christian name familiarity seems a desirable prelude to that infinitely more intimate one. Don't you agree?"

His high-flown language soared over her head, but she caught the gist of it and, grudgingly, conceded that he was right: They had to make a start somewhere, and the sooner the better.

And yet, she stubbornly refused to say so. This marriage was his idea. If he expected her to make it easy for him, he had better think again!

In turn, he took her silence for dissent.

They jounced along in stony silence, each alternately scowling and trying to ignore the shadowy form on the opposite seat. The only sound was the racket of the carriage and the driver's occasional shout to his team. Deciding that he must early put down a firm, husbandly foot if he was to nip such impertinence in the bud, Seymour spoke first.

"This has been a trying day for you, I know. But that is no excuse for—"

"Ye can't know! Ye've not been taken from yer family and friends, hustled off without so much as a last look by some fancy stranger who acts like he owns ye! 'Tisn't yer home that's fallin' farther and farther behind every minute!"

"Neither is it yours. Like it or not, girl, your home is now with me."

Through the ever-deepening dusk, Jane stared daggers at him. But, despite her fury, tears burned behind her eyes, and her throat ached with trying not to cry.

Seymour stared at the milky blur that was Johanna's face. He could not see her expression, but he would bet his last shilling that it wasn't contrition! She was every bit as stubborn and hot-tempered as . . . as he was himself. That hardly excused her. Two wrongs never made a right. If they were to have a companionable marriage—it clearly would never be happy—one of them had to make a change in attitude. By glory, it wouldn't be him!

And yet, in spite of his anger, he found himself feeling sorry for her. She was little more than a child and life had already given her a drubbing. He supposed this marriage must seem the last straw to her. Granted, when it came to their marriage, he was as much a victim as she. The difference was that he had, so to speak, allowed himself to be victimized, while she . . .

He snorted derisively. By the faith, he was making her out to be a martyr and himself an altruist! He had sacrificed nothing to marry the girl. He had merely fulfilled a contract. There was honor in that, to be sure, but not so much as he might like to think.

Jane dashed the tears from her cheeks, then swiped at her dripping nose with a finger.

"A lady employs a handkerchief," he said, stuffing a square of spice-scented linen into her hands. Timing his move to the random lurch and sway of the carriage, he joined her on her seat and, wrapping an arm about her shoulders, pulled her against his velvet and lace covered chest.

Jane stiffened and tried to right herself, but he held her close and his words rumbled like a dirge through the chest beneath her ear.

"We are man and wife, Johanna. There is naught to be done about it now but to make the best of it."

# 2

The carriage jolted and swayed violently. Jane was tossed from the seat and onto the floor as if she were a rag doll. It was an unpleasant way to wake up.

"Eb-ben-neeezer!" Mr. Seymour roared. The carriage slowed and stopped. "Are you all right? Were you hurt?" Seymour asked with genuine concern as Jane tried to right herself.

"I'm—I'm fine. I think," she said, trying to disentangle herself from the heavy, voluminous heap of fur and velvet that seemed intent on smothering her. "What happened?"

"That is what I should like to know!" he growled, furiously throwing open a door. A blast of rain-laced wind caught him full in the face. "Ye gods, man! What are you trying to do, batter us to death!"

"Ah's sorry, suh. Ah's sorry. Dis night's black as pitch, suh. Can't hardly see da road."

"Well, what do you want me to do about that? Light your way with a torch?"

Ebenezer, his dark, wet face glistening in the feeble glow of a side lamp, bowed humbly. "Ah's sorry, suh."

"Is there damage to the carriage?"

"No, suh. Not as I can see, suh."

"Very well, then. Give us a moment to repair ourselves . . . then take it more slowly!" Muttering blackly under his breath, he slammed the door.

Jane had regained her composure and sat staring at him from where she huddled, shivering, in a corner. She had never known a man to bellow so! Or to be so bullyish.

"What the blazes have you done with my handkerchief?" he demanded.

" 'Tis there. With yer cloak."

Something in her tone grated. He shot her a glance. The candle lamp, thanks be to its gimballed bracket, had survived the calamity intact; by its light he read disgust in her eyes. "And why do you look at me like that?"

"I don't see as ye've cause to be so angry. 'Tisn't as though he did it o' purpose. And 'twas *me* got bounced about!"

He held her eyes as defiantly as she held his, then reached for the handkerchief and wiped his face. "The cloak is yours," he said tightly, angrily.

Jane looked in disbelief from his sternly set face to the soft pile of fur-lined velvet on the seat beside him. " 'Tis mine?"

"Did I not say so?" he snapped. "Put it on before you catch your death."

She stroked the rich, loden-green velvet wonderingly, then burrowed her fingers into the soft, gray fur. " 'Tis—'tis beautiful! I never thought to have a thing so grand. Thank ye."

"I am delighted you like it," he snarled. "Are you hungry?"

"Oh. Ah. Aye," she said, her voice still breathy with wonderment.

Watching her drape the cloak about her shoulders and lovingly arrange its heavy drape over her lap, he realized how well it became her; how very young and vulnerable and, yes, beautiful she was.

"I, ah—I am not in the habit of taking a noon meal.

Forgive me for not considering that you are. We shall have a fine supper when we reach the inn."

She looked up at him quickly. "We'll not be in Williamsburg tonight?"

"Williamsburg? We are not bound for Williamsburg."

"But ye live there." At the look of stunned surprise on his face, she asked with marked uncertainty, "Don't ye?"

"No."

"But ye came from there this morn! Mam told me!"

"I have been visiting in Williamsburg. Perhaps, you misunderstood her."

"Nay. She said nothin' of visitin'. Nothin'!"

"But, she well knows that I make my home in Maryland." He saw a medley of emotion play across her face. Shock and horror lingered there the longest. "I am sorry that comes as such a surprise to you," he said, aghast at learning just how much of a stranger he was to her. "I had no idea you were so—ill-informed."

"Maryland? Ye're takin' me clear to Maryland?"

He nodded. "I cannot imagine why she did not tell you."

"I never thought to ask. The last time, the first time, ye came, Pap said ye'd come from Williamsburg, too. So I thought . . ." Her eyes found her lap.

He studied her down-turned face for a while before he said more sharply than he meant to, "We are bound for Maryland. Moping will not change that."

Her head snapped up. "I'm not mopin'! I'm just tryin' to get used to it, is all. Here, for all this time, I thought that—" Jane startled at the sudden thumping on the carriage roof and looked anxiously upward.

"Not to worry. That is only Ebenezer letting us know we have reached the inn."

The landau rolled to a stop. It bounced on its squeaky springs as the driver climbed down, and again when Mr. Seymour joined Jane on her seat. Bending double, he slid open the woodwork under the facing seat and hauled a caped greatcoat from the concealed storage space. Then, and not without difficulty because the quarters were cramped and he was large, he shrugged it on and again bent low to reach under the seat. This time, he withdrew a silver-headed, ebony walking stick.

"This was my father's," he said, presenting it for Jane's inspection. "One day it shall be my son's."

Jane fingered the cool wood gingerly, taking the point of his words like a dagger in the pit of her stomach: That son would be hers, too. And, perhaps, conceived this very night! Unable to force a sound from her fear-constricted throat, she wordlessly handed the stick back.

He made no move to take it, but curled his fingers over hers, tightening her grip on the shaft. His ungloved hand was warm; the look in his golden eyes was even warmer. "You are trembling."

" 'Tis cold."

"You need not fear me, Johanna," he promised softly.

"I do not." Pride forced her to lie.

Through the door, the driver called, "All's in readiness, suh." And Mr. Seymour reclaimed both his hand and his stick.

The inn's public room felt stiflingly warm after the coolness of the carriage and the night. A fire blazed on the fireplace wall's stone hearth, and dozens of candles oozed thick tallow onto the bare tables or dripped the floor from sconces afixed to the walls. Each contributed a flame's worth of warmth to the room. Jane dropped her hood on account of the heat. Then, never having been in a public house, she looked curiously about.

The inn's other patrons—perhaps a half score of men—seemed unbothered by the heat. Some sat alone, sipping at tall tankards and watching the doings of the rest. Others hunched over their meal or talked with table mates. At the far end of the room, a group of four suddenly exploded into bawdy laughter at which the serving girl, who was clearly the object of their jest, shifted the heavy-looking tray of pewterware braced against her hip and stuck out her tongue at them.

Jane blushed at the obscene gesture and looked away—straight into the admiring eyes of a stranger. He winked and smiled. She looked at the floor and sidled closer to her husband.

"Never fear," he said, staring the brazen man down. "We will not be supping here but upstairs, in the room I have taken." Raising a hand, he caught the serving girl's eye.

She acknowledged him with a weary nod, then called toward an open door behind the serving bar, "Mistress Pound! 'Tis the gentleman!"

Jane had never seen such obesity as that which presented itself in the form of Mrs. Pound. The woman's apron-covered breasts and belly seemed to have life of their own; they moved quite independently of each other as she waddled across the room. And when she led them up a steep, narrow rise of stairs, her hips bumped and scraped the walls, and the boards under her square feet groaned so loudly in complaint that it seemed they must give way. Jane was greatly relieved to reach the upper floor; even though the hallway smelled of wet wool and sour bedding, it afforded the substantial woman ahead of her more space, and the flooring complained less vigorously at her step.

"Here we be, sir," Mrs. Pound puffed, stopping and giving the last door on the left an inward shove. "Finest in the house, so 'tis, sir. Just like you wanted."

"And my trunk?"

"Arrived this forenoon, sir. Never been touched but for movin' it in. You'll find nothin' missin'."

Seymour nodded. "You will have our meal sent up?"

" 'Twill be right along. Candle's lit for you and the fire laid."

"Thank you for your trouble." Seymour dropped several coins into Mrs. Pound's fleshy palm.

"Thank you, sir." Her eyes, small dark currants in her doughy face, flitted over Jane. "I trust you'll pass a pleasant night, sir." Then she lumbered off, sniggering as she went.

Seymour scowled briefly after her, then urged Jane into the room. Closing the door behind them, he viewed the room with a critical eye. "I suppose it will serve."

Though she dared not say so, Jane thought the room would more than just "serve." To her mind, the large, battered four-poster with its twin pillows, sagging bed-ropes, candlewicked counterpane, and woven coverlid —the latter cunningly folded and draped across the foot of the bed so as to hide a fraying center seam—represented the utmost in comfort and luxury. While she judged the room's other simple furnishings no less grand—the moth-nibbled tapestry swagged across a corner in lieu of a dressing screen was magnificent, indeed—she deemed the fireplace opposite the foot of the bed the most marvelous of them all. A fireplace in a bedchamber! Fancy that!

The fireplace was the focus of Mr. Seymour's attention, too. As promised, kindling and logs lay on the grate; all he need do was light them. But the wood was none too dry and the chimney's draft poor. What seemed a simple task became a frustratingly smoky one.

He could have put it off awhile—the room was cool but comfortable—but he never procrastinated. Even when it would be easier, even when it wouldn't matter, he refused to put things off. So he spent some time on bended knee, occasionally muttering under his breath, before the flames flickered to life.

"May I take your cloak?" he asked, standing and

turning to Jane.

He hung it on one of the pegs on the wall near the bed and did likewise with his coat and the hat he had doffed upon entering the inn. He propped the walking stick against the wall. His eyes lingered on the bed for a moment before he dismissed the pleasant turn his thoughts had taken and crossed the room to the small table and two straight-backed chairs under the only window. Repositioning the table between the hearth and the bed, he flanked it with the chairs, gave its stained, wrinkled linen cloth a tug to even its skimpy drape, then eyed the results with a disgruntled sigh.

Jane's sigh was one of pure rapture—she had never eaten off linen—and when Mr. Seymour took the two pewter candlesticks from the mantel shelf and placed them on the table, she couldn't help but exclaim, "Oh! 'Tis grand!"

Seymour shot her a look and, seeing her sincerity, smiled a condescending sort of smile. "I am glad you think so." He lit the candles.

Wondering how he could view such elegance so scornfully, she dared to ask, "Don't ye think so, too?"

"It will serve," he repeated, walking back to the window.

"D'ye mean to say ye live grander than this?"

Seymour's hand grasped the faded, dusty curtains as he turned to stare at her. "Did the McPhees tell you nothing of me?"

"They . . . They said ye grow tobacco and raise horses. And that ye don't want for much."

He smiled at the understatement. "Neither will you, from now on."

He sent one half of the pair of curtains skittering along the rod, but he hesitated in his reach for the other. The window reflected the room and the girl behind him and, though her image was distorted by the warped and bubbled glass, he could not tear his eyes from it.

*She's a beauty and no doubting it*! he thought, leisurely taking in the size and shape of her as he had meant to do that morning before the babe stopped his eye. She was small, to be sure, but slender; that slenderness gave her the illusion of greater height. And, if the graceful drape of skirt from waist to hem spoke true, her legs were coltishly long. She was a bit too flat in the bosom to suit him, but if there was any other flaw in her form or her face it was for keener eyes than his to discover.

As for the rest of it: She held herself well; possessed a poise and innate elegance of which she seemed completely unaware. Of course, that shouldn't surprise him. She was a well-bred little filly. What ill-effect she had suffered from grazing the McPhee's mean pastures could be set to rights quickly enough by a good tutor. He would ask his uncle, who had raised seven daughters, to recommend one.

He drew the second curtain to meet its mate, then turned to her. "You are lovely, Johanna. A man could not ask for a more comely bride."

Jane felt herself blush. Though many men had taken more than passing note of her—two had even asked to pay her court—none had ever paid her compliments; Pap and Jacob had seen to that! Her eyes on the knot-hole in a scuffed and scarred floorboard, she said, "I'm—I'm glad ye're pleased, sir."

"Damon," he corrected, softly. "But, what of you? Do I please your eye?"

Surprised by the question—surely, he knew he was a fine-looking man—Jane looked up to find him awaiting her answer.

"Aye," she said, managing to swallow the "sir."

He covered the distance between them in three, long-legged strides. "And, does my touch please you?" Lightly, he stroked her hair. "It is fitting that a wife be pleased at her husband's touch."

A nervous shudder rippled through her as his fingers

came to rest at the nape of her neck.

"Aye," she said, but her voice betrayed her.

Seymour raised her face to his and promised softly, "You need not fear me, Johanna. Not this night, nor any other. I will be gentle with you. And as patient as I am able."

Then he drew her against him and Jane stood stiffly in his embrace, listening to the strong, rhythmic pounding of his heart until he reluctantly put her from him to answer the rap on the door.

The supper was like no other Jane had eaten. She had never had fish, fowl and flesh all in the course of one meal. There were also carrots stewed in molasses; boiled potatoes served with dill butter; fragrant wine; and bread made of fine, white flour. She had never had so much elbow room at a table, or the luxury of tending her own plate without having to tend others first. And her eyes lit up at the sight of plum pudding drizzled with hard sauce. Such a dessert had been a rare and special treat back home.

But despite her gnawing hunger and the splendid meal, Jane could eat little. With each mouthful, she thought of the simple but hearty wedding feast she and Mam had spent the morning preparing. And she couldn't forget the sacrifices her family had made to provide it.

"Is the food not to your taste?" Seymour asked.

"Nay. 'Tis wonderful fine."

"Why, then, are you not eating?"

Unwilling to put her heartache into words or to share it with the stranger who was the cause of it, Jane wagged her head and dutifully turned back to her plate.

When Mr. Seymour had eaten his fill—and he had a remarkable appetite—he leaned back in his armless chair and slowly sipped at a dram of something he poured from an oddly shaped, silver flask produced from inside his coat. "I would offer you some, Johanna, but brandy is not a lady's drink. Will you have more wine?" He reached for the bottle.

"Nay, thank ye," she said, politely keeping her distaste for the stuff to herself.

Settling comfortably back in his chair again, he studied the liquid in his glass. "It occurs to me that what has passed for conversation between us has been largely initiated by me and pertained to you." She looked at him blankly. "In other words, is there nothing you would ask of me?" Jane nodded uncertainly. "Ask then," he said with an encouraging smile.

She hesitated, then blurted, "Why'd ye want to marry me?"

He looked startled for an instant, then he chuckled ruefully. "I was given Hobson's choice, the same as you were. For pity's sake, girl, ask me something reasonable." He saw confusion cloud her eyes—pretty eyes they were, too—and so he explained, "Hobson's choice means no choice at all."

"Aye, I know what it means. But ye had yer choice and ye chose me. 'Twas *me* got no choice but Hobson's!"

He smiled. "Ah, I see. You think, being as I'm considerably older than you are, that I had some say in the matter, hm? Indeed, I did. Unfortunately, my objections went unheeded." The glass he raised stopped halfway to his lips. "Why do you look like that?"

"If ye had objections, then why'd ye marry me!"

He very nearly gaped at her. "By the gods! Did not McPhee explain? Did he tell you nothing of the contract?"

"The contract?"

Seymour stared at her incredulously and it took him some moments to find his voice. "Johanna, you and I have been betrothed since you were but a child of four and I a lad of sixteen."

Jane felt suddenly light-headed. "That can't be so. Ye

must be wrong." Seymour shook his head. "But ye're sayin' Pap lied to me. Pap never lied! Not ever!"

"I fear he did. Although, clearly not convincingly, else you'd not have asked me. What did he tell you?"

Her voice light and breathy with shock, Jane said, "He said ye—ye took a fancy to me when I was small and—and that ye'd asked after me in letters ever since. And then, last year when ye came to the farm, he said ye told him ye wanted to marry me soon's I turned sixteen." She looked up from the napkin she had been twisting in her lap. "It's that last I didn't understand: Why ye should want to marry a girl ye didn't know and hadn't so much as set eyes on for years and years!"

"I can see how that might confound you," Seymour said, flatly. "Did you put the question to him?" She nodded. "What was his answer?"

"He said 'twasn't for me to question."

Seymour added more brandy to his glass. How dare McPhee go against his instructions in this! He had betrayed a trust; broken a bargain. Worst of all, he had broken his word!

"If what ye say is true, then—"

"It is."

"Then, ye've no more fondness for me, than I have for ye?"

"No." He heard the misdirected anger in his voice and regretted it. "That is no fault of yours, Johanna. You are very lovely. I'm sure that in time I will—"

"I think ye're fine lookin', too," she interrupted, meeting his eye. "But that has naught to do with fondness."

His eyes smiled. "Have you never liked anything purely for its prettiness?"

"Aye. Flowers and the like; not people."

"Ah. What say you to this then?

There is a lady sweet and kind,

Was never face so pleased my mind;
I did but see her passing by,
Yet will I love her 'til I die.

Poetic drivel, do you think?"
" 'Tis a nice thought, but—"
"Then you are not of the opinion that it is a much simpler matter to grow fond of someone who is easy on the eye, than of someone who is not?" He smiled handsomely.

"Aye. I s'pose I am."

"So am I," he said, toasting her with his glass. For the first time that day, Jane's smile was genuine. "You've a pretty smile, Johanna." Watching the blush brighten her face, he could not resist teasing, "And an unruly complexion, too, I see." He laughed as Jane's face blazed redder.

But she blanched when he tossed back his brandy, then said as casually as if this were not his wedding night, "We need to make an early start in the morning. It is time we retire."

He stood, intending to round the table and hold her chair. But Jane stood unassisted and took several hasty steps away.

"All the amenities are there," he said, indicating with a glance the washstand and commode partially obscured by the shabby tapestry. "I shall leave you to your undressing."

"I—I haven't my bundle. My rail's in it."

"You've no need of night dress tonight, Johanna," he said, snatching his coat from its peg.

"But—"

"I shall return shortly." And he left, closing the door soundly behind him.

After a visit to the stables to see that his horses and driver were properly quartered, and a trip to the reeking public privy nearby, he took an impatient, bone-chilling stroll through the windy but, thankfully, no longer rainy night before he returned to the room. He found Jane standing just as he had left her; but for the shawl which she had carefully folded and draped over the back of a chair.

"I can't manage the laces," she said to the toes of his muddy boots.

"Laces?"

"On my dress. Down the back." She ventured an upward peep at him and saw him sweep a wind-tousled lock of wavy, chestnut hair back toward the ribbon-tied queue at his nape.

"Turn around, then."

Mortified at having to ask his help, Jane nevertheless turned her back. She heard him hang his coat on the peg and latch the door before she felt him tugging and pulling at the laces in imitation of her own futile efforts over the last quarter hour. Then, taking her by the shoulders, he guided her toward the light of the guttering candles on their supper table. Suddenly, the tightness around her waist eased and she felt his fingers working upward along her spine. She felt his breath coming hotter and faster against her neck, too, the closer the laces came to being undone. But when the pale blue and white striped dimity gaped wide, she heard his breath catch in his throat.

"What mode of dress is this?" He turned her around to face him then, and wasted not a moment in stripping the bodice from her shoulders and exposing the broad, muslin binding about her chest.

His mind's eye filled with the memory of his first sight of her; a suckling babe cradled in her arms. He knew enough of women to know that their breasts were bound to suppress milk upon the death of an infant. It stood to reason that the same would be done should a nursing mother be separated from her child.

"Answer me! I would know why you are bound!"

Mute with shock and shame, Jane could only gape at him.

Furiously, he demanded, "Answer me! Have you played me for the fool? Was that babe this morn your own?"

"Nay!"

"Then explain that!" he seethed, his angry eyes darting to the muslin.

Her face crimson and her eyes wide with fear, she whispered, " 'Twas too small. 'Twas Polly Norton's 'fore 'twas mine. It wouldn't fit 'less I was bound."

"The dress, do you mean?"

"Aye. I let it out all I could, but 'twas still too small. I've—I've grown of late."

His angry scowl softened and the fingers gripping her arms lost some of their strength. But doubt and suspicion still lingered in his eyes. "I'll not be duped, girl. If you are lying to me, I'll know it soon enough, and there will be the very devil to pay!"

" 'Tis true!"

"We shall see."

But when he applied his lean fingers to the knot in the muslin, Jane gasped and pulled away; her arms crossed protectively over her chest.

"Do not impede me, girl," he said, catching her wrists and forcing her arms down.

Although Jane's hands tightened into fists, she kept them at her sides while he untied the knot. But it was not his tone or Meg McPhee's admonitions concerning wifely obedience that made Jane stand her ground when the muslin gave way, her closely guarded modesty drifting to the floor with it. It was pride—the selfsame "proudness" she had despised in him but which she was too unschooled to call by its rightful name: Dignity.

Had she been vain, she would have exulted in his huskily voiced praise and the admiring caress of his hands. As it was, she spun away and, hauling the dimity up to cover herself, demanded indignantly, "Why'd ye shame me so?"

"You've nothing to be ashamed of, Johanna. Faith, you have not!" he whispered throatily. "Look at me." And he turned her to him and cupped her chin so that she had no choice.

His eyes glowed warm and golden, sparked by the light of some inner flame, as he ran his fingers through her hair, lifting it and spreading it like a mantle over her shoulders. "Golden as the summer sun," he said, his voice husky and low. "Ye gods, Johanna, you are truly a beauty!"

Then he bent to kiss her, urging her mouth to his and keeping it there with the hand behind her head. His lips were hot and moist, but they lingered only a moment before he turned away.

Jane's relief was quickly replaced by horror when, right before her eyes, he began stripping off his clothes. She watched him drape his coat, waistcoat and frill over her shawl on the chair, but when he unbuttoned his breeches and hauled the hem of his blouse free, she looked away. She heard the chair creak under his weight, and then his boots thumped one after the other to the floor.

"Come here, Johanna."

Venturing a peek at him, she was was relieved to find he was still wearing his breeches. But she stood her ground.

"Come here. Give me your foot." He patted the chair seat between his muscular thighs. When she hesitated, he teased, "Do you sleep in your shoes, then?"

Jane smiled despite her nervousness and shyly presented her foot. Her mud-crusted shoe soon joined his boots under the table. But before she could retrieve her leg, one of his hands encircled her ankle and the other ran up under her skirts and inside the wide leg of her drawers until it found the rolled top of her stocking.

Embarrassed and painfully self-conscious, Jane tried to pull away, protesting, "I can do that for myself."

"I haven't a doubt that you can," he said, smiling up into her eyes but making no move to release her.

Jane felt the worsted wool begin a leisurely slide down her leg. The caress of his fingers did odd things to her as they worked the stocking off—odd things, but delightful ones, too. When the time came, she needed but little prodding to offer the other leg.

When that one had been as leisurely and pleasantly bared as the first, Seymour stood and said, "Now, the rest."

Brooking no argument, he stripped her dress and petticoat off as one. Then, trampling the jumble of cotton underfoot, he slowly, resolutely drew her toward him.

"A man delights in his wife, Johanna," he said, feeling her resist the pressure of his hands. "He delights in her beauty; in her touch; in touching her."

His breath came warm and soft against her face, and his eyes were fairly ablaze with the light of his inner flame as he pressed one of her trembling hands against the coarse, curling hair of his chest. She felt the wild hammering of his heart beneath it.

He gently cupped her breast. "And, if she but allows herself, a wife can find much delight with her husband." With his lips touching her hair, he implored, "Do not impede me, Johanna. Let me delight you."

Then his mouth was on hers, his lips gently teasing until hers softened and parted to accept his kiss. She was surprised by the heat of his mouth and the strong taste of what must be brandy that lingered there. But no more surprised at that than she was to find that she liked what he was doing to her. Though he was still an arrogant, hot-headed stranger, she liked the way his lips nipped and nibbled at hers, then danced away to her cheek, her temple, her ear, where they nuzzled softly before returning to tease at her mouth again. And she liked the way his hand skimmed along her arm and over her shoulder to the back of her head, setting her atingle with gooseflesh when his fingers burrowed into her hair. She liked the way his busy fingers played at her breast, too, sending warm tinglings sparking through her as they flicked and circled and rubbed at the tip of her. Never had she felt such sensations! Or so much sensation at once. But, oh, she liked it!

Timidly at first, more boldly when she sensed his approval, she kissed him back, imitating the movement of his lips and the dartings of his tongue when it slipped between her teeth to play with hers. And when her neck began to ache with straining upward, she stood on tiptoe and dared to raise the hand that had been at his chest to his firmly muscled shoulder.

His kisses grew more demanding then; his tongue more searching. And when he left her to throw back the bed covers, she felt a wholly unexpected flutter of anticipation. And if the fingers she placed in his outstretched hand trembled, it was with excitement, not dread.

Warmth radiated from him like heat from a fire as he drew her to the bed, but the coarse cotton sheeting was cool against her skin. Stretching out beside her, he braced himself on an elbow and stroked the hair back from her temple. "You are beautiful, Johanna," he said in a voice that was husky and low. Then his eyes left her face to follow his hand as it wandered downward over the hill of a breast; into the valley of her waist; up the gentle rise of cotton-covered hip.

His mouth found hers again before it trailed a

molten path along her neck, past the throbbing pulse in her throat and downward. When his lips found the nubbin at the peak of one breast, she caught her breath in a gasp only to released it in a cooing moan when he played at it with his tongue. She was startled that such a sound had come from her, yet it did again when he sought out the other breast and dallied at its expectant crest like a child savoring a peppermint drop; wanting to make it last.

His hand was busy, too. Gliding over her hip, it skimmed along her thigh to her knee and back again, stroking, stroking and, gradually, with each sensuous, velvet-soft sweep, encompassing more of her.

He felt her tense each time his hand strayed to untouched flesh; evoked heretofore unknown sensations. And he took care to go slowly. Seducing a virgin was like gentling an unbroken filly: Patience had its reward. It was all a matter of that: Patience. And trust.

"Trust me, Johanna," he whispered huskily.

And she did. Even when he loosed the drawstring at her waist and eased her drawers well down, she trusted him. She had often witnessed the mating of livestock and had dreaded the day when some man would make similarly crude use of her. But this was nothing like that! He was delighting her as he had promised to do, and in ways she had never dreamt possible! She had even begun to think that people were somehow different from animals, above such a degrading act . . . until he stripped off his breeches.

The ending was not nearly so delightful as the beginning had been. She hadn't expected it would hurt. And even though the first pain was as sharp and quick as the slash of a knife, the searing fullness of him where there had been nothing but emptiness before knocked all thought of delight right out of her. And while she wanted to believe what he told her when it was done, that soon she would take as much pleasure from him as he took from her, the painful throbbing of that wounded part of her defied his words.

He must have read that in her eyes, because he smiled softly and said, "Patience, sweeting. Rome was not built in a day." Then he kissed her gently and, having tucked the covers warmly about them both, promptly fell asleep.

Sleep came less easily to her. She was unaccustomed to the commotion of a public house: strange voices filtering through the wall, unfamiliar steps shuffling beyond the door and drunken curses bellowing in the room below. And, try as she may, she could not adjust to the softness of a bed; to the press of ropes through a mattress.

Watching the candles gutter out one by one, she longed for the familiar sounds of home and the firmness of the floor under her straw pallet. Like a pup newly taken from its littermates, she whimpered her loneliness and, cuddling close, took what comfort she could from the nearness of a gentle stranger.

# 3

The next morning they crossed a rain-swollen river on a ferry so overloaded that Jane feared it would capsize and send them all to the bottom, then continued their northward journey through a capricious spring storm which lashed the carriage with hail and rain. Jane could not help but pity Ebenezer, exposed to the elements as he was. But when she mentioned her concern to her husband, he dismissed it with a curt answer, never raising his eyes from the papers which held his attention.

With nothing to occupy her, Jane spent much of her time thinking of home and, when that became too painful, wondering at the change in the man on the opposite seat. He was different than he had been the day before. Whereas he had made an effort at conversation after the previous night's supper, at breakfast he had hurried through the meal with scarcely a word but to urge her to do the same. And once they settled into the carriage, he behaved as though she wasn't there. When he wasn't worrying over the pages of heavily inked rag paper and vellum on the jolting lap desk on his knees, he sat staring morosely out a rain-drizzled window, lost in his own thoughts.

He looked different, too. Rather than fine velvet and

lace, today he wore a brown leather jerkin, a full-sleeved, white cotton blouse, doeskin breeches and a pair of well-worn, brown boots. And when the carriage became mired, which it did several times, he threw on not the elegant greatcoat of the previous day, but a beaver pelt cape and plain black tricornered hat to help his "outriders" and Ebenezer—who had also shucked his finery—shoulder it out of the mud.

The transformation in him left Jane feeling hurt and mightily confused. His aloofness after the married intimacy they had now shared put her off completely, while his rustic manner of dress made her feel more his equal. By the time darkness fell and Ebenezer's pounding on the carriage roof announced their arrival at the night's stopping place, Jane felt that Mr. Seymour was more of a stranger than ever.

Again he spared no expense in providing their supper, the first meal they had taken since breakfast—Jane was beginning to think he meant to starve her to death before they reached Maryland—and which they again took in the privacy of their room. But he did not linger over his sip of brandy: Leaving her as soon as he had eaten, he descended to the taproom to "raise a tankard or two," as he said, with his men.

As this night's bedchamber did not boast a fireplace and the night was cold and damp, bed seemed the warmest place to be. So, Jane retired without him and, feeling homesick and abandoned, cried herself to sleep.

As the next morning dawned bright and sunny, Jane's spirits lifted a bit when she saw that the rear half of the carriage bonnet had been folded down. After a day and a half of being shut within four walls, she welcomed the fresh air on her face and the unobstructed view of puffy white clouds scudding across a rain-washed sky. But she could not stop herself from wondering if those same clouds might not also drift over the farm and the family she had left so far behind. That thought, and others like it, subdued her.

"You are solemn of a sudden," her husband said, seeing the down-turned face of the girl on the seat beside him. "You seemed in a quite good humor when we set out."

"I was."

"What has happened that you aren't now?"

Defensively, she parried the question with one of her own. "Have ye no papers to look at today?"

"It is not worth the trouble to begin on them. We will reach the river shortly."

"We crossed a river yesterday, but that did not keep ye from yer papers."

"Ah, so that's it. You want all my attention for yourself, do you?" he teased.

"Nay, not all. But some of 'twould be nice."

"But you have my full attention now; as you had at breakfast . . . and before," he said with a twinkle in his eye. "God's truth, girl, if you continue at the pace you've set, you'll wear me out!"

Jane flushed hotly, remembering their several, not unpleasant, predawn awakenings. "I told ye, I was cold. I'm not used to sleepin' . . . without a rail."

"Ahhh. Then perhaps with the coming of summer and warmer nights I shall get some rest, hm?"

Tilting her face to his, she said with what he found to be admirable pluck, "Ye needn't of made so much of it if ye hadn't wanted to. I was only tryin' to get warm."

He grinned and chuckled deep in his throat. "Cannot you tell when I'm baiting you, girl? I've no complaint with you. Far from it! But you've a mighty lot to learn of me yet, if you think I will not respond appropriately when you snuggle that bare, shapely little rump of yours against me."

Her face aflame, she said in all seriousness, " 'Tis true enough. I do not understand ye."

"Am I such a puzzle?"

"Aye!"

He turned to face her, surprised by so emphatic a reply. With a shoulder resting against the raised half of the carriage bonnet, he asked, "How do I puzzle you?"

"Ye're . . . Ye're different!" She eyed his neat, black frock and the tidy, dove-gray silk cravat stuck with an initialed gold stickpin just above where it disappeared into his black, silver embroidered waistcoat. "Ye've shown yerself to me as three different men in as many days."

"Do you mean this?" He looked down at his chest and fingered a narrow, cotton lapel. "I dress as suits my purpose, Johanna. For my wedding, I wore finery; for a day's hard and muddy travel, I chose clothes suitable for such; for today, a modest traveling suit. It is only the clothes that have changed. The man is still the same."

She could have argued, but deemed it wiser not to risk spoiling his rare good humor.

"I would I had a change of clothes," she said, looking forlornly down at her muddied and wrinkled dress. "I should have, had *he* not lost my bundle!" she added, shooting an icy glare in the direction of the driver.

Seymour cleared his throat uncomfortably, unwilling to place the blame for the "losing" of her wad of shabby clothing where it rightfully lay. "That will be remedied shortly. I have arranged for some clothing for you. You will find it aboard the sloop."

"Oh. Thank ye," she said, surprised by his thoughtful generosity. He nodded acceptance of her gratitude, then looked away. "What's a sloop?"

"A small ship."

"Ye have a ship!"

"No. It is my uncle's. We will sail up the Potomac to his estate—to visit for a time."

Jane didn't think he sounded pleased at the

prospect. "Don't ye like yer uncle?"

He looked at her in quick surprise. "On the contrary. I well like him." But, seeing that his misery had been discovered, he sighed leadenly and fixed his eyes on a distant point on the road behind them to confess, "It is my cousins—most of them—that I could well do without! Six of the seven will likely be at Langdale to meet us; husbands and rambunctious broods in tow, no doubt." He sighed again. "How I wish I could spare you, Johanna. But there is nothing for it. We are expected."

Jane's gaze fell from his handsome, aristocratic profile and skimmed down the front of his grand "traveling suit." She studied the black, broadcloth breeches buckled below his knees, the length of well-muscled calf covered in black cotton hose, the shiny, silver buckle at the high throat of one polished, black shoe.

With a sigh of her own, she said, "I think 'tis more that ye wish to spare them me."

"Why do you say such a thing?" he said, staring at her sharply.

"I'm not of yer class! Like ye said yerself, I'm not the bride o' yer choice, but one that was forced on ye. Ye could've done better than me, a fine gentleman like yerself. We both know that to be true. I'll—I'll shame ye before yer family."

He eyed her steadily for some time, while one lean, manicured finger tapped an annoying tattoo on his knee. Then he said, "It is true that you have not been schooled in the social graces. You are not possessed of a glib tongue, the ability to prattle endless mundanities over tea, and you're beyond so dubious a virtue as false modesty. God be thanked, you are not a silly, giggling coquette given to dramatic swoons! You are, however, genuine, pleasant, reasonably bright, I think, and most certainly pretty. I am not ashamed to present you as my wife."

He watched one of her small, work-roughened hands ineffectually smooth at her wrinkled skirt.

"And if it is the matter of your dress that troubles you, rest assured that you will be as finely and as stylishly garbed as any of them by the time we arrive. But—I would have you bear one thing in mind." Curling a finger under her chin, he raised her face to his. "No matter how grand the apparel or how bedazzling the jewels, they are only pieces of cloth and bits of shiny rock: They adorn us, Johanna, they do not make us." He smiled ruefully. "And there is the lesson some of my cousins would do well to learn. Several of them are sorely lacking in humility."

He looked at the road again for a thoughtful moment, then said, "I suppose, as I have mentioned them, I ought to tell you something of my cousins.

"There are seven, as I think I said, and all are female, more's the pity. Penelope and Elizabeth are the eldest—considerably my senior—very nearly old enough to be your mother twice over. They will undoubtedly be as overdressed and overbearing on this occasion as they are on every other.

"The next eldest is Priscilla. She has fearfully poor eyesight, but vanity forbids her wearing spectacles. She will peer at you. Like so." He raised his chin, furrowed his brow and squinted down his nose at her.

Jane couldn't help but laugh. He smiled.

"After Priscilla comes Lucrecia. She is the prettiest of the lot—and knows it. But, as I believe she is still with child, we may be spared her and her incessant posing and prinking.

"Next in line is Marianne." He paused to smile. "She is much like you, I think, and not too many years your senior. She and her husband Robert Drake—he's a fine fellow, by the way—live on Maryland's Eastern Shore. We shall see them, now and again, once we are home.

"Lastly, the twins, Daphne and Delia. Taken by them-

selves, they are charming young ladies. But put them
together . . ." He finished the thought with a moribund
sigh and a headshake. "But, as they celebrated their
eighteenth birthday last summer, they are the closest to
you in age. Daphne married at Christmastide. Perhaps,
being as you are both newly wed, you will find some
common ground." Jane didn't think he sounded very
hopeful.

"Delia is—giddy. She giggles at nothing at all. She
has recently become betrothed to the grandest fop I've
yet to see. Of the pair of them, I think he is the more
delicate. He's a good match for her, though: Lord Some-
body-or-Other, here in the colonies looking after his
family's considerable interests."

Jane felt her stomach tighten. A lord. Practically
royalty! "Will he be there, d'ye think?"

"Possibly. But you needn't concern yourself with
him—or with any of the other gentlemen—beyond a
polite word or two."

Jane smiled nervously. "I don't think I'll remember
all ye've said. Who d'ye say is most like me?"

"Marianne."

"Marianne," she said, committing the name to
memory. "And Penelope squints."

"Priscilla," he corrected with a fleeting smile. "Never
fear, you will come to know them all. I only thought to
give you an idea of them."

Jane nodded, feeling like a hen about to enter the
fox's den, while Seymour likened himself to an ancient
Roman jailer who, despite his conscience, must obey
orders and send an innocent to the lions.


Jane had never seen a ship and certainly had never
expected to be aboard one. But it was not the trim little
sloop with its pretty blue hull, varnished red oak deck,
and luxuriously appointed, mahogany-paneled cabin
which awed her; it was the clothes: two huge trunks full

of them.

When Mr. Seymour had said he had arranged for some clothing for her, she had not suspected such finery. Or so much of it! There were gowns, corselettes, underdrawers, petticoats, panniers—Jane had never seen such contraptions and had no notion as to what she might be expected to do with them—stockings of silk, satin garter ribbons, dancing slippers, dainty shoes, gloves, fans, hankies, bonnets and parasols. There was another elegant cloak, this one plum-colored satin lined with white silk, and a lace shawl which put the one she was wearing to shame. The shoulder scarves, of which there were three, were made of a fabric so sheer as to be transparent, and the ruffled, lace-trimmed night clothes were prettier than anything she had yet worn even by day! But most mind-boggling of all was the title Mr. Seymour had casually tacked behind the name of the woman who had displayed all the finery: lady's maid.

"May I prepare you a basin now, ma'am?" the woman asked, laying away the last of the shoulder scarves.

"What?" Jane said blankly.

"May I prepare you a basin, ma'am? Before taking his leave, Mr. Seymour suggested that you might wish to bathe before dressing, ma'am."

"Oh. Ah. Aye."

Dropping a curtsy, the maid folded back the Chinese screen which obscured one corner of the small room and proceeded to fill with warm water the enormous, flat-bottomed basin set on the floor. When she added a dollop of something from a stoppered phial and gently swirled it through the water with her fingertips, the musty cabin suddenly filled with the scent of wild lilies. Having thus prepared the bath, she dried her hands on her impeccably white apron, then turned them to the laces at the back of Jane's dress.

Not daring to protest lest her modesty be inter-
preted as dissatisfaction with the woman's service, Jane
submitted to being bathed in a manner to which she was
not at all accustomed; her usual method of bathing
had nothing to do with floor basins, scented water
or other persons. The woman's attentiveness embarrassed Jane nearly as much as her wedding night had
done.

Mistaking her mistress's nervous trembling, Nancy
asked solicitously, "Is the water too cool, ma'am?"

"Aye," Jane fibbed, hoping to put an end to her
ordeal.

But Nancy merely added more warm water to the
basin in which Jane stood, lathered the plump sponge
with the bar of Castile soap, and asked as she went back
to work, "Is that better, ma'am?"

So Jane reluctantly submitted to be washed, dried,
powdered, lotioned and perfumed—to her horror even
her toenails were pared—by the maid who acted as
though pampering an unclad female was the most
natural thing in the world. Then, while Jane stood trying
to conceal her embarrassment—and herself as best she
could behind a skimpy, linen towel—Nancy turned to the
array of clothing.

Jane soon found herself bedecked in french linen
and silk undergarments. Then the panniers were tied
about her waist so that a set of hoops jutted
out—comically, she thought—over each hip, and a crisp
ruffle- and bow-trimmed petticoat was draped atop
them. A frothy, pink and lavender gown made of an
incredibly fragile stuff which Nancy called "superfine"
and ornamented with deep lace flounces at its elbow-
length sleeves and beribboned square neckline, was
guided over her head and laced snugly, rather too
snugly, down the back from neck to waist.

Feeling trussed like a turkey from the waist up but
oddly and uncomfortably bare below due to the

pannier-spread skirts, Jane dutifully slipped her silk-stockinged feet into the low-heeled, bow-trimmed, pink satin pumps Nancy knelt to offer. Jane marveled that they, and everything else, fit. How had Mr. Seymour known her size? After all, he had been wrong about the wedding ring.

Next Nancy respectfully announced that she would arrange Jane's "coiffure." Not sure she had one of those but trusting that it, like everything else, would be provided, Jane carefully settled herself on the chair before the dressing table. The image the elaborately framed mirror threw back was not her own, Jane was sure. She had never worn anything finer than the dimity dress which lay in a shabby heap on the cabin floor where Nancy had disdainfully tossed it. But it was this "coiffure" business which wrought the most astonishing change in her.

Nancy brushed Jane's golden tresses until they gleamed, then, with the aid of a slender rod which she heated over a small brazier, she coaxed the hair into a cascade of plump ringlets near Jane's left ear and arranged the rest in thick coils, loops and puffs at the back and crown, securing all with small, silver combs. When asked if she approved of the style, Jane could only nod in amazement.

Lifting the protective towel from Jane's shoulders, Nancy asked, "Shall I inform Mr. Seymour that your toilette is completed, ma'am?"

Uncertain what a "twa-let" was, but positive that if Nancy said so, she must have completed it, Jane breathed an "aye" and sat staring at herself.

Her astonishment seemed to be contagious. Damon Seymour stood in the open doorway with the late afternoon sunlight glowing around him, staring mutely at her, for what felt like an eternity to Jane.

"Ye're not pleased?" she finally dared to ask, the suspense worse than she supposed his disapproval could be.

"On the contrary. Quite the contrary!" he said, smiling and shutting the door.

Jane smiled, too, then laughed with nervous relief as he crossed the cabin to stand behind her. "I can scarcely believe 'tis me I'm seein'," she said, meeting his admiring eyes in the mirror. "Thank ye for all the beautiful things."

"A wealthy gentleman's wife is expected to be beautifully gowned. And jeweled." From the depths of a coat pocket, he produced a velvet jeweler's pouch, the contents of which he spilled onto the table before her. "My wedding present to you."

Jane stared, wide-eyed, at the glittering violet stones of the necklace. "Oh, 'tis so beautiful!" she breathed. Then, again, she met his eyes in the mirror. "But I've—I've nothin' to give ye."

He smiled and, bending low, kissed her cheek. "I have had my gift already."

She read his meaning in the warm, amber depths of his eyes and, with a blush and a shy smile, lowered hers.

He chuckled softly and said as he fastened the flashing amethysts about her flushed throat, "You, my dear Johanna, are the quintessential bride."

"Is that—bad?"

"No. It's charming," he said, kissing her again and letting his hands linger warmly at the base of her neck long after the clasp was fastened.

But when a rap sounded on the door, he stepped a respectable distance from her and called commandingly, "Come!"

Nancy opened the door and dropped a curtsy almost in the same movement. "The captain sent me, sir. He said to tell you we're in sight of Langdale."

"Thank you."

The maid bobbed another curtsy, then snatched the discarded towels, dress, and shawl from the floor on her way out.

"Wait! My brooch!"

Nancy extracted the cameo from the jumble of fabric, placed it in Jane's outstretched palm and, with yet another curtsy, made for the door.

"And my shawl!" Jane yelped, leaping to her feet.

Though she looked surprised, the maid handed over the ancient piece of mended lace. "You don't want this dress, do you, ma'am?" she stated more than asked.

"No. Discard it," Seymour answered for his wife. And when Nancy had gone, he fairly demanded, "What do you want with that shawl, Johanna? You cannot possibly wear it."

Jane clutched the lace to her breast. " 'Twas Grandmam's, like the brooch, and I would keep it."

He scowled but said nothing as he reached for the plum-colored cloak Nancy had left draped over the lid of a trunk.

Jane worried at a mended spot in the lace with a newly manicured fingernail. "Can I ask ye somethin' that's been troublin' me?"

"Certainly."

"If it wasn't yer idea, whose idea was it for us to marry?"

"It was your father who suggested the match."

She should have known, Jane thought glumly. Why had Pap lied about it? Why hadn't he told her the truth? And why had Mr. Seymour's father agreed to such a mismatch?

"Why'd yer father agree to it?"

"He would have been foolish not to. He had nothing to lose by it and considerable to gain," Seymour said easily, draping the cloak about Jane.

"I don't understand. What'd he gain?"

He smiled sadly. "Had he lived to see us marry, the terms of the contract were such that your property would have fallen to him. As his heir, it is now mine."

She stared at him. What property? She had brought nothing but a bundle of clothing to the marriage—and that had been lost!

Seeing her confusion, Seymour said gently, "Another matter McPhee failed to explain to you, hm?" He gave her shoulders a consoling squeeze. "Well, as it is thoroughly done with now, there is no point in troubling over it, is there? Come along. I should like you to see Langdale as we approach it from the river; it's a very pretty sight."

But Jane *was* troubling over it. There was too much that she did not understand to simply let the matter drop. But he was already making for the door and there were all those awful cousins of his waiting. . . .

Determining to pursue the subject at a better time, she turned and laid the shawl and brooch on the table behind her, catching sight of herself in the mirror as she did so.

"Damon?" She had to say it twice before he turned to face her. And when he did, he wore the slightly startled expression of a man who has been mistaken for someone else. "Ye said I should call ye that, when we're alone."

"Yes. Yes," he said, the surprise leaving his face.

"Will ye—when we're alone—will ye call me Jane?"

"I have told you I prefer Johanna. Jane is far too common."

"Aye, for the likes of her!" she said with a scathing glare at her reflection. "But if what ye said this morn is so, if 'tis not what we wear that makes us, then inside me—where it truly counts—I'm Jane."

He smiled slowly. "Very well, Johanna. Jane it shall be . . . now and then."

# 4

Standing on deck beside her husband as the sloop
docked at the Langdale pier, Jane looked as composed
as a statue. But had she been aware of her audience, she
would have felt even more anxious and looked less self-
assured.

As Damon had predicted, six of his seven cousins
were on hand to witness the arrival of the girl they had
come to call among themselves "The Seymour Mare." It
was an unoriginal title, borrowed from history. King
Henry's Jane Seymour had worn it first, but the cousins
thought it suited Damon's bride at least as well, and they
were eager for a good, unobtrusive stare at the filly.

"My word! He's married a Lilliputian!" Penelope
cried, expecting that her witty opinion would be
seconded.

Elizabeth didn't disappoint her. "Indeed! For a fact,
that statuesque Townsend woman would have suited
him better."

"You cannot be serious," Priscilla huffed, never one
to be left out even if she couldn't clearly see what was
going on. "Even a diminutive bumpkin is a more suitable
match for a man of Damon's caliber than a . . . a
strumpet!"

"Lilith Townsend is a strikingly handsome woman,

Prissy. Even you must have seen that," Elizabeth defended. "And Damon was more faithful to her than to any other."

"Humph!" Priscilla snorted, unable to rebut her sister's statement; Cousin Damon's attentiveness to Miss Townsend was too well—and scandalously—established. "He was only biding his time until this little plum was ripe for the picking, as any lusty young gentleman would do. He could never have married her. Propriety aside, there was the contract to prevent that."

"Still and all, I fail to see what he will find in common with her. She's a child, for mercy's sake! And living with a family of tenant farmers all those years. . . . I shudder to think how crude she must be! I shall never understand why Uncle Bertram made such an arrangement. The child would have been incalculably better off here at Langdale."

"It *is* possible that some provision was made for her schooling." Penelope said. "She may be better educated than we have been led to expect."

From the room's other window, Daphne put in her tuppence worth. "I daresay, Cousin Damon will see her educated as suits him—in bed, at least!"

"Daphne, really! What a thing to say!" Delia scolded from her twin's elbow. "Ever since your marriage, that is *all* you think of!"

"I can hardly expect you to understand," Daphne retorted loftily. "And I have doubts as to whether you ever will, married to Lord Snuff-and-Sneezes. I declare, it will be a wonder if he beds you at all. Why, 'twould muss his hair!"

Delia roiled, and was about to defend her elegant fiance's honor or, at least, his masculinity, when Penelope intervened. "Enough, you two. They are disembarking. Let's see how she carries herself."

Five pair of eyes, one squinting myopically, followed Jane's progress along the wooden pier from which their father's tobacco crop was shipped, then up the long, gentle slope toward the house. Delia giggled when Jane, unaccustomed to heeled shoes, stumbled against Damon's side.

"Bumpkin is the word for her," Elizabeth said with a smug smile.

"I don't deny that," Priscilla said. "I merely made the point that a bumpkin in the family is preferable to a strumpet."

The women exchanged forced smiles and turned back to the window.

"Oh, we've all turned an ankle, haven't we?" Daphne said. "I think she's pretty."

"Very," Penelope agreed. "She carries herself well, too. I will even go so far as to say that she has an innate grace. What do you think of her, Marianne? You've been quiet as a church mouse. Marianne? Why . . . Wherever did she go? She was here, only a moment ago."

"There!" Daphne and Delia yelped in tandem, staring down at the expansive lawn before the house.

"Egads! Has she no decorum?" Elizabeth gasped. "I knew it was a mistake for Father to consent to Robert Drake's suit. Ever since she married that *farmer* . . ."

Damon was the first of the newlyweds to note Marianne's exit from the house. He gave the small hand clutching at his sleeve a reassuring pat. "That is Marianne coming to meet us. She is friend, not foe."

Jane forced herself to smile weakly up at him. But his consolation did nothing for her knotted stomach and watery knees.

"Damon! Oh, how good to see you!" Marianne chortled, extending her hands toward his, then warmly kissing the cheek he lowered to her. "And this must be your Johanna," she said, turning her radiant smile on her new cousin.

"Yes. Johanna, may I present my—our—cousin, Marianne Drake?"

"I'm pleased to meet ye," Jane said, wondering if the family resemblance was as strong between Damon and his other cousins as it was between him and this one.

Marianne's hair was the same shade of chestnut as Damon's, and she had the same strong, square jaw and straight, high-bridged nose—not as attractive on a woman, unfortunately. Her eyes were not amber, but a clear, sparkling blue and they, and her pretty, contagious smile, gave her face such animation that its shortcomings were easy to overlook.

"And I am delighted to meet you," Marianne said, kissing Jane's cheek, too. "I hope you will forgive my manners in dashing out at you like this, but sometimes excitement gets the better of me. Did Damon tell you we are neighbors?"

Jane looked surprised. He hadn't said exactly that.

Damon laughed. "That's an exaggeration, isn't it? We do have the Chesapeake Bay between us, you'll recall."

"Oh, bother! Compared to the distance between Hook's Head and Langdale, Raven's Oak is a hop, skip, and jump." To Jane, she said, "My husband and I make our home near Hook's Head. Robert grows tobacco. Although, not on so grand a scale as Father and Damon do. Particularly, Damon!"

"Did Robert come with you?" Damon asked quickly, hoping to steer the conversation from the path it seemed about to take. He never boasted and didn't care to have it done for him.

"You don't think Robert would allow me to come all this way by myself, do you?"

"I thought you might have come from Annapolis with Daphne and Paul."

"Goodness, no! The lovebirds would not have appreciated my company, I'm sure. Nor I, theirs!"

Damon chuckled. "He is here, then. Good. Are the Fairfaxes here, too?"

"No. Why?"

"Isn't that their carriage?" Damon nodded at the phaeton in the carriage drive beside the house.

"Oh! Yes, yes it is. Lord Pomeroy is here. He's visiting with the Fairfaxes at Belvoir which, of course, is much more convenient to Langdale—and Delia—than is Mary's Hill. And, as Mother tells me he is here nearly every day for tea, well . . ." She lowered her voice to a conspiratorial whisper to add, "Everyone is walking on eggs around him, Damon. He insists on talking politics and Robert, and Father especially, must be careful how they tread. You know how he is: One hardly dares take a glass of *water* without toasting King George when Pomeroy's about! You will be careful what you say, won't you? For Delia and Father's sakes?"

"Never fear. I can toast our monarch, tongue in cheek, with the best of them. Who else is here?"

"Everyone except Lucrecia and Charles: She can hardly be expected to travel in her condition, you know." She saw Damon toss Jane a knowing glance. "Ah, you've forewarned Johanna of my sisters, I see. Good. I didn't think you would send an innocent to the lions unprepared."

Damon scowled and cringed inwardly at Marianne's unfortunate choice of words. Jane looked horrified.

"Oh. Oh, what an awful thing for me to have said! I make my sisters sound positively ferocious, don't I?" she said with a nervous little laugh. "They're really very nice, Johanna. Aren't they, Damon?"

Damon shot Marianne an exasperated smirk, then said to Jane, "Don't let them put you off. You are as much a member of this family, now, as they are."

Jane returned his encouraging smile with a weak one while Marianne cast about frantically for a means of changing the subject.

"What do you think of Father's newest addition to the house?" she asked, her eyes fastened on the home's

Doric-columned portico.

"It's . . . imposing," Damon said.

"Ostentatious, you mean," Marianne said, smiling.

"That, too, of course."

Marianne laughed and, tucking her hand through Damon's free arm, urged her cousin and his bride toward the house.

Marianne's remark about her sisters and lions had done nothing to bolster Jane's courage. The closer they got to the wide span of brick steps, and the trial that awaited her beyond them, the weaker Jane's knees became. So she held tight to Damon's reassuring arm, and took comfort in the thought that, if his cousins didn't like her, the feeling would probably be mutual.

Even so, within minutes of her introduction to them, Jane wanted to bolt from the house and run all the way back to the farm where she belonged. By no stretch of the imagination did she belong here, in this elegant place, with these arrogant people! She had no sooner returned Damon's aunt's warm greeting with a nervous, "I'm pleased to meet ye," when the two elder sisters exchanged deprecating glances and one of the twins giggled behind her fan. And, though Jane had been warned, Priscilla's myopic staring, her slow, head-to-toe scrutiny, unnerved her completely. Fortunately, the gentlemen viewed her much more appreciatively. Even Lord Pomeroy was polite. Only the restraining pressure of Damon's hand at her elbow kept Jane rooted to the magnificent carpet under her feet and propelled her toward what Aunt Hortense called the "withdrawing room" where they were all to have tea.

But once in that spacious, richly appointed, high-ceilinged room, things only got worse for Jane. Too awed by her surroundings to consider her pannier-altered shape, her skirt swept a small vase from a low table and sent it crashing, posies and all, to the floor.

With her face strawberry-red, Jane gasped an

apology to Damon's Aunt—who accepted it with a gracious smile. "Don't give it a thought, dear. Accidents do happen."

Jane immediately stooped to clean up the mess.

"Leave it," Damon said, pulling her up by an arm.

"But—"

"The maid will do that." And he deposited her in a chair while everyone except the giggling twin pretended not to notice.

In fact, for the remainder of the excruciatingly long hour, almost everyone contrived to ignore Jane. Even Damon excused himself from her side after tea and cakes had been served to join his uncle and the lanky, dark-haired Robert Drake where they stood talking across the room.

Initially, Jane was glad to be left alone; she had embarrassed herself enough already. But when her self-consciousness eased enough for her to listen to the ladies' conversation, she realized that her exclusion from it was, in itself, an embarrassment. She could not have joined in even if she'd wanted to. She had no knowledge of the books, music, friends, and relations the other women discussed with easy familiarity. Neither did she have children, household concerns, or problem servants to compare. So she answered the few questions tossed her way, concerning the weather and her trip, politely but shortly, then spent the remainder of the time trying to quiet the nervous, china-chatter of the dainty cup and saucer in her calloused hands.

When the ordeal was over and she had dutifully allowed herself to be tucked into an elegant, canopied four-poster to rest before supper, she lay staring up at the shirred and ruffled fabric arching overhead, comparing herself to the rest of them. She was like a frost-frozen apple, she decided: as beautiful and rosy-red as any picked in season, but with its pretty exterior hiding the slushy pulp within. Nobody liked frozen apples.

*  *  *

"You're dressed already," Damon said, entering the room and ordering Nancy from it with a glance. "You look lovely. That color becomes you."

Jane didn't hear the compliment, her mind was too full of the recitation she had prepared. Nervously fingering the froth of gold-embroidered lace that softened the deep, square-cut neckline of the topaz silk gown and matched the flounces edging its elbow-length sleeves, she said, "I'm sorry for shamin' ye, Damon. Truly I am. I don't know how to do things, or what to say, like the rest of 'em do. But I'll learn. I'll watch 'em real careful, and maybe soon I'll—"

"Have I said I am ashamed of you?" he said with a scowl.

"Nay, but—"

"Then stop this nonsense."

Startled, Jane looked up and saw him disappear behind the dressing screen drawn across a corner of the room. Miserably contrite, and not at all reassured, she perched on the edge of the room's only chair to wait.

She was already familiar with the sounds of his daily ritual: the energetic scrubbing as he washed his hands; the slap of his razor against the strop; the clink of his shaving brush against the rim of the soap mug; his melodious gargling. She could gauge the state of his readiness by the sounds issuing from behind the screen. When she heard the soft whisper of fabric slipping over fabric as he pulled on his coat, she stood expectantly.

He was wearing the same clothes he had worn on their wedding day, but with white hose and fancy shoes in place of his boots. Consulting his pocket watch, then perfunctorily tucking it away, he met her eyes. "We've a few minutes, yet."

Turning to the window, he caught the lace curtain back in a hand and stood staring out into the night; his handsome, sternly set face reflected in a windowpane.

"You will go into supper on Uncle Cyrus's arm. He will show you to your seat at the table. Aunt Hortense has arranged for you to be seated beside Robert Drake and opposite Marianne. Uncle Cyrus will be at the head of the table to your left, so you will be in friendly waters, so to speak."

Miserably, Jane sighed. So they'd been talking about her, arranging how to deal with her. Aloud, she said, "Where will ye be?"

"At the other end of the table, partnering Aunt Hortense." With only a space for breath, he resumed his recitation. "I know you do not care for wine, Johanna, but there will be toasts proposed to His Majesty and to us, as newlyweds. You need take only a small sip to be polite. Thereafter, you may ignore the wine completely if you wish. Water will be served.

"Each dish will be presented to you by the butler, and you will be expected to help yourself from the platter. If you do not care for any of what is being offered, you need only raise your hand above your plate or tell him 'No, thank you,' and he will move on. You are under no obligation to sample everything.

"Following the meal, you and the other ladies will adjourn to the withdrawing room. I and the other gentlemen will join you there, after a time." He turned to her then, his eyes smoldering with suppressed anger. "And as to the matter of shame . . . if there is shame to be felt, Johanna, it is my cousins who ought to be feeling it." He offered his arm. "Come along, now."

Supper progressed exactly as Damon had said it would. But he had failed to mention the mind-boggling display of cutlery and crystal Jane found flanking her plate. It was Robert who came to her rescue.

In a whisper, he said, "Use the fork and spoon farthest from the plate first, whichever is appropriate to what is being served, and work in toward it. If you lose your place, watch Marianne." He winked. "That's what I do. And don't worry about the glasses. It's the butler's job to know which wine goes where."

Inexpressibly grateful for his advice, and for Marianne's lighthearted chatter from across the table, Jane made her way self-consciously through the meal. And, when it was over, she joined the exodus of females Aunt Hortense led into the adjoining room.

Once there, Aunt Hortense and her two eldest daughters quickly formed a cozy little circle around a table and began chatting and doing needlework. One of the twins sat down at the harpsichord and, with a giggle by which Jane was able to identify her as Delia, began to play a melody of such intricacy, Jane marveled that her fingers didn't tangle. The other twin suggested that the remaining foursome, Jane included, might play a game of whist, "But not for stakes, of course."

There was nothing for Jane to do but admit she didn't know the game, at which Daphne and Priscilla exchanged glances and Marianne suggested that "our new cousin" might care to learn it. Not wanting to be contrary, and thinking that a game, even a genteel one, could not be so hard to learn, Jane said that she would. But never having seen a deck of playing cards, she had to master even such rudiments as distinguishing the suits, the values of the face cards, and the art of fanning a hand. The complexities of bidding were hopelessly beyond her.

Having established that whist was not a game Jane could master in an evening, and after ascertaining that she was ignorant of board games as well, the others seemed at a loss as to what to suggest next. But Delia, who had apparently tired of her musical exhibition, determined that they should have a game of pantomime, and promptly explained the game to Jane. It sounded simple enough, not unlike games she had played at home. Feeling certain that here, at last, was something she could do right, Jane eagerly agreed to play.

Marianne went first and masterfully pantomimed the fable of "The Fox and the Grapes." Daphne made a convincing Delila, shearing poor Samson's strength. Even Priscilla joined in, casting down Rapunzel's hair from a footstool tower.

Confidently, Jane stood to take her turn. But when the slip of paper she drew from the enameled bowl read, "Cleopatra barging on the Nile," all confidence vanished. She had no idea who Cleopatra was, although she quickly deduced that the Nile must be a body of water . . . somewhere.

An awful silence filled the room as she stood staring blankly at the piece of paper that had proved her undoing. And she flushed deeply with embarrassment when Aunt Hortense suggested, "Take another, dear, if that one is too difficult."

But when Jane's trembling fingers unfolded the slip reading, "Juliet's suicide—from Shakespeare," her eyes glazed with tears at finding another riddle.

Daphne sniggered to Delia, behind her fan but loud enough, "We should have taught her to read, first."

"I *can* read," Jane defended, rounding on her antagonist.

"Then, do what it says," Daphne taunted.

There was an awkward moment of silence. Then, mortified beyond endurance, Jane bolted from the room.

"If she can read," Daphne snorted, "I can fly!"

"You told me you could read, Johanna," Damon said, his tone mildly accusing as he eyed his bride reproachfully from the chair in their room.

"I can!" Jane cried, throwing back the bedclothes and flouncing to her feet.

Damon grunted as he pulled on a riding boot. "But Marianne said that you were having a game of pantomime last night and you couldn't make out the—"

"Aye! But not because I couldn't read 'em!" she shouted, furiously straightening the tangle of nightdress about her legs.

"Lower your voice, Johanna. A lady does not shriek. Particularly, at her husband. And especially not in a sleeping house before dawn!"

" 'Tis clear enough after yesterday: I'm no lady!" she said, but more softly.

Damon ignored the statement and addressed the problem. "If you can read, what gave you trouble?"

"I never heard of 'em! The others got easy ones, but I never heard of mine. Who is Cleopatra?"

"Cleopatra was an Egyptian queen."

"And . . . And Juliette? And Shakespeare?"

"Ahh, I see," Damon said, standing to put on his riding coat. "Shakespeare was a writer. He wrote plays about both Cleopatra and an unfortunate young lady named Juliette. I expect Uncle Cyrus has copies of the plays in the library. If not, you may read them at Raven's Oak."

"Oh. I never heard of 'em," Jane repeated, lamely.

"Why didn't you say as much last night?"

"I was goin' to. I was goin' to ask Marianne, but then Daphne said—"

"Yes. I know what Daphne said," he muttered disgustedly. "You need to realize, Johanna, that if your positions were reversed, Daphne would be completely out of her element on a farm."

"Oh, aye. I know that for a fact! But I wouldn't make sport of her for not knowin' how to milk a cow!"

He smiled at that, then turned to leave.

"Where are ye goin'?"

"Uncle Cyrus has arranged a hunt."

"What'll ye hunt?"

"Actually, nothing. Fox hunting is a sport, not a legimate hunt at all. You see, a pack of hounds flushes a fox and the riders chase it until it runs to ground. Or is caught by the dogs." He stepped quickly back to the chair to retrieve his quirt.

"What's the point of chasin' a fox ye'll never catch?"

"As I said, 'tis purely sport."

"Sounds silly to me."

He smiled at her around the edge of the door as he closed it. She heard him exchange hushed good mornings with someone in the hall, then a soft rap sounded on the door. Quickly smoothing her sleep-tousled hair, Jane called out nervously, "Come in?"

"Good morning," Marianne said. "Damon told me you were up."

"I'm used to risin' early," Jane said, feeling defensive; wondering if that, too, would be held against her.

"We have that in common then." Marianne smiled, closing the door. "Early morning is such a lovely, peaceful time of day," she said, crossing the room to the window and, as Damon had the previous evening, pulling back the curtain in a hand. "The slug-abeds don't know what they're missing, do they?"

Jane had never considered the aesthetics of rising early; on the farm it had been a necessity, not a luxury. She had rarely had time to enjoy the apricot and saffron hues of a sunrise, as Marianne was doing now, and had always been too busy with egg gathering, or milking or dressing youngsters to even think to call that frantic time of day "peaceful." It came as a shock to her to realize that now she could rise with the sun or not, as she chose.

"I hope he doesn't break his neck," Marianne said with quiet fervor, watching the hunters gather in the yard below. She raised a hand and waved, mouthing through the glass, "Be careful!" Then she smirked in annoyance at what must have been her husband's gestured reply.

"Is this fox huntin' so dangerous?"

"It can be for someone of Robert's limited ability. He's not the best horseman in the world." She tossed Jane a smile, then turned back to the window. "But Damon will keep an eye on him for me."

Jane thought, *Like ye tried to keep an eye on me for Damon last night.*

As if she had read Jane's thoughts, Marianne said, "I came up a little while after you did last night. I suppose you must have been asleep and didn't hear my knock."

Jane reached for her chamber robe, snatching at the same time at the excuse Marianne had given her. "Aye. I must've been."

"I want you to know, Johanna, that I feel perfectly awful about what happened. Daphne was frightfully rude!" She faced Jane. "But if you had only confided in me that you don't read, I may have been able to—"

"Do ye think me liar as well as a dunce?"

"Why no. Of course not."

"Then, since I told ye last night that I can read, why do ye say I can't?" Seeing that Marianne had no answer, she went on, "I haven't been schooled like ye have. I haven't read Mr. Shakespeare's plays; 'twas not somethin' needed knowin' on a farm. But I'm no dullard, Cousin Marianne. I know what I know and I'll learn all that ye do. And be twice as wise when I have done!"

Marianne was shocked and looked it. She could manage nothing more than a breathy, "I'm sure you will."

The newlyweds stayed three more days at Langdale. Damon spent most of his time with his uncle and the other men, leaving Jane to be entertained by the ladies. Unfortunately, Robert's responsibilities to his farm took Marianne away on the day after the fox hunt and, after the pantomime incident, for which Daphne apologized without sounding apologetic, the consensus of opinion among Jane's other new cousins seemed to be that she, like poison ivy, was best left alone. For the most part, despite their mother's efforts to include Jane in their activities, that was how they left her—which suited Jane perfectly.

"Happy to be leaving?" Damon asked from the facing seat of the landau which had caught up with them during their stay.

"Aye," Jane admitted.

"So am I. I long to be home."

Jane longed to be home, too. The week since she had left the farm seemed more like three! She fairly ached with longing for the family and the familiar sights and sounds and smells, even the tiresome chores, that were all so very far behind her now.

"How long 'fore we're there?"

"Two or three days."

Jane cringed inwardly at the thought of spending those long, boring days jolting over roads that made her bones ache despite the padded seats and the cushioning of the carriage springs.

"Barring anything unforeseen," Damon added, belatedly.

"D'ye mean it could take longer?"

"We have enjoyed a remarkably trouble-free journey thus far: no highwaymen; reasonably good weather; no lame horses, broken wheels or the like." He smiled. "It seems that you bring luck with you, little bride." Then he turned his attention to his lap desk.

Stifling a sigh, Jane turned hers to the scenery. But there was little to see and nothing of interest. Then she remembered the book of verses Aunt Hortense had given her. But the motion of the carriage made it difficult to read, and the book itself served as an ugly reminder of the library at Langdale and the conversation she had overheard there.

She had not meant to eavesdrop; she had been intent only on trying to find the plays about Cleopatra and Juliet. But the library doors had been closed and, uncertain whether to knock or to enter unannounced, she had lingered indecisively in the hall and had heard Damon and his uncle talking.

"She's a pretty little thing, I will grant you that. Willing enough, too, if that sparkle in your eye is any measure," Uncle Cyrus had said. She had heard Damon chuckle. "But, is she the right girl?"

"What do you mean?"

"How can you be certain, with so much at stake and knowing the Ralstons as we both do, that another child was not substituted in her place years ago . . . with us none the wiser?"

"I cannot believe, Uncle, that McPhee would take part in such a deception."

"But you have told me yourself that the girl has no knowledge of the situation. Does not that raise questions in your mind?"

"Father trusted McPhee, as did you, Uncle. I will grant you, I am perplexed as to why he did not tell her of the contract as per our agreement, but as for the rest, he took great pains to ensure the child's welfare. He and his wife, both."

"Do you think they would not have taken pains to ensure the welfare of *any* child had they been shown profit in it?"

"If you doubted McPhee's integrity, why did you not say so when the child was placed with him?"

"I did not doubt it then! But now, after what you have told me—"

"What does it matter, Uncle? If Ralston has duped us, what does it matter now? The contract is fulfilled, the land ceded, the marriage consummated. What does it matter?"

"It will matter, my boy, when and if Ralston shows

proof that she is not who we believe her to be. All our efforts—all *your* efforts—will have been for naught!''

"That is not true, Uncle. I have served my purpose in marrying her. Albeit, that purpose was not yours or my father's or *her* father's, but I have done what I set out to do!''

The room went quiet, and Jane knew she ought to have left then. But they had been talking about her. They had been talking about Pap and her! She hadn't been able to make her feet move.

After a little time, she had heard Uncle Cyrus say, "You are right, son. Of course, you are. May the devil take the rest of it, you've done the right thing, the best thing, for the girl.'' She had heard the clap of a hand on a shoulder or back. "But it *is* unfortunate, McPhee's dying. How I would like to have a word or two with him about this! Unconscionable, that you were not informed of his demise.''

"It seems, but for Johanna, none of them write. And as she had been kept ignorant of matters—''

"Um. I see. I suppose you are looking for a new tenant. I know of an able fellow. Shall I recommend him to you?''

*Tenant?* she had thought dazedly. *Pap had been Damon's tenant?*

"No, thank you, Uncle. I have decided to give McPhee's son a trial. He seems a capable sort, and I should not like to uproot a widow and her family unnecessarily.''

"Business and sentiment do not mix! How often have I, and your father before me, told you that?''

"Often enough so that I have never yet allowed the one to be damaged by the other.''

"I cannot argue that,'' Damon's uncle had said in a smiling voice. "Your returning to Raven's Oak—and assuming its management—speaks well of you, son. You've good judgment. I ought to know better than to question it.''

"Thank you, sir. I must confess, though, that after what Colonel Washington told me the other morning, I am beginning to fear for your judgment. You deeded Pomeroy two hundred prime acres?''

"Delia's dowry. His father has been after that land for years! Have sons, my boy. Marrying off daughters is hellishly expensive!''

The men's conversation had turned to estate matters then, and Jane had blindly made her way upstairs, where she spent hours pondering what she had heard. Who were the Ralstons? What was at stake? Of what "situation" was she still ignorant? And, most troubling of all, they had made it sound as though she wasn't a McPhee! Who did they think she was?

She had intended to demand answers to all those questions that night, when Damon joined her in bed. But the look in his eyes stopped her. For all his adamance of the afternoon, his uncle's uncertainty had clearly been at work on him. But as he did not give voice to the questions she saw in his eyes, neither did she ask hers.

Looking at him now, watching his brow furrow, then smooth as he studied the ledger on his lap, she saw not the man with whom she had begun to feel at ease; the man in whose strong, patient, practiced arms she was learning the delights of the marriage bed. She saw, instead, a man who, though he was handsome and generous and kind, was also capable of deceit.

# 5

In the middle of the night on their third day of travel, Damon gently roused Jane from sleep. Yawning and pulling her cloak snug against the night's chill, she stepped groggily out of the carriage and into the glare of torch light. Shielding her eyes with a hand, she squinted at the massive structure before them.

It was like no inn at which they had yet stayed. Set well back from the road at the end of tree-lined lane the mansion was built of irregularly shaped stones. The leaded glass of its multipaned windows glinted yellow-red in the flare of the stanchioned torches flanking the path to the stone front steps. Its chimney-pricked roof-line blackened the sky a full three stories above her, and its wide, iron-studded door looked more forbidding than welcoming.

"Welcome to Raven's Oak," Damon said from her side. When her wide eyes found his face, he smiled and swept her up in his arms.

The door swung open, magically, at their approach and he tarried a moment on the threshold to plant a kiss on her gaping mouth before setting her on her feet inside. From nowhere, a lanky, dark-liveried, white-haired man appeared to accept the traveling cloak Damon was already shedding.

"Welcome home, sir."

"Thank you." The man glided about them like a graceful shadow, then accepted Jane's cloak. "Johanna, this is Simon, our butler and my valet. He has served at Raven's Oak for many years."

If he had said the man had served there for centuries, Jane might have believed him; Simon looked positively ancient. "I'm pleased to meet ye," she said.

"It is an honor to serve you, madam," he said with a respectful if rusty-hinged bow, his arms still full of outerwear.

Then, his hand beneath her elbow, Damon turned her toward the stairs and the line of women which, Jane was sure, had not been there a moment ago.

"Your household," he said, urging her toward the assembled group and the robust, middle-aged woman heading it. "This is Mistress Oswald, the housekeeper; Mildred, the cook; Janet the parlor maid; Eulalia, the scullery maid and . . . Opal, who helps where she can. Curtsy to your mistress, Opal." And, sleepily, the little Negro girl complied.

With the introductions completed, Damon looked to his wife and added offhandedly, "There will be time later for you to meet the others: groundskeepers and the like."

Jane was sure her jaw dropped, but if Damon or the others noticed, they pretended not to. Instead, they looked at her expectantly, and Jane had the awful feeling she was supposed to say something.

"I—I'm pleased to meet ye," she said, uncertainly. But when they still looked as if they were hanging on her every word—all but Opal, who yawned languorously— she added, "Thank ye for stayin' up so late to—to welcome me."

The line dipped unevenly as each of the women and the little girl curtsied again. Then the housekeeper took a step forward and said in a voice that echoed through the cavernous entry hall. "Welcome to Raven's Oak, madam. We of your household wish you good health, long life, and much happiness here." Then, releasing a chain from about her thick waist, she handed it, and the enormous, jangling key ring it held, to Jane.

Hesitantly accepting the odd gift, Jane murmured her thanks and her husband dismissed the staff.

Simon, who had hovered somewhere behind them during the proceedings, and Janet, the maid, immediately ascended the broad, straight staircase which opened onto a narrow balcony over the rear half of the entry. Turning left at the top of the stairs, they disappeared down a lighted hallway. The other women quietly melted into the blackness of a hall behind the rise of the stairs.

Jane looked again to the keys in her hands. "Why'd she give me these?"

"Tradition. You are the mistress of the house, Johanna. Those are the keys to every lock on every door, cabinet, and callar in the house. Although it is little more than a symbolic gesture. Most of those are duplicates." He took the key ring from her. "Most, but not all. These are the keys to our apartment. There are no duplicates for these."

"Two keys for one door?"

"Two keys for two doors. We have separate bedchambers adjoined by a sitting room. Come. I'll show you."

But at the top of the stairs, he hesitated, then steered her toward the back wall of the little balcony. "Let me show you these, first." Stopping before the first in a line of portraits, he said, "This is Sir Thomas Seymour, supposed progenitor of our line. This next, is my great-great-grandfather; a man of little importance in human events, I'm afraid. This is our common great-grandfather, Rendell Seymour. It was he who built Raven's Oak in 1664." He moved on the the last two portraits.

"This is Rendell's son, my grandfather. His name was Renwick."

" 'Tis an odd name!"

Damon looked at her quickly, a brow arched in surprise. But he smiled a little when he said, "Yes. I suppose it is. But it is said to mean 'from the place where the ravens nest' and, as he was the first heir born here, it seems suitable."

He urged her on to the last portrait and Jane, feeling no need of an introduction, said, "This must be yer father. Ye look like him."

"Yes. His name was Bertram Renwick." He smiled. "Quite a mouthful to say."

Jane smiled, too. "Why isn't yer picture here?"

"It will be, one day. But as I am still very much alive, my portrait hangs in our sitting room."

He led her down the short hall to the left of the stairs and, when it ended into another hallway, turned her left, toward the front of the house. Like the balcony, this hall was lined with portraits; these, of ladies.

"Who are they?"

"Past mistresses of Raven's Oak."

"The wives of the gentlemen back there?"

"Of those who lived in this house, yes."

"But, seems there are more wives than husbands!"

Damon laughed. "Each of the gentlemen outlived one wife—in great-grandfather's case, two—and so remarried."

"Oh. Which one is yer mother?"

"Mother's portrait is in the withdrawing room. It is a family custom to display the portrait of the current, or most recent, Mistress Seymour over the hearth there. Your's will soon replace Mother's. I have engaged an artist to paint it." He stopped before a heavy-looking door on their right and, depressing the ivory handle, threw it wide. "Your bedchamber."

Jane thought she was prepared for anything after the

grandeur of Langdale, but she stood transfixed in the doorway, too bedazzled even to breathe.

Deeper than it was wide, the room was large by any standard—by Jane's, it was enormous—and the sheen of candlelight on cherry wood and damask-pink satin endowed it with the roseate glow of a misty sunset. The furnishings blurred before her eyes: the canopied bed with its head against the far wall and its gleaming rose satin curtains caught to the bedposts by gold-tasseled cords; the twin armoires with the pierglass between them; the glass-fronted cabinet with its sparkling array of crystal and porcelain; the tall chest of drawers; the candlestands flanking the bed, each bearing a silver candelabrum. She didn't even see the small, round table between the room's twin windows or the pair of painted silk, Chinese screens to her immediate right. Such opulence was blinding.

From behind her, Damon said, "If there is anything not to your liking, feel free to change it to suit you. You need only tell Oswald what you wish done and she will arrange it for you."

Jane nodded, but she couldn't imagine wanting to change a thing. Or where to start if she did!

"I'll leave you to your toilet, now," he said, and added in a seductive whisper, "and join you later, hm?"

Again, Jane nodded mutely and, when he had moved off down the hall, dared to set foot in the room. The floral-patterned, hooked rugs which almost entirely covered the floor were thickly padded with straw and as soft and deep underfoot as she supposed clouds must be. For some time she stood in the middle of the room, trying to take it all in. Then Damon's words registered in her bedazzled brain, and she wondered what kind of toilet he expected her to perform without the trunks that were still in the wagon on the road behind them.

But, as he hadn't complained the first night when she had lacked scented lotions and the like, Jane decided that soap and water would do and set about looking for the washbasin which, surely, must be somewhere in this forest of furnishings. She was about to peek behind the newly discovered Chinese screens when, as if from nowhere, Janet appeared. Feeling like a child caught trespassing Jane let her hand fall guiltily from the frame of the screen she had been about to fold back.

"Oh. I beg your pardon, ma'am. I didn't know you had come up," Janet said, dropping a curtsy. "May I be of some service to you, ma'am?"

"Ah. Aye. I was lookin' for a washbasin."

"Yes, ma'am. It's just behind the screens." Stepping quickly to Jane, she folded back a screen to expose a deep alcove. "I'll light the candles for you, ma'am."

When the candlewicks blossomed into flame, Jane was astonished to see a cozy little room which held a mirrored dressing table arrayed with the toilet articles she had thought were still far behind her; a low, wooden cabinet which, since leaving the farm, she had learned discreetly housed a chamber pot; a washstand with a white porcelain pitcher and basin, each garlanded with painted flowers; and what looked like an oversized, enameled scuttle minus the handle.

"May I turn down your bed, now, ma'am?"

"Oh. Ah, aye."

Dropping another curtsy, the maid went efficiently about her business. Tossing back the gleaming, satin coverlet, she folded the bedding down on the side of the bed nearest the windows, then plumped the near pillow and stepped around the bed to plump the far one. But rather than turning the bed clothes down on that side, she merely untucked them.

Jane felt herself blush at the invitation to intimacy the gesture implied, but appreciated its subtlety. She wondered if Damon's bed had been similarly prepared. Or if it had been prepared at all.

"May I get you anything, ma'am?" Janet asked,

straightening and turning. "Something from the kitchen, perhaps?"

Still unused to going without a noon meal, Jane was hungry. But, not knowing what to ask for, and thinking that to ask for anything at all at this hour of the night would surely upset the cook, she shook her head.

"I'll bid you a good night, then, ma'am." With a bob of a curtsy, Janet left. But the door had scarcely closed behind her when a brusque rap on it presaged a breathless Nancy's arrival.

"I'm sorry to have kept you waiting, ma'am." She offered a stiff-jointed version of Janet's graceful curtsies, feeling the battering her body had taken during the three and a half days she had spent, as propriety dictated, riding atop the carriage beside the driver.

"Ye've not kept me waitin', Nancy. I've only been here a bit myself." Jane's eyes swept the room. "Have ye ever seen anythin' so grand?"

Nancy's smile was forced, and Jane failed to hear the envy in her voice when the maid said, "Indeed not, ma'am. I'm told Mr. Seymour had this room completely redone for you."

"Did he?" Jane gasped, eyes popping. "For me?"

Nancy nodded, still wearing her sugary smile. "Every stick and stitch. Have you seen these, ma'am? Embroidered with your initials, as all your linens are." Jane accepted the linen hand towel Nancy offered and traced the elaborately scrolled "J.S." and its garland of dainty flowers with a fingertip. "He wanted everything new for you, ma'am; nothing to remind him of the last mistress, so they tell me." Dazedly, Jane handed the towel back. "Have you seen the clothes, ma'am?"

Thinking Nancy meant the tardy luggage, Jane said, "No. The wagon with my things broke a wheel or somethin'."

"Those are only your traveling clothes," Nancy said, hoping the disparagement she felt for the bumpkin she was forced to call mistress hadn't come through. Sweetly, she added, "I was speaking of these." Then she flung the doors of one armoire wide to display the fantastic array of clothing inside. "The other is like as full. And the chest of drawers. He didn't spare a penny in outfitting you, ma'am. And he has instructed me to see to it that anything lacking be made up."

"Oh, I'm sure he's thought of everythin'!" Jane breathed.

Nancy reserved comment until she had closed the armoire and was unlacing Jane's dress. "It seems, ma'am, he neglected to see you properly fitted. Your bodices are a bit tight, aren't they?"

"Aye. But I can let 'em out."

"Oh, no! A lady doesn't do such for herself. You'll need a dressmaker. I understand as there's one nearby."

"The one who made all my things?"

"No, ma'am. Mr. Seymour sent to Philadelphia to have your things made."

"Philadelphia! But, why?"

"Perhaps, he thought the Philadelphia seamstress more skillful than the local one. I'm sure the local woman'll do for a bit of altering, though, ma'am. Shall I make arrangements with her for a fitting?"

"Aye. I s'pose so. I wouldn't know how to go about that for myself."

"Nor should you, ma'am. That's why I am here; to do for you all that need be done." She smiled again, and forced herself to flatter. "And I've never had such a lovely mistress to do for, ma'am."

Jane returned the smile. Embarrassed as she still was by such praise, she did not doubt Nancy's sincerity in offering it. The maid had accepted her at face value and that acceptance, made all the more precious by contrast to the enmity she had found at Langdale, had won the woman Jane's genuine affection . . . and friendship.

Jane had been stripped down to her corselette and fancy, bow-trimmed breeches by the time her bath water arrived.

"It's about time!" Nancy scolded, when Opal, with much thumping and sloshing, bumbled into the room; a half full bucket in each hand. And she scolded her again when she dawdled in leaving, peeping curiously at her new mistress through a gap in the screens.

"That one needs a good ear boxing if you ask me, ma'am," Nancy grumbled, having seen the child gone. "She's only tolerated because she's Eulalia's girl. Mr. Seymour doesn't hold with selling a slave from its own."

"Oh," Jane said, watching Nancy pour water into the oversized scuttle. "Has he many slaves?"

"Oh, yes, ma'am. Mostly field hands, but there's a goodly number working in the stables, too." She tested the water temperature with a practiced elbow and added more cold. "Eulalia's the only house nigger, though. Excepting that addlepated child, of course, ma'am. As I say, she needs an ear boxing. But, as Mr. Seymour isn't heavy-handed with his niggers, I don't suppose she'll ever get it. Is the lily scent all right, ma'am?"

"Oh. Aye. D'ye mean, he doesn't whip 'em?"

"I'm told not, ma'am. They say he takes after his father in that. There's not been a whipping here for as long as anyone can recall."

Jane was thoughtfully quiet as Nancy finished the bath preparations. The only slave owner she had known had been a man who called himself Squire Trent, though no one back home had thought him deserving of the title, and she knew his slaves hadn't received kind treatment. They were always running away. And the squire was always paying Pap for the use of his keen-nosed hounds to bring them back again. Which, most of the time, he did . . . though sometimes more dead than alive.

It had never seemed right to her, one man owning another the way he owned an ox or a mule. And learning that her husband was a slave owner didn't set well with her.

But once settled into the hip bath, with the enticingly scented, delightfully warm water sloshing languidly about her, Jane found herself rethinking her thoughts on slavery. If a man had no sons to work his land—and Damon didn't—then he had need of hired workers, be they black or white. And so long as he treated them kindly—and Damon did—she supposed it mattered little if they were slave or free. And if she was to find happiness in this new life where her only friend, aside from Nancy, was her slave-owner husband, she had best not think any harder on the subject than that! Though it still didn't set well with her. . . .

The eyes Jane had blissfully closed snapped open and she started at the soft tapping on her bedroom door.

"Ignore it. She'll go away," Damon whispered huskily, brushing the sheet aside and baring Jane's breasts to his lips.

He had bared much more of her and a considerable portion of himself when, with a loud thump and raucous rattling of china, Opal kicked open the door.

"Damn!" Damon bellowed, throwing himself from Jane and tugging the sheet over both of them. "Damnation! How often have you been told to *await a reply* before entering a bedchamber!"

Opal's eyes were as large and dark as the plump prunes on the breakfast tray in her hands. "I's sorry, suh. I fo'gits." Haltingly, she backed toward the door.

"Leave the tray, seeing as you've brought it," Damon snarled. Then, the thought struck him. "We've not yet ordered breakfast. Who told you to bring it up?"

"Mildred, suh. She say to me, 'Opal, you take dis

tray upstairs.' But Amos, he weren't dere, suh, and dere ain't no way in wit'out Amos—he got de key, suh—so I—"

"Yes, yes! Leave it and go!" Damon snapped, cutting the girl off.

"Yes, suh." But after depositing the heavy tray on the table near the windows, the child stared unabashedly at the mortified, white-skinned, pink-cheeked, blue-eyed, yellow-haired young woman in the bed.

"That will be all, Opal," Damon prodded tightly.

"Lookin' at ma'am's like lookin' at a flower garden. Ain't it, suh?" the girl said breathlessly.

"Opal!"

"Yes, suh. I's goin'."

With that, Opal scuffed across the carpet—obviously relishing the feel of it under her bare, brown toes—and, with another long look at Jane, slowly pulled the door shut behind her.

"Damnation!" Damon seethed. "I'm sorry, Johanna. The girl is a bit dull witted." He smiled. "But I give her credit for her powers of observation; you are beautiful, indeed!" And he wasted not a moment in taking up their loving where Opal's untimely entrance had forced them to leave it off.

The sun was noticeably higher in the sky when Jane, stretching languorously, said with a contented sigh, "Oh, I think 'tis more delightful every time!"

He laughed softly and smoothed the blond hair tousled by sleep and her wild abandonment to their lovemaking. "*You* are delightful, Jane."

She smiled. "Thank ye for callin' me that."

"I said I would, now and then. And a gentleman must keep his word. His honor depends upon it." Tossing back the sheet, he disentangled his robe from the jumble of bedding and stood to put it on. "What do you say to a ride after breakfast?"

"All we've done for days is ride!"

"I meant a ride on horseback," he said, rounding the foot of the bed and walking to a window where he pulled the drapery back in a hand and leaned against the frame in what Jane now recognized as an habitual pose. "It seems we've a fine morning for it."

She watched him open the window and drink in the cool morning air before she miserably admitted, "I'm sorry, Damon, but I don't know how to ride."

"I'll teach you," he said easily. "And, as you are quick study, I've no doubt that you will excel at riding as quickly as you have at . . ." he tossed her an intimate smile, "other things."

In spite of her effort not to, or maybe because of it, Jane blushed. Hiding her face before he could tease her, she scooted to the far side, "his" side, of the bed and quickly retrieved her dressing gown from the floor where he had tossed it the night before. "Who is Amos?"

"What?"

"Who is Amos? Opal said she was takin' that tray to him."

"Oh. Yes. Amos is . . . a servant. He has a room upstairs. As they all do."

Jane looked at his strong, stern-jawed profile against the dawn. "D'ye serve all yer servants meals in their rooms?" she fairly gasped.

"Certainly not!" He looked at her and, just as quickly, away again. "That is, not as a rule. Amos is—he has been unwell of late."

"Oh," Jane sighed, turning her attention to the ribbon ties on the front of her robe. " 'Tis very kind of ye to take such care of yer servants. And yer slaves."

Damon slowly pivoted to face her. "What do you mean?"

"I was thinkin' of Opal, mainly. 'Tis kind of ye to keep her; not sell her away from her mother."

"Oh? How do you know I won't do that?"

"Ye won't, will ye?"

"Who has been talking to you?"

"Nancy. She said ye don't hold with sellin' a slave from its own. Or with whippin's, neither. She said that ye treat yer slaves . . . kindly," she finished, weakly.

But as he stormed toward her, Damon's eyes looked anything but kind!

"I'll not be the subject of gossip, Johanna. Particularly, not under my own roof! Is that clear?"

"Aye, but—"

"Is that clear!" he demanded, gripping her shoulders so strongly that it hurt.

"Aye," she gasped.

He released her abruptly then, and left through the door which, Jane supposed, led to the sitting room between their bedchambers, slamming it angrily behind him. Staring after him, she sagged onto the bed.

It was well into the forenoon when a very subdued Jane, perched precariously atop a pretty little dappled mare, accompanied her husband down the tree-shaded drive. Damon's spirited sorrel gelding pranced and side-stepped, eager for a run. But when his rider would have none of it, he settled into a sedate walk and cast an envious eye at the long-legged, black colt cavorting gaily at its dam's side.

"Hold the reins loosely, Johanna; don't clutch at them. The reins are used to guide and instruct the animal, not as a point of balance for the rider."

"But there's nothin' else to hold on to," she cautiously complained. "It looks easier to sit yer way."

He smiled for the first time since the episode before breakfast. "I've no doubt it is. But a lady does not ride astride."

"Why not?"

"For one thing, her skirts prevent it. And for another," he cleared his throat, "a lady does not spread herself. Now, then. Sit tall; back straight. No, don't raise your hands, keep them low and over the withers—fingers facing, thumbs on top—yes. Elbows in closer at your sides. Good. Now, relax. No, no keep your back straight; don't slouch.'' He eyed her critically for a long moment. ''You want a suppleness of waist, Johanna. Relax your legs; don't grip the saddle so tightly. A rider's movements must be as fluid as those of his mount.''

Jane relaxed by cautious fractions, trying to keep all his instructions in mind at once. With so much to think about, she wondered how anyone could enjoy riding. ''Am I doin' somethin' else wrong?'' she asked miserably, feeling him watching her.

''No, you are doing quite well. I was just thinking how well you look in burgundy. I've yet to see you in a color that does not flatter you.''

''Ye've not seen me in gray.''

''Ah. Are any of your dresses gray?''

''I don't know. I haven't had time to look at all of 'em.''

''Well, should you discover a gray one, set it aside. I shall see it is replaced with one in a more flattering shade.''

Jane looked at him aghast. ''Just like that?''

''It is a simple enough matter to return it and request a replacement. Which reminds me, do the gowns fit you as well as it appears they do?''

''Well enough. How did ye know my size?''

''I told McPhee to have his wife supply your measurements to the dressmaker last year.''

''Oh.'' Jane swallowed thickly. ''Mam didn't tell me.''

''There seems to be a duced lot the pair of them didn't tell you,'' he said, sounding annoyed. But the aggravation had left his voice by the time he said, ''We will be turning into that pasture ahead. To make a horse turn, the rider lays the reins against the animal's neck on the side opposite to the new direction. To turn left, you will lay the reins on the mare's right, and vice versa. Like so." He demonstrated, weaving his gelding in a sweeping, serpentine curve. "You try it. Excellent. To make your horse stand, bring your hands gently in toward your body. Thusly. Fine. Wait here while I open the gate."

Jane watched him bend low over his horse's neck and effortlessly lift a rope loop from a gate post. Swinging the gate wide, he waited for her to follow him through, coaxed the colt along after her, then closed the gate and redeposited the loop.

"This way."

The direction he took led them through a copse alive with birds whose orange and black plumage contrasted strikingly with the sun-dappled, spring-green foliage. The woodland gave way to a sloping, flower-dotted field with a swiftly flowing, tree-lined brook at its bottom.

"This is Ravenswood Creek. We'll cross, there," he said, nodding downstream and to their left at the narrow bridge that spanned the turbulent water.

Once across, they followed the creek bed for some distance before Damon turned his horse up the steep, wooded side of the escarpment to their right. Drawing rein at the summit, Jane found herself looking down into a pretty, river valley.

"The Patapsco. It marks the southern boundary of Raven's Oak," Damon explained. "Baltimore lies some fifteen miles downstream, as the crow flies."

Jane looked at him quickly. "D'ye mean, all the time we've been ridin' we've been on yer land?" He nodded. "And, how far do ye own toward Baltimore?"

He stretched out an arm and pointed through the trees. "Do you see that promontory where the river makes a sharp bend?"

"Clear to there?" Jane asked incredulously, judging the distance in miles.

Damon smiled. "Come along. There is something else I want to show you."

They descended toward Ravenswood Creek again, and this time rode upstream along its shady bank.

When they had gone some distance, Jane asked, "And I s'pose this is yer land, too?"

"Yes. As far west as the township of Rendell." He smiled at her. "It was named after my great-grandfather. When he built Raven's Oak, he found it necessary to import the labor to do the job. By the time the house was finished, the workmen were so well established in their own community that they decided to stay. They named the place Rendell. Personally, I've always thought they lacked imagination."

Jane smiled. "'Is it far from here?"

"A mile or so. A bit more, from the house."

"Is there a dressmaker there?"

Damon looked at her sharply. "Why do you ask?"

"Nancy said there's one close-by, and I thought she might have meant in Rendell."

"What else did Nancy say of her?" he demanded, sounding as angry as he looked.

"N—nothin' else."

"Then, why mention her at all?"

"My dresses need some lettin' out. Nancy said she'd arrange for the dressmaker to—"

"I thought you said your dresses fit you well."

"I said, 'well enough.'"

He took in her shape with a practiced eye. "Have you taken to binding yourself again?"

"Nay. Not exactly."

"What do you mean, 'not exactly?' Either you have or you haven't."

"A corselette can be laced as tight as need be. 'Tis almost the same as being bound."

"In that case, I'll have your things returned to Philadelphia for alteration."

"But, with a dressmaker so close, that's silly!" Jane yelped.

"They were made in Philadelphia. They will be altered there."

"But it'll take weeks and weeks to send 'em all off and get 'em all—"

"Enough said!"

Angrily, Jane clamped her mouth shut. It took her awhile to decide that he probably knew best; that he undoubtedly knew the local woman's reputation and found it wanting. Having determined that she was being ungrateful, she tried to make amends.

"Those are fine lookin' horses," she said, nodding toward a half-dozen mares and their foals grazing near a pasture fence. "Are they yers?"

"Didn't Nancy tell you I breed horses?" he sneered, sarcastically.

"I didn't ask, did ye breed 'em. I asked, do ye own 'em. Surely, ye can't own everythin' hereabout!"

A smile threatened to erase his scowl, but he managed to contain it. "Yes. They are mine." He paused. "What songs do you know?"

"Songs?"

"Songs. As it seems we are unable to speak civilly for more than a sentence or two, I thought we might try singing. What shall we sing?"

"Oh. Ah. Whatever ye like."

But Jane was familiar with none of the tunes he named. And even when he ran out of titles and resorted to singing a stanza or two of each song, she was forced to wag her head miserably.

"Very well, then. You sing one. Perhaps I'll know it."

Jane hesitated. She had never sung with or for anyone but her family and friends, and she felt her voice was not nearly as good as his. Then, too, the songs he had begun were fine, lilting melodies. The songs she knew best were children's rondelays or simple country tunes. Nevertheless, she shyly began, "I know a man who has a dog. 'Tis a rare dog. 'Tis a whistlin' dog. And he keeps it in the valley."

"Go on," he urged when she stopped and looked at him miserably.

"Heigh, ho, 'tis a whistlin' dog, he keeps down in the valley. Ho, heigh, it whistles away, away down in the valley-o."

"You've a fine voice," he complimented sincerely. "And that's a catchy tune. How does it go again?"

Jane sang the ditty again, adding sheepishly, "Ye can put in anythin' ye like in place of the dog."

"Very well. A toad."

"A toad!"

"You said anything I like, and I like a toad." He grinned. "And I will have my toad juggling rather than whistling, if you please."

Jane laughed. "But, 'tis silly. A jugglin' toad!"

"And a whistling dog is not?" he said, jovially. "You start it, and I'll join in."

They sang verse after verse, taking turns supplying lyrics each more ludicrous than the last and actually enjoying themselves until Damon stopped singing abruptly, midway through the verse about a tickling hare, and scowled at an ancient oak tree situated atop a nearby knoll.

"Wait here," he ordered. Not giving Jane time to question him, he cantered off toward the tree.

She watched him dismount and, with his quirt, prod at something on the ground. She couldn't see what it was, but she sensed it was dead by the manner of his approach to it. Then, not far from Damon, a movement caught her eye. A bird, a large, black bird was flapping and fluttering helplessly in the grass. Damon saw it, too. Striding to where it lay thrashing, he took a quick look at it, then crushed its head with his heel. Even from a distance, the look on his face said it was more than an injured bird he wanted to kill.

With little more than a glance at her, he called, "Ride back. Follow the brook. I've business in Rendell."

Stunned, and not a little irritated at being left on her own in the middle of nowhere, Jane watched him ride off. But by the time she had reached the bridge over Ravenswood Creek, she was surprised to find herself enjoying the solitude. She had almost never been completely alone on the farm. And on those rare occasions when she snatched at a solitary moment, she had inevitably felt guilty: That precious time had been stolen from someone or something else. But here, no one and nothing awaited her. Time was hers for the taking!

Such leisurely freedom was heady. She revelled in it, and in being totally, completely alone . . . until she encountered the pasture gate.

Knowing full well that if she dismounted to open it, she would be unable to remount, Jane struggled with the rope loop her husband had so easily mastered, very nearly tumbling headlong from her horse before she finally lifted the loop over the post. Then she spent what seemed like an eternity trying to close the gate behind her. It opened inward, away from the road, and with her stable so close at hand, the mare protested being turned from it to go back and latch a gate. But when Jane had at last swung the thing shut and redeposited the loop, she found that the little colt had been left on the other side. Frustrated to tears, she went through the whole, exhausting procedure again.

It was with a feeling of triumph that she at last approached the stables. Like the main house, and the carriage house close behind them, they were built of rough-hewn stone blocks, which exuded an air of permanence; of somber indomitability. They had withstood more than a century, they seemed to say, and would be here long after her fragile flesh had turned to dust.

That thought sobered her, as it seemed to have done others. There wasn't a smiling face in sight when she drew rein near the mounting block in the stable yard. The head groom, a Negro called Noggin, was scowling as he wordlessly caught the mare's bridle to keep the animal still while Jane ineptly dismounted. And Ebenezer, who emerged from the stable's cavelike interior, glowered at her almost menacingly. Even a stable boy, a little pickaninny like Opal, stopped cleaning out the stalls and leaned upon his muck rake to stare at her in solemn wonder.

Aware that she had made some mistake, but at a loss to imagine what it was, Jane lamely bid the mute assemblange a ''Good mornin','' though it was well past noon, and set off for the house. Her greeting there was little warmer.

Entering through the kitchen as she would have done at home, she was met with the horrified stares of the cook, the maid, the scullery woman, and Opal. Mrs. Oswald, the housekeeper, leveled a tight-lipped, unquestionably displeased glare at her over the rim of a teacup. Too flustered to know what to say to them, Jane said nothing at all but hurried across the room and through the first door that presented itself. Unfortunately, this gave access to the servants' stairs, not the front hall as she had expected. But, rather than face those in the kitchen again, Jane pridefully hoisted her skirts and took the stairs. They went up, and up was where she wanted to go.

Stiff and sore from her stint on the mare, it was no easy climb. And the stairs turned back on themselves so sharply at each of the numerous landings she passed, that the effect was dizzying. When, at last, she found a door, she all too eagerly abandoned the stairs, which continued their convulted climb to the left, and opened it.

It swung outward on well-oiled hinges, but not into

the hallway lined with ladies' portraits as she had hoped. Her heart plummeting, Jane surveyed the expansive chamber before her. Heavy, dark draperies were drawn across the several windows, but here and there a dagger of sunlight pierced through a gap, faintly illuminating the room and the dust moats that swirled in the draft her entrance had stirred. The air was hot and heavy with the smell of disuse. What furnishings there were, were shrouded in sheets and clustered toward one end of the room which, Jane miserably decided, must be the attic. With a leaden sigh, and wondering how she could have missed the door to the second floor, Jane turned back to the stairs. From the corner of her eye, she caught the gleam of something bright and brassy at the far end of the room: a door handle!

Her hurried footsteps echoed in the dusky, silent space, and her movement stirred a new flurry of dust moats as she followed an ill-defined but discernible path in the dust powdering the solid-sounding flooring. Encouraged by this evidence that others had come this way, she confidently applied her hand to the cool, brass handle. Surprised when it resisted the considerable pressure she applied to it, and deciding that it must be stuck, she gave the door a shove with her shoulder.

There was a scuffing sound on the other side, not unlike the sound of shuffling feet, and the quiet chatter of china. A teacup rattling in a saucer?

Jane took a startled step back. Clearly, this was not the door to the hallway.

"May I be of assistance, madam?"

Jumping like a startled cat, Jane spun to face the man who stood at the mouth of the servants' stairs. "Oh! I—I was tryin' to . . . 'Tis stuck."

"It is locked, madam," the butler corrected. "This floor is not in use. If I may show you to your—"

"But there's someone there. I heard . . . him," she argued, even as she wondered what had made her think there was a *man* beyond the door. "And there are footprints in the dust."

"What you heard, madam, must have been me climbing the stairs. And, as this room is used for temporary storage, the servants do come here, occasionally." The parchmentlike skin of the man's gaunt, ancient face creased in what may have been an attempt at a smile. "I beg your pardon for alarming you, madam, but if you will be so kind as to allow me to show you down?"

Walking slowly back, Jane turned his explanations over in her mind. She couldn't question what he had said about the room being used for storage, and she knew that sounds carried easily up stairways, which would account for the scuffing she had heard. But there was still the rattling china. There was someone on the other side of that door . . . Of course! Amos, the servant; the man whose breakfast she had eaten.

"I hope I didn't disturb him," she said to Simon in a hushed whisper.

"Madam?"

"Amos," she said, adding with a glance at the door, "That's his room, isn't it?"

Simon stiffened and brusquely cleared his throat. "If you will follow me, madam?" And he led the way back down the stairs.

She forgave herself for missing the second floor door when Simon pushed through it, then held it open for her to follow. Nothing more than a hinged panel set in the landing wall, the hidden door opened without benefit of latch or handle. Unless one knew where it was, one might never find it. If she hadn't seen it opened, she would have thought it as solid as the rest of the woodwork.

"This way, madam."

Moving ahead once more, Simon led her past two doors, one on each hand, and across the hall which led to the balcony before Jane found herself in the portrait-lined hall she had been searching for. This house was even bigger than it looked!

Swinging her bedroom door wide, the butler solicitously asked, "May I send a maid to attend you, madam?"

Seeing no need to send for Nancy, but suspecting that if he had suggested it, it was probably the proper thing to do, she answered with a small nod and Simon promptly closed the door behind her. Jane heaved a sigh of relief at being "home" at last. As alien as it still was, the room was a welcome sight, if an overpowering one. After the homey clutter of the kitchen, the oppressive stairwell, and the dusty dimness of the room upstairs, it looked even grander and brighter and cleaner than she had remembered it. She doubted she would ever get used to such grand accommodations.

Or to having maids. The bed had been made up in her absence, the breakfast tray removed from the table. The screened-off dressing room had been tended, too. Fresh towels hung on the pegs on the washstand, and the chamber pot and bath had been emptied. A pretty, buttercup-yellow frock, dotted with embroidered blue flowers and trimmed with lace and blue ribbons, had been carefully draped over the back of the little chair before the dressing table, and the toes of a pair of dainty blue house slippers peeped out from beneath the spread of its skirt. Her toiletries had been neatly rearranged, too, to make room on the table for a large, elaborate wooden box.

Fingering the mother-of-pearl inlays of the lid, Jane decided that whatever the box contained must be intended for her and cautiously peeked inside. Jewels. What must surely be a king's ransom in jewels sparkled and glittered at her from within the velvet confines of their case. Opening it wide, a collection of necklaces, dangling from hooks inside the lid, first caught her eye.

She hardly noticed the amethyst one Damon had given her, so awestruck was she by the other three. The most breathtaking of those was made up of brilliant, crystalline stones which sparked and flashed every hue of the rainbow. Similar, smaller stones had been used in the other necklaces to frame the large, rectangular green jewels in one, and smaller, oval-shaped blue stones in the other. Stunned, Jane stared at them, gingerly touching each in turn, before she dropped her bedazzled eyes to the other treasures in the case.

On the first of its three shelves—each of which lifted out by means of corded loops at the sides—were the wristlets. Two of them matched the green- and blue-stoned necklaces; one was gold inlaid with sparkling red gems; another polished silver and beautifully engraved with flowers and birds and grape clusters; the last, silver set with pearls. The next shelf housed the earbobs—she would have to have her ears pierced, she supposed—and the rings: as many rings as she had fingers! Then came the brooches. She was relieved to see her grandmam's cameo there. There were also cloak clasps and several strings of pearls, one a double strand. The bottom compartment of the box was expectantly empty.

The breath that had repeatedly caught in her throat left Jane in a rush of a sigh and she whispered, "As if there could be more!"

"Madam?"

The maid's voice from the other side of the screen startled her, and Jane quickly replaced the shelves and closed the jewel case before she called a tremulous, "Aye?"

"You sent for me, ma'am?"

Stepping around a screen, Jane said meekly, embarrassed at having to correct the woman, "I—I sent for Nancy, I think."

Janet looked uncomfortable. "Nancy is not here, ma'am."

"Oh. Wh-where is she?"

"She left without saying where she was going, ma'am. If you would like to change after your ride, I shall be happy to assist you."

"Thank ye," Jane said, miserably wishing she could manage her elaborate dresses for herself.

Janet bobbed a quick curtsy and smiled a nervous smile before she set to work helping Jane change. Clearly out of her element in the role of personal maid, Janet said no more than necessary and, when the heavy, burgundy twill had been exchanged for the dainty cotton frock, was as happy to be gone as Jane was to have her go.

But as quiet as Janet had been, her meager company was better than none. The bedroom was grand and beautiful, but it afforded nothing by way of entertainment. After examining the lovely furnishings and brick-a-brack, the fabulous array of clothing, the incredible collection of jewelry again, Jane found nothing else to do. She was standing at the one of the windows, staring out at the tree-filled elipse between the curving front drive and the road, wondering if anyone at the farm on Moss Creek was missing her, when she remembered that she had yet to see the sitting room.

The door, through which Damon had entered and exited several times since last night, was closed. She opened it only a crack and peeped cautiously into the empty room before she dared to enter. The sitting room was only half as large as her bedroom, but no less elegantly appointed. Two comfortable-looking wing chairs, with a graceful, straight-legged table between them, faced the small fireplace to her right. There was a divan under the wide window to her left and this was flanked by a small, round table on one side and the twin of the curio cabinet in her room on the other. Directly opposite the door was another, closed as hers had been, which undoubtedly gave access to her husband's room. On the short wall beside it, stood a glass-fronted bookcase and a low cabinet bearing a silver tray arrayed with two glasses and a decanter half full of an amber-colored liquid: Damon's brandy, she supposed. On what was clearly "her" side of the room, a small secretary stood against the wall and, beside it, a stand topped with a bouquet of flowers. But the most arresting of all was the imposing portrait above the mantel.

Barely aware that she did so, Jane walked to the center of the room and stood staring up at her husband's stern-jawed likeness. That it had been recently painted she had no doubt; he was wearing the same velvet jacket and lacy flounce he had worn on their wedding day. She didn't recognize the boots and breeches. But, although it was undoubtedly appropriate to the wealthy master of so grand an estate, the pose seemed wrong; out of the character for the humble man she knew Damon to be. He looked decidedly arrogant standing there, one hand resting on the head of his father's walking stick and the other fingering his heavy gold watch. And there was something of a swagger in the lift of his chin. Of course, she reminded herself, remembering the overheard conversation at Langdale, she knew almost nothing of him at all. Perhaps the painter had known him better. He had certainly been a master! It was Damon to the very life! Except . . . Jane held the portrait's steady, penetrating gaze—and shuddered with a prickly chill. For all that they were mightily familiar, there was something odd about those eyes. Unnerved, and rubbing the gooseflesh from her arms, she looked away.

The bookcase caught her attention and she spent awhile choosing a book with which to pass the time until . . . When? Tea? Dinner? What did the wives of wealthy gentlemen do?

With a leaden sigh, she settled onto the divan to read. She had turned only a few pages when she heard men's muted voices in the hall, then Damon's quite clearly as he entered his room.

". . . has promised to set a few days aside. See that Father's violin is in tune for him."

"Very good, sir."

"Ives will be coming, of course. And Pemberton, no doubt. Lay in a supply of the light rum they favor."

"Yes, sir. What of . . . ladies, sir?"

"No ladies," Damon growled.

"Yes, sir."

Jane thought Simon sounded relieved.

"Did my wife return safely?"

Jane stiffened and strained to hear the butler's hush-voiced reply. Damon's mirthful chuckle reached her clearly enough. Furious that he should laugh at her—she had long ago concluded that whatever her mistakes had been, she would not have made them had he not deserted her—Jane took an angry step toward Damon's bedroom door, intending to defend herself or, at least, accuse him. But his laughter died abruptly and the anger in his voice froze her in midstride.

"How!"

"It was unavoidable, sir. Oswald said Madam bolted from the room before any of them had time to gather their wits from the surprise of seeing her there. Unacquainted with the house, sir, she quite innocently took the wrong stairs. No harm was done, sir."

Jane's heart warmed toward the old butler; he sounded kind as he defended her.

"You're certain?"

"Quite, sir."

"Good. Where is she now?"

"I showed her to her room, sir. I believe she is still there."

At the sound of purposeful footsteps, Jane realized Damon's intent and made a dash for her room. He opened the door on his side before she reached the one on hers. Looking as guilty as she felt for her inadvertent eavesdropping, she turned to find Damon eyeing her as steadily as did his portrait. Her skin crawled under the intense, double scrutiny.

"You overheard me speaking with Simon, I presume."

"I heard ye laughin' at me plain enough," she said, angrily holding his eyes. "I do not like bein' laughed at, Mr. Seymour, any more than ye like begin' talked about. And I do not like that very much, either!"

He glared back at her. "I merely inquired as to your safe return home."

"Aye. And *then* ye laughed!"

Seymour momentarily dropped his eyes. "Did you have any difficulty finding your way back?"

"Nay. My trouble started once I got here."

"Yes, well, give me a few minutes to change, then I'll show you about. That should eliminate any future 'trouble,' hm?" He turned and reentered his room, calling behind as he went, "Have you eaten?"

"Nay."

"Why not? I told Mildred to prepare your supper."

Not wanting to admit that she had been too shy to ask for anything, she said, "I wasn't hungry," which was half true, anyway.

"Simply because it is not my habit to take a noon meal, do not think you must forgo one."

Eager to shift the conversation from herself and her blunders, she asked, "Why don't ye sup at noon?"

"What was that? Come in here, Johanna. I can scarcely hear you." She went as far as the door. "Now, what was that you said?" he asked while Simon helped him out of his jacket.

"I asked, why don't ye sup at noon?"

"I rarely have time. An estate the size of this one does not run itself." Untying his stock, he handed it to the valet, who draped it atop the jacket over his arm. "Thank you, Simon. You may go." Then, disappearing behind his dressing screen, he said, "I am usually up at cock's crow and off soon after, especially at this time of year. I rarely find time to return to the house much before tea. But," she heard water splash into a basin, then the sound of hands being lathered, "that is no reason for you not to take supper. Or to rise so early."

"I'm used to risin' early," she said, letting her eyes freely roam the place now that Simon was gone.

The room was as masculine as hers was feminine. And, though she was sure the rooms must be the same size, the dark, wood-paneled walls, russet-colored draperies, and massive, ornately carved furnishings made this bedchamber appear the smaller of the two.

He laughed shortly. "I'm sure you are, what with the milking to do."

"Julia did the milkin'," she said, testily, irritated by what she took for mockery. "I helped Mam with the babes and breakfast."

"But I thought you said you can milk?"

"I can. And gather eggs, set bread to rise, and dress three youngsters all before first light!"

It was very quiet behind the screen. After a while, without a hint of ridicule, he said, "It was a hard life you led, Johanna."

" 'Twas not so hard as some others," she said, quietly. "And 'twas all I knew, 'til now."

She heard the rustle of clothing before he spoke again. "What is your earliest memory, Johanna?"

"What do ye mean?"

"What is the first thing you remember?"

"I—I think 'tis of Pap, ridin' me pickaback 'round the yard. Why?"

"How old were you then?"

"Five or six, I s'pose."

"You remember nothing earlier than that?"

"I don't think so. Why do ye want to know?"

"I thought you might remember an afternoon when you were three. I can recall it quite clearly." He stepped around the screen and reached for the frock coat Simon had laid out. "You were running about the lawn with a collie pup, chasing after it. I watched you from the road for a while. By the time I reached the house, it had allowed you catch it and you brought it to show me. I told you it was the finest puppy I had ever seen. And you gave me a kiss—a very moist kiss—just here." He touched his left cheek. "Do you remember that afternoon, Johanna?"

Jane thought she ought to remember it, and, not wanting to disappoint him, she tried. But ultimately she was forced to wag her head.

Disbelief, disappointment, anger, resignation . . . she saw each of them race through his eyes in the few moments before he turned his back and shrugged into the coat. "It's probably just as well," he said, more to himself than to her. "It makes no difference." Then he turned and, wearing a soft smile, offered his arm. "Come along, Mistress Seymour, and I'll show you your house."

Jane tried to concentrate on Damon's running discourse as he led her from one room to another—four more bedrooms and another sitting room upstairs; the withdrawing room, dining room, music room and study on the lower floor—but questions kept intruding: Where, on the farm, was there a lawn? Fields aplenty, but a lawn? A collie pup, had he said? There had been only Pap's hounds on the farm.

By the time they reached the library, the end of the tour, Jane's troubled thoughts had folded in on themselves completely. Had the conversation she had overheard between Damon and his uncle troubled Damon more than she thought? Had it been Uncle Cyrus's question, "But, is she the right girl?" that had prompted Damon to fairly plead with her to remember a day and a meeting which, as far as she was concerned, had never happened?

"Tea, Johanna?"

"Wh-what?"

"Where would you like to take tea?" he said, sounding annoyed; looking it, too.

"Oh. Wherever ye want."

"Downstairs, thank you, Janet." he said to the maid Jane had not noticed standing in the library doorway. With the woman gone, he turned his eyes back to Jane. "Have you been paying any attention at all?"

"Oh, aye. 'Tis all very . . . impressive."

"I am not trying to impress you, Johanna. I am trying to acquaint you with the house." He eyed her steadily. "I don't suppose you can find your way to the withdrawing room from here, can you?"

"Nay. I don't s'pose I can. I'm sorry. I've been tryin' to remember, that's all."

"Remember what, for pity's sake?" he snapped.

"The day ye said ye saw me playin' with the puppy."

His annoyance vanished like smoke in a stiff breeze. "You cannot discover a memory that is not there, Johanna. You were little more than a baby at the time, and far more taken with the pup than with me. I should never have mentioned it."

"Ye'd think I'd remember the dog, then," she muttered to the floor. But she raised her face to ask, "A collie pup, ye said?"

He smiled. "Put it from your mind. It's of no matter."

"But it is! Ye said I was playing on a lawn. There are no lawns on the farm. Nor collie dogs, neither!"

"Of course, there are not. But you did not spend your entire life on that farm, Johanna." Stunned, she stared at him, and he cautiously asked, "Do you remember nothing of Southwind?"

"What's the wind got to do with anythin'?"

Now it was Seymour who stared. Then, clearly choosing his words carefully, he said, "Southwind is an estate. On the James River. You lived there as a child. You do not recall it?"

"N—nay."

"And, McPhee did not prompt you. . . . He did not mention it to you?"

Slowly, Jane wagged her head. Seymour turned and strode a few paces away, a thoughtful finger tapping his lips. When, after a minute or more, he turned back to her, Jane thought he looked extraordinarily pleased; as if he had reached some happy conclusion.

"As I said, you lived there as a child. It was there that I saw you playing with the dog. But, as I also said, you were very young. It is not surprising that you cannot recall it. Or the dog." He smiled. "Here, now. Let me show you these."

Unwilling to put the subject aside, but too confused to rationally pursue it, Jane numbly accepted the hand he offered.

Drawing her close to him, Damon guided her around the large, rectangular table in the center of the narrow room and toward several bookcases. "Here, arranged alphabetically by author, are the novels; plays; poetry; collections of stories." He pointed to a lower shelf. "You will find your Cleopatra and Juliet down there. Over here," he hurried her past a wide, deep alcove, partially obscured from view by generously swagged draperies, and led her over to the cases against the opposite wall, "here are the histories, biographies, etcetera. And in this case are the treatises on politics, theology, philosophy, and the sciences. I doubt they will interest you overly much. Then, over here, the tag ends: almanacs, journals, atlases, and the like. You will find portfolios of artwork and some rather fine woodcuts and lithographs under here." He opened the doors at the base of a broad-shelved cabinet and, after she had peeped inside, closed them again. "You are free to read anything you like, but with one caution." He paused. "You *are* paying attention."

"Oh, aye!"

"Some of the books are very old and the spines and pages have become brittle. I trust you will treat them gently."

"I'll be most careful," she promised, solemnly. "Have ye read all these?"

"Not all of them, no, but most, I think."

"And those upstairs, too?"

"Yes. Is that what you were doing, reading?"

"Aye. But I hadn't got much of a start before ye came home and . . ." She shrugged the rest away.

"Um." His hand at her back, he steered her toward the door and the hall beyond it. "What book were you reading?"

"*The Life and Opinions of Tristram Shandy, Gentleman.*" Damon choked. "Are ye all right?"

"Fine," he croaked, turning her right and indicating with a wave of his hand that she should precede him down the narrow hall. After several coughs, he said, "There are several fine books of poetry there. Why did you not select one of them?"

"I thought, since I've married a gentleman, I'd better learn somethin' about 'em."

He coughed again. "Some things are best learned by experience, Johanna," he said with the sound of a smile in his voice. "I am sure you'll find . . . No, this way . . . I am sure you'll find more suitable reading matter in the library." The works of Shakespeare were hardly that, he knew, and he cringed at the thought of her reading them. But he took some comfort from knowing that Shakespeare's more objectionable passages were couched in Elizabethan terms—unlike Laurence Sterne's ribald innuendo—and might go over her pretty, innocent, little head.

Jane looked around the drawing room as if seeing it for the first time, even though it had been less than half an hour since she had been there. Four tall windows facing the east and south sides of the house let in much light, but there was no direct sun at this time of day. This, and the clear blue of the walls above the gray-white wainscot, made the room seem cool. The silver-shot blue damask of the draperies and upholstery reminded Jane of the flash of a minnow's belly in still, deep water, although she was sure a more sophisticated description was better suited to such an elegant room.

" 'Tis very grand," she said, looking up at the crystal chandelier suspended in the center of the high-ceilinged room.

"It's grand enough," Damon said, urging her toward a pair of comfortable-looking chairs. Having settled her in one, he prepared to take the other. Flipping his coattails over his lap, he said, "I have been thinking of having a French window installed in the music room. It's dark as a tomb in there. And access to the back lawn would be nice. What do you think of the idea?"

"Sounds fine." Having no idea what a French window was, she hoped he wouldn't press her for a more specific reply.

"Do you think you would like to learn to play the clavichord?"

"The what?"

He smiled. "The clavichord. There's one in the music room. You really weren't paying attention, were you?" Jane looked contritely down at her hands. "Would you like to learn to play?"

"Aye. I think so."

"Good. It will be nice to have music in the house again."

Before Jane could wonder aloud who had last played it, Janet arrived with the tea cart. And by the time the

maid had served their tea and left, Jane had discarded
that question in favor of another, more pressing one.

"What did I do that was so wrong this afternoon?
Aside from takin' the wrong stairs and endin' up in the
attic, I mean."

"You did nothing 'wrong,' Johanna. This is your
home and you may come and go from it as you please.
But it is more usual for the lady of the house to enter it
from the front."

"But that would have meant walkin' all the way
'round! The kitchen's closer to the stables."

"True. But had you left your mare in front, one of the
grooms would have taken her to the stable for you."

"Oh."

"And you were not in the attic. That was the ballroom. It has not been used in years."

"Aye, that's what yer butler said—that it's not in use.
But if Amos has a room there, then . . ."

"What makes you think he has?" Damon interrupted
sharply.

"I—I heard him."

"That is not possible. Amos, like the other servants,
has quarters in the attic."

"Then, whose room is at the end of the ballroom?"

Damon stiffened in his chair. "No one's. What was
once a small parlor, where my parents' guests could sit
and rest their weary feet, is now used for storage."

He looked very sure of himself—which, as master of
the house, he must be—but Jane shook her head
woefully. "I could've sworn I heard somebody on the
other side of that door!"

"What, ah, did you hear?"

"Somebody movin' around—'course that was
prob'ly just the butler comin' upstairs, like he said—and
china rattlin'. Like this." She picked up her cup and set it
unsteadily back in its saucer. "Aye. Just like that."

Damon relaxed and smiled. "You undoubtedly

heard someone in the kitchen. The ballroom was designed with fine acoustics so that music would carry well there. Unfortunately, other sounds carry well, too. The servants' stairwell funnels sound up from the kitchen, and the room bounces it around until it seems to come from all directions at once. I've been in the ballroom, when the house was otherwise quiet, and heard the clatter of a ladle in a pot."

Jane remembered Mrs. Oswald's glare over her teacup. Convinced, she nodded slowly. "Aye. But I'd have taken an oath on the Bible that sound was comin' from behind the door."

Damon smiled again. "Now you know better, hm?"

Jane smiled, too, but sheepishly. "Aye. Why don't ye use it—the ballroom?"

"Father closed it off after Mother died. I've seen no reason to reopen it. But, now that Raven's Oak has a new mistress, perhaps, one day, I will." He took a sip of his tea and lifted his eyes to the portrait over the mantel. "It's time we find a place for that upstairs."

"Yer mother was very pretty."

"Yes, she was."

"How old were ye when she died?"

"Nearly six."

"Ye haven't many memories of her, then."

"Oh, no. I remember her quite well. At least, I think I do. Father spoke of her so often that it is difficult to know which memories are mine and which were his."

Jane studied the portrait. The woman's hair was darker than Damon's; her nose shorter; her face a softly rounded oval with not a trace of Damon's strong, squarish jaw. That, like his hair, he had gotten from his father, but still, there was a resemblance.

"Ye favor her, I think, about the—" Breaking off, Jane gaped from the portrait to her husband, then back again.

"You were saying?"

"Ye have the same eyes!"

"No. Mother's were blue, as you see."

"Aye, but yer's have the same look about 'em. 'Tis odd!"

With mock affrontery, Damon said, "I beg your pardon, but I do not think either my mother's or my own eyes 'odd.' "

" 'Twas not what I meant," Jane said with a quick shake of her head. " 'Tis only that the other portrait, the one of ye . . . The eyes are different."

"How do you mean?"

It was more a challenge than a question, and Jane, thinking she had offended him by criticizing an otherwise flawless likeness of him, quickly assuaged, " 'Tis a fine paintin' of ye. I recognized ye at once. I'm sorry if I hurt yer feelin's by faultin' it."

"No, no, it is hardly that. I am only curious to know what you mean."

"Well," she began cautiously, looking at the portrait again, "yer mother's eyes have a sort of . . . warmth about 'em. Like yer's do, most times. But it seems to me that whoever painted yer picture, painted yer eyes cold. I've never seen 'em look so. Not even when ye're angry." Damon was silent and she tried to gauge his reaction. His face was as blank and unrevealing as the craggy stones of the Raven's Oak mansion. Nervously, she added, "Of course, I've not known ye long. Mayhap yer eyes do look so, now and again. And, like I said, 'tis a fine likeness of ye all the same."

He was quiet for a time, as if deciding what to say or whether to say anything at all. Jane thought he looked much like a child who was trying to decide whether or not to confess his involvement in some misdeed. In short, he was a man doing battle with his conscience. And, when he abruptly changed the subject, Jane had the unsettling feeling that his conscience had lost.

"Have you had an opportunity to look at your wardrobe?''

"Aye. Everythin's beautiful. Thank ye."

"You're welcome. But I only asked because you mentioned earlier that gray is unflattering to you, and there is a silver and blue gown which I had hoped you would wear for your sitting."

"My sittin'?"

"For your portrait. Did you see the gown?"

"Aye. 'Tis the grandest of 'em all!"

"But will it become you, do you think?"

"Oh, aye. The bodice is mostly blue, but for the lace, and so long's the gray's not next to my skin 'tis all right."

"Fine. You shall wear it for your portrait, then. It will go well with the necklace." He looked at his mother's portrait again. "Every bride of Raven's Oak has been portrayed wearing it, and it graced the throats of Seymour ladies for more than a century before that. It has quite a history." He smiled over at Jane. "You see, in 1547 when the piece came into the possession of his presumed paramour, Thomas Seymour was Lord High Admiral, Baron Seymour of Sudeley. As the story goes, the necklace was ill-gotten gains acquired by the admiral in his dealing with the very pirates it was his duty to suppress."

Eyes popping, Jane studied the heavy-looking necklace. Three large, pearly gray stones—the centermost of which was pear-shaped and larger than the other two which were simple ovals—were framed by massive, silver filigreed settings linked to one another by a double strand of large pearls from which strands of tiny pearls draped in a profusion of little scallops. Pirate booty or not, she thought it a gaudy thing. But if she was expected to wear it, and clearly she was, she would. She didn't expect ever to like it.

"You don't like it?" Damon asked.

" 'Tis . . . quite somethin'."

Humor sparked Damon's eyes and the hint of smile

played about his lips. But he said with perfect sobriety, "Ah, yes. It is that. A truly monumental piece!"

"Aye. But I don't think 'tis as pretty as the other jewelry," she dared to say.

Damon smiled and laughingly confessed, "Nor do I. Father called it 'the moonstone monstrosity' and never insisted that Mother wear it once her portrait was done. Would you very much mind wearing it just the once? It *is* a family tradition."

"Nay. I won't mind," she said. But she couldn't suppress a grimace when she looked back at the thing. "So long as it's only the once."

Damon laughed again—a warm, rich, rolling laugh that seemed to come from deep inside him. She liked the way he laughed; the way his eyes sparkled; the gleam of his even, white teeth. She liked the way he laughed very much, even if he was laughing at her.

"So," he said, still chuckling, "you discovered the jewel case. Then, you have already seen the necklace." Jane's smile faded. "It's in the case."

"I didn't see it," she said, dubiously.

"You must have. How could you have missed it?"

"But, I didn't. I don't think 'twas there."

Damon's smile disappeared. "I put it there myself only this morning. It's in a velvet pouch in the lowest compartment."

Jane wagged her head. "There was nothin' in a pouch."

"You must be mistaken," he said, straightening in his chair.

"I'm not. I looked at everythin' very close. I'm sure there was no—"

Damon's teacup teetered precariously in its saucer as he all but threw it onto the table and stormed from the room. Jane followed, having no doubt as to his destination. Or as to what he would find—or not find—in the jewel case.

"Who was with you when you opened the case?" he demanded when Jane breathlessly arrived in her room.

"No one. Nancy was gone when I got back, and I put everythin' away before Janet—"

"Nancy," he seethed, his voice cold with anger. "I should have known! Stay here!"

Jane resented the order, but didn't dare disobey it. Damon's fury was intimidating. Straightening up the disheveled jewelry case, she decided that his anger was probably justified. He prized the ugly necklace as a family treasure. And, if he had put it in the case himself and it was now gone . . . What if Nancy had taken the awful thing? Jane had assumed that the servant had only gone to see the dressmaker in Rendell. If she was wrong, if Nancy had stolen the hideous necklace, whatever did she expect to do with it? Not wear it! If she had been so eager for jewelry, one would think she would have taken one of the prettier pieces. That Nancy had stolen the moonstone necklace, seemed too ridiculous to consider!

"I've every confidence that we shall have it back," Damon said, striding into the room and startling Jane. "If the maid did make off with it—and it seems certain she did—she'll not get far. I've sent Grimes and Bundy after her."

Jane had no idea who Grimes and Bundy were, but she let that pass and said confidently, " 'Twas not Nancy who took it. I'm sure she's only gone to Rendell to see the dressmaker."

"She may have gone to Rendell, but not in your service. I dismissed her."

Jane gasped. "Ye what? But, ye said she was *my* maid!"

"She served you but she was employed by me."

"But ye said I may have her as long as she pleased me."

Damon glowered. "I received a reply to my query of

her last employer—the one she wisely failed to give as a reference. I will not tolerate women of low moral fiber serving in this house! Neither will I tolerate gossips!"

"She was not a gossip," Jane said, defending the woman as best she could.

"All servants gossip among themselves—Simon being the exception which proves the rule—and there is nothing to be done about that, short of cutting out their tongues. But I will not abide a servant who does not know her place and carries tales to her mistress!" He stepped closer, intimidating Jane with his nearness and his size. "Neither do I approve of that mistress encouraging servants' gossip. In future, Madam, when you have questions concerning Raven's Oak or its master, you will address them to me!"

Bravely, Jane met his eye. "I would have asked ye about the slaves, but ye were not here. Just as ye weren't here to ask about the stables or comin' in through the back!

"Ye go about yer business, whatever 'tis, and leave me to bumble along as best I can. Then, when I make a mistake, ye laugh at me and get angry 'cause I've asked help of somebody else! And now, ye've sent away the only one here who was friendly to me just because she—"

"Enough!" Damon roared. But when he continued, his voice was low and controlled, though Jane thought it took a mighty effort for him to keep it that way. "I apologize for leaving you to your own devices this morning, and I take full responsibility for your errors upon myself. But I will not—"

"Takin' responsibility for 'em is one thing! Sufferin' the embarrassment of 'em is another!" she cried, knowing she was getting too angry to keep her tongue in check. "Ye treat me like one of yer slaves: orderin' me about or pushing me aside, as the fancy strikes ye! Well, I'm not yer slave. And I'm not a maid ye can keep or let go as it suits ye, either!"

"Unfortunately, that is the case," he growled with tenuous self-control before he pivoted on a heel and made for the door.

Jane's anger flared all the hotter. "I didn't ask to wed ye, either!" she shrieked.

The door slammed behind him.

# 6

Jane awoke with a start. The candle on the stand beside the bed had long since guttered out. But the pillow next to hers was still empty. She felt a stab of conscience: If Damon had kept to his own bed last night, he must still be angry.

Jane cringed and snuggled deeper into her pillow. Drawing the sheet over her eyes against the glare of the rising sun, she tried to silence the voice in her head. "Humble pie is a woman's dish, gal. Bitter as 'tis, ye'd best learn to choke it down if ye wed a man as proud as yer Pap."

Jane gave vent to a moan of pure misery. Damon was at least as proud as Pap. And she must be prouder than Mam because just the thought of being first to apologize made her bristle. But maybe if she didn't apologize for *what* she had said, only for *how* she had said it . . .

With her pride rebelling despite her concession to it, she snatched her robe from the foot of the bed and advanced on her husband's room. There was no response to her rap on his closed door. She opened it a crack. "Damon?" Nothing. Not even a snore. And, when she ventured a peep, she found the bed not only un-occupied, but unrumpled. He had gone out soon after their shouting match. Had he been gone all night?

More puzzled than worried, and grateful for her reprieve, she went back to her own room and was nibbling at a leftover crust of bread on her dinner tray—and wondering if it was too early to call for Janet to help her dress—when the sound of hooves drew her to the window. Shielding her eyes with a hand, she squinted into the sunrise and saw a man on horseback and a wretched-looking Nancy jouncing on the animal's rump behind him. Jane's heart instantly went out to the woman. And her sympathy redoubled when the man, a brutish-looking fellow dressed in work clothes, drew rein before the house and roughly swung Nancy to the ground where she crumpled like a rag doll.

Despite her haste, the entry hall was empty when Jane reached it, but the sound of Nancy's snivelling and her burly escort's angry orders led Jane toward the hall behind the stairs. She followed the now muffled sobbing to Damon's study. She paused in the hall for a moment, summoning her courage, then stepped into the room.

The man, a robust fellow in his prime with a few day's growth of dark beard on his meaty face and a nose that looked like it had been broken more than once, was standing in profile to her, near the desk. Nancy, her face buried in her hands, huddled in a nearby chair.

"Hush, Nancy. 'Twill be all right."

The man, clearly startled, looked to Jane and swept his tricorn from his head to expose a balding pate. Just as startled, Nancy raised her tear-streaked face and, with a swipe of a sleeve under her nose, blubbered, "Oh. Oh, ma'am! I didn't do nothin' wrong. God's truth, I didn't!"

"Hush. I believe ye," Jane said with a wan but sympathetic smile. Then, her eyes left the pathetic woman's and met the man's.

"Luther Grimes, ma'am. At your service." He made an awkward but respectful bow.

"Mr. Grimes," Jane said by way of acknowledgment and, she hoped, by way of dismissal. But Mr. Grimes stood his ground. "I'll look after Nancy, now, thank ye."

Grimes cleared his throat. "Not to be contrary, ma'am, but I'd best keep my eye on 'er 'til Mr. Seymour gets here."

"Ye may go, Mr. Grimes," Jane said levelly, marveling at her courage in contradicting a stranger and such a surly looking one at that.

The man's bushy brows knitted over his battered nose, and the dark eyes beneath them held the same disparagement she had seen, too often of late, in others. But he muttered a "Yes, ma'am,"—the respectful term grudgingly given—and eyed Jane calculatingly all the way to the door.

"Oh, thank you, ma'am!" Nancy breathed fervently when Grimes had disappeared down the hall. "He frightens me half out of my wits. He's a brute, that's what he is: A brute! And—and he said I stole something. Something of yours, ma'am. By all that's holy, I swear I took nothing!"

Weak-kneed, Jane made her way to a chair before the fireplace and dropped into it. " 'Tis all a mistake, Nancy. I know ye wouldn't steal from me."

"Bless you, ma'am." Nancy sniffed and gave her nose another swipe with the sleeve.

Jane looked at her, wondering how on earth the maid could prove she had *not* stolen the necklace. "Where were ye when he found ye, Nancy?"

"Baltimore, ma'am. I thought to look for employment there." Her eyes darted downward and she said miserably, "Mr. Seymour dismissed me."

"I know," Jane said, sounding no less miserable.

Nancy's head came up. "I know what you must think, ma'am, but it wasn't like that. I never encouraged young Mr. William—not for a moment. He took the thought into his own head. And what was I to do but give in to him?

He threatened to see me dismissed if I didn't. Said he'd tell his father I had led him on, that it was *me* who made the advances. I had no choice, ma'am. You can understand that, can't you?" Jane stared at her blankly. "I mean, it was tryst with Mr. William, or out I'd go. It isn't as though posts as lady's maid grow on trees, ma'am. I was only looking out after my interests. And—and it was only a few times. I'm not a . . ." Fresh tears welled in the maid's blue eyes and spilled down her cheeks. "I'm not a light-o'-love, ma'am. I only bedded with him a few times, and only because I had to. I'm not what Mr. Seymour thinks, ma'am! And I'm not a thief, either."

Shocked, Jane heard herself murmur, "I'm sure ye're not."

"I knew you would believe me, ma'am. If only Mr. Seymour did!"

"He—He can't accuse ye without proof, Nancy."

"He's already done, ma'am. That's why he sent Grimes after me, isn't it: to drag me back here as if I were a common thief? And the worst of it is, I can't prove him wrong!" She covered her face with her hands and sobbed throatily. "I don't even know what it is I'm supposed to have taken!"

"A necklace. There's a necklace missin' from my jewel case."

Her head still in her hands, Nancy blubbered, "I'd never take anything of yours, ma'am. You're the dearest, sweetest mistress in all the world. How could I steal from you? You're as dear to me as a sister."

Jane's heart ached with affection and pity. "Don't worry, Nancy. I'll stand up for ye. Ye're dear to me, too."

But despite her confident tone and her sincerity, Jane was terrified at the prospect of standing up against her husband. In her mind's eye, she saw him as he had been the previous afternoon: a towering giant with the very fires of hell in his eyes. And the forty-odd minutes that she had to dwell on the vision before the reality finally arrived, did nothing to bolster her courage.

"Madam," he said sternly, his expression as dark and foreboding as the somber black he wore. The quirt in his black-gloved fist tapped an angry tattoo against one highly polished black boot. "I will see you in your chamber when I have concluded my business here."

Squaring her shoulders and raising her chin, Jane met his menacing advance with a bravado she was far from feeling. His eyes, smoldering like golden embers, seared Jane's when hers met them. Dropping her gaze to the only spot of color in the black he wore—the simple, gold stickpin securing his stock—she said, as levelly as she could, " 'Tis my business, too. The necklace was mine."

She saw his chest swell, but the angry outburst she braced herself for never came. "Very well. Stay. But I will brook no interference. Is that understood?"

"I don't want to interfere. I only want to defend Nancy."

"Can you defend her?"

The note of challenge in his voice made Jane look up. She found mocking self-assurance tempering the anger in his eyes. "I can say I don't believe she stole it; that she's not a thief."

"That is your belief; it is hardly a defense."

"Can ye prove she did take it?"

Damon didn't answer but, for the first time since entering the room, turned his attention to the maid who had abandoned her chair and now huddled on the floor in a posture of abject humility. "Look at me!" The upturned, tearstained face brought a fresh stab of sympathy to Jane. It appeared to have no such effect on her husband. "Get up!" When Nancy stood, trembling, before him, he demanded, "Did you or did you not take the moonstone neckpiece?"

"Not, sir."

"Would you care to reconsider that answer?"

"I did not take it!" Nancy cried, turning imploring eyes on Jane. "Tell him, ma'am. Tell him I wouldn't steal from you!"

"Please, Damon. I'm sure ye're mistaken. Nancy would have no use for—"

"Simon!" Damon bellowed, cutting her off and adding even before the man appeared, "Show in the gentleman. Have Bundy wait."

The man who Simon ushered into the room was a prosperous looking middle-aged gentleman wearing a charcoal gray coat with cuffs and lapels of jade velvet and a multitude of glittering silver buttons. His dove gray waistcoat matched his breeches and was very nearly the same color as the peruke he sported; the queue at the back of it was tied with a flamboyant green bow. Rings sparkled on several of his pudgy fingers as he shifted his walking stick in his hands.

After exchanging an acknowledging nod with the man, Damon demanded of Nancy, "Are you acquainted with this gentleman?"

Nancy's eyes widened and she swallowed nervously, but denied knowledge of him with a shake of her head.

"Then allow me to introduce him. This is Mr. D'Ancel; formerly of Philadelphia, late of Baltimore. Mr. D'Ancel is a pawnbroker by trade." His gaze shifted to the man. "Do you recognize this woman, sir?"

"Indeed, yes. I made her acquaintance yestereve."

"You're mistaken! I've never laid eyes on you!"

"Is it possible you could be mistaken, Mr. D'Ancel?" Damon asked, coolly.

"No, sir. She is the same woman who caused me no small inconvenience by appearing at my place of business as I was preparing to close for the day."

"And . . ." he shot a glance at Jane, "how did she introduce herself to you, sir?"

"She told me that she was Mistress Seymour, your wife."

Jane's eyes popped and darted in quick succession from D'Ancel to Damon to Nancy, where they stayed.

"But, as you see, she bears no resemblance to my wife."

"So I do see, sir. Madam," he said, offering an elegant bow which Jane was too benumbed to acknowledge. "However, being new to this area and unacquainted with either you, sir, or your lovely wife, I had no reason to doubt her veracity. And, as I am a businessman and the surety she offered to secure the loan was adequate, I could see no reason to refuse her the funds."

"So, you granted her a loan of two hundred fifty pounds."

"I did, sir."

Jane gasped audibly at mention of that staggering sum: More than several years' profit on the farm, she was sure. And Nancy cried, "No! It wasn't me! It was someone else!"

"It was you, right enough. If I may, sir?" D'Ancel asked, producing a velvet pouch from one of the coat's roomy pockets. When Damon waved him toward the desk, he released the purse's drawstring closure and spilled its contents onto the blotter. Gently arranging the necklace into roughly the shape it would assume about a lady's throat, he said, "And this is the surety you offered me."

Recognizing the necklace as the one in the portraits, Jane slowly raised hurt and disillusioned eyes to the maid.

"It's lies! All lies! I never went to him. I never took it! Tell them, ma'am!"

Jane looked away. Damon barked toward the hall, "Bundy!"

Jane recognized the young man who answered the summons as one of the two outriders she had seen on her wedding day—and belatedly recognized Grimes as the other.

"You spoke with the ships' agents?" Damon asked.

"Yes, sir. Miss Brown—" he indicated Nancy with a scathing glance, "booked passage for Boston under the name Wilde, sir. I recovered her passage ticket and nearly two hundred pounds. She had the money sewn in the hems and linings of her garments, sir. It's all here."

Accepting the leather packet Bundy extended, Damon turned to the maid. "Where is the rest of it?"

A coldness settled into her tear-reddened eyes, but Nancy said nothing.

The room was silent for a moment. The men merely stared or glowered at the thief, and Jane was too hurt to bear to look at her. Then Damon summoned Grimes into the room and instructed in a voice cold with anger, "Escort 'Miss Wilde' to the constable in Baltimore. Tell him I will call upon the magistrate and swear out a complaint against her, later this morning. And while you're in town, see what you can do about recovering the fifty or so pounds this lacks." He hefted the packet. "Sell her passage ticket and whatever valuables you find. You know how to go about it."

"Yes, sir." With one meaty paw clamped tightly about the firm-jawed maid's upper arm, Grimes hauled her toward the door.

"Wait!" All eyes were on Jane, as she asked, "Why, Nancy? Why?"

"All my life," Nancy began with a sneer, "I've done for others: Laid out the ladies' pretties; pampered them; bowed and scraped to them. But you . . . you were the last straw! When I saw you, a simple, ill-bred bumpkin, plopped in the middle of all this," she gestured wildly about them with her free arm, "that was the last straw! I'm better than you are. It was my turn for a bit of it! The price that necklace fetched would have set me up like a lady long enough for me to catch a gent the likes of him.'' She indicated Damon with a thrust of her chin. ''Or better!''

Jane's eyes pricked with tears. It wasn't her fault, or Damon's either, but if he hadn't married beneath him, if she wasn't so simple and ignorant, maybe then . . .

''I'm sorry, Nancy,'' she said in a choked whisper. ''Truly sorry.''

D'Ancel looked uncomfortable. So did Bundy. Damon shot Jane a reproachful look. Grimes hustled Nancy away.

Turning to the moneylender, who stood beside the desk ostensibly intrigued with his examination of the necklace on the blotter, Damon said, ''I will, of course, reimburse you the loan you made in exchange for the promissory note Miss Brown signed.''

Looking relieved to be getting down to business, D'Ancel smiled and presented a folded document for Damon's inspection. Having read it through and examined its content, Damon opened a locked desk drawer and withdrew a deep, brass bound box, which he placed with a soft thump beside the necklace. He took a key from a waistcoat pocket and opened the box.

Jane looked away. She found it impossible to understand the greed and envy that had motivated Nancy toward dishonesty. And, if she hadn't heard them with her own ears, she would never have believed it possible for anyone to tell such bold-faced lies. Or to tell them so convincingly. And today hadn't been the first time she had lied! That was the most painful truth of all: Nancy had used her, courted her friendship and favor as a means to an end, to afford herself a protector if her plans went awry. Her friendship and affection had been a sham.

But, hurt as she was, the sad irony of the situation wasn't wasted on Jane. She, who had never aspired to it, held the position Nancy coveted dearly enough to risk the gallows.

Jane shuddered and unconsciously raised a protective hand to her throat. Only then did she realize she had been staring blindly at young Mr. Bundy who stood, hat in hand, across the room. But if he was bothered by her staring, he didn't look it. He smiled. Embarrassed, Jane looked away.

Damon was returning the strong box to the desk, and Mr. D'Ancel was fondly patting an inside coat pocket. Jane supposed that, being a moneylender, money meant a great deal to him. It didn't seem to mean as much to Damon. He hadn't even flinched at the enormous sum of two hundred fifty pounds. And doling it out—plus a bit more for Mr. D'Ancel's "trouble"—had left him equally as unmoved.

Her eyes slid from her husband's handsome, composed face to the necklace still on the blotter. Was it truly so valuable? It didn't look it. It was even uglier than it looked in the portraits . . . and more massive. She was wondering if her slender neck could support such a heavy-looking thing when Damon snapped her from her musings.

Bidding Mr. D'Ancel a good morning, and echoing her husband's thank you for the man's efforts in seeing the stolen property restored, Jane watched as Damon left to show the man to the door. As their footsteps faded down the hall, Jane became aware that Mr. Bundy was still in the room, and that he was taking his turn at staring at her. Having had more than enough of being gawked at by servants, Jane shifted her eyes challengingly to his.

"Ma'am," he said.

"Mr. Bundy."

"Not 'mister,' just Bundy," he corrected with a smile. "It's a nickname of sorts, though I can't rightly say how I came by it."

Jane smiled back, liking the man's easy manner. He reminded her of Jacob, though Bundy was probably a year or two older and his face was more pleasant looking, if not handsome. But her too recent, too painful experience with Nancy warned her not to like the man Bundy too much.

"So," he said, feeling the silence grow awkward, "that's the necklace I've heard so much about. Might I take a closer look? It ain't every day a man in my position sees such finery as that."

Jane nodded, painfully aware, now that the excitement was over, that she wore only her dressing gown and slippers. When he stopped beside her, she asked nervously, "What is yer position here, Mist—ah—Bundy?"

He flashed an even-toothed grin at her quick correction. "Jack of all trades, master of none, that's me, ma'am."

"But, what do ye do?"

"Head hostler's the title Mr. Seymour's tacked on me. Mostly, though, I do whatever it is he needs done," he said, but thinking, *She smells like roses; even her hair*. Staring at the necklace, he said, "That is something ain't it? Mighty fine piece of workmanship."

Jane looked at his face in quick surprise, expecting to see anything but the sincerity she found there.

"Don't you think so, ma'am?"

"Oh, ah, I s'pose so."

Bundy smiled. "It ain't real pretty, but it's put together real fine."

His eyes seemed more gray than blue now that she was close to them, and they crinkled at the corners with his smile—just like Jacob's did. Suddenly, she missed Jacob and Mam and Julia so awfully much!

"Are you still here, Bundy?" Damon said from the doorway, his tone more chiding than surprised.

"Oh. I, ah, I was just going, sir."

Walking into the room, Damon passed Bundy on his hurried way out. "Oh, Bundy," he called softly. The man did a neat little pivot on a heel. "You've forgotten your hat."

His face suddenly ruddy under its tan, Bundy took a few steps back and accepted the hat Damon extended. "Thank you, sir. Day to you, ma'am."

"Good day," Jane said, a little breathlessly.

Damon looked down at her quickly. She was staring after Bundy with such wistful yearning that he asked, sounding as suspicious as he felt, "Do you know him?"

"What?"

"Do you know him from somewhere else?"

"Nay."

He held her eyes for a moment before he lowered his gaze to the necklace. Picking it up, he let it droop in his hand and pushed his suspicions and possessiveness aside. "An unpleasant way to start a day."

"Aye," Jane miserably agreed.

"A shrewd man, that D'Ancel. This is worth half-again what he gave for it. Had we not discovered it missing as promptly as we did, he would have disposed of it for a tidy profit." He dropped it into its pouch.

"But he seemed glad to return it."

"He had no choice." Pocketing the pouch, he called toward the door, "Simon." The man appeared so quickly Jane thought he must have been awaiting the summons. "We will breakfast in the dining room."

"Yes, sir."

Turning back to Jane, Damon eyed her critically. "Why the long face? We have the necklace back."

"I—I thought we were gettin' to be friends, Nancy and me."

"A mistress and her servant can never be 'friends.' Nor should they be."

"Ye're friendly with Simon."

"Simon is a trusted servant whom I have known

longer than either of my parents and for whom I feel a certain fondness and even respect. He is not my friend. Nor will he ever be. Friendship requires mutuality of interests and station, familiarity, confidentiality. It cannot exist between master—or mistress—and servant." When Jane looked contritely at the floor, he lifted a long curl of her hair from her shoulder. "And now, we must set about finding you a new maid, hm?"

"I don't need a maid," Jane said, with a slow shake of her head. "I don't want one. Janet can lace my dresses."

"A lady should have a maid," he disagreed, gently rubbing the silken hair between thumb and forefinger. "Someone skilled in hairdressing, hm?" Jane said nothing. "Take heart, girl. We've all been shammed one time or another. Mark it down as a lesson learned." Dropping the curl, he stepped back to the desk and the packet still atop it.

"What'll happen to her?" When Damon didn't answer, Jane turned and found him counting the money the packet had contained. "Will they—hang her?"

He was thoughtfully quiet for a time. "Hanging her will not recoup the money I have lost. I would prefer to see her indentured for the amount which I am still owed plus whatever fines the court levies against her." He returned the money to the packet, then tossed it back onto the desk. "I shall suggest that to the magistrate, in fact. Given Miss Brown's aversion to servitude, I doubt no more fitting a punishment could be found for her." He smiled, fleetingly. "Let's go in to breakfast, shall we?"

Jane had paid as little attention to the dining room as she had to the withdrawing room the day before, and cared even less about it now. But the long table in the center of the room with its blinding expanse of white linen was, like a virgin snowfield in full sun, a sight not easily ignored. When her eyes adjusted to the glare, she discovered that the table was flanked on both long sides by four chairs—though it could easily accommodate twice that number—and by a single chair at each end. Several, triple-branched, silver candlesticks marched single file down its center.

Her attention thus captured, Jane eyed the rest of the room. Framed by leaf-green draperies, two tall, latticed windows on each of its outside walls gave views of the paddocks and stables on the north side, and the grassy hills and orchards to the west. Like all the other rooms in the house, it had been richly but tastefully decorated. The gleaming paneling above the painted wainscot was hung with paintings of prettily arranged food and flowers, and the fireplace was surrounded by marble.

Damon's hand at her waist urged Jane into the room and toward what looked like a banquet. "This is a buffet, Johanna. One takes a plate and serves oneself. Let's see what we have."

Moving down the length of the table, he raised one lid after another, revealing in turn a steaming dish of oat porridge, sausages, fried ham, coddled eggs, and a slimy-looking mass of something. He barely gave a glance to the fragrantly steaming basket of muffins and the bowl of oranges that had already set Jane's mouth to watering.

"It seems ample enough, hm?"

"All this . . . for just us?" she said, knowing the answer even before he nodded it. "Seems so wasteful!" Damon smirked in annoyance. "All I mean is," she hastily tried to amend, "there's enough here to feed my whole family and more besides."

Damon said nothing, but retraced his steps and pressed a plate into Jane's hands. With a sweep of an arm, he indicated that she was to precede him. Dutifully, even contritely, she did, taking a token serving of everything but the oatmeal—she had had more than enough of that on the farm—until she came to an unidentifiable, fishy-smelling mass. "What is it?"

"Steamed oysters." Jane wrinkled her nose. "Try one."

"No, thank ye."

Reaching in front of her, he plopped one onto her plate, then drizzled it with a spoonful of drawn butter. "Try it. There is nothing tastier than Chesapeake Bay oysters. Except, perhaps, soft-shelled crab." Jane grimaced. "Reserve judgment until you've tried it," he said, helping himself to a generous portion.

Trying to ignore the buttery goo that was oozing its way toward her sausage, Jane topped off her plate with a muffin and a plump orange. She waited until Damon had done the same before she turned toward the intimidating table.

It looked even more intimidating—and much longer —from her chair, which was separated from his by the snowy expanse of linen and the forest of candles. They ate in silence, the distance between them inhibiting conversation and making Jane feel excruciatingly self-conscious. It wasn't until Jane had cleaned her plate, but for the pile of orange peelings, that Damon finally spoke.

"Did you like the oyster?"

" 'Twas a bit chewy, but I didn't mind it."

He laughed in delight. "Would you like tea?"

"Aye."

"Give the bell a jingle."

Jane glanced uncertainly at the small, china bell near her plate which was not so different from the one Damon's Aunt Hortense had jangled almost continuously throughout the meals at Langdale. At Damon's encouraging nod, she rang it.

She was surprised when Eulalia answered the summons, entering the room through a door near the sideboard and behind her: She had thought the negress was only kitchen help. But when the woman dropped a curtsy and stood expectantly awaiting instruction, she said, "Tea, please?"

"Yes'um." Then, turning to Damon. "Will you take your coffee now, suh?"

"Yes. Thank you." But when the woman turned away toward the kitchen, he said, "Clear away the plates first."

"Yes'uh."

No wonder poor little Opal was dull-witted, Jane thought.

But when Eulalia had left, Damon explained in a loud whisper, "She is being trained to wait on our table. Simon is getting too old to carry the heavier platters and trays, and his hands are not as steady as they once were. I trust you'll be patient with her."

"Aye." She returned his smile and, after a moment, added, "Ye're a kind master."

He shook his head. "A practical one. It would not do to have a hot platter dropped into a guest's lap, now would it?"

They said nothing more, and as soon as Damon had drunk his coffee—which he did quickly, not savoring it as Jane did her tea—he excused himself from the table and left with the promise to return by teatime. Jane heard him speak briefly with Simon before the front door closed solidly behind him.

Dejectedly pushing her half-full teacup away, she watched the creamy-tan liquid slosh into the saucer. What was she supposed to do all day?

"What do you mean, she is 'missing?'" Damon demanded, handing his hat, gloves and quirt to Simon who, as always, had greeted him at the front door.

"Precisely that, sir. We have searched the house thoroughly and her horse is still stabled."

"Perhaps she went walking."

"That was my thought, too, sir. I sent Bundy in search of her. He returned after more than an hour without seeing any sign of her."

"Ye gods, Simon!" Damon bellowed. "Cannot I trust you to look after a slip of a girl for a day?" Simon accepted the chastisement as his due. "How in heaven's name did you 'lose' her?"

"Immediately after you left this morning, sir, I returned the necklace to Madam's jewel case, as you had instructed, then attended to the matter of the money packet." He fished into a pocket. "The key to your strong box, sir."

"Thank you. Go on."

"Having acquitted my duties, I made my way to the dining room to inquire after Madam's wishes. She was not there, sir."

Damon tensed. "You looked upstairs, of course?"

"Yes, sir. I took it upon myself to look there immediately when I discovered the dining room empty, sir. Nothing had been disturbed."

"Do you mean, then," he said, visibly relaxing, "that no one, *no one*, has seen her all day?"

"No one, sir. Madam did not even summon Janet to assist her in her dressing, sir."

"Well, she must be here somewhere. She can't have evaporated!"

"No, sir. But it is puzzling, sir. We searched the house most carefully."

"Search it again!" he roared, heading down the hall to his study. "Great gods and little fishes," he muttered, storming into that room, then stopping short in the middle of it to stand, arms akimbo, staring blindly at the desk, trying to think where a lonely, homesick girl clad only in a robe and slippers could possibly go. And how she could have gone anywhere without at least one member of the household having seen her.

"Damnation," he grumbled. Then, with a snap of his fingers he turned and strode into the adjoining library.

Fully expecting to find her sitting in, and dwarfed by, one of the room's several large wing chairs, his face fell when they proved to be empty. But a quick perusal of the bookcase showed he had been at least half right. Shakespeare was missing.

"All right. Where has she taken it?" he wondered aloud, stepping to the window alcove and, habitually, pushing the swagged drapery aside to lean against the frame.

"Pardon me, sir. It has just occurred to me that . . ."

With a finger pressed to his lips, Damon silenced the man, then motioned him closer. When Simon stood beside him, Damon said in a whisper, "Searched the house most carefully, did you?" Then he nodded at the window seat.

"Oh my, sir," Simon murmured, looking down at Jane who was curled up like a kitten in the corner of the alcove, her damask-pink robe a near match for the seat's velvet cushions. "I cannot think how we missed seeing her there, sir."

"Mmm," Damon growled in response to Simon's sarcasm. "Tell the others I've found her."

"Yes, sir."

Looking down at her, watching her sleep, Damon was struck by how very small and vulnerable, how very young she was. He felt a sudden surge of paternal protectiveness toward this child he had taken as his wife. But the longer he stood there watching the gentle rise and fall of her bosom; her slightly opened, soft-lipped mouth; the silken cascade of her unconfined hair, the less paternal he felt. And he hadn't been standing there long before he wanted to touch her breasts and kiss her lips in a manner far from fatherly! Lowering himself to the seat near her feet, he lightly stroked her hair.

Her eyes snapped open and found his face in the same moment. "Oh! Oh, I—I must have fallen asleep," she said, sitting up quickly and knocking the book off the seat. Their heads met with a dull "thunk" when they both made a grab for it.

"Allow me," he said, rubbing his temple and reaching for the book again.

"Is it all right?" she asked, massaging her forehead.

He checked his fingers for blood. "I think so."

"I meant the book."

He smirked at her. "The book is fine."

She smiled sheepishly. "I was readin'."

"So I see. Shakespeare, hm?"

"Aye." Her eyes brightened. "I read about Romeo and Juliet before I started readin' about Cleopatra. Oh, but 'twas a sad story! Here I was just startin' to think they'd be happy forever after and . . . 'Twas so sad!"

Looking suddenly pensive, Damon stared out the window. "Not all lovers come to a happy ending," he said. And he was quiet for some time before he looked back to her and added, "Fortunately, neither do they all come to such a tragic end. Now, then. Would you care to dress for tea?"

"Is it so late? Oh! I've been here for hours!"

He stood and offered her a hand. "Since shortly after I left you at breakfast?"

"Aye. But how'd—Ow! My foot's asleep! How'd ye know that?"

"You've had the household bedeviled trying to find you. The next time you decide to curl up with a book, be so kind as to tell someone, will you?"

Hobbling along beside him, she said, "I didn't think anybody'd miss me."

"You are the mistress here, Johanna. Of course, you were missed!"

Jane limped a few steps in silence, then said miserably, "I s'pose I should apologize, then, for causin' so much worry."

Damon stopped short. "A master, or mistress, does not apologize to servants. You may, if you feel it necessary, explain your actions—in this case, your absence—but you must not apologize for it. Do you see the difference?"

Jane nodded, though she wasn't sure she did. She felt badly for having caused others to worry and, hard as it might be to do, she knew she would feel better if she could apologize. But, since Damon said that wasn't done, she decided to bear her guilt as punishment and thought, not for the first time that day, what an awful thing it was to be a mistress.

But it did not take her long to find that her position had its compensations, not the least of which was abundant free time. Throughout the next week, while Damon spent his days attending to business, she spent hers curled up on the window seat, devouring Shakespeare. And when she proudly announced one night over dinner that she had read all the plays, Damon smiled indulgently and said, "There is more to literature than Shakespeare, girl." So she devoted the next two days to Chaucer.

But, determined as she was—as she had always been—to finish what she started, the archaic language of The Canterbury Tales soon proved her undoing and she reluctantly returned it to the shelf. She enjoyed The Life and Strange Surprising Adventures of Robinson Crusoe much more, and was well into The Fortunes and Misfortunes of Moll Flanders when her reading was interrupted by the arrival of the portrait artist.

Never having met an artist before, Jane didn't know what to expect of the man. But upon introduction to Mr. Peale, she realized that she hadn't expected he would be so young—or so unpretentious. But, as he was both, as well as Damon's friend, she felt comfortable with him at once and readily agreed to call him Charles in exchange for what he said would be his "great honor" in calling her Johanna.

With their introduction behind them, and formality discarded, Peale smiled into her eyes and said, "You are a lovely subject, Johanna. My fingers fairly itch for my palette and brush. However," he went on, looking at Damon, "I fear that when I have done the portrait, I will be accused of having painted the figment of our combined imaginations."

Damon chuckled, tossing a smile at Jane. Clearly pleased that his friend was so taken with her, he parried the compliment with one of his own. "Come, now, Charles. You are accustomed to comely ladies. Your own Rachel is lovely, indeed."

"Oh, I'll not dispute that," Peale heartily agreed.

"I had thought she might accompany you on your visit. It would be a pleasant and, I'm sure, welcome change for Johanna to have a female companion."

"I should have liked that. Of late, I've seen little enough of Rachel myself. But," he spread his hands helplessly, "she had cause to stay at home with the girls. Our youngest has been unwell."

"Nothing serious, I trust."

"I trust not. She appears to be on the mend."

"And how was your stay in London?" Damon asked, allowing Charles and Johanna to precede him into the drawing room.

Jane hung on Peale's every word as he spoke of his recent sojourn in England. She had never heard of most of the people he mentioned; friends he and Damon had in common; political figures; the artist Benjamin West, his mentor. But she had, of course, heard of King George, and her eyes bulged when Peale said he had refused to remove his hat when the king's coach passed him in the street.

Far from sharing her dismay, Damon clapped Peale soundly on the shoulder. "Hurrah for you, Charles! But it is some wonder a head still sits on these shoulders, my friend."

Peale snorted derisively. "I do not uncover to tyrants, whatever the price. But, I confess, I am relieved to still be possessed of my traitorous head. And to be back in the colonies, in the company of like-minded friends."

Damon smiled, but said solemnly as he settled back in his chair, "Friendships are being strained nowadays, Charles. Take care that you do not assume too much of even a friend." Peale's brow furrowed slightly but, after a significant glance at Jane, Damon dispensed with his serious tone and said, "But, as the subject of friends has come up, I put in a word for you with one of my uncle's."

"What sort of word, and with whom?"

Damon grinned. "A good word with Colonel Washington. His wife is anxious for a portrait of him. Or so I was told." In an effort to include Jane in the conversation, he said, "You recall Colonel Washington, don't you? He brought his hounds to the hunt at Langdale. Sat a chair or two down and across from you at breakfast."

Jane conjured up the image of the commanding, handsome, but rather florid-faced gentleman in his late thirties. "Oh, aye. I didn't know he was in the army, though." She added a bit sheepishly, "I took him for a gentleman farmer, like yer uncle."

"And so he is, now," Damon said. "But he was quite the hero a few years past in our war with the French and the Indians." He looked back to Peale. "I did not think you would mind my mentioning you to him."

"Hardly! What did he say?"

"Well, he is not as eager for the portrait as his wife. But, from what I know of that lady, I believe she will have her way. And when she does, perhaps it will be your name that comes to his mind."

"Better mine than Copley's or Hesselius's," Peale

said, smiling. "It will do my reputation—and my purse—no harm to portray such an illustrious, prosperous gentleman."

Damon laughed and poured them each another glass of wine. Jane sipped at her tea, content to listen as the men talked, which they did, including her whenever they could, until it was time to dress for supper.

It wasn't until dessert was being served by a nervous Eulalia—and under the watchful eye of an equally anxious Simon—that their conversation lagged and Jane found space to state the obvious. "Ye've been friends for a long while, haven't ye?"

Peale nodded and swallowed his mouthful of raspberry-topped blanc mange. "What is it now? Ten years?"

"Nearly that," Damon said, unobtrusively pushing his untouched dessert away.

"How did ye come to meet?"

The two men exchanged glances, then Peale laughed and said, "I think you had best be the one to tell her. You'll paint it in a better light than I will, I've no doubt."

Damon cleared his throat uncomfortably. "I deserve to hear your version of the story, Charles. Although you are probably right, I would treat the callow fellow I was more kindly than you will."

"Callow! This is being kind!" Peale exclaimed. Turning to Jane, he said, "Brash is what he was. An arrogant, swaggering, hot-headed young buck, if he was anything at all."

Jane looked down the table at Damon. She had never seen him swagger, but arrogant and hot-headed seemed right. Reading her thoughts, Damon shrugged and offered by way of defense, "I was young—nineteen."

"And arrogant and swaggering and hot-headed," Peale repeated with a grin. Then he said in a confidential aside to Jane, "He had been keeping the wrong company 'til he met me.''

Jane laughed and prodded, "And how did he do that?''

"I was a saddler at the time, having inherited my father's business. Young Master Seymour,'' he nodded at Damon, "being a gentleman of means, employed my services.'' He jabbed an accusing finger at Damon. "I was a fine craftsman. You'll allow that!''

"I allowed that at the time, else I would not have patronized you.''

"Um,'' Peale grumbled. "In any case, my brother and I constructed a saddle for your husband. And a fine one it was, too. I put hours into tooling the leather to Damon's peculiar specifications: He wanted acorns and oak leaves and birds all over the thing. When it was done, it was nothing short of a masterpiece. Being quite proud of my handiwork, I delivered it in person. And what do you think?''

"He did not like it?'' Jane cautiously guessed.

"Right. Wanted it redone. 'It is not at all what I had in mind.' said he. 'Well,' said I, 'if you want it redone, it'll cost you double.' That did not set well with him, I can tell you. We exchanged words—more than a few—one thing led to another and . . . he called me out.''

"He what?''

"Challenged me to a duel. A duel, if you can believe it, over a saddle! Now, had it been over a point of honor or an affair of the heart, I might have understood. But, a saddle? I laughed in his face.''

Jane ventured a glance at Damon, who was sitting with an elbow propped on the table, smiling behind his hand. She thought it was safe to ask, "Did *that* set well with him?''

Peale laughed. "No, it most certainly did not. He was purely incensed! He tried everything he could think of to get onto the dueling field, including casting aspersions against my parentage. But the angrier and nastier he got, the more stubborn I got. What it was boiling down to, you see, was a contest of wills. He was bound and determined to put me in what he considered to be my place, and I was just as determined that he would not."

"It seems to me, ye were a bit arrogant yerself, Mr. Peale."

Peale tossed an amused but approving glance at Damon, then conceded Jane's point with a nod. "And as it appeared that we had each met our match in that respect, there came about a grudging truce."

"Did ye redo his saddle?" When Peale nodded, she looked down the table. "And did ye pay him double?"

"I paid him half again the price of the original."

"Then, seems my husband bested ye, Mr. Peale."

"It was to be Charles, remember? And no, he did not. I asked twice the payment I expected to receive, knowing full well he would wrangle me down. I was most happy to settle for exactly the price I wanted in the first place!"

Jane laughed girlishly and even Damon chuckled. Grinning himself, their guest quickly launched into an anecdote the story had brought to mind. Jane laughed at that too, feeling happier and more at ease than she had since leaving the farm.

She was enjoying herself so much that she hated to see the meal end, and she felt a stab of envy at being excluded from the man's lively company when Damon invited Charles to take a brandy with him in his study. But, as banishment was inevitable, she accepted it graciously and, since they had lingered longer than usual over supper and the hour was late, she bid both men a polite good night.

She was surprised when Damon hung back. "You know where the study is, Charles. I'll join you in a moment." He waited until Peale had disappeared around the corner, then took both of Jane's hands in his. "Can you wait up for me?" he whispered. "I'll not be much longer."

The flicker of desire in his eyes sparked an answering glimmer in Jane's. "Aye," she promised, breathily.

He left her with a kiss and a smile. Jane was smiling with anticipation, too, when she turned to the stairs. But halfway up, she decided to take a book into exile with her; just in case Damon's talkative friend kept him from her longer than expected.

The connecting door between the library and study was closed when she quietly retrieved the copy of *Moll Flanders* from the window seat, but Peale's smiling voice reached her quite clearly.

"Charming. Completely unspoiled. You aren't thinking of changing that, are you?"

"She has much to learn of etiquette and the social graces, Charles."

"That will come with experience and exposure. Let her see some ladies and she'll soon be one—more's the pity. She's a delight just as she is."

"I'm glad you like her."

"Indeed, I do like her. But more importantly, do you?"

Though Jane found herself listening breathlessly, if Damon answered it was in a voice too low for her to hear.

Later, she asked the question for herself. "Damon?"

"Mmm?" he hummed, nuzzling her hair and seeking out her breast with a hand.

"Do ye—do ye like me?"

He kicked at the bedclothes entangling their feet and slipped his knee between hers. "Of course, I like you," he mumured huskily, bringing their hips on a level and pulling her under him. "You're exquisite. Exquisite!" he fairly groaned, possessing her.

It was the answer she wanted to hear. And yet, it wasn't.

*  *  *

Stiff and self-conscious, Jane sat on the chair where Charles Peale had stationed her while the artist paced to and fro before her. With a thoughtful finger tapping against his pursed lips, he paused to study his subject.

"Relax your shoulders." Jane tried. "Perhaps, you would be more comfortable holding something."

Casting about the withdrawing room, his eyes lit on the bouquet on the mantel and he extracted a heavy-headed lilac blossom from the arrangement and wiped its dripping stem on his breeches before handing it to Jane. Dutifully, she allowed him to arrange the flower and her hands just so in her lap.

"Better. But not right," Peale muttered from behind the thoughtful finger. Then, dropping his hand, he said confidently, "What we have here is a basic contradiction." Jane arched her brows quizzically. "I was commissioned to paint Mistress Seymour, a grand lady. But the Mistress Seymour I see . . . What is needed, I think, is a fresh approach. An approach as simple and unassuming as Mistress Seymour, herself." He smiled and gestured at her with a vaguely circling hand. "This is not right for you. The gown, the jewelry, your hair . . . they overwhelm you."

Jane hastily lowered her eyes. Though she was sure he meant well, she was hurt by the criticism. The gown was the very one Damon had selected for her portrait; the only jewelry she wore, aside from her wedding ring, was the moonstone necklace; her hair, painstakingly arranged, was of the latest style. Damon had said she looked lovely when she had arrived—half an hour late—for this first sitting. So had Charles. But now . . .

"I see I've offended you," Peale said regretfully but without apology. "I wish to portray you as you are, Johanna: the essence of you. And all that," he swept his hand at her, "hides you." Turning, he pointed to the portrait of Damon's mother over the mantel. "When you look at that, what do you see?''

Jane hesitated, reluctant to state the obvious. "A pretty lady.''

"Precisely. Not a whit more. When people look at your portrait, I want them to see more than a pretty lady. I want them to see *you.*'' Hurrying back to her, and with a belated, "Forgive me, but may I?'' he pulled the combs from her carefully arranged coiffure and, when the coils and ringlets tumbled down, swept the hair back and cupped it lightly against the back of her head. "Simplicity suits you,'' he said, smiling into her shocked face. "That decides it. If you will rearrange your hair—simply, please—I shall see to the other arrangements.''

"What arrangements?''

"You should be portrayed against nature, Johanna. Your hair gilded by the sunlight, your eyes reflecting the sky, the—Yes! The raven's tree as your backdrop!''

Jane looked dubious, but hesitated to argue in the face of his enthusiasm. He was the artist. And, before leaving to go about his business, Damon had said that Charles was to do whatever he thought best regarding the portrait. But still . . .

Looking down at her silk and lace and raising a shy hand to the necklace, she said, "Won't I look silly dressed like this, sittin' in the middle of a field?''

"No. No, certainly not! And you will not be sitting—I don't think. But the contrast . . . that is the point, don't you see? That very contradiction is the epitome of you.''

He spoke with such fervor and was so obviously eager for her to share his conviction that Jane dared not hesitate further. "I'll see to my hair.''

"You're not convinced, are you?'' he asked as she walked to the door. Turning, Jane shook her head. "Very well. If you are not satisfied when the painting is done, if you do not like it, I will redo it until it pleases you.''

Jane smiled, but eyed him slyly. "For double the price or only half again?"

Charles laughed. "Not a penny more than half. You've my word."

Jane held her breath. From Damon's elbow, Charles asked the question she dared not. "Well? What do you think?"

"An excellent likeness."

"Of course, it's an excellent likeness. But what do you think of it?"

"It's . . . not at all what I had in mind." He shot the artist a scathing, sidelong glance. "But, you've caught her." He grinned. "I like it, Charles. Very much. What do you think, Johanna?"

"I like it, too," she said, shyly. "But it gives me a queer feelin', lookin' at a picture of me."

Damon smiled at her fleetingly; dispassionately. The smile Peale gave her was far warmer. "You'll become used to that, soon enough," he said, before turning to Damon to ask, "Shall I arrange the framing for you? I've a commission in Philadelphia next week. I can have the portrait framed for you there, if you like."

His eyes on the painting, Damon nodded. "You know, of course, that you are welcome here until such time as you must leave for Philadelphia?"

"Much as I appreciate your hospitality, I'll be off in the morning. Humble though it is, I miss my own hearth."

"Of course." Damon turned from the easel. "Come into my study and we shall deal with the finances of this matter so that you are not detained on that account in the morning."

Watching Damon walk toward the drawing room door, Peale glanced at Jane, then asked, "Didn't Johanna tell you?"

Damon pivoted in the doorway. "Tell me what?"

Jane looked quickly from one man to the other. "I—I thought ye would speak with him yerself," she said, lamely. How could she admit that she had not been alone with Damon in the several days since Charles had made the gracious offer?

"Tell me what?"

"I thought to make the portrait a wedding gift."

For the first time since she had met him, Jane found Damon at a loss for words. "Oh, Charles, no. I can't possibly accept. Your time alone is worth . . . That's far too generous a gift, Charles."

Peale looked resolute. So did Damon. Diplomatically, Jane ventured, "I don't see how we can refuse a gift, Damon. 'Twould be rude."

"She's better mannered than you are, you oaf," Charles said, smiling at Jane.

Heaving a sigh, Damon acquiesced and, striding back into the room with his right hand extended, said sincerely "Thank you, Charles."

Peal grasped his friend's hand. "You are most welcome."

"But," Damon added, strengthening his grip when the artist moved to withdraw his hand, "I will stand for the framing."

"Indeed you will!" Peale said, well knowing the price of a picture frame.

Both men smiled and, with Damon leading the way, retired to the study when Damon would sign a blank voucher to cover the cost of the framing. Damon had total confidence in his friend.

Miserably, Jane watched him go, her eyes on her husband's broad back. He had said scarcely a word to her in a week and had been sulking like a child who had lost his favorite toy. It wasn't her fault she was a woman and bore Eve's curse every month, was it? Not considering that Damon's sullen behavior might stem from his bitter disappointment at her failure to conceive rather than from chagrin at having been denied her bed, Jane gave an indignant little huff and turned back to the portrait.

Charles had painted her prettier than she was, she thought, but she recognized herself easily enough. He was a wonderful painter! The way he had caught the play of sunlight on her hair and on the silk, the silvery shimmer of the moonstones and the milky glow of the pearls, was an absolute marvel to her. And she could almost feel the press of the breeze against her skirt—a sensation that had gone all but unnoticed by her at the time, but which Charles had miraculously captured. It seemed everything had captured his attention, even the bumblebee sipping at a clover flower near her left toe! And the raven which had jeered at them mercilessly, the sole survivor of the tragedy which had befallen his fellows, hung suspended in flight over the ancient tree which generations of his kind had claimed as their own and from which Raven's Oak had derived its name. Charles had even caught a sunbeam winking from the ring on her finger which, she noted with a smile, he had painted hugging her knuckle; looking every bit as oversized as it was.

She looked down at her hand and toyed with the ring; rotated it with her thumb and little finger; watched it glint in the candlelight. How often she and Julia had lain awake at night, giggling under the covers of the pallet they shared, wondering who they would marry. She had never doubted it would be one of the neighbor boys. Luke Trent or Adam Bodey, most likely. But it might have been George Thomas; he had been making calf eyes at her for as long as she could remember. Until last year when Pap had told everyone she was spoken for.

Why had he lied? Why hadn't Mam told her the truth? She must have known it! And why . . .

"He's a wonder with paint, isn't he?" Damon asked quietly from behind her.

Startled, Jane rounded on him. "I thought ye were in yer study."

"Charles has gone up. He wants an early start in the morning." He closed the space between them and stopped beside her. Looking at the portrait, he asked, "Why didn't you tell me he wanted to make a gift of it?"

"I've not seen ye except when he's been about."

"Through no fault of mine," he said tightly.

"Nor of mine!"

He shot her an accusing look that said he disagreed. But, turning away, he changed the subject. "Charles mentioned you are interested in learning to paint."

"Aye," she said, as eager for a neutral topic as he was. "He showed me a bit about drawin'; how to look at things and really see 'em. He makes it seem so easy!"

"He has a rare talent. Perhaps, we can find someone to instruct you. And while we are on the subject of lessons—" He clasped his hands lightly behind his back and began to stroll about the room. "I have engaged a tutor for you. He will be arriving tomorrow. As you have much to learn, I trust you will be an attentive pupil."

"Wh—what will he teach me?"

"Music, dance, etiquette, diction—that sort of thing."

"What's diction?"

"The art of speaking properly."

Jane bristled, as much at his patronizing tone as his implication. "Don't I speak good enough to suit ye?"

Her argumentative tone pivoted Damon on her. Hands still clasped behind his back, he said with a tight smile, "I would prefer we not argue tonight, Johanna. It has been a long week."

But an argument, Jane realized, was exactly what she needed. She had been walking on eggs around him for the whole of his "long week," trying to smooth the feathers she had unavoidably ruffled. A good argument was just what she needed!

"Aye, it's been a long week. And ye've said scarce a word to me through all of it! And on account of somethin' that's no fault of mine!" Damon glowered at her darkly, but Jane went recklessly on, "I'm not good enough for ye other ways. I don't dance or play yer clavichord or 'speak' good enough for ye, but I'm good enough for . . . for *that*!"

"Any woman, Madam, is good enough; it takes little talent! But, as you are my wife and the only woman available to me . . ." Damon broke off, suddenly realizing what he had said.

Jane stared at him, mouth agape. But, she supposed, he was right: any woman would do. A ram wasn't choosy about nannies nor a cock about hens. Still, it hurt to hear him say it; to admit he valued her *only* for that, and didn't value her that much even then.

"I'm sorry, Johanna," he began, looking more apologetic than he sounded, "but the simple truth is that you are my wife. As such, you have a duty to me."

"Aye." she hissed through anger-clenched teeth.

Now it was Damon who stared miserably after her as she stormed from the room.

Jane fumed as Janet unlaced her dress and readied her bath. What a fool she had been! She was no Juliet and *he* was certainly no Romeo! This marriage had not been a love match, and it never would be! What a fool she was to ever have thought . . . hoped . . . but she *had* thought, and she *had* hoped. What a foolish, silly, romantic little girl she had been! Well, no more. Nevermind that she enjoyed, revelled in, their lovemaking. Nevermind that it was the only time she felt even remotely his equal. Or that it was the only part of their lives they shared. Nevermind any of that! It was her duty. That was how *he* saw it. That was how she would see it from now on. That was how it was!

Damon felt his heart cringe as he watched her march resolutely toward him and her bed. He hadn't meant to be so sharp with her; he certainly hadn't meant what he had said—not the way it had sounded. She was wonderful in bed! She had an exquisite talent for lovemaking. But now . . .

"D'ye want the candle?" Jane asked stiffly, stopping beside the bed and avoiding his eye.

"Yes. Leave it.' Hearing the bite in his voice, he said more gently, "You know I like to see you. You're a beautiful woman, Jane."

She glared at him in tight-lipped silence, then turned her back and removed her robe. She slipped out of it and slid under the covers quickly, careful to allow him no more than a glimpse of her. And she kept well to her own side of the bed, not cuddling into his arms as he liked her to, but tucking the sheet securely under her chin and laying there stiffly, waiting. Staring up at the canopy, she thought smugly, *There. I've presented myself. Let him do the rest!*

Damon growled a sigh. "I'm pleased with your portrait."

"So ye said. Charles would've been disappointed if ye weren't," she said, deliberately turning aside what she knew he intended as a compliment.

"What, ah, what were you thinking about in the drawing room?"

Jane traced the thoughts he had interrupted to their conclusion, then said, "I don't think ye'd like to know."

"I would not have asked if I did not want to know!" he barked, instantly regretting his tone.

"I was wonderin'—or about to—why this mismatch was ever arranged. Why ye didn't marry one of yer other cousins."

Damon looked at her impassive profile. "Would you rather I had?"

She continued to address the canopy. "Any one of them would've suited ye better than me."

"How can you know that when you don't know them?"

"I know me. And I know ye—well enough."

Something in the way she said "well enough" made Damon's pride bristle. "Do you dislike me so much, then?"

She shrugged. "Ye're kind enough when it suits ye."

"Damme, girl!" he cried, shoving himself up onto an elbow and peering into her face. "When have I been anything *but* kind to you? I've given you everything: clothes, jewels, a fine house, a staff of servants! And when have I not been patient and gentle with you? And has kindness begotten kindness? Hardly! You approached this bed like a convict going to the gallows!" He paused, as if expecting her to answer, but Jane turned her face away. "Damnation, Johanna! I have asked little enough of you. Cannot you give me what little I ask?"

Her face snapped back to his and her dark eyes met his steadily. "I've given ye all I can! I came to ye with nothin' but my body and my pride. Ye've taken the one. I'll not be robbed of the other!"

"I'm not trying to rob you of your pride, Jane," he huffed disgustedly. "All I ask is that you be a wife to me. Is that asking too much?"

"Askin'!" she cried. "Ye're not askin', ye're demandin'! But seein' as ye've bought and paid for me—as ye've just gone to so much trouble to point out—I s'pose ye've a right to take the price out of my hide, same as ye do with *all* yer slaves!"

His pale expression revealed his shock. "Is that how you see it?"

"That's how it is."

"Damn!" he seethed, catapulting from the bed, taking the bedclothes with him., "You are the most insufferable, infuriating, ungrateful—''

Protectively dragging the covers back, she shrieked, ''Ye're no great prize yerself!''

Straightening to his full, impressive height and with his broad, darkly furred chest heaving, Damon glared down at her for what seemed an eternity before he snatched his robe from the foot of the bed and stormed from the room. Jane jumped when the door slammed behind him, but rather than feeling relieved at his departure, she felt nothing but dreadful regret.

# 7

Charles Peale was gone, and Damon with him, when Jane went down to breakfast the next morning. She was as sorry to have missed the artist as she was glad to have missed her husband.

"Pardon me, madam," Simon said in his stuffy manner and with his usual, rusty bow.

Jane stopped idly toying with her oysters and looked up from her plate. "Aye?"

"Bundy has asked to speak with you."

"What does he want?"

"I do not know, madam. Shall I tell him you will see him when you have finished your meal?"

"Oh, I'm not very hungry. I'll see him now."

Fighting down the butterflies in her stomach while she waited for Simon to show Bundy into the withdrawing room—this was her first summons as lady of the house—Jane hoped Bundy wasn't going to ask her something about his job. If he was, he had come to the wrong Seymour. The running of the estate was Damon's business, and he never spoke of it with her.

"Good mornin', Bundy," she said nervously when Simon had shown the man in and bowed his way out.

"Morning, ma'am," Bundy said, looking nervous himself as he shuffled the hat in his hands. "I'm sorry to have interrupted your breakfast, ma'am. I wouldn't have minded waiting 'til you were done."

"That's all right. I wasn't hungry."

He smiled fleetingly, then, with obvious reluctance, came to the point of his call. "I, ah, I came to talk to you about your riding, ma'am. Mr. Seymour had a word with me before he left for Baltimore this morning and . . ."

*Baltimore?* Jane thought. *Damon went to Baltimore?*

". . . said I was to—to teach you to ride, ma'am."

"Oh," Jane said, dully. She had expected that Damon would continue to teach her himself. They had been out several times together and he had seemed to enjoy it as much as she had. But, of course, after last night . . .

"He—Mr. Seymor that is—he suggested that we might start this morning, ma'am. Of course, any time you say, ma'am, is fine with me."

"Oh. Well. I—I have to change." She flounced her mint green skirt. "Is half an hour all right?"

"Any time, ma'am, any time you say is fine."

Jane smiled sheepishly and, with a little shrug, said, "Half an hour, then."

Bundy smiled broadly and Jane was again struck by his likeness to her brother. Except that Bundy's hair was sandier and his shoulders narrower than Jacob's. They were about the same height, though; several inches short of being tall. Neither would stand out in a crowd.

"I'll see to the horses, ma'am, and be waiting out front. If that's all right, ma'am?"

"I'm sure it's fine."

"Yes, ma'am." And, with an awkward bow, he left.

They rode eastward, away from the pasture land and the raven's tree with which Jane was now well familiar, and for all that he was supposed to be her teacher, Bundy said little; nothing at all instructive. It wasn't until they drew rein in the shade of a tree atop a rise that he offered more than two words together.

"You sit a horse real fine, ma'am."

"Thank ye. I'm not so nervous as I was at first." They exchanged smiles. "What's that down there?"

Bundy followed her nod. "That's wheat, ma'am."

"I thought Mr. Seymour grew tobacco."

"He does. But some of the farmers hereabout have been having fine luck with wheat, ma'am. It's easier to grow than tobacco." Seeing her interest, he explained, "You see, ma'am, tobacco's hard on the soil; leeches it out real quick. That being the case, tobacco fields have to lie fallow after a few crops. It takes a mighty lot of land to profit from growing tobacco."

"And Mr. Seymour doesn't have enough?"

She had asked the question in all seriousness, but Bundy seemed to take it as a joke. He laughed and said, "That's a good one, ma'am."

Jane smiled diffidently. "Then, why's he growin' wheat?"

"Like I said, ma'am, it's easier to grow. Brings in a nice profit, too, seeing as it can be sold local. Same with corn. The real trouble with tobacco, so I understand, is the export tariffs. Plenty of planters are grousing about those, and more'n a few have been out-and-out ruined on account of 'em." He had let his gaze wander from her as he spoke, and now he looked quickly back to her. "Not that I'm saying Mr. Seymour's in either group, ma'am. Not at all! But I do think, ma'am, he's right smart putting in wheat. And in taking such care to do it right, too. Everybody's real impressed by the way he's been overseeing the plantin' himself. Everybody but Flygher, of course. Now there's a man doesn't like his toes stepped on, even when they ain't his to call his own!" Then, like a boy who knows he has spoken out of turn to his elders but hopes not to be taken to task for it, he grinned nervously and said, "But I expect you know that, ma'am. We can ride down this way." And he eagerly led the way.

Jane knew nothing, least of all who Flygher was. But she thought better of asking and, letting her eyes wander over the landscape as her mare obediently followed Bundy's gelding down the grassy hillside, asked instead, "Those fields over there, is that wheat, too?"

"No, ma'am. That's tobacco."

"And those men, are they slaves?"

"The most of 'em, yes, ma'am."

Jane studied the workers intently. She had never seen slaves actually working a field, and these men—some three dozen of them—didn't fulfill her expectations. Rather than being half-naked, as Squire Trent's slaves had been, these wore baggy shirts and trousers of what appeared, from this distance, to be homespun. Some wore wide-brimmed straw hats, but most of them were bareheaded. Their demeanor was as expected, though, for they went about their hoeing and weeding with steady diligence, never raising their heads or straightening their backs from the chore. The breeze-fragmented tune they were singing had the rhythmic, mournful quality of a dirge.

"What's that they're singin'?"

Bundy wagged his head. "I wouldn't know, ma'am. Ain't nobody knows where they get their songs. Seems they mostly make 'em up."

"That man on the horse, who is he?"

"Why, that's Mr. Flygher, ma'am. The overseer."

She heard the incredulity in Bundy's voice and kept her eyes glued to the fields yonder, looking away from the man who had turned in his saddle to look at her.

"Forgive my asking, ma'am, but, hasn't Mr. Seymour shown you 'round?"

"He—he hasn't had time," she said, grasping at the excuse Bundy had given her. "What with the plantin' to see to. And I've been havin' my portrait painted, too."

"Oh, yeah. I should've remembered that, seeing as

that artist fella was out pitching the bar with us only last Sund'y. He's got a good arm, too. Amos was the only one could best his pitch. 'Course, Amos bests everybody. Even Mr. Seymour!''

''Oh! Then, he's recovered?''

''Ma'am?''

''Amos.'' Jane drew abreast of Bundy, who was waiting for her, and reined in. ''He's recovered from his ailment.''

''Pardon me, ma'am, but you must have him confused with somebody else. Amos ain't had a sick day since I've been here.''

''Oh. How—how long's that?''

''Let's see . . . 'Sixty-six. Just four years, ma'am. Four years this month.''

Jane looked away. ''Is there another man called Amos here, besides the one ye spoke of?''

''No, ma'am. There's only the one.''

Jane offered him a lame smile. ''Then ye must be right; I misunderstood,'' she said, knowing she hadn't. She looked quickly away again. ''What else is there to see besides the fields?''

''Well . . .'' Bundy hesitated, scratching his head. ''I, ah, I don't think I oughtta be showing you 'round, ma'am. That's for Mr. Seymour to do.''

''But ye've already shown me the fields and, as busy as he is, Mr. Seymour may not find time to show me the rest.'' Jane unwittingly beguiled him with a smile. ''What else is there?''

''Well, there's the curing sheds and storage barns—for the tobacco—and the dock. Nothin' much of interest to you there, ma'am, not this time of year. Then there's the gristmill Mr. Seymour's building over on Stoney Creek, but that ain't finished yet. There's the paddocks and stables and the slave quarters and—''

''Oh! I'd like to see where the slaves live, please.''

''No, ma'am,'' Bundy said, firmly. ''It ain't for the

likes of me to be introducing you 'round down there."
Jane's disappointment was evident, so he added
solicitously, "But I think it'll be all right for me to take
you on up to Stoney Creek and—and on our way back, I
can show you the breeding stock, if you like."

"All right."

Bundy smiled. "We can ride along the edge of this
field, then cut through them woods, ma'am. There's a
trail."

The ride to Stoney Creek was a pretty one, and while
Jane enjoyed looking at the scenery, Bundy enjoyed
looking at her. He had seen plenty of pretty women in
his travels, and had bedded more than a few, but he had
never seen one quite as pretty as her. He was hard
pressed to keep his eyes from her for more than a
minute or two during the ride, and it was only the
presence of the dozen laborers—eight of them slaves,
the rest freedmen—and the estate foreman, Grimes, who
was overseeing construction of the mill, that cured him
of his incessant staring.

"Good morning, ma'am," Grimes said with no small
surprise. Doffing his hat to the lady, he shot Bundy a
suspicious and accusing glance.

"Good morin', Mr. Grimes," Jane said, not liking the
man any better on their second meeting. "I asked Bundy
to bring me. I hope you don't mind?"

"Why, not at all, ma'am. It's a pleasure to have your
company." He smiled a genuine smile. "Would you like
me to show you around, ma'am?"

Jane glanced over his head at the workmen, a
number of which were staring back. "N-no, thank ye. I
can see everythin' fine from here."

"Stop your gawkin' and git back to work!" Grimes
bellowed, seeing the cause of Jane's nervousness. "I'm
sorry, ma'am. Niggers ain't well-mannered. But they'll
be no bother to you, should you like to look around."

Jane soon discovered that she had been right; there

was no more to be seen from the ground than from the saddle. But she did get a feel for the size of the place. Not yet half completed, the mill was large enough to accommodate the McPhees' entire house. The water wheel, so Grimes informed her, would stand more than a story high, and the two grindstones—which were being shipped and should arrive any day—would each weigh better than a quarter of a ton.

"When will it be finished?"

"In time for harvest, ma'am," Grimes said, adding with a glance at his work crew and a hand on the hilt of the coiled whip at his waist, "Guaranteed."

Jane didn't like Mr. Grimes, at all.

"He's just like Squire Trent," she muttered, her thoughts still on the man who she and Bundy had, by now, left well behind.

"Ma'am?"

"Nothin'." But a moment later she asked "Would Mr. Grimes use that whip on 'em, Bundy?"

"I don't s'pose he'd have to, ma'am. They're a real good crew o' workers, those. Would you like to see the breeding stock, ma'am?"

But as capable and knowledgable a guide as Bundy was, and as interesting as Jane found her tour of the breeding stables, her eyes and attention kept wandering to the long, tidy row of freshly whitewashed houses. With their complement of outbuildings, the structures made up a small village some distance from the main house. During one of her surreptitious peeks at the place, she recognized two of her dresses and several of her petticoats fluttering on a clothesline. Inadvertently, she gasped, "Oh, my!"

"I told you, ma'am. It ain't my place to take you there. Now, this mare here is Raven's Night. She's got about the best bloodline you'll—"

"But, those are my clothes on that line!"

He looked at her incredulously. "Who do you think

does your washing, ma'am?"

"Oh."

"Like I was saying, ma'am, Raven's Night here has about the best bloodline of any mare this side of the Atlantic. Her foals have—"

"Do they do yer washin', too?"

Bundy smirked. "Yes, ma'am, they do."

"What else do they do?"

"Just about everything, ma'am," he said. Relenting, he stretched out an arm and, pointing to each structure in turn, rattled off, "That there's the carpenter shop; weaving shed; smithy; curing shed; tanning shed; cow barn; chicken coop; back of that—you can't see 'em from here—are the hog pens and the kennels. The negroes take care of all o' that and do the vegetable gardening and the pickling and preserving; tend the orchards and the grape arbor, and do the picking and the drying, and make the cider and—they do just about everything, ma'am."

"And they live in those houses?"

"Yes, ma'am."

Jane gave him a grateful smile. "Now, what was that ye were sayin' 'bout Raven's Night's foals?"

Bundy smiled back at her and felt his heart warm him from the inside out.


"Pardon me, madam. Mr. Seymour has returned with Mr. Cullingford and requests the pleasure of your company in the withdrawing room."

Certain that after last night Damon would take no pleasure in her company, Jane attributed the polite phrasing of the order to Simon and asked, "He's back with who?"

"Mr. Cullingford, madam. Your tutor."

The tutor! She had forgotten all about him!

"Tell 'em I'm comin', will ye please?" she said, tossing her book aside and jumping to her feet.

"Yes, madam. Do you wish tea served?"

"Oh. Ah. I—I should, shouldn't I?"

Simon poorly suppressed his warm smile. "I shall see to it, madam."

"Thank ye, Simon." The butler bowed and moved to leave the library. "Simon!"

"Madam?"

"Am I . . . Do I look all right for meetin' a tutor?"

Simon eyed the modestly cut, pink cambric afternoon dress. "I should think so, madam. If I may be permitted to say so, you look quite lovely."

She flashed a nervous smile. "Thank ye, Simon."

Despite her apprehension, Damon greeted her very politely, wearing a half-smile and a look in his eye which Jane couldn't quite decipher but which didn't look ominous. She half-smiled back.

"Mr. Cullingford, may I present my wife? Johanna, this is Mr. Cullingford, your tutor."

"A pleasure, madam," the tutor said, bowing grandly.

He was a sliver of a man, and barely taller than Jane herself. He wasn't very old, either; thirty, perhaps. His mouse-brown hair was caught back in a queue, the style most gentlemen favored, and had been elaborately poofed over his high forehead and formed into two tight curls over each prominent ear. But, as the entire arrangement was slightly askew, Jane decided it must be a peruke. His pale blue eyes were poorly aligned, the left being higher than the right, but whether their asymmetry was a genuine error of nature or an illusion caused by the listing wig, Jane couldn't be sure. There was nothing illusory about his nose. It was hooked and outsized for his narrow face, dwarfing his thin-lipped mouth and all but nonexistent chin. He was the least attractive specimen of manhood Jane had ever seen, and her husband's virile good looks and handsome physique only served to accentuate poor Mr. Cullingford's numerous shortcomings.

Straightening from his bow, Cullingford smiled condescendingly. "I trust ours will be a most propitious acquaintance, Mistress Seymour."

Jane smiled wanly but said nothing, having no idea what she might be getting herself in for if she agreed.

"I am certain it will be, sir," Damon said smoothly. "Will you have a seat?"

With a gracious nod of acceptance, Cullingford waited until his employer had seated his pupil before he flipped the tails of his drab brown coat over the lap of his drab brown breeches and settled—somewhat daintily, Jane thought—into a chair. Damon continued to stand, looming over them both and with that unfathomable expression still in his eyes.

"I have told Mr. Cullingford, Johanna, that in addition to the course of study he will prepare for you, you are taking riding instruction. Did you benefit from Bundy's instruction this morning?"

Jane hesitated, not wanting to get Bundy into trouble by telling the truth, but not wanting to lie, either. "I learned a good deal," was all she could honestly say.

"Excellent. I shall see that he devotes an hour to your instruction each morning. I trust that will not interfere with your schedule, sir?"

"Not at all, sir. Not at all," Cullingford said, smiling ingratiatingly at his employer, then turning to Jane. "However, I might suggest that you ride early. It has been my experience that pupils are most attentive early in the day and I should not like to delay beginning your lessons beyond nine-of-the-clock." Jane smiled tightly, not liking the man's condescending tone and supercilious manner. "Of course, a great deal of my instruction will not be confined to the hours allotted to your intellectual betterment. In the matters of etiquette and deportment, for example, it has been my experience that practical application—seizing the moment throughout the day, so to speak—is the most effective and beneficial mode of instruction. In point of fact," he went on, his limpid eyes appraising, "there is no time like the present to begin." His gaze slewed to Damon. "With your permission, sir?" Damon nodded. "If you will rise, please, madam?"

Self-consciously, Jane did, pushing herself up from her chair with a hand on each of its arms. Cullingford stood, too, his thin lips pursed like the drawstring closure of a small pouch.

"A lady does not *heave* herself from a chair, madam. A lady *does* rise and seat herself slowly and gracefully. Like so." He demonstrated, lowering and raising himself from his chair with more grace than Jane could ever hope to achieve.

His high-browed stare clearly implied that Jane was to follow his impeccable example, which she did several times until Cullingford conceded that she had made some improvement, retook his seat and, finally, stayed there. Jane promptly settled comfortably back in hers.

"Ah-ah!" Cullingford cautioned, wagging a delicate finger. "A lady's back never touches that of the chair. Sit tall, madam, with your back erect."

Reluctantly, Jane straightened, feeling the muscles of her lower back—still stiff from a morning in the saddle—rebel.

"Much better," the tutor lauded with an approving smile for his pupil, then a hopeful glance at her husband.

"Oh, yes. Much better," Damon agreed, taking the chair next to Cullingford's and, to Jane's chagrin, making much of settling well back into its upholstered softness and crossing his long legs comfortably at the knee.

He met Jane's withering glare with a complacent smile. Suddenly, she understood: He would have his revenge for last night. He would torture her to death with this awful little man!

Simon's arrival with the tea cart elicited another

round of instruction. Dismissing the butler with a haughty, "That will be all, thank you," and shooing him out with a fluttering hand—thereby earning for himself the man's undying enmity—Cullingford proceeded to instruct Jane in the ritual of serving tea. By the time she had poured, sugared, creamed and served for the three of them; passed around the plate of rusks, the marmalade and the jam; been criticized for clattering her spoon as she stirred; taught how to properly balance her saucer and hold her cup; and remonstrated twice for "slurping," she was ready to explode with anger and frustration. She did not enjoy the tea hour one bit, but she exalted in having borne it.

Given Cullingford's attentions at tea, she should have been prepared for the rigors he had in store for her over supper. He was relentless. Jane was told that she ate "too quickly," took "too large" mouthfuls, chewed "too vigorously," applied her napkin "too crudely," and had the "vulgar habits" of hunching over her plate and resting her forearms on the table. He seemed not to notice—or if he did, not to care—that Jane was "too happy" to have the meal end.

But even when it had, Mr. Cullingford's instruction did not. He reseated her at the table repeatedly, reminding her to raise herself "a *soupcon*" above the chair in order to accommodate the gentleman to whom the honor of seating her had been given. And when he finally allowed them to withdraw, Jane found herself rigidly poised on the edge of a drawing room chair, being subjected to a lecture on "The Art of Genteel Conversation," as Mr. Cullingford titled it. Then she was forced to participate in a stiflingly polite and boring exchange with the man while Damon smugly sipped his brandy. She was hard pressed to know which of the men she detested more.

At the end of an agonizingly long hour, Mr. Cullingford outlined the course of study he had determined would be "most advantageous to this particular pupil." There would be, he informed Damon, in addition to the lessons in deportment and etiquette he had already begun, the usual instruction in music—both vocal and instrumental—the dance, diction, and dramatic reading. But he also proposed to include lessons in grammar and vocabulary "as the pupil exhibits severe deficiencies in these areas," and to defer her instruction in French "until she has mastered her mother tongue."

Having received Damon's murmured approval of his plans, Cullingford then informed "the pupil" of the schedule he expected her to maintain. Grammar and vocabulary lessons would begin promptly at nine, followed by lessons in diction and dramatic reading. Following the noon meal, she would take instruction in music and the dance until teatime and, of course, the matter of deportment and etiquette would be "dealt with throughout the day."

Then, smiling benevolently, he said, "I trust, madam, that with perseverance on both our parts, you will be the very embodiment of refined gentility at the end of a year's time."

"A year?" Jane cried, erupting from her chair and aiming herself at her husband. "A year? Ye expect me to put up with this—with him—for a year!"

Damon shrugged. "If that is Mr. Cullingford's estimate. He is the authority on the matter, my dear." Then he frowned and, before Jane could say more, chastised, "I believe I recall telling you that a lady does not raise her voice."

"And I told ye, I'm no lady!" she shrieked defiantly, shifting her furious glare to Cullingford. "And I'm not so sure I want to be one!"

"My word, sir!" Cullingford gasped as his pupil sped up the stairs, intent on gaining her room before Damon's anger could manifest itself.

But, to her utter incredulity and outrage, Jane heard

Damon explode with laughter.

Jane stared dumbly at the neatly numbered list of carefully printed words on the page Mr. Cullingford extended to her across the library table. There were fifty of them; most she had never seen before.

"Punctilious?" she asked, slowly raising her eyes. "What's that?"

"That, madam, is what I intend to make you," he said, stiffly. "You hold the first vocabulary list. You are to learn the correct spelling, pronunciation and usage of each word. Those that are unfamiliar to you, you may research in the dictionary. By tomorrow morning, you will have written each word thrice and penned its definition in the space I have provided. At that time, I will ask you to spell each of the first ten words and to use them in sentences."

"All that by tomorrow?"

His answer was a pompous nod. "If you will put it aside, please, we shall adress ourselves to your rather quaint speech patterns. I am referring specifically to your use of 'ye' for 'you,' and 'aye' and 'nay' for 'yes' and 'no,' respectively. You will use the correct pronunciation—you, your, yourself, etcetera—and dispense of 'aye' and 'nay' beginning now." Having delivered this dictum, Cullingford turned away and, while Jane stared daggers at his back, scanned the shelves of a bookcase. He selected a volume and returned with it to the table, opening it at random, then he extended the book to Jane. "Read, please. Aloud. You may begin at a paragraph."

"If ye're trying to find out—"

"If *you* are," Cullingford interrupted to correct.

"If *you* are tryin' to find out if I can read," Jane seethed, "I'll save ye—*you*—the trouble. I can."

"If you will begin at a paragraph, please?" Cullingford said, tightly.

Glaring at him, Jane accepted the book and, in a voice taut with anger, read:

> The Reader may please to observe, that in the last Article for the Recovery of my Liberty, the Emperor stipulates to allow me a Quantity of Meat and Drink, sufficient for the Support of 1728 'Lilliputians.' Some time after, asking a Friend at Court how they came to fix on that determinate Number; he told me, that his Majesty's Mathematicians, having taken the Height of my Body by the Help of a Quadrant, and finding it to exceed theirs in the Proportion of Twelve to One, they concluded from the Similarity of their Bodies, that mine must contain at least 1728 of theirs, and consequently would require as much Food as was necessary to support that Number of 'Lilliputians.' By which, the Reader may conceive an Idea of the Ingenuity of that People, as well as the prudent and exact Oeconomy of so great a Prince.

Before Jane could begin on the next paragraph, Cullingford reached for the book and said, "That is sufficient, thank you."

Closing the book, Jane read the title on the spine before handing it back: *Travels Into Several Remote Nations of the World* by Lemuel Gulliver.

"You are unfamiliar with Dr. Swift's works, I see," he said, accepting the novel.

"Swift? But 'twas written by Lemuel Gulliver."

Cullingford smiled deprecatingly. "A pseudonym— or nom de plume, as the French say—employed by Jonathan Swift to protect his identity as author of this rather scathing satire and which lends a farcical touch of authenticity to the fiction." He smiled again, self-righteously this time, and returned the book to the case.

Watching him correctly file it among the Ss, not

where he had found it among the Gs, Jane wondered
how many Lilliputians he equalled, and decided it
couldn't be more than a thousand.

"That was nicely done, madam. You read well and
expressively." He turned to her and, lest the
compliment should go to her head, said, "However,
your enunciation is atrocious. Say, 'Last night I caught
sight of the flight of a bat.'"

"Last night I caught sight of the flight of a bat?"

"Final 't,' madam. Let me hear it."

"Las-t nigh-t I caugh-t sigh-t of the fligh-t of a ba-t."

"Better. Now. Walking, talking, standing, sitting.
Repeat." When Jane had echoed him, Cullingford
snapped. "'G,' madam. There is a final 'g.' Say, bringing,
ringing, singing."

"Bring*ing*, ring*ing*, sing*ing*."

"Walking or talking or standing or sitting, we are
bringing and ringing and singing. Repeat."

"That makes no sense!"

"Repeat after me, madam."

Cullingford launched into the nonsense sentence
again. And no sooner had Jane repeated it than he sent
forth a barrage of other, equally nonsensical rhymes and
ditties. By the end of the hour when he remarked upon
her verbal improvement, Jane's head fairly swam with
the phrases. And by the end of the second hour, which
she spent researching the impossibly long list of
impossible words, her head was throbbing.

The tutor's niggling corrections over dinner did
nothing to ease her headache and, under his relentless
scrutiny, her appetite deserted her—even though she
had foregone breakfast in order to ride early and had
been famished all morning.

But her flagging spirits rose when the time came to
take her place on the small bench before the clavichord
and mimic her tutor's fingering of the keys. Though the
scales he set her to practicing were monotonous, Jane

sincerely wanted to learn to play and kept at them diligently for the full hour. She was surprised that the time passed so quickly, and disappointed when Cullingford announced it was time for her vocal instruction.

She had been embarrassed to admit her musical deficiencies to Damon, but she was mortified at having to reveal her limited repertoire to Cullingford. He rolled his eyes heavenward—they were correclty aligned today, as was his peruke—and sighed ponderously each time she confessed ignorance of the tune he effortlessly coaxed out of the clavichord. But she almost forgave him his arrogant chagrin when his lower jaw sagged in awe as she sang one of the lullabies she knew so well.

"My word. That was extraordinary," he announced when she was done. And after she had sung a few scales and a gibberish of elongated vowels, he said, "In your case, madam, vocal instruction per se would be painting the lily. All you require is a knowledge of civilized music."

He was less impressed with her aptitude for dancing. Used to lively reels and gavottes and the flings Pap had taught her, she felt awkward and self-conscious as she tried to imitate the graceful dips and slow turns of the staid minuet chosen for their first lesson. And the more self-conscious she felt, the more awkward she became. She had stumbled through the dance twice when she was instructed to drop a deep curtsy to her partner. Jane was no less appalled than her tutor to realize she didn't know how. What remained of her afternoon was spent in learning.

Escorting her toward the drawing room where tea—and another round of instruction, Jane was sure—awaited them, Cullingford said, "I confess, madam, you have surprised me. Your attitude of cooperation—with only a few exceptions—has been most satisfying, even exemplary. After your outburst last evening, I had anticipated less diligence and enthusiasm than you have shown."

Jane forced a smile. She hardly felt enthusiastic—
except about the music lessons. Frustrated, angry,
resentful, embarrassed, hungry and tired, yes;
enthusiastic, no. Determined was more like it. She would
see this tutoring business through and as quickly as
possible—may Cullingford's year be hanged!—and if
being cooperative and pleasant would speed the
process, she would be the most brilliant, *amicable
abcedarian*—words two and one on her vocabulary
list—the man had ever taught. Then she would be rid of
him all the sooner for it . . . and teach her arrogant
husband a lesson about pride in the bargain!

But, for all her resolve, after four months of suffering
Cullingford's arrogant criticism, Jane's meager store of
patience was running low. She was tired, sick and tired,
of guarding every word she spoke, every gesture she
made; of not being able to stand or sit or read or eat a
meal without being monitored; of never, in all her
waking hours, being alone; and of being too much alone
the rest of the time.

Fairly, she admitted that Cullingford wasn't responsible for that last. Much as she detested the man,
she could not lay the blame for Damon's disinterest in
her at Cullingford's feet—even if she didn't know where
else to place it. Surely, the fault was no longer hers. In
the last four months she had gone out of her way to be
pleasant to her husband: smiling at him sweetly;
glancing at him from beneath coyly lowered lashes;
speaking to him politely and with proper wifely respect;
making genteel conversation over meals and tea. She
had practiced every one of Cullingford's lessons in
ladylike comportment. And still, in all the months since
her tutor had arrived, Damon had not once approached
her bed.

She had thought of going to him—had almost done it
several times when the appetite he had awakened in her

kept her tossing and turning with longing far into the night—but she had never been able to summon enough courage or choke down enough pride to cross the sitting room and risk his rejection. Or worse, be met with his smug I-knew-you-would-come acceptance.

If Damon had similar nocturnal difficulties, he, too, kept them to himself. Though he had been at home more often during the summer—it being between the busy seasons of planting and harvesting—Jane had seen little of him. Her lessons had kept her occupied all day, and he had stayed out of the way, working at his desk in the study. But she suspected he kept an ear to what was going on in the adjoining library: She had heard him laugh once while she was reading an amusing story aloud to Mr. Cullingford.

But now that it was autumn, Damon spent a large portion of his time supervising the final preparations for the forthcoming harvest fair and horse auction: the local Event-of-the-Year.

She had gleaned that tidbit of information from Bundy. Damon still never spoke of estate matters to her, but Bundy . . . Bundy knew everything that went on, and wasn't shy about discussing it with her. Jane suspected that was because he thought she knew as much about Raven's Oak business as he did. With a duplicity that was new to her, she was careful not to let her ignorance show. But, now and then, she gave herself away. Like the morning when, during one of their rides, Bundy mentioned the eleven head of horses Damon was putting on the auction block.

"They ought to bring the best prices Raven's Oak has seen in recent years," he remarked.

"Eleven? But, I thought there were only six two-year-olds."

"There are. But he always auctions off the less promising yearlings and some of the brood mares. The ones past their breeding prime. Didn't he tell you?"

"It must have slipped his mind. Will he be replacing the mares?"

"I expect so. He'll have a fine lot to choose from. Breeders come here from all over for the auction."

"Here? They're coming here, to Raven's Oak?"

No, not *here*. Over to Auction Meadow, outside Rendell. I showed you the place a couple o'weeks ago, remember? I don't think you listen to a half of what I tell you."

"Yes, I do! I hang on your every word. You're teaching me to ride. I would break my neck if I didn't listen to you."

"Well, if it's your neck you're worried about, you'd best not be hanging on your tutor's every word. You could break it doing that, too, as highbrow as he talks!"

Jane enjoyed his teasing. He teased her often, and never called her "ma'am" anymore unless someone else was around to hear. She liked that. It made their rides friendlier. Her excursions with Bundy were the one enjoyable thing in her life. He was uncritical—praising what she did right, not criticizing what she did wrong—and had proven himself to be a fine teacher. She had mastered her mare's gaits and loved to canter over the rolling, grassy pasturelands of Damon's property. She enjoyed Bundy's undemanding company so much, in fact, that over the course of four months, she had gradually extended the hour allotted to their rides to an hour and a half by starting out a little earlier each day.

It was a practice Damon had noticed. And this morning, he watched from Jane's bedroom as the pair rode side by side down the drive. The sight of Jane laughingly tilting her face skyward irked him.

It had been a hellishly long time since she had laughed with him like that. And hellishly longer since she had been a wife to him!

Admittedly, he may have been wrong in demanding his conjugal right. But, by damn, it *was* his right, and if the measure of blame could be weighed, she would be shown to have been the more wrong: She had denied him what a good wife didn't! And why? For the sake of pride? Damnation! If she had a whit of pride she'd be ashamed of her conduct as a wife! Didn't a wife take pride in fulfilling her duty; in giving her husband children?

By damn, what was the matter with her! It wasn't as though he had made it unpleasant for her. He had seen to it that she took as much pleasure from him as he did from her, hadn't he? Damned right, he had! And despite her stubborn pride, the woman wasn't made of ice. He had heard her tossing and turning in her bed like a fish thrown up on a river bank. She was hot as a poker. Hotter! So what the deuce was the matter with her? She knew where his bedroom was. She knew . . .

Damon smashed a balled fist into an open palm. "There's the answer, you idiot!" he seethed, watching the couple disappear beyond the frost-bronzed foliage of the trees in the elipse. "Even a second-rate stallion has his romp now and again!" he muttered, then bellowed to the man two rooms behind him, "Simon! Send for my horse!"

"Pardon me, sir?"

"I said, send for my horse," Damon repeated, striding through the sitting room.

"But your carriage is waiting, sir. I thought you had business in Rendell this morning."

"I don't pay you to think!" Damnon snapped, hastily tying his stock.

"Quite so, sir. That is a service I willingly render without remuneration." And he went back to brushing up the nap on the velvet jacket in his hands.

Damon snatched the coat away. "Send word to the stables, Simon, that they are to saddle Gilyad's Sun. And tell them I want him five minutes ago!"

* * *

Jane looked at Bundy curiously as they walked their horses, cooling them down after the canter. It wasn't like him to be so serious. Or so quiet. He had said almost nothing since they had left the house. He was usually full of teasing, and always asked to hear an account of the previous day's lessons with Mr. Cullingford. But today . . . Bundy was different today.

"I'm learning a new dance," she said, and was disappointed when Bundy continued to ride morosely on. "It's called 'Oaks and Willows.' The gentlemen dance the part of the oak trees, all regal and strong, and the ladies are supposed to be the willows." She waited, but still Bundy said nothing. "Mr. Cullingford says I'd do better as an oak. He called me 'graceless.' Said I 'completely lack the required suppleness of movement.' He made a beautiful willow!" She laughed a little, but Bundy didn't. "Did you hear me?"

"I heard you."

"Do *you* think I'm graceless, too? Is that why you don't think it's funny?"

"Criminy sakes, no!"

The look of misery on his face made Jane flinch. "Wh—what's wrong?"

"You really don't know, do you?"

"Is it—is it that I was making fun of Mr. Cullingford? I know that's rude, but . . ." With a moan of a sigh and a disgusted headshake, Bundy looked away again. "What is it, then?"

"Nothin'."

"That's not true. For goodness sake, I'm not clairvoyant, Bundy. How can I know what it is if you won't tell me?"

"There's some things shouldn't need explaining. If they do, they ain't worth wasting breath on."

"I don't understand."

"I know."

She watched his resolute profile. A muscle jumped

near his jaw, as though he was gritting his teeth. Hard. "Won't you explain it to me? Whatever it is, whatever I've done, I shouldn't want to do again if it upsets you so."

"You won't. You'll have nothing more to do with me after today."

Jane reined in sharply and sat staring after Bundy as his horse paced on. "Bundy!" He reined in but didn't look at her. "What are you saying? That we won't be riding together anymore?" He nodded, curtly. "But, you promised to teach me to jump!"

"No."

"Yes, you did! And you know Mr. Seymour wants me to learn."

"Then he'll have to get somebody else to teach you."

"I don't want anyone else to teach me." Jane nudged her mare forward until she stood beside Bundy's gelding. "Or is that you don't *want* to teach me anymore?"

"No. No, it ain't that!" he said, looking at her quickly and as quickly glancing away. "It's that I can't."

"Why not?"

"It's--it's the auction. It's so close I can fairly touch it and I've got more work yet to do to get ready for it. I just plain can't be wasting my time, riding all over the countryside with you, when there are more important things I should be doin'."

The rejection in his words stabbed painfully at Jane. "I realize how busy you must be. But, if Mr. Seymour thought you were needed elsewhere—"

"There's no 'buts' about it. And Mr. Seymour don't know the problem."

"Oh, Bundy, I'm sure you're wrong. You told me yourself he has been very busy with arrangements for the auction. I'm certain that if he thought our rides were taking you from more important duties, he would have—"

Bundy's icy stare stunned Jane to silence. "He don't know the problem, I told you."

"I'll—I'll take it up with him, then," Jane said, self-consciously using the stilted phrase Cullingford had taught her. "I'm sure, once he realizes how pressed you are for time, he will assign some of your duties to some-one else and we can continue our rides."

"He can easier assign the riding to someone else," Bundy said, stonily. "For that matter, he ought to be teaching you himself; he's the best horseman on the place. Maybe *that's* what you ought to 'take up with him,' ma'am."

Jane looked down at her hands. He had slammed a door in her face and, with that one, last word, turned the key in the lock. She ought to be furious, she supposed. Riding was her only pleasure and Bundy her only . . . friend.

But whether or not he was truly her friend, with no one else to take her riding—for surely, Damon wouldn't make the time—she would sorely miss it!

"After you've put your little mare there through her paces and shown Mr. Seymour what you've learned, will you do me a favor, ma'am? Just to make me look good, don't tell him you're a natural born horsewoman."

"Certainly, I won't," she said in all seriousness, worrying at the reins with gloved thumbs. "It wouldn't be true."

"Yes, it would be. You took to riding like . . . like a flower to the sun."

Something in his tone made her look at him, and she discovered a strange turmoil in his eyes.

Turning his horse in a tight circle, he said, "I'll take you back now, ma'am."

"Now? But we've more than an hour before I have to start with Cullingford."

"Yes, ma'am. And, like I said, there's a hundred things I oughtta be doing but this."

"Can't one of them wait just an hour? Please? Oh, Bundy, please?"

From the concealing shade of tree, Damon watched the impassioned exchange in the meadow. Knowing full well that things were not always what they seemed, that perception of any given situation was in the eye of the beholder, and also knowing that he was predisposed to see the present situation in an ugly light, he tried to be objective. But even though their words were lost to him over the distance, his wife's imploring manner and his hostler's frequent headshakes, led him to only one conclusion: He was witnessing a lover's quarrel; an assignation gone awry.

Filled with righteous indignation as the party sorely wronged by this tête-à-tête, he shortened rein and was about to ride in on them when, abruptly, the couple parted: Bundy riding back toward the house; Jane kicking her mare into a hell-bent gallop the opposite way. He hesitated, his head swiveling in a rapidly increasing arc from one to the other, as he tried to decide which guilty party he would take to task first.

Jane had crested a low rise when the sound of fast approaching hooves caused her to throw a puzzled glance over her shoulder. She was more than surprised when she recognized the rider close on her heels—and getting closer. And she had barely started to rein in when Damon's powerful stallion drew abreast of her little mare.

"What are you trying to do—ruin her?" he yelled, leaning low to catch the mare's reins and hauling both horses to a prancing stop.

"I was having a run," Jane said, still breathless with exertion. "I do it every morning. She's used to it. Bundy says a good run every day—"

"Bundy," Damon sneered, letting go her reins as if they burned. "He's made a rider of you, I'll give him that much," he said. But he thought, *And a cuckold of me in the process!*

"What are you doing out here? I thought you were in Rendell making arrangements for the auction."

"Did you?" he said, the bitterness still in his voice. "And who told you that?"

"Simon did, when I asked if you would be joining me for breakfast. Why are you staring at me like that?"

Inexplicably, Damon found himself unable—or, at least, unwilling—to put his accusation into words. Turning away, he asked, "And where is Bundy?"

"He—he went back."

"Why?"

"He had business to see to, preparations to make for the auction." The look in his eyes warned her that this was not the time to be asking favors, but she said, anyway, "I would like to speak with you about that. About Bundy."

Damon straightened in his saddle. "Would you, indeed?"

"Yes. It seems that the auction, coupled with my riding lessons, has put a great strain on his time. I thought that you might assign some of his duties to others—just temporarily, of course—so that he might continue to instruct me."

Damon smiled a tight, cold smile. "You wish me to relieve Bundy of his burdensome chores so that he will have more time to apply to you?"

"Yes," she said, her smile hesitant but hopeful.

"By damn, woman!" he roared. "I was not born yesterday! Do you think I don't know what has been going on? I'm not so big a fool as you take me for, madam!"

Jane swallowed convulsively, startled and as shocked as she was baffled by his furious outburst. But as he continued his harangue, the light of understanding dawned. Stunned by the charges he was levelling against her—and poor Bundy as well—her mouth worked impotently for some moments before she found the strength to give her words voice.

"How dare you—how can you even imply—"

"I make no implication, madam, but an accusation!"

"He has taught me to ride. Nothing more!"

"I hardly expected a confession," Damon sneered, his handsome face grown ugly with anger and disgust. "A woman who stoops to such a deception hasn't the character to admit of her wrongs!"

"I've stooped to nothing! I've done no wrong!" But she saw that he didn't believe her and knew that nothing she could say would convince him of the truth. So she stiffened and, hating herself for the tears that welled in her eyes, spoke with a dignity she had not known she possessed. "Think whatever you will of me, then. I'll not lower myself to pleading forgiveness of an offense I did not commit."

Then, with a poise that astounded him, she turned her horse and slowly moved away. And he thought, as he watched her go, what a lady she was and how much good the tutor had done her. And how very much he loved her.

"No! No, no, no, no, and no!" Cullingford cried, leaping up from his seat at the clavichord and advancing to where Jane stood glaring at him. "Lithe, supple, graceful movements, madam. Your arms are supposed to be green willow boughs, not dead sticks. Please do try to remember that!"

"I am trying! Why don't you teach me another dance since you find me so inept at this one?"

"Would that I could, madam. Would that I could! But your husband expressly directed that you should learn 'Oaks and Willows.' Therefore, learn it you shall. Though it be the death of us both!"

"I have no desire to *die* in an effort to please my husband," Jane said, gathering up her skirts and heading for the music room door. The massive form blocking it brought her up short.

"Rest assured, madam, I will never ask so weighty a sacrifice of you." His eyes bored into hers for a long moment before they leapt to Cullingford. "What seems to be the trouble?"

"Your wife is experiencing some difficulty dancing 'Oaks and Willows,' sir. I am certain, however, that with perseverance and patience, she will achieve the level of grace the dance requires, and which she presently lacks."

Damon's eyes recaptured Jane's. "I do not find my wife lacking in grace, sir. Nor in any virtue," he added, softly. "But as you are of other opinion, I should like to discover the extent of her deficiency for myself. Will you be so kind as to provide the musical accompaniment?"

"Certainly, sir. Of course."

"Oh. Oh, no, I don't want to—"

"Madam," Damon intoned firmly, offering his arm.

Jane felt her stomach knot as Damon led her to the center of the room and bowed gracefully as Cullingford struck the opening chords of the dance. Jane responded with a stiff curtsy and a furious scowl. If he was trying to make a fool of her with the intention of laughing in her face, she thought, gingerly accepting his hand and stepping into the first figure of the dance with all the grace she could muster, she wasn't going to make it easy for him!

But as they moved together, then apart, each dancing an assigned role, each complementing the other, Jane found herself responding to her new partner as she never had to Cullingford. Damon *did* look as majestic and proud as an oak, and he made her feel delicate and, yes, even graceful beside him. And, as it wasn't necessary to duck under his arm as was the case with Cullingford's, even the turns went smoothly. For the first time since all this dancing business started, she felt that she was actually doing well. She was even enjoying herself. She was even smiling!

Damon was smiling, too. And looking at her as he hadn't in a very long while; in that special, warm sort of way. Despite what he had said that morning—the horrible accusation he had made—she found herself fairly melting under his warm gaze.

Then she remembered that he owned her; that any other woman would serve him as well; that she was only the "available" one. She wasn't smiling when the dance ended and she melted into a curtsy amid a billow of skirts. She wanted to refuse the hand Damon offered to help her rise, but that wouldn't have been polite, and Cullingford would make an issue of it. And she wanted to reclaim her hand quickly, but Damon's thumb closed over her fingers and held it fast. The kiss he gave it, as his eyes held hers, was lingering, sensual, and far from polite.

His voice was more than polite, too, when he murmured for her ears alone, "You dance beautifully, Jane. I find no fault with you at all."

Then, tucking her hand into the crook of his elbow, and holding it there, Damon turned to the tutor who sat at the keyboard wearing a look of utter astonishment. "I fail to find justification for your complaint, Mr. Cullingford. I thought my wife the epitome of grace."

"Yes. Quite so, sir."

"Perhaps, all that was needed was the proper accompaniment. You have been playing the duel roles of partner and accompanist. A difficult task, at best."

"Yes. Yes, indeed it is, sir," Cullingford said, shaking off his surprise and adding, "If I may suggest that, hereafter, you partner your wife while I provide the music? That would seem to be in the pupil's best interest, sir.''

"My thought, exactly. Shall we commence the new regimen tomorrow? If you will excuse us, my wife and I have a matter to discuss.''

Jane looked up at Damon in surprise and dismay while Cullingford protested, ''But I had thought, sir, that as Mistress Seymour has mastered 'Oaks and Willows' at last, that we might begin on—''

"Tomorrow," Damon interrupted, spiriting a wary Jane toward the door, where he paused to toss over his shoulder, ''You will forgive us, I trust, if we are not present for tea? Our discussion may prove a lengthy one.''

"If it is your intention to resume our 'discussion' of this morning—'' Jane began indignantly, when she was sure they were safely out of Cullingford's hearing.

"Nothing of the kind," he assured her with a warm smile. Then, to Simon who they met in the front hall, Damon said, ''See that we are not disturbed.'' And he urged Jane up the stairs.

He said nothing more until they reached her bed-chamber. ''Shall we go into the sitting room?''

Once they were there, he seemed to lose his voice altogether.

"What did you want to discuss with me?''

He paced away from her, toward the window. He would have leaned on its frame as he did against that of every other, but the divan prevented that. He stuffed a hand into a pocket, instead. ''Nothing.''

"Then why—''

"I wish to apologize. I misjudged and offended you this morning.'' He faced her. ''I ask that you accept my most humble apology.''

"What made you change your mind?''

He paced obliquely away from the window. ''I—had a word with Bundy.''

"And you believe him over me?" she said, indignantly.

"I do not know you well enough, Johanna, to know what sort of person you are," he said as if that explained it.

"And you know Bundy better, so you think the worst of me?"

"Only a fool trusts blindly. My reputation and my honor, to say nothing of my self-respect, were at stake here!"

"And what of my reputation and honor and self-respect? Or do you believe such things are of no matter to a woman?"

"Certainly, I don't believe that."

"But you act as though a woman is a—a sort of commodity, the sole purpose of which is the physical gratification of men! And if she's not serving that purpose for one man, she must be doing so for another!"

"I do not view you—or any woman—as a commodity. However, as to a woman's 'purpose,' her duty is to her husband." His eyes and voice softened as he walked toward her. "And when that husband has gone to great lengths to ensure that his wife finds her duty to him not unpleasant, he is hard-pressed to understand why she refuses to fulfill it."

She couldn't look him in the face; she stared at the silver buttons on his blue coat, instead. "Because you—you make me feel like one of your brood mares. I'm nothing more to you than that, then you demand of me that I—"

"I'm not demanding, now, Jane," he whispered, his voice as soft as the expression in his eyes.

"N—Now? But, 'tis the middle of the afternoon!" she gasped, retreating from his advance.

"What difference does that make?"

" 'Tis broad daylight!"

"We'll draw the drapes."

"But how will that look? Everyone who sees 'em will know—"

"Then we'll leave the drapes and draw the bed-curtains," he reasoned, a note of impatience in his voice.

Jane continued to back away. "It—it doesn't seem right . . . somehow."

"Whatever a man and wife choose to do together, and whenever they choose to do it, is right," he said, following her and unbuttoning his coat as he went.

"What about the rest of my lessons?"

"I've excused you for the day." He took off the coat and tossed it blindly at a chair, then swiftly unbuttoned his waistcoat and flung that aside.

"But—but what about tea? You must be hungry after missing breakfast and dinner."

"I had a bite when I came in." His stock missed the chair by a foot and a half.

Backing through his bedroom doorway, Jane gulped reflexively when she realized where her retreat was taking her. "But—"

"Stop playing coy, Jane. You want this as much as I do. I saw that on your face while we were dancing," he said, undoing his cuff buttons. "Don't you think I've heard you at night, as wakeful as I've been, and for the same reason? You want me as much as I want you!"

His lips were hot against hers, his kiss hard and demanding. Jane shrank from it, squirming her arms between them, trying to push him away. But he pulled her all the tighter against him as he loosened the lacings down her back. Then, pushing the fabric aside, he turned his desperate fingers to the strings about her waist.

With her petticoat puddled about her ankles and her

drawers in jeopardy, she twisted her mouth from his. "Nay! Damon, don't!"

"You want it, too," he whispered, harshly, his breath coming hot and ragged against her face. "Why pretend you don't?"

"I don't!" she said, meaning it. Lovemaking was what she wanted—if she wanted anything at all—and this was a far cry from that!

But she may as well not have said it; his hand, hot as molten metal, freed her drawers and slipped inside, kneading her firm flesh as he brought her hips harder against his. Jane felt a dreadful stirring of panic when his other hand burrowed into her hair, forcing her mouth back to his, and his weight tumbled her backward onto the bed.

It seemed to swallow her up. The down-filled mattress with its deep velvet coverlet enveloped her like a dark cloud as he lowered himself on her. The pressure of his mouth against hers pushed her head deeper into the yielding bedding and her nose into the fleshy part of his cheek. She fought for air. With her hands pummeling ineffectually at his back and shoulders, she kicked at his heavily booted shins with dainty, slippered feet while he worked at her skirts; jerked and tugged them up, even as the hand that had been at her head pulled her bodice down.

Air! She must have air! Desperately, she heaved and twisted, squirmed and writhed. But the more she struggled, the tighter he held her; the harder his mouth pressed on hers; the more weight he brought to bear on her chest. Air! She had to breathe!

Damon wished she would stop fighting him. He had never used force on a woman, though he had heard tell that some of them liked it. But he had always preferred to approach lovemaking with tenderness. He had thought that was what Jane liked, too. But, as there seemed no doubt that she was as eager to be bedded as he was to bed her, he was willing, for a while, to humor her mock resistance as a female whim and give her the fight she seemed to want. And he had to admit, she put up a good one. But enough was enough.

Raising his face from hers, he was about to tell her so when he realized that something was wrong. Something was terribly wrong! Her eyes were wide with terror, her face a sickly shade of gray, and she was fighting for breath; gasping like a fish drowning in air.

Levering his weight off her with desperate haste, he asked, "Jane? What's wrong? Can't you breathe?"

Eyes bulging, mouth working, Jane struggled up onto her elbows.

"No. No, don't do that. Lie back. That's right. Breathe easy. You'll be fine in a minute. Just fine." And when she collapsed back against the bed, eyes closed, breathing deeply, he said, "I'll get you some water."

Walking back to the bed from his dressing corner with the glass of water in his hand, he was struck by how very small she looked there, in his bed. There had never been a woman in that bed since he had been sleeping in it—before that, there had been a veritable parade of them—and it was oddly comforting to see Jane there, even in her desperate state. He couldn't help but wonder again why she hadn't come to him in all the long, lonely nights over the past four months. She had been as starved for him as he had been for her! It could have been so good between them this afternoon, if she hadn't carried her foolishness so far. Why in hades had she done that?

"Here," he said, more sharply than he intended and urging the glass on her.

Weakly, Jane shoved herself up against the headboard and gingerly accepted the glass. The water was tepid and flat, but it felt wonderful sliding down her throat.

"Better?" She nodded. "What the hades was that all about?"

"I couldn't breathe."

"Obviously! I meant the rest of it. Why did you have to spoil it by fighting me like that?"

"Spoil it! I told you I didn't want to!"

"What you *say* you want and what you want are obviously two different things!"

"I said I didn't want to and I meant that! You forced me. You—you tried to—" But she couldn't bring herself to say the ugly word.

Damon stared at her, watching the tears roll one after another down her still girlishly rounded, thankfully once again flushed cheeks. How dare she blame him! How dare she even imply rape!

But even as he huffed self-righteously, nagging doubt crept in: Maybe he had been overeager; maybe he had misinterpreted her struggles; maybe—just maybe—he had been on the verge of . . . But, blast it! It wasn't *his* fault! She was the one who had gotten contrary all of a sudden! By damn, he ought to take her. He had the right. She was his wife! She was supposed to be the mother of his children. He would never have children at the rate things were going!

But, no matter how close he may have come to it in a moment of mindless passion, now that he was thinking again, rape didn't appeal to him in the least. As much as he wanted her, he wouldn't have her that way. Now now, not ever. He could wait. He would wait. By damn, he'd make her *want* him. She'd come begging by the time he was through with her! And then, maybe then he'd give her a dose of her own medicine. The thought made him smile.

"Are you certain you're all right now?" he asked.

"I'm fine." She hauled her bodice up, protectively.

"More water?"

"N—no, thank you."

He held out his hand for the empty glass and let his fingers rest warmly over hers for a moment before he pulled the heavy, cut crystal from her hand. "I promise you," he began with a soft smile, but an insistent knocking on the door cut short his resolution. "Go away, Simon! I told you we were not to be disturbed."

"Forgive me, sir," came the butler's door-muted reply, "but it is a matter of utmost urgency."

Damon considered for a moment, then put the glass on the candlestand beside the bed before heading for the door. Bracing the door open against his shoulder, effectively blocking the man's view of the room and the bed, Damon demanded, "What is it?"

Jane heard Simon's well modulated whisper and watched Damon's back stiffen. "I'll be right there." He started to close the door, then yanked it quickly open again to call down the hall, "Keep that jackass Cullingford out of the way!"

"What's wrong?" Jane asked, when he turned his worried frown on her.

Moving toward the bed, he said with quiet urgency, "I want you to do as I tell you. Don't ask questions and, just this once, don't argue! Where are the keys Oswald gave you?"

"In my jewel box."

"Get them. Well, go on! Hurry!"

A dozen questions flooded her mind, but Jane bit them back and made her way to her own room as quickly as her loosened dress and underpinnings would allow. She had only just reached her dressing corner when Damon called impatiently, "Have you got them?"

"Almost." Giving up her struggle with her sagging underdrawers, Jane kicked them off, dumped the glittering contents of her jewel box onto the dressing table and emerged from behind the screen with her bodice clutched in one hand and the keys in the other.

"Here. Give them to me."

She watched as he locked her door, then fairly dashed back toward his room.

"You'll have to lock my door behind me," he called as he went. And when she panted into the room behind him, he said, "It's this key. Give it a full turn and don't leave it in the lock." The other keys on the chain jangled raucously as he inserted the proper one into the lock. "Don't let anyone in until I get back. I don't know how long I'll be gone, but stay here until I get back. And don't open the doors! Do you understand?"

"Yes, but—"

Stepping into the hall, he closed the heavy door soundly behind him. "Lock it."

When she had, she heard him try the handle before his hurried footsteps faded down the hall.

Jane stared at the closed door for what seemed a long time, tormented by the questions and fear Damon had left with her. What could be wrong? Why had he locked her in? What—or whom—was he locking out?

But, as there were no answers and nothing for her to do but wait, she heaved a sigh and retraced her steps to her own room, picking up discarded bits of clothing along the way.

The warm, Indian summer day was fading into cool twilight when a knock and a quiet, "It's all right, Johanna. It is I," sounded at Jane's bedroom door.

It took her only a moment to toss the dress, whose tight bodice she had been altering, into concealment under the table, but considerably longer to find the right key among the jumble on the ring. But at last the one she put to it fitted the lock and she swung the door wide, brimming with questions. Damon's appearance made her draw hastily back.

"What happened? You look like you've been in a fight!"

He said nothing until he had fallen heavily into a

chair near the window. "Some trouble in the slave quarters."

"You had a fight with the slaves?"

"Hardly," Damon scoffed, fingering the ugly bruise on his left cheekbone.

"Then, who'd you fight?"

"Flygher."

Jane's eyes popped. "The overseer? Why?"

"Later, Johanna. Later." He let his head fall back against the chair and closed his eyes.

Jane had seen enough bruised and battered menfolk to know what was needed: Jacob had been quite a scrapper and, more times than she could count, John had taken on one of the Tompkin boys—sometimes all three at once. In no time at all, she was calmly and gently wiping the sweat-streaked dust from her husband's face. But gentle as she was, when she dabbed at the crusted blood at the corner of his mouth, he winced.

"I hope your Mr. Flygher is in worse shape."

"He is," Damon promised, still not opening his eyes.

Jane didn't doubt that. She had met Flygher on the tour Damon had given her of the slave quarters and had seen him several times since then on his way to or from a consultation with her husband in the study. He was a wiry man without Damon's height or brawn. But his movements had a quickness about them, and his small, dark eyes held a cunning glint. He had put her in mind of a ferret. And, for all their small size, ferrets could be nasty.

"You have a fine start on a shiner," she said, inspecting the swollen bruise under his eye. "Why'd you wait so long before coming home?"

"Later, Jane," he said wearily. But when she quickly left him, he raised his head and peered at her with his good eye. "Where are you going?"

"To get a poultice for your eye. 'Tis prob'ly too late for it to do much good, though."

"Simon is already seeing to that."

"Oh." Pulling up a chair beside his, she turned her attention to his bruised and battered knuckles.

He settled back again and closed his eyes. He liked the feel of his hands in hers as she bathed each raw knuckle in turn. It had been a long while since she had shown him tenderness. This was a moment worth savoring, worth capitalizing on, too.

"I could stand getting out of this blouse," he said, watching her reaction through slitted eyes, "but I doubt I can manage it with these hands."

"Sit up and I'll help you." When Damon had slowly straightened, she yanked his shirt free of his trousers—but missed his lopsided grin as she tugged it off over his head. "What you could stand is a wash," she concluded, tossing the dirty, sweat-stained French linen aside.

"Whatever you say, Jane. I'm at your mercy, it seems." He fell back against the chair.

Jane eyed him suspiciously. True, he looked the worse for wear, but she had seen Jacob worse off than this and *he* had never been so weak. Concern quickly replaced suspicion. "Do you hurt anywhere?"

"I hurt everywhere," he groaned.

"I mean, do you hurt inside?"

"Huh?"

"Once, back home, George Tompkin got in a fight and got hurt real bad inside. Broke his ribs and—Oh, I don't know what all else. He was abed for most of a month."

"Oh?"

Jane nodded emphatically, and laid a small, cool hand lightly on her husband's naked rib cage. "Do you hurt here?"

Damon squinted at her and wondered how far he should carry this sham. It wouldn't be too bad having her worry about him a bit, even pamper him. And there were all sorts of tantalizing possibilities in having her tend him in his bed for a month! But . . . the auction was next week, and he had house guests coming. Then, too, there were appearances to consider: It wouldn't look well, him being laid *that* low by Flygher!

"No," he regretfully admitted, "I'm all right inside."

Her smile of relief almost made his being whole worthwhile. Maybe she cared something about him, after all. Maybe bringing her around wouldn't be as difficult as he had supposed!

"I'll wager all you need is a good liniment rub. I'll call for Janet to bring some up."

Damon caught her wrist as she moved to leave. "No. Stay here. We'll send Simon for it after he's brought the poultice," he said, thinking what wonders could happen if she gave him a liniment rub! "How do you know so much about all this?"

"My brothers. Jacob and John, mostly."

"Tusslers are they?"

"It was John who laid George Tompkin low."

Damon laughed, gripped at his midsection, and sobered instantly. "A rub, you say, hm?"

"I hope that's all you need."

"I'm—I'm sure it is," he said, his hesitation calculated to convey uncertainty.

With worry creasing her brow, Jane folded a towel into a neat little compress and, soaking in the tepid water in the basin, laid it carefully over his swollen eye.

"That feels wonderful, Jane." He reached for her free hand and gave it a squeeze. "Thank you."

"You're welcome."

His thumb stroked the back of her hand. "I had forgotten, until we were dancing this afternoon, how small your hands are."

"It's not that mine are small, it's that yours are big."

"Is that what it is?" He gave her a weak smile. "You know, much as I hate the idea of being laid up, maybe a day or two wouldn't hurt."

"If—if there's a doctor in Rendell, maybe we ought to send for him. The Tompkins had a doctor for George, and he said it was a good thing they sent for him else George would've been up and about and, like as not, would have done himself *real* harm: poked one of those broken ribs through some *important* part of him!"

"I don't need a doctor. There's nothing broken, I'm sure."

"But—"

"All I need is a bit of rest and . . . a bit of company while I get it?"

"If you're certain that's all you need." she said, suspicion returning at his seductive tone, "I'll be happy to read to you. Mr. Cullingford says I read very expressively."

"You do. I've heard you." He sandwiched her hand warmly between both of his.

Withdrawing her hand, Jane busied herself with rinsing and refolding the compress. "I wonder what's keeping Simon with that poultice. Your eye is looking worse by the minute. What is he putting in it, do you know?"

Damon rolled his head against the chair. "Eulalia makes them up. I don't know what she puts in them, but they're pure magic."

"She's made poultices for you before?"

"Now and again."

"Really." Jane dropped the towel into the basin with a plop and a splash. "I would never have taken you for a brawler. Mr. Cullingford says *gentlemen* don't do that sort of thing."

Damon huffed derisively. "What does that popinjay know about being a gentleman?"

"I suppose you're right. He mustn't know as much as he claims," she said, sweetly. "You're a gentleman and you brawl."

"I do not brawl!" Damon yelped, sitting bolt upright.

Jane looked at him in mild surprise. "But you do heal quickly, don't you?"

Damon looked genuinely miserable now. "That was a low trick, Johanna."

"No lower than the one you were trying to play on me!"

"How else am I supposed to get a little tenderness out of you?"

"Like begets like, Mr. Seymour."

"Ha! That's a crock! And you, madam, are living proof!" Heaving himself out of the chair, he charged into the sitting room.

"And you, sir, are an unconscionable charlatan!" she shrieked at his vanished back.

"I heard that!"

"You were supposed to!"

He reappeared in the doorway, one raw-knuckled hand gripping the frame, and stood glaring at her for a long minute before he snapped, "Give me the keys!"

"The keys?"

"Those keys!" He jabbed a finger at the table. When Jane stubbornly stood her ground, he stalked back across the room. "You're like a petulant child," he sneered.

"There's the pot calling the kettle black," she muttered when he turned away.

Jane knew he heard her; his step faltered in midstride. But it wasn't until he was once again dwarfing the doorway, that he pivoted on a heel and said with a smug, if lopsided, smile. "By the way, you are once again without the services of a maid. Janet left with Flygher when I booted him off the place. Have a pleasant supper with your tutor, madam. I am going to bed!"

Cullingford's eyes were bright with excitement, more animated than Jane had ever seen them when she met him in the drawing room before going in to supper.

"Oh, good evening, madam!" he fairly chortled, turning away from his study of her portrait over the hearth. "My, you look lovely this evening."

"Thank you," she said, surprised. She had expected to be chastised for wearing the simple, front-lacing frock rather than proper evening attire and for appearing a full thirty-seven minutes late.

"Won't Mr. Seymour be joining us?" Cullingford asked, expectantly eyeing the hall.

"No. He is . . . indisposed."

"What a pity. I do hope it is nothing serious."

"No, no. He's a bit tired."

"I can certainly understand that. Certainly! Does that sort of commotion occur often here in the plantations?"

"I—I don't believe so." Jane smiled at him wanly. "I wasn't aware you had heard about the 'commotion.'"

"My word, madam! One can hardly be present on an estate of this size during such a calamitous event and remain oblivious to it, can one?"

"No. I suppose one cannot," she said, angrily thinking, *Unless, of course, one's brute of a husband has locked one in one's room!*

"I must say, madam, that I have nothing but the utmost respect for your husband."

"You have?"

"The utmost!"

"Oh. I'm sure he will be pleased to know that." Cullingford smiled. "But it was my impression that you were—I thought you said gentleman didn't do that sort of thing."

"Madam?"

"Brawl."

"Brawl?" Cullingford tittered in the affected way he had. "My dear madam, to refer to the events of this afternoon as a 'brawl' is tantamount to calling the Bible an evening's light reading."

Jane's brows shot up. "What would you call the events of this afternoon, then?"

"I would say, unequivocally, without reservation and with no fear of contradiction, that this afternoon was one of the most—*the* most—"

"Yes?" Jane prodded, hanging on his next words.

"Quite frankly, madam, words fail me! I have never witnessed such sheer courage as your husband exhibited in the face of—"

"You saw it?"

"Oh, yes. Oh, my, yes! From a safe distance, to be sure, but I saw it all," he said, proudly. "Your husband, madam, thrust his way through that vicious mob, that bloodthirsty throng of depraved savages, and with every likelihood that they would take their aggression out on him—redirect, so to speak, the thrust of their anger toward their master for his intervention on behalf of his hireling—he leapt, unarmed, upon the wagon where the overseer stood, bound hand and foot and with a noose about his neck, mere moments from death, and laying himself open to a deathblow—"

"Stop! D'ye mean they were goin' to hang Flygher?" she gasped, forgetting her "you" and her "ing."

"Most certainly they would have, had not your husband intervened when he did. Did not Mr. Seymour tell you?"

"He, ah, he said . . . He didn't go into detail."

"Yes," Cullingford said with a knowing nod, his eyes bright with admiration. "Yes, I can understand that. I have been aware for some while now, as you must be as well, that modesty and humility are two of your husband's greatest virtues. That is so often the case with men of intrepidity, is it not?''

"Y—yes," Jane stammered breathily, lowering herself weakly into a chair. "But, if he saved Flygher from hanging, how'd he come to fight him?''

"Ah, therein lies the tale," Cullingford said with a smug smile, flipping the tails of the better of his two evening jackets over his lap as he settled on the divan opposite her chair. "But, as Mr. Seymour's modesty forbids him to recount his valorious conduct, perhaps I should not be so presumptuous as to—''

"But you've got to tell me! How else will I ever know?''

"You do have a point there, madam. Reticent as your husband seems to be to 'toot his own horn,' as the saying goes, it is unlikely that you will hear of the heroic episode from him." He looked thoughtful for a moment or two. "And I believe you do have a right to know the full extent of your husband's valor.''

Jane smiled. "Thank you for understanding that.''

"Not at all, madam. Not at all. Now, then, where was I?''

"Mr. Seymour had leapt upon the wagon and—You said something about a 'deathblow.' ''

"Ah, yes! The Africans had armed themselves, you see, with all manner of farm implements: mattocks, hoes, pitchforks. The last being, I would suppose, their most effective weapon, it being light and easily wielded and having, by and large, the properties of the lance or spear. Most intimidating. Although, I understand, a sharpened hoe can be a quite formidable weapon.''

"Yes, yes, I'm sure. What happened next?''

"Having placed his own life in jeopardy—he had instructed that his supporters, your riding instructor among them, stay well back—your husband faced the irate mob, raised and spread his arms in a gesture of pacification." Cullingford leapt up and onto a footstool where he flung his arms wide in imitation of Damon's gesture, "and thus baring his brave breast to a death-blow, restored order out of bedlam! Then, pointing an accusing finger at what must have been the instigators of the revolt," he aimed a finger at Jane's nose, "he demanded that all weapons, such as they were, be laid aside. In the space of time it takes me to tell it, and with a clang and clatter that rent the prevailing stillness, their weapons were, indeed, cast down. And for no other reason than that your courageous husband commanded it so!" Cullingford puffed out his chest as proudly as if the triumphant moment had been his own. "Then, he turned to Flygher, who stood behind him, craning his neck to ease the pull of the noose still about it, and freed him of his bonds. At which a great hue and cry went up from the African mob, filling the air with such anger and portending such brutish violence that, again, I feared for your husband's life!

"But *he* showed no fear, madam. Solid as a rock he stood and, again, faced them down. And only when they had quietened did he speak." Staring, as if enraptured, at the chandelier overhead, Cullingford stood motionless on his stool.

"What did he say?"

"Alas, I was unable to hear his words. But his gestures, his gestures, madam, bespoke patience and, yes, even kindness. And when the bloodthirsty rabble had again been placated, he turned once more to the overseer. Again, from my vantage point, I was unable to hear what passed between them, but from the look of outrage on your husband's face, I judged he was not well pleased with Mr. Flygher. It was not until later that I learned of the grievous wrongs the man had perpetrated against your husband's Africans. Vile actions which had so incensed them, they rose up in revolt against the blackguard."

"He mistreated them, do you mean?"

He nodded curtly. "However, I beg you do not ask me to recount the nature of the atrocities he committed upon them. It is not a tale for a lady's ears." Then, as if only just realizing where he was, he smiled sheepishly and abandoned his stool.

"Is whatever he did so awful?"

"Heinous, madam. Heinous!" he said, smoothing the waistcoat and stock his theatrics had disarranged, then more or less straightening his listing peruke.

"But I still don't understand. Why did Da—Mr. Seymour fight Flygher?"

"That was not your husband's choice, madam. The overseer struck the first blow. As I understand it, Mr. Seymour, upon learning of the man's sadistic bent, ordered him to depart the premises immediately and with no more than the clothes on his back. Mr. Flygher apparently took umbrage at so abrupt a dismissal and thought to take Mr. Seymour to task for it."

Cullingford pursed his lips disapprovingly before going on. "I have always found fisticuff exhibitions boorishly vulgar. But I confess, I admire your husband's proficiency. I have never witnessed a more brutal contest. It is amazing to me that Flygher survived the match. As I said earlier, madam, your husband has earned my sincere respect and admiration. He is a man of honor, admirable courage, and humanitarianism.

"Which, of course, is not to say that he is likely to allow such anarchic behavior as the Africans exhibited to go unremarked. I feel certain he will take disciplinary action against them, if he has not done so already. Ah, yes," he sighed, "the entire episode will make a most lively chapter in my memoirs. I did tell you that I am writing my memoirs, did I not?"

"N—no. I don't think so," Jane said, absently.

"Oh? I was certain I had. I have been compiling notes—keeping extraordinarily detailed journals—since leaving England some six years ago. However, I have only recently begun the rather tedious business of actually writing. I have decided to call the book, 'A Sojourn in the Colonies: A Scholar's Memoir.' I have no doubt that it will be well received. I have had some rather remarkable and unique experiences which, I am certain, will enthrall, enchant, and enlighten those of my countrymen who, unlike myself, choose to find adventure vicariously through the derring-do of others." He smiled and offered his arm. "I shall tell you more about it over supper, shall I?"

For the sake of politeness, Jane tried to concentrate on her supper partner's self-righteous monologue, but her mind kept slipping back to his account of the afternoon's crisis. Discounting Cullingford's remarks about "disciplinary action"—for, surely, having taken the slaves part against Flygher, Damon would not punish them—she took as gospel the rest of his account, and could clearly imagine Damon shouldering himself through the outraged mob; Damon standing in the wagon, his feet firmly planted, his shoulders squared, his hair shining russet in the afternoon sun as with kindness and reason he wrought order out of chaos. And she was awed by his courage: He could have been killed! Is that why he had locked the doors? Had he thought he might be? Had he been afraid that, with the master gone, the slaves would turn on the mistress? Had he considered her safety above his own?

Jane shuddered and pushed that last thought away a dozen times between appetizer and dessert. And yet, there it was, back again, as Cullingford continued his arrogant prattling over a glass of sherry in the drawing room.

"Please do forgive me, Mr. Cullingford," she said, interrupting him because that was the only way to get a word in edgewise. "As exciting as your adventures are, and as eager as I am to hear more, I'm afraid I am frightfully tired. Will you excuse me, please?"

"Why, certainly, madam. I quite understand. It has been a long, eventful, day. I shall defer the remainder of my account until the morrow."

"I look forward to it," Jane said, hoping her grimace didn't show.

"As do I. May I bid you a pleasant night?"

"Thank you. Good night."

Through the half open door to his room, she could hear Damon snoring. She wanted to tell him how sorry she was for having goaded him to anger. She wanted to tell him how much she respected him for doing what he had done; to thank him for the precautions he had taken to protect her; to hear his heart pounding strong and fast beneath her ear; to tell him she was proud to be his wife; to show him that she meant it. But she merely stood there, listening to him sleep.

"Johanna. Johanna, wake up. I want to talk to you."

"Mmm? What?" Squinting against the morning light, Jane peered groggily up at Damon's silhouette. "Oh. Good morning. How's your eye?"

"Better." He sat on the bed near her feet, his face no longer in shadow.

"It looks better. Eulalia's poultice *must* have been magic."

He threw her an exasperated smirk. "As you pointed out, I'm a quick healer." Contritely, Jane lowered her eyes. "I'm sorry to have awakened you, but I wanted to make certain I caught you before you went out. I have business in the quarters this morning and would much prefer it if you kept to the house 'til I have done."

"You're going there again?" she cried, sitting bolt upright. "After yesterday? Do you think it's safe?"

He turned his face away in disgust. "Of course, it's safe! And what do you know of yesterday?"

"Mr. Cullingford told me what happened. He said you could have been killed! He said, the slaves were armed and—"

Damon snorted derisively and stood. Crossing to one of the windows, he huffed to the sun-drenched landscape beyond. "The man is as ignorant as he is arrogant!"

"But he saw it, Damon! He told me. They were armed with pitchforks, and they were going to hang Mr. Flygher!"

"No, they were not going to hang Flygher," he snapped.

"But Mr. Cullingford said—"

"And I said," he barked, rounding on his wide-eyed wife, "they were not! They were only trying to bring an ugly situation to my attention."

"Sure seems they could have found a simpler way of doing that!" she muttered, but said more loudly, "Why didn't they just tell you he was mistreating them?"

"They shouldn't have had to," Damon said, guiltily, turning back to the window. "And they couldn't; it doesn't work that way. A slave has no direct access to his master. It is the overseer who deals with him. The master tells the overseer what he wants done; the overseer tells the slave. And it works the same in reverse. If the slave has a problem of which the master is unaware—which should *never* be the case—it is the overseer who brings it to the master's attention."

"But, if the *overseer is* the problem, do you mean they can't do anything about it?"

"They did something about it yesterday," he said, drily. "And today, I must do something about that."

Jane swallowed thickly. "You're going to punish them?" Damon said nothing. "Mr. Cullingford said you would, but I couldn't believe it. Why? If they meant Flygher no harm . . . If they were only trying to make you see—"

Pivoting on a heel and striding toward the hall, he said, "Keep to the house this morning, Johanna!" He punctuated the order with a slam of the door.

Throwing herself from the bed, Jane stood staring impotently after him, wanting to do something about this awful situation. Hearing Simon puttering about in his master's room, she ran through the sitting room to demand, "What's he going to do, Simon?"

"Good morning, madam."

"Morning. What's he going to do?"

The valet went back to the chore her entrance had interrupted. Laying a freshly laundered shirt away in a drawer, he said quietly, "I wouldn't know, madam."

"Yes you do. You know everything. He's going to whip them, isn't he?" The man said nothing but reached for another shirt. "Oh, Simon, I can't let him do it! It isn't right. They were only standing up for themselves!"

"Forgive me, madam, but they did not 'stand up,' they rose up against their master."

"They didn't! It was Flygher! And they were justified!"

Turning compassionate eyes on his tender-hearted but naive young mistress, Simon said, "Justified or otherwise, madam, they revolted against those in authority over them. Harsh as it may seem to you, an example must be made, a precedent set."

"But it isn't fair. You don't think it's fair, do you?"

"As Mr. Seymour recently pointed out, madam, I am not paid to think." Closing the drawer, he turned and offered, "May I see to anything for you, madam?"

After a moment of consideration, she said firmly, "Yes. You may send Opal—or someone—up to help me dress. And then you may send word to the stable to saddle my mare. Thank you."

Seeing the fire of determination in her eyes and the rigid set of her jaw, Simon implored as she turned away, "Please, madam, I beg you, do not interfere. There is nothing you can do to alter the set of his mind. Mr. Seymour will do what must be done."

"I can try!" she cried, looking over her shoulder into the old, rheumy eyes within their frame of drooping lids and wrinkles. Her own eyes sparked with tears. "I must try! It isn't fair."

"Perhaps not, madam," he said with a compassion that matched her own. "But it is necessary."

Jane kept to her room all that morning, not wanting to see or hear what was happening in the little village behind the house, and equally as reluctant to subject herself to memoirist Cullingford. So she paced about her elegant prison cell, too agitated to sit still for long or to concentrate on her sewing or reading or even drawing with the sketch pad and pencils Charles Peale had sent her. But when she heard Damon come in just before noon, she marched straight into his room.

"Did you whip them?"

In the process of changing his sweat-stained blouse, Damon rounded on her quickly. "No. I had Grimes do it for me. He's the new overseer."

"Grimes! You replaced Flygher with that—that brute Grimes?"

"As I should have done long ago. I take it you don't approve."

"I disapprove of more than that!" she said, infuriated by his implacable calm. "But you don't give tuppence for what I think, do you?"

"On this subject, not a penny," he corrected, tossing the soiled shirt aside and disappearing behind his dressing screen.

He was surprised when she didn't come back at him with an insult. And even more surprised to find his room empty when he crossed it to get a fresh shirt.

"Aren't you feeling well?" he asked, entering her room. Jane said nothing, refusing to look up from the sketch pad on her lap. "You let me have the last word back there. That's not at all like you. Are you ill?"

Jane glared at him, bit back an angry retort, and lowered her eyes to her drawing again.

"What are you drawing?"

"That," she said, jerking her head at the scene beyond her window.

Crossing the room, he stopped beside her chair and canted his head for a look at the sketch. "It's very good."

"And *your* opinion, of course, counts for something."

"So does yours—on certain matters."

She stared daggers at him. "Not on important matters!"

"Not on *estate* matters. I don't tell you how to manage the household; you don't tell me how to manage the estate."

"I don't manage the household. Mistress Oswald does."

He cocked the brow over his healthy right eye. "Perhaps it's time you changed that."

"I—I wouldn't know how."

"Tell Oswald what you want done, how you want things managed, and she will tell the others. She is *your* overseer, Johanna." He turned to leave.

"What shall I tell her I want done?"

"You complained about the excess of our buffet one morning, as I recall. And you might do something about Opal . . . and her shoes."

"And how do I go about finding a new maid?"

He stopped and looked back at her. "I'll see to that for you. Next week. Until then, use Opal."

"I tried Opal this morning. The poor little thing can't thread laces or even tie a bow!"

After a moment, he said with a seductively soft smile. "I'm quite good with laces—and bows."

"Oh, but I couldn't ask you to—"

"You didn't. I offered." And he disappeared toward

his own room.

It was an offer Jane was reluctant to accept, given the look in his eye as he made it, so she appeared for dinner in the same dress she had worn to supper the night before, and parried the questioning glances Damon tossed her down the length of the table with sweet, only slightly smug, smiles.

Cullingford didn't notice. He was far more interested in seizing the rare opportunity his employer's presence at the noon meal provided to speak with the man about the meting out of justice which—from a discreet distance—Cullingford had witnessed that morning. He had been surprised, puzzled and secretly disappointed that the whipings were such mild ones and so quickly, almost bloodlessly, accomplished. He was eager to expound his own ideas as to what would have been a more fitting punishment for so serious a crime. But when he managed to insinuate the matter into the sparse conversation, Damon stopped him cold by turning the talk to his wife's lessons.

Cullingford was no more surprised than his pupil—though he was decidedly more chagrined—when Damon said he wanted some changes made: Vocal instruction was to be set aside and the time previously allotted to it applied to the clavichord lesson; the study of French would replace the vocabulary lesson; instruction in the management of household accounts and ledgers would replace dramatic reading.

Jane smiled gratefully down the table; she wouldn't miss the eliminated subjects a whit! But Cullingford sputtered indignantly, "You overstep yourself, sir! How dare you impugn my ability as an educator?"

"I impugn nothing, sir. I merely wish my wife thoroughly educated."

"Are you implying, sir, that my instruction has been less than thorough?"

"Certainly not, sir. You have been thorough to the

point of redundancy. Particularly with respect to my wife's vocal instruction. You will implement the new course of study beginning tomorrow, sir."

"I am the educator, sir. By what right do you presume to usurp *my* authority in that area?"

"By right of being the gentleman who employs you, sir."

Cullingford, his feathers badly ruffled, turned his attention back to his poached fish. But, as soon as the meal had ended, he took his anger out in the only way—and on the only person—available, and was even more demanding and critical than usual during the course of Jane's lengthened clavichord lesson.

He was fully prepared to be equally as obnoxious during the dancing lesson, but found himself little more than a convenient accessory once his pupil's new partner arrived. Even he could find no fault with her, then, and dared not invent any. Her clumsiness vanished like mist in sunlight as her husband led her through the several dances it had taken her months to learn, then easily taught her in the space of one afternoon the complicated figures of a lively reel.

From his seat before the keyboard, Cullingford watched the handsome couple; he saw the woman smiling up admiringly at the man. The tutor's jealousy might not have been so biting had Seymour's wife been the only woman to look at Damon Seymour like that. But there had been that statuesque Townsend woman whose acquaintance Cullingford had made aboard ship enroute here from his last post in Jamaica. She, of the voluptuous bosom and entrancing, blue-green eyes, had smiled at Seymour in just the same way when their paths had crossed on the Baltimore pier. May the Devil take men like Damon Seymour! They had it all!

# 8

As much as she had been looking forward to the Rendell Auction, and as carefully as she had dressed for this, her first local appearance as Damon's wife, now that she was here, Jane wished Ebenezer would turn the chaise right around and head for home! The moment they had turned off the road into Auction Meadow, she had felt eyes sizing up the new mistress of Raven's Oak.

"It seems awfully rude of us not to have invited Mr. Cullingford to join us," she said, purely for the sake of making conversation.

"I've had more than enough of that arrogant popinjay. I left a horse at his disposal. He can ride over if he's interested," Damon said, eyeing the hawksters' wagons and the local merchants' stalls. And when his eyes lit on the dressmaker's, he labeled himself a fool for thinking she might not be represented here. No *one* missed the Rendell Auction; the local event of the year.

He heaved a quiet sigh. He had been living in a fool's paradise since Lilith Townsend had left for Jamaica last year. He had hoped she would stay away. What had brought her back? Business? Now that, he chided himself, was wishful thinking! Her business had not suffered from her absence. Her sisters were doing very nicely, so he had heard. No, it wasn't business that had brought her back. She must have tired of playing nurse-maid to her widowed brother's children. Or maybe he had taken another wife, leaving Lilith free to come home. But, damnation, he had told her to forget him, to consider Damon Seymour dead! He had done a fine job of forgetting her! Maybe he shouldn't have. Maybe he should have prepared himself for the day when Lilith Townsend returned to reclaim her lover!

Damon's hand was less than steady as he helped Jane out of the chaise. Thinking his anxiety was because of her, she promised softly, ''I'll try not to embarrass you in front of your friends, Damon. I'll be the finest lady I know how to be.''

His expression was nothing if not pained. ''You'll not embarrass me, Johanna. It is I who hope not to embarrass you.'' Then, before she could put her surprise at the remark into words, he tucked her hand into the crook of his arm and led her toward a double string of horses.

Even before she saw the placard with the drawing of an oak tree crowned with flying ravens suspended high over the animals' heads Jane recognized the horses from the paddocks at home. Glancing at the men who were currying them, she spied Bundy among them. She hadn't seen him in more than a week and couldn't hide her blush when she did now. How, oh, how could Damon have thought such a terrible thing!

''Good morning, sir. Ma'am,'' Bundy said with a tip of his hat. But that was all he said to her before he turned his attention to her husband to discuss the horses.

Having ascertained that all was in order with his property, Damon abruptly turned Jane toward another string of horses. The placard over these read: ''Brook Hollow.''

''Morning, Seymour,'' a man called from somewhere in the animals' midst. ''Git over there!'' Jane heard a hand whack against horsehide as a black mare wheeled away to expose a short, heavy-set middle-aged man who, Jane suspected, would be more comfortable in work clothes than the gentleman's garb he wore. "Fine day we've got for it, eh?"

"Couldn't be finer," Damon agreed, meeting the man's reach. "That's a nice-looking string."

"None better here today. Yours included."

"I wouldn't say they're that fine," Damon countered with a smile, then he indicated Jane with a nod. "May I introduce my wife? Johanna, this is Mr. Slater. His farm, Brook Hollow, borders Raven's Oak on the north."

"A pleasure, ma'am," Slater said.

"I'm pleased to meet you, Mr. Slater," Jane said, smiling, but feeling her skin crawl under the man's appraising stare.

"And what do you think of our auction, Mistress Seymour?"

"I've not seen much yet, but I expect to enjoy it."

"I'm sure you will," he said, tearing his gaze away from her too-tight bodice and focusing on Damon again. "Hear you had a bit of trouble over your way last week."

"We had some excitement."

Slater guffawed. "So, that's what you're calling it. Always were one for a good tussle, weren't you?" Jane thought she saw Damon cringe. "I must say, you don't look the worse for wear. Talk has it, you near did Flygher in. Broke his jaw, so they say." Damon said nothing. "Got everything back under your thumb, have you?"

"Just where it ought to be."

"Good. That's real good. Wouldn't want any of *my* Africans getting any notions. Not that they would. I don't have freedmen putting ideas in their heads. I saw you've got your mill in operation. What're you asking to crack a bushel o' corn?"

"How many bushels do you want cracked?"

"That all depends on the price."

"The price depends on the quantity. Why don't you take it up with Bundy, over there. He's my new foreman."

Jane concealed her surprise as best she could, busying herself with snapping open her parasol while Slater asked, "What happened to Grimes?"

"He replaced Flygher as overseer."

Slater guffawed again and gave Damon's shoulder a solid whack. "By jiminy, boy, you do have it under your thumb, don't you!"

Damon smiled tightly. "If you'll excuse me, Mr. Slater, I'll be showing my wife around before the area gets too crowded."

"Surely, surely. Again, ma'am, a pleasure. Good luck to you today, Damon."

"Thank you. The same to you." Squiring Jane away, he asked, "What would you like to see first?"

"Why didn't you tell me you'd made Bundy foreman?"

"Why didn't you tell me you were planning to starve us to death?"

Jane looked up at him sharply and drew a breath, but thought better of saying anything. Since she had mentioned the extravagance of the breakfast buffets to Oswald, it *had* seemed as though the woman was intent on starving them. Even Cullingford, who ate like a bird, raised quizzical brows at the meager fare that now made up their meals. And Damon had taken to eating dinner regularly, not trusting the other two meals to satisfy his appetite. Unlike her husband, she didn't have her part of the estate under her thumb quite yet.

"Is Mr. Slater a married gentleman?" she asked, eager to change the subject.

"Mr. Slater is no kind of gentleman at all. But, no. He's a widower. Why?"

"I thought that if he had a wife, I might call on her. Just to be polite."

"It is not for you to make the first call. It is for them to call on you." He looked at a cluster of women who, seeing his glance, avoided his eyes.

Jane glanced at the women, too, and smiled. She was hurt and puzzled when they turned away. "Why haven't they?"

Damon hesitated before saying with a smile, "Perhaps they're intimidated by the thought of calling on a genuine lady."

Jane smiled back at him, but wanly. That wasn't the reason, and she knew it. It was something else, something more.

Not giving her time to dwell on the matter, he said, "Now, then. What would you like to see?"

"Whatever you like."

"Let's take a look at the vendors' stalls, then. Maybe you'll see something that strikes your fancy."

"Buy something, do you mean?"

"Yes, if you see something you like."

"But I don't need anything."

"Buy something frivolous, then. Who knows? We may find your heart's desire." He looked down at her. "And what would that be?"

"I don't know."

"Come, now. There must be something you've always wanted." He saw her eyes brighten an instant before she lowered them. "I thought so. What is it?"

"Nothing. There's nothing."

"Yes, there is. Out with it! What do you want?"

Jane stopped and looked up at him, her eyes and tone imploring. "Promise me you won't laugh if I tell you. Promise?"

"I promise."

"I always wanted a—a shiny red hair ribbon. A wide one. Like so." She indicated a width of about two inches with her fingers. "But it seems silly, now. You've given me so many beautiful things, that—"

"Do you mean to say, I neglected to supply you with a shiny red hair ribbon?" he said, feigning horror to camouflage his surprise at such a simple little wish.

"You're mocking me. I knew you would!" Spinning on a heel, Jane stormed away, grasping the handle of her beruffled parasol with both hands and shunning the arm he again offered.

Damon sighed miserably. This was all he needed: Johanna with her dander up! It wasn't bad enough that everyone knew about the business with Flygher. Now it was going to look as if his slaves weren't the only ones he couldn't control!

"Johanna!" he barked, albeit quietly, keenly aware of their public situation.

Not looking at him as he fell in step beside her, she snapped, "You promised you wouldn't laugh."

"I didn't laugh."

"You mocked me. It's the same thing. Worse!"

"I was not mocking you. I was only surprised that something so simple as a hair ribbon could mean so much to—"

"I'm sure you were! I don't suppose you've ever wanted anything you couldn't have."

"As my wife, neither shall you."

"I *don't* want for anything. You've given me everything."

"You want a red ribbon. And a red ribbon, you shall have." Securely gripping her elbow, he aimed her at a neatly lettered sign which proclaimed the wagon beneath it to be the property of Josiah Reed & Co., Purveyors: Dry Goods & Sundries.

"I don't want it anymore," she snapped, pulling against his hand.

"I want you to have it," he seethed.

"Why? So everyone will see how generous you are, buying frippery for your wife?"

"Damn, Johanna! Why must you be stubborn?"

"Me stubborn!"

He scowled but said nothing as they stopped to wait their turn at the smooth-surfaced plank set atop kegs which served as a counter. Most of those people about them contrived to avoid meeting their eye. But, to the one or two gentlemen who bade Damon a "good day," Jane smiled politely, lest she break her word and shame her villainous escort before those he called "friend."

But she was perversely pleased to hear the clerk say in response to Damon's request, "I am afraid I haven't any red, sir. But I have a lovely magenta—"

"Thank you, no," Damon said. Then, turning Jane brusquely away, "We'll try another."

"Damon, really. I don't want—"

"Damon! Damon! Johanna! Yoo-hoo!"

"Marianne!" Damon called, grinning as he turned Jane toward the frantically waving woman. "Why, hello! I was hoping you would be able to make the trip."

Marianne blushed and pulled her lacy shawl more closely about herself in an effort to hide her pregnant belly. "Shame on you, Damon," she chided. "Calling attention to such a thing and making a lady blush."

"I only said, I'm glad you could make it," he chuckled, planting a fond kiss on his cousin's cheek. "How are you?"

"Well. Wonderfully well! Hello, Johanna. It's so good to see you again. And how lovely you look!"

Jane returned Marianne's warm hug and the compliment, although she thought Marianne's eyes had lingered longer than necessary at her slender waist. Of course, that was probably to be expected. The whole family must be waiting for her to give Damon his heir.

"And how are you?" Marianne asked, straightening from their embrace. "He doesn't beat you, does he?"

"No. But he's grand at tongue-lashings," Jane said, surprised at her audacity.

Damon looked surprised, too, and said in all

seriousness. "For which, I will have you know, cousin, I receive punishment in kind."

Marianne laughed. "I must say, it sounds as though you have thoroughly settled into marriage." Then, looking up at Damon, she suggested, "Shouldn't you be looking at horses or something?"

"Ah . . . I intend to, a bit later."

"No time like the present," Marianne said, tucking her arm through Jane's. "You'll find Robert over there somewhere, searching for a new carriage horse. He could use your advice. You know what a terrible judge of horseflesh he is. Johanna and I want to browse a bit. Don't we, Johanna?"

"Yes," Jane said, firmly, suddenly realizing that was just what she wanted, if it meant being rid of Damon for a while.

"Very well, then, I shall meet you in . . . an hour? By the carriage?" Jane eyed the sun to gauge its height and nodded. "Fine. Oh. Here." Damon pressed the coin he withdrew from a pocket into Jane's palm. "On the chance you see something that strikes your fancy. Have a pleasant time." With a tip of his tricorn, he turned and merged with the milling crowd.

"A guinea!" Marianne chirped, eyeing the gold coin. "My! Damon's generosity is exceeded only by his good looks."

Jane stared at the coin, too. She had never held more than a shilling before. A guinea was worth twenty-one shillings! If ribbon was four pence the yard, and a shilling worth twelve pence, at three yards for a shilling, she could buy a length of ribbon for every woman in sight!

"Best tuck that away," Marianne urged, and when Jane had dropped the money into her reticule, asked, "Would you like to look for anything in particular?"

"No. You?"

"I thought I might look at some yardage for baby

things." Marianne beamed. "I haven't wanted to get my hopes up much before this—I've miscarried four times, you see—but as it seems I'll carry to term this time, I really should have something to dress him in."

"You think it's a boy?"

"I don't know. Robert would like a boy, of course, so I've gotten into the habit of speaking of the baby as 'him.' Just between us, though, I'd sooner it be a girl. Never having had brothers, I'm a little frightened of having a boy. I don't think I'll quite know what to do with one. Of course, that won't present a problem to you," she said, a question in her smiling eyes.

Jane pretended not to notice it. "When do you expect the baby?"

"Just about Christmas, as near as I can figure." She lowered her voice to an intimate whisper and leaned close. "Mother said, the rule *she* always used was to count three months back from her last menses, then add ten days for good measure. She was never more than a week off with any of us." Having no notion at all of how such a thing was figured, Jane squirreled the information away in case she should ever need it, and Marianna went on with a radiant smile. "Oh, Johanna, I'm so excited! Finally, a baby after so many disappointments!"

Jane returned Marianne's smile, hers more thoughtful than excited. She had not thought much about having a child. It was something women did; something that just happened. Surely, it was nothing to get excited about. Mam never had. She had always seemed resigned to it. Babies were a lot of work, and a great worry when they were sick. And it wasn't a good idea to get too attached to them for the first year or so. She had learned that the hard way only last winter when they had buried sweet little June beside Pap. No, having a baby was no cause for such excitement. But, they were endearing little things. And when they started smiling and cooing, they were awfully cute. But even so, she couldn't imagine ever being so giddy at the prospect of having one.

"Oh. Oh, Johanna, look!" Marianne sighed ecstatically, holding up a tiny, ruffle- and lace-trimmed christening gown and matching bonnet. "Isn't this the most precious . . . How much?"

The young woman smiled over her counter. "One and six."

Looking crestfallen, Marianne shook her head and regretfully laid the dress back on the pile of others. Jane was surprised. She had assumed the Drakes were well enough off. But, one and six *was* a lot of money!

"I'll give you a pound for it," Jane bartered.

The woman's eyes narrowed speculatively. "Look at the lovely embroidery, miss. I couldn't possibly let it go for less than . . . one and four?"

"Oh, Johanna, no. I can't let you—"

"One and tuppence, then," Jane said firmly, ignoring Marianne.

"This fabric is imported from London, miss. And the lace is French!"

"One and tuppence."

"I suppose I can see my way clear to let it go for one and three."

"Done." Jane smiled and presented her guinea.

"Oh, Johanna, I really can't accept it," Marianne protested.

"Of course you can. It's a gift for the baby."

"But what will Damon say?"

"He gave me the money to buy something, didn't he?"

"Something for yourself."

"He didn't say that. Besides, I have plenty left." Jane held out her hand for her nine pence change and watched as the woman wrapped the fragile little garment in soft paper, then tied it securely with string.

"What do you want to buy?" Marianne asked.

"Oh . . . some ribbon," Jane said, offhandedly. "If I can find the right shade."

Hearing the exchange, and not wanting to turn such an obviously well-heeled customer loose, the clerk said, "What shade have you in mind, miss? I have quite a selection. All imported!"

Jane looked at her steadily. Of course, the ribbon was imported. Where else could it have come from, if not Europe? "Red," she said, evenly. "About so wide."

"I've just the thing!" Turning to the wagon behind her, the vendor dragged out a box. "Here we are. Satin and cotton, both. Which would you like?"

Jane felt her heart flutter. Red ribbon. *Shiny* red ribbon! "The satin, please. One yard," she said, a bit breathily.

The clerk measured off the length from nose to thumb along her outstretched arm, discreetly subtracted an inch, then snipped the scarlet streamer with a scissors. "That will be six pence, please."

"Six! Ribbon sells for four at Reed and Company."

"Oh, does it?" the woman said innocently, not lowering her price.

"Come along, Marianne. I'll get my ribbon elsewhere."

"But I've already measured it out!" the clerk yelped.

"So you have. And a bit short, at that. I'll give you four for it." Jane plopped her coppers on the plank, snatched up her ribbon and Marianne's parcel and, annoyed at the woman's attempt to cheat her, tossed over her shoulder as she left the stall, "And it is mistress, not miss. *Mistress Seymour.* Good day."

Sarah Townsend's eyes widened and her mouth formed itself into an "O." Wait 'til she told her sister about this. Just wait 'til she told Lilith!

Damon was a careful shopper, too. It wasn't that he minded spending money, that was money's function, but he wanted to get its worth.

"What do you think of her, Robert?" he asked the man standing at his elbow.

"I'm not much of a judge but, if she's as advertised, I think she's a good buy. You want her for Johanna?"

Damon nodded, mentally taking stock: clear eyes, strong of tooth and limb, no deformities that he could detect. "Good temperament, has she?" he asked the seller.

"The best, sir. Very obedient. She gave my late wife no trouble at all. In fact, my wife was quite fond of her."

Damon considered a moment. "One hundred, you said?"

The man laughed shortly. "I said, one hundred *fifty*."

"I'll split the difference: One twenty-five."

"She's worth more than that, Mr. Seymour, as a gentleman with your fine eye can surely see. One forty-five."

"One thirty is my final offer. It's the best you'll hear today, I'll wager."

The man nodded and smiled. "She is yours, sir, for one hundred thirty pounds."

"Will you accept my voucher?"

"Certainly, sir."

With the transaction completed, Damon took the end of the leather thong which bound the slave's wrists in front of her.

"Her name is Venus, by the way."

"Thank you, Mr. Courtland. Good day to you."

"And to you, sir."

With his purchase, her eyes on the ground, stepping smartly along behind him, Damon returned to the carriage. "Ebenezer, this is Venus, Mistress Seymour's new maid. See that she is taken back to the house and given over to Mistress Oswald."

"Yes, suh," the negro driver said, eyeing the young woman every bit as critically as her new owner had.

Watching the pair move off, Damon tossed several parcels onto the carriage seat, then wondered aloud, "I wonder what's keeping our wives. They ought to have been back here by now."

Robert chuckled. "Mari's been hoarding her pin money for months. It'll take her more than an hour to spend it."

"Well, then," Damon said, shoving the packages out of the way, "we may as well get comfortable." Climbing into the chaise, he whacked the seat beside him invitingly.

The two men sat, elbow to elbow, in silence for some minutes, each content to leave the other with his thoughts and to keep his own to himself until Robert said, "I heard a bit of talk before I ran into you this morning. They say that's what you get for working freemen in with your slaves."

"Do you really think I care what they're saying?" Damon challenged, coolly.

"They may have a point, you know. A freeman just might put ideas into a head that oughtn't to have room for them."

"Freedom does not make a man a thinker, Robert. God granted *every* man a brain," Damon said, eyeing his cousin-in-law. "How was your harvest."

"Better than last year."

"Did your wheat do well?"

"Very. How about yours?"

Damon smiled. "I'm turning another ten acres over to it next spring."

Robert grinned. "I was thinking of putting in another four, myself." He took off his hat and perched it on his comfortably crossed knee. "I hear Lilith Townsend is back."

Damon looked at him sharply. "Isn't there anything you don't hear?"

"Now, that I wouldn't know, would I?" Robert said,

still grinning. "What are you going to do about her?"

"Nothing."

"Nothing? Don't you think you ought to see her? Talk to her?"

"I did talk to her. Last July, before she left. I said all that needed saying."

"Apparently, she wasn't listening: She's back."

"And that has nothing, nothing whatsoever, to do with me," Damon said hotly.

"What about Johanna?"

"What about her?"

"It could get stickier than a honeypot for you if Lilith figures things out and *that* gets back to Johanna!"

"Lilith Townsend has no reason to suspect I am anyone other than who I am supposed to be. Neither has anyone else. Nothing is going to get back to Johanna."

"But what if it does?"

"It won't," he said, adding significantly, "unless someone I trusted with the truth proves unworthy of my faith in him. Or her."

"By the gods, man! She has a right to know!"

"Do you intend telling her?"

Robert met and held Damon's eyes. "I gave you my word. You ought to know better than to ask that."

"What about Marianne, then?"

Robert sighed and looked away. "She hates it. She likes Johanna and . . . she cannot understand why you put yourself—all of us, Johanna included—in for this!"

"She knows damned good and well why I did it! So do you!"

"Yes," Robert said, raising angry eyes. "Yes! But that was six months ago! She . . . *we* never thought you intended to carry it this far! We thought, by now, you would have told her."

It was Damon's turn to look away. "Things—haven't gone as I expected."

"And how long do you expect us to keep up this charade? It isn't easy, you know. Mari and I weren't raised as liars!"

"Do you think I was?" Damon seethed. "Do you think it's easy for me?"

Robert saw the pain in the other man's eyes and implored, "Then tell her!"

"I can't. Not now. Not yet."

"When?"

"When the time is right," he said, sadness rampant in his eyes. "When she's given me a son."

"Oh, Marianne, it's so late! Have you everything you want? We should be meeting Damon."

"Damon won't mind waiting," Marianne said, accepting yet another parcel from yet another clerk. "He's the very soul of patience."

"Not with me, he isn't," Jane said ruefully.

Marianne looked surprised but, in the face of Jane's conviction, decided not to argue and fell into step as the anxious young wife set a brisk pace toward the rendezvous. But her pregnancy made keeping up difficult, and they had not gone far when she puffed, "You go on ahead. I'll catch up. Where is your carriage?"

"Just over there; near the horses. Are you certain you don't mind?"

"Positive."

"All right. Let me take your bundles for you."

"Thank you. I feel enough like a beast of burden without them." Marianne smiled a smile that said, "Isn't that wonderful?" Then she added, "If Robert is there, tell him I'll be right along, will you?"

With her arms filled with parcels, Jane hurried off. She found Damon and Robert standing in the shade of a frost-gilded oak tree near the carriage. They were engaged in conversation with a man Jane did not know.

Tall, slim, and raw-boned, the sandy-haired fellow was dressed like a gentleman in a well-tailored blue coat and buff breeches and had an earnest demeanor that she could read even from a distance. Not wanting to intrude on the man's conversation, she slowed her step to a snail's pace and was glad when Damon caught sight of her and excused himself to meet her.

"I—I didn't want to intrude," she said with an apologetic smile. "I'm sorry I'm late."

"It's of no matter. I see you found a few things." He relieved her of the packages.

"These are Marianne's."

"What? Nothing for yourself?"

"I . . . I found the ribbon."

He smiled. "The right color?"

"Yes. It's just what I wanted. Thank you."

Wearing a satisfied sort of smile, he stood looking down at her for a few moments before he remembered the others. "There is someone I want you to meet." And he steered her toward the tree. "These are yours, Robert," he said, handing over the paper-wrapped heap.

"For me? Why, Johanna, how thoughtful. Alas, I fear I did not buy you anything," he quipped. Then, grinning, he gave her cheek a cousinly peck.

Jane laughed. She had forgotten what a tease Robert was and how much she enjoyed him.

"Come to think of it," he said, straightening, "I haven't bought Marianne anything, either. I suppose I had best do that if I am to have any domestic tranquility at all. Where is she?"

"Just coming."

"Ah, so she is. If you will excuse me, Johanna; gentlemen? A pleasure to have made your acquaintance, Mr. Jefferson. I hope we will have time to talk again."

"Likewise, Mr. Drake," the man said, accepting

Robert's hand and giving it a hearty shake before Robert dashed off to intercept his wife.

Still smiling, Jane met the stranger's hazel, gray-flecked eyes as Damon made the introductions. Though Jefferson's smile softened his angular features, Jane thought he still fell well short of being handsome. And while he was impeccably polite and well-mannered, he was not friendly. She sensed a restraint, a reserve in him which led her to label him a cold fish.

"Thomas will be staying with us for a few days. A week, if I can twist his arm."

"Thank you for the invitation, but I can manage only three days, Damon. Any longer is impossible."

"What business will take you from us after so brief a stay, Mr. Jefferson?" Jane asked.

"The law, madam. I am a member of that profession whose trade it is to question everything, yield nothing, and talk by the hour."

Jane was taken aback by the remark; shocked by his criticism of so esteemed a profession. Particularly, since he was a lawyer, himself.

Seeing Jane's surprise, Damon said, "What Thomas has neglected to say is that he was elected to the Virginia House of Burgesses last year. And it is my opinion," he eyed his friend significantly, "that his future lies there: in politics. But, meanwhile, he delights in biting the hand that feeds him."

Jefferson smiled. "That same hand feeds *you*, indirectly. I have my eye on that chestnut over there. Is he as sound as he looks?"

"He's the best of the lot."

"What price do you expect him to fetch?"

"Oh, forty or a bit more. Depending on how high you are prepared to push the bidding."

"I'll push it no higher than that, I warrant you!"

Damon chuckled. "Well, if he's too rich for your blood, that black there ought to suit you. But he hasn't the spirit of the chestnut.''

Jefferson shot Damon a glance. ''You are forgetting that yours are not the only horses at auction here today.''

''No. I didn't forget. But I was hoping you might. Does friendship count for nothing?''

''In the matter of horses,'' Jefferson said, earnestly, ''the animal's pedigree counts for more.''

Smiling, Damon took the man's forthrightness in stride. ''And you'll find no pedigree finer than theirs. Both were sired by Gilyad's Sun. The chestnut is out of Titania and the black out of Raven's Night.''

Jefferson nodded appreciatively, but said, ''I have heard much good said of Brook Hollow Farm. I understand your neighbor has outstanding mares.''

''He has. But he hasn't a stallion the likes of Gilyad.''

Jane let the horse-talk eddy around her as her eyes wandered over the crowd. There were more simple folk here now, easily recognizable by their weathered complexions as farmers. Their families had had the morning's chores to finish before joining the gentry for a day's sport.

The entertainers had arrived, too. Over near the pastry vendor, the scalloped yellow awning and fluttering vermillion and blue banners of a puppet theater beckoned all to come and enjoy the show. The instinct was strong to reach down, grasp a small hand in each of hers, and rush off with the youngsters she always had in tow at the fairs and auctions back home. The urge would not leave her until she forcefully reminded herself where and who she was.

But it quickly returned when she saw the tumblers. And again when she spied the wagon with iron bars at the back and bold red and yellow lettering on the side: ''Goliath the Dancing Bear.'' Oh, how little Jillian had loved and feared the dancing bear at the fair in Four Corners last year!

How she missed them all! Jackie, with his dark curls and soulful eyes; Jillian, with her sweet smile and dimples; Jonah and his chubby-armed hugs; Jeremiah, the baby. Goodness! He must be crawling, nearly walking, by now! And how were the others? Had the crops been good this year? Were Julia and Jenny being enough help to Mam? And Mam, how was she?

Oh, how she longed to hear from them! Why hadn't they answered her letters? She knew, of course, that none of them could write. Jacob and John could barely manage their signatures; Mam, Justin, and the older girls, not even that. Pap had been the learned one. It was Pap who had taught her by flickering candle light, at the end of his own long workday, to read and write. She could still remember the feel of her hand in his as he taught her how to hold the quill and guide it over the page; the scratchy day's growth of whiskers on the cheek pressed to hers; the snug, secure feeling of his arms about her as she snuggled into the nest of his lap. And she could remember the smell of him, too: the smell of sweat and leather, loam and lye soap. In that moment she missed him with a poignancy that brought her to the verge of tears even while she chastised him for dying; for not teaching Jacob his letters; for leaving no one behind to comfort her with news of home.

Despite the questions that had been recently raised concerning her childhood years, Moss Creek Farm was her home. And the McPhees, whether she was truly one of them or not, were her family.

So, why hadn't she heard from them? Surely, Parson Dye had delivered and read to them the letters she had written. Why hadn't he answered? Why hadn't she heard?

Still fretting over those questions, she heard Damon ask Mr. Jefferson a quite different one. And when he accepted Damon's invitation to share their picnic hamper, she found herself worrying about a more immediate problem.

Oh, please, she prayed with silent fervor, let there be enough! And when she saw that there was, and an extra place setting, too, she breathed a grateful sigh. But it didn't take her long to figure out what Damon already had: No matter how niggardly Oswald had been with their meals of late, she would have packed the hamper for three, expecting that Cullingford would join them.

With that worry gone, Jane thoroughly enjoyed playing hostess at the simple meal. She even began to enjoy Mr. Jefferson. He was really quite charming, and very intelligent. He knew everything about anything: literature, music, dancing, even French! And he said that he considered thoroughbred horses a "necessary luxury," an incongruity that made Jane laugh, but which obviously pleased Damon no end.

But Damon was less pleased when, with their picnic finished, Mr. Jefferson excused himself and made his way toward the horses from Brook Hollow Farm. "There goes a man who knows his own mind," he muttered miserably.

"Don't worry. He'll buy your chestnut stallion."

"Oh, will he? And how can you know that?"

"I saw the way he looked at him. Just like me and red satin ribbon."

Damon grinned. "And where is your ribbon?" Jane patted her reticule. "What else would you like?" he asked, suddenly anxious to spoil her, to indulge her every whim.

"I'd like to see the mime. May we?"

But after they had watched the show and Damon had contributed as the hat was passed, he asked, again, "Didn't you see anything else you wanted besides the ribbon?"

"I bought a christening gown for Marianne's baby. She wanted to buy it but . . . I thought it would make a nice gift."

Damn smiled knowingly. "As expensive as that, was it? I'm sure she appreciated it. But, didn't you find anything else *you* wanted?"

Jane shook her head quickly and looked at the juggler, who had taken the mime's place in the center of the circle of spectators. He was just launching the fifth of the seven balls he had proposed to keep aloft.

"Are you certain?" Damon prodded, reading her face. Jane nodded again. "Then, why do you look like that?"

"Like what?" she said, staring straight ahead.

"Like *that*."

"I don't know what you mean. Oh, look! He's juggling all seven! I've never seen the like!"

"Amazing," Damon said with never a look at the marvelous man. "If you saw something else you wanted, why didn't you buy it?"

"I—I didn't have enough money."

"Oh, for mercy's sake," Damon muttered. "Come along, then. We'll go buy whatever it is."

"Oh, no! You can't come with me. I have to buy it by myself."

"Why?"

"Because . . . I have to."

After a glance at the mobbed hawker's stalls, Damon wagged his head. "I will not have you wandering about in that crowd by yourself. I'll go with you."

"But you can't!" she implored. "I'll only be a few minutes. I promise."

He shook his head with a resolve Jane recognized as unbendable and sidled closer to her, rudely jostled by two new members of the juggler's audience.

"Oh, all right. But you mustn't peek."

"For pity's sake, why not? It's to be mine, isn't it?"

Jane smirked, annoyed that he had guessed she was buying something for him. "Eventually, yes. But not until I'm ready to give it to you."

"Fair enough. Lead the way."

"May I have the money first, please?"

"Don't you trust me?" Damon chuckled.

"You promised not to peek. If you're standing right next to me while I—"

"All right, all right. Will a guinea do?"

"A guinea! I only want a crown."

"Is that all?" Jane nodded. "You're certain?"

"Positive."

Fishing the silver coin from a pocket, Damon dropped it into Jane's open palm then, with a hand resting familiarly at her waist, steered her away.

The two men whose belated arrival had crowded Damon looked after the couple. "Did you hear that?" one incredulously asked the other.

"I sure did."

"Weren't that Mr. Seymour?"

"I believe it was."

"He just go hisself married, didn't he?"

"So I heard."

"Yuh. So, what's he doin' buyin' a doxy?"

"Dunno. But she's a fine-lookin' one, I'll say that."

"Yuh. For only a crown, too! I once paid twice that for ol' Moll down ta Sawyer's Gap."

"You don't say it! That old hag?"

"Well, when a man's got a need, he's got a need."

"I ain't never had the need that bad."

"You don't suppose," the one said to the other after a thoughtful moment, "that after Seymour's had his roll with her, you and me might—"

"Now there's a thought."

The men grinned at each other, then the first one sucked his teeth and said, "Sure will be a fine change from ol' Moll!"

Damon waited impatiently a discreet distance from the stationer's stall while Jane transacted her secretive business. But the smile he wore to greet her return faded when he saw her empty hands. "What happened?"

"Nothing."

"Then where's my—your parcel?"

"I'll pick it up a bit later."

Damon's smile renewed itself and, consulting his pocket watch, he said, "We've about half an hour before the auction begins. What would you like to see?"

"The puppet show?"

He offered his arm. He was enjoying squiring her around. He knew people took notice of her; had heard more than one appreciative murmuring between gentlemen as they passed. He liked knowing there were those who envied him such a pretty bride—even if those same men would envy him far less if they knew what went on, or what didn't, behind the walls of Raven's Oak. But all that was going to change. Soon. He would see to that, if it took every ha'penny he had! He'd dicker with the angels over the price of the moon if she asked for it. Or sell his soul to the devil if that would make him welcome in her bed again.

"Why, Damon. How nice to see you again," the woman purred.

Damon's head swiveled sharply to the right. "Miss Townsend," he said grimly. "What a surprise."

"Not such an unpleasant one as that, surely," the woman countered with a flirtatious smile.

Jane looked around her husband at the tall, slender, strikingly handsome brunette who had drawn his attention from her.

"Allow me to introduce my wife," Damon said coolly, but with a strong emphasis on "wife." "Johanna, Miss Townsend."

"Oh, really, Damon, such formality between old friends," Miss Townsend chided with a moue. Leaning across Damon so closely that her breast brushed his arm, she said to Jane, "It's Lilith, please."

"How do you do?" Jane said, taken aback as much by the woman's forwardness as her apparent intimacy with Damon.

"I am very well, thank you. And yourself? Are you enjoying being Mistress Seymour?"

"Y—yes. Thank you."

"I was certain you must be," Lilith purred, adding with a significant glance at Damon, "How could you not?"

Damon stiffened. "If you will excuse us, Miss Townsend, my wife and I were about to—"

"Oh, Damon. You aren't going to dash off just as Johanna and I are getting acquainted, are you?" Her eyes skimming Jane's figure, she said sweetly, "My, what a fetching little frock. Who is your dressmaker?"

"Oh, ah . . . Mistress Graystone, in Philadelphia."

"Really. I had heard she was quite good." Lilith appraised Jane's snug bodice. "But then, we do all make mistakes, don't we?" Blushing, Jane lowered her eyes. "No offense intended, of course, my dear. Only another dressmaker would be likely to notice."

"You're a dressmaker?"

"Why, yes."

"Oh!" Excitedly, Jane looked up at Damon. But the eyes he held leveled on Miss Townsend were cold as ice, and his expression stony. She didn't dare ask the obvious question.

Miss Townsend had no qualm about it. "Shall I call at Raven's Oak and make a few alterations for you?"

"That won't be necessary," Damon said even as Jane smilingly drew breath to accept the offer. "My wife's new maid is an excellent seamstress."

"My new maid?"

Damon smiled down at her. "Yes. You asked about having a new maid last week, remember? I thought to surprise you, darling."

Jane was surprised, all right! "Darling," had he said?

"Oh, dear, and I made you spoil your surprise,"
Lilith pouted. But she brightened quickly enough and
added with a sultry smile at Damon, "Why don't you
stop by sometime, whenever it's convenient, and let me
make it up to you?" Then she turned a facade of a smile
on Jane. "So nice to have met you. Don't hesitate to
send for me should your maid's talents fail you." And
she swept gracefully away, her head held regally high.

Jane stared after her, her mind a muddle. Only one
thought, one jarring jolt of feminine instinct loomed
clear: When a woman looked at a man the way Lilith
Townsend had looked at Damon . . .

"Johanna?" Jane looked up quickly. He, as quickly,
looked away. "The show is beginning."

Jane didn't enjoy the puppet show. She didn't even
see it. All she could see was Lilith Townsend in Damon's
arms.

The pale green foolscap was boxed and ready when
Jane presented her claim check to the stationer. But he
bade her wait just one moment while he dashed to the
wagon behind him to retrieve the seal it had taken an
engraver the better part of an hour to decorate with a
raven on the wing. After presenting it for her inspection,
he dropped a blob of sealing wax onto a sheet of paper
thickly dotted with others and pressed the seal into it.

Forcing a smile and an exclamation of delight, Jane
tucked the slender package under her arm and turned
away. But she didn't head back toward the auction
ground where she had left Damon. She needed time to
think. Time alone to sort out the jumble of emotions in
her head . . . and her heart.

Assuring herself that Damon was too preoccupied to
notice how long she was gone—or that she was gone, at
all—and certain she would be back before he missed
her, Jane set off across a grassy, goldenrod-flagged
field, toward the tree-lined brook beyond.

She had reached the trees but had made little headway in fathoming out how to deal with Lilith Townsend, when a man's voice hailed from close behind her. "Afternoon, missy." Startled, Jane turned and found not one but two men, both grinning broadly.

"Good afternoon," she said, wondering who they were and what they wanted with her.

"By golly, but you're a pretty little thing," one of them said, exchanging an excited glance with his cohort who bobbed his head in hearty agreement. "We was wonderin' if, ah, if you're free now."

"I'm sorry. I don't know what you mean."

The other man, the younger of the two, spoke up this time. "Are you meetin' anybody out here?"

"N—no."

"Then, you're free," he concluded with a happy grin.

"Which one of us do you fancy first?" the other asked, giving his wrinkled jerkin a downward tug. Jane shook her head in confusion. "Well, then, seein's you ain't got no favorite, and seein's as it was me spotted you walkin' this way, I reckon I'll take first roll. All right with you, Ben?"

"Seems fair," Ben said, sounding disappointed.

"Right enough, then. We can jus' duck ourselves back in there, behind them bushes." He reached for her arm with a dirty hand.

Jane took a quick step back. The men's talk might be baffling, but their intent was suddenly crystal clear!

"Aw, come on, now," the man said, matching Jane's retreat step for step, "You ain't gonna play coy, are you?"

"Hey, Jack?" the younger man said, seeing the fear in Jane's eyes, "I think you're scaring her. She's mighty young. Can't of been at this long. You're scaring her, Jack."

"Naw, she ain't skeered. She likes to play a bit o' come and git it, is all. Ain't that so, missy?" he said, plunging a hand into a pocket and coming up with a silver coin pinched between the grimy nails of his thumb and forefinger. "You jus come and git this, then, and I'll git a bit o' you in exchange. Fair enough?"

Still backing away, Jane shook her head frantically. "No. No, please. You—you've made a mistake!" she said, looking beyond the men to the auction grounds across the sunny field. The auctioneer's babble carried faintly to her on the breeze. There was no help coming from that quarter.

"I think she's right, Jack," Ben said, his tone worried. "I think we mighta made a mistake."

"Ain't no mistakin' what we heard back there!" Jack snarled, impatience making him angry.

"I dunno. She's dressed mighty fine for a doxy."

"She's high class. Figures she's too high class for the likes o' us. Well, this here crown's as good as Seymour's!"

He lunged for her and Jane screamed, dropping the package as she turned and ran. But Jack was faster than he looked. Catching hold of a fistful of skirt, he hauled Jane back.

"Jack, don't! She ain't what we thought! Can't you see that?"

Jack ignored his friend and, countering Jane's dodgings, grabbed her hard by the shoulders.

Kicking, twisting, and squirming so violently that her bonnet went askew, Jane screamed again. This time her cry was loud enough to make Ben look apprehensively over his shoulder, then implore, "Let her go, Jack. Jus' let her go!"

Tearing at the filmy triangle of gauze tied about Jane's shoulders, Jack ripped it off and crammed the coin into the cleavage of her breasts. "There, now, missy. All bought and paid fer!" he sneered, forcing her back toward the bushes he had eyed before. "Primed as you got this ol' pump, this ain't gonna take more'n a minute o' your time!''

Damon looked around. Where the devil had she gone? She was right here a minute ago! ''Bundy,'' he called in a harsh whisper to the man who stood a few paces away. When Bundy stepped closer, he asked, ''Have you seen my wife?''

''I saw her heading over toward the peddlers a bit ago, sir.''

Damon cursed under his breath and extracted a packet from inside his coat. ''Here. Fill in the seller's name and the amount of the sale. I'll sign them when I get back. You know what to bid on?''

''Yes, sir,'' Bundy said, accepting the bank vouchers.

''I won't be outbid on that bay, Brook Hollow mare.''

''No, sir.''

When Damon reached the stationer's, Jane was nowhere in sight. ''Pardon me,'' he said to the clerk who was packing up for the day.

''Yes, sir. May I be of assistance?''

''I'm looking for a young woman. She was to call for an order here.''

''Could you describe her, sir? We have done a good deal of business today and—''

''Fair hair, about so high, wearing a yellow dress and a straw bonnet.''

''Oh, that young lady! Yes, she was here. Quite recently, in fact.''

''Did you happen to see which direction she took as she left?''

''As a matter of fact, I did. One doesn't often see such a pretty—''

''Yes, yes, I know. Which way did she go?''

Annoyed by Damon's curtness, the man said tartly, ''Toward the meadow. I lost sight of her behind that wagon.''

''How long ago?''

"As I said, quite recently. Within the past quarter hour, I should think."

"Thank you."

Striding away in the direction of the man had indicated, Damon eyed the expansive field and the woodland beyond. He was probably worrying for nothing. She was undoubtedly over there relieving herself. As modest as she was, she would shun the public privy and find the most out-of-the-way spot she could! he thought as he leaned against a wagon to wait for her.

But he couldn't shake the niggling worry; the feeling that told him he had better look for her. Knowing that his instincts were more often right than wrong, he set briskly off toward the trees. He had barely reached them when a viciously snarled, "Bite me, will ya?" preceded the sound of a slap and a woman's sharp cry.

"For God's sake, Jack, let her go! Think what you're doin'!"

"Git off me, whelp!"

Damon spun toward the voices and, some way off, through the sparse, October foliage, he caught a flash of yellow.

"Ow! Why, you little she-cat! I'll take that outta yer hide if it takes me—"

The rest of Jack's threat was cut off by the pressure of his collar about his throat as Damon, suffused with an anger as great as any he had ever known, dragged the filthy, rutting animal off his wife. Jack's eyes bulged, and his mouth worked convulsively as Damon's fist plowed into the flab of his belly. But the cry that made its way up his throat stuck there, strangled by the nooselike tightness of the fabric about his neck. Damon drove his fist home again, then a third time, letting the force of the last blow send Jack reeling into the bushes where he lay sprawled on his back, gasping for air. Grabbing a handful of jerkin, Damon hauled the man up to meet the fist he aimed at his face. He had drawn his arm back for a second blow when it was caught from behind.

"Don't! You'll kill him!" Ben screamed, wisely letting go and stepping well back when Damon turned on him. "Let's—let's talk reasonable, Mr. Seymour," he said, holding his open hands at shoulder height and sounding scared. "Nothing happened. I swear to you. Nothing! It was all a mistake."

"You're damned right it was a mistake!" Damon growled, dropping the senseless body he still held aloft by its clothing and advancing on the man. "She's my wife!"

Terrified, Ben backed away, pleading as he went. "You've no quarrel with me, Mr. Seymour. I never so much as touched her. Never laid a finger on her. I swear it! Ask her if you don't be believe me. Ask her!"

"It—it w—wasn't him. He tried to st—stop it," Jane sobbed from where she huddled on the ground, her skirts in wild disarray.

Seething, Damon stopped and glowered at the quaking man. "The other one . . . Did he . . . How badly did he hurt you?"

"I'm all right," she managed to choke out.

Taking a menacing step toward the visibly shaking Ben, Damon ground out between clenched teeth, "Get out of my sight. And take that dung heap with you!"

Ben wasted no time on apology. Warily skirting Damon, he laboriously heaved his unconscious friend's deadweight over his shoulder and made off as fast as he could.

Breathing heavily, more with anger than exertion, Damon turned to Jane. "You're all right? You're—you're sure he didn't . . ."

Jane was crying too hard to answer with more than a nod. And when Damon knelt beside her and tentatively took her in his arms, she snuggled close and buried her face against his chest. Her wrenching sobs shook him, too.

"Sssh. Hush, now. They're gone," Damon crooned, stroking her disheveled hair and marveling at the surge of tenderness he felt.

"They—they followed me," she sobbed. "And there w—wasn't anyone else . . . I tried to get away. I tried! Oh, Damon! It was so awf—ful. I was so scared!"

"Sssh. It's all right, now. You're safe. I'm here." He kissed her hair, suddenly feeling the strong, competent male; the heroic defender; the antithesis of everything *she* was. And he liked being made to feel that way; strong and compassionate all at once. Why didn't she let him be tender with her? Why had it taken something like this? Why were they always at each other's throat? He kissed her hair again, and held her tightly until her sobbing eased.

When she had wiped her face and heartily blown her nose on his handkerchief, she said, "I'm so glad you came when you did. It was even worse than last week."

"Last week? Dear God, what happened to you last week?"

"You," she accused, meeting his shocked stare with red-rimmed eyes. "You happened to me!"

The tenderness he felt for her disappeared like smoke up a chimney. "You little idiot! What that animal was doing—what he would have done if I had not arrived when I did—makes our little tussle look like a romp in a haystack!"

"Well, if that's what you call it," she said, yanking her skirt from beneath his knees and struggling clumsily to her feet, "from now on you can do your romping with that—that dressmaker!"

Stunned, Damon sat back on his haunches and stared after her as Jane flounced angrily toward the stream several yards away. Lilith had been obvious, cer-

tainly, but as naive as Johanna was, he had thought . . .
But then, a body could get a fine education from reading
Shakespeare!

"Well," he said, mildly, "since you're so worldly
wise, what happened with those men just now oughtn't
to have come as much of a surprise to you. You were
asking for it, tramping about all by yourself."

He saw a shudder ripple through her, but she
squared her shoulders and countered, "We aren't
talking about me and them. We're talking about you
and . . . her."

"No, we are not. We will never talk about her. She is
water under my bridge, to turn a phrase. Now, pull
yourself together and we'll be getting back."

Standing, Damon picked up her bonnet and reticule,
then her shoulder scarf and the slender package that
had been the cause of all this. Stationery. The last thing
in the world he needed. He had just ordered four quires
of vellum—embossed with the Seymour crest—from his
stationer in London.

"Here are your things," he said with a quiet sigh.

"Thank you," she said stiffly, accepting everything
but the package. "You may as well keep that. It's for
your birthday, belatedly."

"And how do you know my birth date?"

"I asked Simon." She looked up at him. "I wasn't
prying. I just thought that was something a—a wife
should know about her husband, that's all." Turning her
eyes back to the stream, she laid her bonnet and the rest
on a rock and began rearranging her hair.

"Thank you. It's . . . very thoughtful of you."

"It's ridiculous," she said, tying on her bonnet and
tucking a few stray tendrils under its brim. "Not only is it
two months late, but I bought it with *your* money."
Pulling the neckline of her dress away from her as far as
its snug fit would allow, she withdrew the coin just as *he*

had: pinched between two fingers. Battling tears of humiliation, she handed it to him.

"What's this?"

"Some good comes from everything, Mam always said. That's your crown back. He paid me. He thought I was a—"

"Why, that bastard! That filthy son of a worthless—"

He hurled the tainted coin into the stream where it disappeared with a tiny and wholly unsatisfying silver splash. For a long, thoughtful time he stared after it, watching the lazy slide of water over the satiny boulders of the stream bed. When he finally spoke, the abruptness of his words startled Jane almost as much as their content. "About Miss Townsend. I took vows on the day we married, Johanna. Granted, they were unsupported by emotional commitment, but I am, nevertheless, bound by them. I promised, among other things, to be faithful to you. I do not give my word lightly. I made the promise; I will continue to keep it." He faced her then, and offered his arm. "I think it is time we get back."

Jane stared at him for a moment, then busied herself with her skirt, fastidiously brushing away bits of leaf and smudges of dirt to avoid meeting his eye and taking his arm.

Damon glared down at her, puzzled, even angered, by her rejection of what had been his declaration of lifelong fidelity. What was the matter with her? What the hades did it take to touch her? By damn, but she was cold! he thought, unaware that she had not heard a profession of fidelity, but an admission of the sacrifice his sense of honor had cost him.

Bundy watched the couple walking back across the meadow. She looked miserable, absolutely miserable, trying to keep pace with her husband's long-legged stride. Why don't he ease up on her? Bundy wondered, angrily. Couldn't he see how unhappy she was? Didn't

he know all she wanted was a gentle hand on the rein,
not a curb bit jammed in her mouth?

"How did we do, Bundy?"

"Ah . . . you got the bay mare, sir."

"Excellent! And the others?"

Dear God, Bundy thought, she looked as if she'd
been crying! What'd he do to her out there? He couldn't
have taken her out there to . . . He couldn't have forced
her to . . .

"Well?" Damon snapped, impatiently.

"Keller's black went to Lem Baxter. I didn't think
you'd want to go over twenty for her."

"That's true."

"We picked up the other four. Three of 'em were
right in line, price-wise. I might've gone a bit high on that
blazed chestnut from over in Reistertown: thirty-two.
But seeing as your friend Mr. Jefferson bought your
chestnut stallion for better than forty, I figured it'd be all
right to spend a little more for the mare."

Damon laughed delightedly. "Did you hear that,
Johanna? Thomas bought the chestnut, just as you said
he would." Jane smiled fleetingly and again lowered her
eyes. "You did a fine job, Bundy. Thank you."

"You're welcome, sir," Bundy said with a noticeable
dearth of feeling. "I filled in your vouchers like you said,
and the gents were willing to trust your honor in making
good on 'em. And this is what you're owed." He thrust a
small stack of papers at Damon.

"I trust I came out on the plus side," Damon said
coolly, wondering at the man's demeanor.

"Far and away, sir."

"Well, I'll say it again—you did a fine job."

"Thank you, sir."

"See to it that everything gets home all right."

"Yes, sir. Afternoon to you, ma'am."

"Good-bye," Jane said unsmilingly, her eyes slipping
quickly from his.

Bundy felt his heart freeze. Something had happened out there in the woods. Something that had hurt her. He aimed a venomous stare at her husband.

"Is there something else, Bundy?" Damon fairly challenged.

"No, sir."

Damon watched Bundy stride away, then let his eyes slide to Jane. She looked as forlorn as he had ever seen her. Had he been right, after all? Was there something between her and the man who was turning out to be the best foreman Raven's Oak had ever had? Damnation, it surely seemed that way! She had her nerve, carrying on about Lilith Townsend when she had taken a lover of her own! Or had she meant what she said? Did she want him to do his "romping" with Lilith and leave her free to pursue a former stable hand? *That* would be a cold day in hell!

"Well, well," he said with forced lightness as he shuffled through the papers in his hands. "It seems Pemberton made it, after all. He owes me forty quid." When Jane said nothing, he prodded, "He's to be one our house guests, remember?"

"Oh, yes. The magistrate from Philadelphia. Did, ah, did his friend Mr. Ives come, too?"

"He doesn't owe me anything, but he's undoubtedly here. I'll walk you to the carriage, then make good on my vouchers."

"Thank you, but I can find it myself." Stonily, she turned away.

"Don't talk to strangers along the way, will you?"

She shot him a furious look over her shoulder. As she stormed off, Damon found himself thinking I *was wrong. She's not cold. She has plenty of fire.* Unfortunately, it was the kind of flame that burned without giving off any warmth.

It was late afternoon when the Seymours and their

house guests returned to Raven's Oak. Having seen Damon's guests properly welcomed and shown to their rooms, Jane eagerly sought out her own. She had only an hour to bathe and change before she was expected to preside over tea. But as rushed as she was, she stood motionless in her bedroom doorway, staring dumbly at the subservient heap of black serge on the floor in the middle of the room.

It took a minute before she regained herself enough to ask, "Who are you?"

"Venus, ma'am. Your new maid," the negress said, not raising her head or her eyes from the carpet.

"But you're a . . . Are you a slave?"

"Yes'um."

Jane stared at the woman—who seemed to be praying—for a long moment. Then she hurried toward the sitting room door. "Please, get up. I'll be back in a minute." When she had reached Damon's room, she cried, "There's a slave in my room!"

"Oh, yes. I'd forgotten about her. She's your new maid," he said from behind his dressing screen.

"But she's a slave!"

"What difference does that make? She's an experienced lady's maid, and a seamstress, too."

"It makes a difference, Damon."

At the low note of anger in her voice, Damon stopped lathering his face and, with the shaving mug and brush still in his hands, stepped out from behind the screen. "Why?" he asked, knuckling an errant fluff of foam from his upper lip. "Don't you like negroes?"

"N—no. It—it isn't that." His appearance distracted her momentarily. She had never seen him engaged in the strictly masculine act of shaving before. And she had never seen him look more manly than he did standing there, shirtless, a towel casually tossed over a broad shoulder, his face half-covered with froth. "Be—because I don't hold with slavery, that's why. It says in the Bible that we're all children of one father and . . . I won't ask one of my sisters to serve me as a slave."

"It seems you missed reading the part about the sons of Ham," Damon said, looking mildly amused. "You didn't ask her to serve you. She was born to it."

"I will not own a slave!"

"You don't. I do. I bought her; she's mine." He disappeared behind the screen again, and Jane heard the brush clinking busily against the mug's ceramic rim as he worked the collapsed bubbles into a lather again.

"But you bought her *for me*, and I won't have it. I won't!"

"Whether you will or won't is irrelevant. She is bought and paid for and will serve in *this* house in the capacity for which she was trained," he said, amusement replaced by annoyance. "And, madam, as you purport to be a lady, she will serve you!" Slamming his mug and brush down, he began furiously stropping his already sharp razor, muttering under his breath with each violent stroke. Jane caught the word "ungrateful."

"I am not ungrateful, Damon," she said in what she hoped was a conciliatory tone. "I appreciate what you tried to do. Truly. But I . . . I just don't feel right about people owning people."

But for the swish and splash of water as he rinsed the razor after each stroke, all was quiet behind the screen. And when Damon suddenly appeared around it again, toweling off his face, Jane jumped like a startled cat. "Very well. You may as well learn right now how slaves are dealt with here. I will see you and 'your' slave in the sitting room."

"What are you going to do?" Jane gasped, fearing the worst.

"Go get her."

"If you intend to—to harm her, I want you to know right now that I—"

"By damn, woman!" he roared. "Just this once can't

you do what you're told without an argument?''

Head bowed, eyes respectfully lowered, Venus followed the mistress whose face she had yet to see into the adjoining room. And she worried as she went. What had she done to offend? Not daring to presume the familiarity with this new mistress that she had taken as a matter of course with Miss Emily, she had been respectfully humble. And she hadn't spoken out of turn. Of that, she was sure! So what had she done to be called before the master?

Stopping just inside the sitting room and a re-spectable distance from where her mistress stood, Venus began reciting the prayer Miss Emily had taught her. But when she got to the line, ''Thy will be done in earth, as it is in heaven,'' she stopped. Why had God willed that dear, sweet Miss Emily should die? And why had He willed that Master Courtland should sell her off instead of keeping her to serve the new wife everybody said he was taking? She had never imagined her life without Miss Emily. She had *never* thought to find herself sold; dragged along a dusty road at the end of a leash by a no-account stable nigger who was as far below her, a house servant, as she herself was below her mistress. She had never thought the day would come when she would be learning a new mistress's ways!

But learn them she'd better, and right quick. She didn't mean a thing to these Seymour folk. If she didn't please them, they would turn right around and sell her again. She didn't ever, not ever, want to go through another day like this. Not if she could help it. No matter how bad things were here, she didn't ever want to be sold again! Not ever in her life! ''I'll do anything they tell me, Lord,'' she found herself praying, ''even lay with the new master like I had to do with Mr. Courtland since You took Miss Emily away. I'll do anything at all, Lord, if it means I won't never be sold again!'' And she concluded with a silent but fervent, ''Amen!''

Jane studied the woman who stood obediently, and as motionless as a black pillar, awaiting whatever was to come. She was tall and slender—"willowy" was the word, Jane supposed—and the maid's uniform that had been Janet's was several inches too short for her. The ruffled cap on her head covered most of her hair, but Jane could see that it was short and tightly curled. Her face had a delicate softness about it; her features were not blunted and coarse as were those of most negroes Jane had seen. And her skin was a beautiful chocolate color.

"Good afternoon, Venus," Damon said, entering the room and jarring Jane from her thoughts.

"Afternoon, suh."

He stopped beside Jane—who, he thought delightedly, looked more nervous by half than the slave—and said, "Come here, Venus. Come closer." Her eyes on the floor, the maid complied. "You have been acquainted with your duties and shown to your quarters, I trust?"

"Yes'uh."

"When I speak to servants, Venus, be they slave or free, I expect them to meet my eye."

The eyes Venus hesitantly raised were large and black and filled with uncertainty. "Yes'uh," she whispered.

Damon smiled at her benignly, aware of the effort she was making to overcome the training that told her she must never raise her eyes to her betters. "You know that I paid a considerable sum for you."

The dark eyes slipped downward. "Yes'uh."

"Look up when I speak to you, Venus," Damon reminded her patiently. When she did, he went on, "The sum I paid for you is roughly equal to the wages I would pay a hired maid to serve my wife for the period of three years. If you serve Mistress Seymour well, Venus, at the end of that time I will consider your debt to me paid."

He heard Jane's soft gasp, but the slave stared at him in utter incomprehension. "What I am telling you, Venus, is that in three years time you will have earned your freedom." Venus blinked twice and her eyes widened until Jane thought they would pop out of her head. "Do you understand?"

"Yes'uh," she replied, incredulous.

"Mind, now, you are not free yet. You must fulfill your obligation to me first. Is that understood?"

"Yes'uh," she said, still clearly stunned.

"Fine. You will be well treated here. You have no need to fear that you will not be. Have you any questions as to your duties and what is expected of you?"

"No, suh."

But Damon saw the shadow of doubt cross her eyes, and said quietly, "You will serve my wife and only my wife, Venus. Do I make myself understood?"

Jane looked at him in puzzled surprise, but Venus showed only relief. "Yes'uh. Thank you, suh."

Damon smiled. So, he *had* been right: Courtland had sold off his concubine. "I understand you are an accomplished seamstress."

"Yes'uh. I made most all of Miss Emily's things, suh."

"Excellent. Mistress Seymour will make good use of your talents, I'm sure. I trust you will not find her *too* difficult a mistress." He met Jane's indignant eyes. "Now, madam, might I suggest you get on with whatever you intend doing? We're expected for tea." With a nod and a smug smirk of a smile, he disappeared into his room.

Pemberton and Ives were already in the withdrawing room when Damon ushered Jane in. Though they had been introduced to her before leaving the auction grounds, this was Jane's first good look at the pair. It was easy to see why they were close friends: They were as like as bookends. Both were impeccably well-groomed and tailored, white-wigged, dandified and arrogant even at a glance, obviously wealthy and apparently partial to snuff. When their host and hostess entered the room, both quickly pocketed snuff boxes and sneezed into lace-trimmed handkerchiefs. Their conversation, Jane soon discovered, was flowery and insipid. Whether that was because they had nothing of consequence to say or because they deemed serious conversation unsuitable in the presence of ladies, Jane would never know. But she was only too happy to leave them to Mr. Cullingford, who seemed cut from the same bolt, while she gave most of her attention to the Drakes and Mr. Jefferson.

As much as she enjoyed the men's lively repartee, she enjoyed Marianne's female companionship more. She hadn't realized how thirsty she was for a woman's company; the indefinable sense of kinship. She soaked up Marianne's company like a sponge, absorbing every drop against the days of drought ahead when she would wring out her memory to quench her parched woman's soul. Though she didn't understand why, she had come to realize that she could not expect a drop of friendship from the good women of Rendell.

From across the room, Damon watched the women, noticing the confidential tenor of their talk. As he remembered what Robert had said, "She hates it . . . Mari and I weren't raised as liars," he felt his stomach knot with dread.

Jane's stomach was so full of butterflies, she was sure she wouldn't be able to eat a bite. She had never presided over a dining table full of guests before, and she wanted to make a good impression. As much for her sake as Damon's, she didn't want his friends to think he had married a bumpkin . . . even though he had.

When she entered the sitting room where Damon was waiting, he took her in from head to toe, his eyes ultimately coming to rest on the diamond and emerald necklace that dipped in glittering splendor toward her gown's daring decolletage. "What happened?" he asked, sounding disappointed.

Jane looked down at herself and smoothed her green silk skirt. "Is there something wrong?"

"Not wrong, exactly. It's just that the last time you wore that gown it—fit differently. What happened?"

"Oh. I let it out."

"Why?" he yelped, looking pained.

"It was too tight. I was practically falling out of it!"

"I know. It was wonderful on you."

"And it isn't wonderful on me now?" she challenged testily.

"Oh, no. No, no! It's still very nice. But I liked it the way it was, too."

"I didn't think you noticed the first time I wore it," she said, remembering the occasion. Cullingford's eyes had nearly jumped out of his head when she had arrived in the drawing room, ready for dinner. But Damon had barely glanced at her.

"A man would have to be blind not to notice you in that." He cleared his throat brusquely and changed the subject. "How is Venus working out for you?"

"Oh, she's wonderful! She knows what I want even before I do, I think."

Damon smiled and, crossing the room to her, fingered a plump ringlet near her ear. "She seems to be accomplished at hair dressing, too."

"Yes," she said, inexplicably unnerved by his nearness. "She's wonderful."

"I'm glad you're pleased with her."

"Oh, I—I am. Thank you."

"You're welcome." He smiled. "And, how do I look? I dressed without benefit of Simon tonight. Is everything—straight?"

He took an obliging step back and spread his arms

for her inspection. Jane did a hasty appraisal. "I think so."

"Would you mind making sure? As fastidious about dress as some of our guests are, I wouldn't want them to find their host less impeccably turned out."

Jane's eyes retraced their downward glide: French lace frill; royal blue jacket; gold silk waistcoat . . . superbly fitted breeches. Her eyes snapped back to his. "I'm sure."

"Even this?" He flounced the cascade of ruffles at his breast, deliberately disarranging them. "I've always had a deuce of a time arranging a frill. Would you mind?"

It was a reasonable enough request, that she tidy his frill, especially since he had just made such a mess of it. But the way he had asked—the way he looked when he did—gave it a significance out of all proportion. This was something he would ask only his manservant or his wife to do. It was a personal, intimate favor, one of the personal, intimate favors a wife did for her husband.

Jane raised troubled eyes to his. Why was he making so much of it? Why was she?

"Do you mind?" he asked.

"No. Of course not."

The spicy musk of his cologne eddied and swirled around her and mingled with her essence of roses as she raised her hands to the wifely task. Their scents mingled and became one, just as male and female, man and wife, became one. Her pulse thrummed in her throat, and she saw the broad expanse of chest before her as she had seen it that afternoon. The lace under her fingers became a furring of crisp, auburn hair; the satin lapels of his jacket, his warm as velvet skin. She let her hands linger there, let her fingers burrow, her palms press as she had not for oh, so long! Such a long, long time!"

Watching her, steeling himself against her nearness and her touch, Damon wondered what she would do if he kissed her. He wanted to. Dear God, he wanted to put his hands around that tiny waist of hers, draw her up against him and do a helluva lot more than just kiss her! But that would spoil it. That would make him hers. What he wanted was to make her his. And he could do that if he was patient. He had seen how she looked at him this afternoon; he could see how she was looking at him now. All he had to do was be patient—and keep Bundy at bay—and she would come to him. By damn, he'd make her want him!

"There. I think that does it," she said, more breathily than she wanted to.

"Thank you."

"You're welcome."

He touched the ruffle of gilt lace framing her low-cut bodice. "I do believe we make quite a handsome pair, decked out in our finery."

"Yes. I—I believe we do."

"You are very lovely, Johanna," he said, his voice dropping to a sensuous whisper. "Very lovely." His fingers provocatively brushed the swell of a breast before they left the place. "Shall we go down?"

Dinner was even more of an ordeal than Jane had anticipated. But for a different reason than any she had foreseen. It was not her management of the meal that caused her trouble; she orchestrated the servants beautifully with jinglings of her little bell. It was Damon. The seductive looks and admiring smiles he sent her way were downright disconcerting. And toward the end of the meal, he gave her a look so bold, so evocative of shared intimacies, that Jane turned as pink as the raspberries topping her blanc mange.

And dinner was but a preview of what was to come. When, after their brandy, the men joined the ladies, Damon suggested a "musical evening." And after everyone had trooped around the corner and down the hall to the music room, he hooked a hand about Jane's waist and said, "Favor us with a song, will you, darling?" And when she had—and an encore, too—Damon took both her hands warmly in his and proclaimed, "You sing like a thrush." A verdict with which everyone agreed. Thereafter, he was never far from her side: blending his baritone with her soprano when everyone joined in the singing; perching on the arm of her chair while Mr. Jefferson entertained them on the violin, and Marianne and Mr. Cullingford took turns at the clavier.

Jane was awestruck by his attentiveness, unnerved by it, too, until she realized that it was all for show. Proud as he was, Damon wouldn't want his family and friends to know something was amiss in his marriage. And, having realized that and knowing that she was critical to the success of his little game, Jane had half a mind not to play along. But she couldn't expose the charade and embarrass him without humiliating herself in the bargain. So, pretending she was as blissfully happy and content as he, she grudgingly helped him paint the charming tableau of a pretty couple. But once, when he was laughing at one of Robert's jokes and looking down to see if she was laughing, too, Jane realized it was a shame that they had to pretend. And, just for an instant, she wondered if they were.

It was nearly midnight when, politely smothering yawns, the guests began to excuse themselves and head for bed. Jane wasn't sorry to bid them good night. She was tired herself, and anxious to be done with Damon's little farce of domestic bliss.

"Will you take a glass of Madeira with me?" Damon asked when the others had left.

"No, thank you. I'm tired. Good night."

"The evening went very well, don't you think?" When Jane said nothing, he added, "Everyone was very impressed with you. And not just your singing. You were the perfect hostess. Anyone would think you had been giving dinner parties and entertaining guests all your

life." He smiled. "Are you certain you won't join me?
There's a claret here, if you would prefer that?"

She drew breath to tell him that she didn't care for
wine, and he well knew it. But, much to her surprise, she
found that she was as reluctant as he to have the
evening, and their little charade, end. "The claret, then,
please. Only half a glass."

Grinning, he reached for the decanter. "Did I tell you
I spoke with Mr. Decker today?"

"No. Who is Mr. Decker?"

"He's the stone mason I've engaged to put in the
French window. He'll start work on it next week."

"The French window?"

"Yes. We discussed putting one in here, remember?
It will brighten the room considerably." He handed her a
glass. "You're a rare flower, Johanna. I won't have you
wilt for lack of sun."

She felt like telling him he could quit his playacting;
there was no one left to appreciate it. But she only said,
"Thank you," and accepted her wine.

"A breath of air would do nicely just now, don't you
think?"

"Now? But it's the middle of the night."

"There's a moon. Shall we?"

Jane had rarely ventured out at night back home,
and when she had, it had only been to visit the
Necessary House. Those times hadn't been especially
pleasant; crossing a farmyard in the dark had its perils,
and she had always hurried along, hoping the occasional
goo underfoot was only mud. Now, it was a novel and
not at all unpleasant experience to walk leisurely across
a shadow-dappled, freshly scythed lawn with an elegant
gentleman at her side.

"It's beautiful. So quiet and still. And the moon looks
almost near enough to touch," she whispered.

Damon looked down at her, keeping his smug smile
to himself. "Shall we walk toward the orchard? I'm

anxious to see how the picking is coming. There's a nip of frost in the air.''

Indeed, there was. The night air was cool against Jane's face and the expanse of skin exposed by her gown's low, square neckline.

''Are you chilly?'' he asked.

''A little. I'm not used to being without a shawl or something.''

''You look lovely without a shawl . . . or something,'' he said, his voice seductively soft. ''Here. Hold this.''

''Oh, but now you'll be cold,'' she protested, holding his glass as he took off his coat.

He ignored her and draped it, still warm from his body, about her shoulders. Their eyes held as he pulled the lapels closed over her breast. ''Warmer?''

''Much. Thank you.'' She felt a vague stirring of excitement begin low and in the center of her when his hands lingered warmly near her breasts.

''You are beautiful, Johanna,'' he whispered, bunching the jacket's soft velvet and satin in his fists and drawing her slowly closer.

And when their lips met, tentatively, softly, Jane felt the little tingle of excitement blossom into a tremor of desire.

As he felt it ripple through her, an answering quickening began within himself. Then she reached hungrily upward for the lips that teased at hers. By heaven, he'd have her tonight! He'd warm her with more than a kiss! But he would have her on his terms; make her come to him; beg for him!

Straightening, Damon slowly smoothed the jacket front over the full curve of her. ''We'll spill the wine,'' he whispered, reclaiming his glass. Then, with a hand at her waist, he resumed their interrupted stroll. And when his hand began a slow caress of her side, reaching higher with every upward stroke until it was caressing her breast, he felt her shudder. ''Are you still cold?'' he asked, feigning ignorance.

"N—no. You?"

"Not at all," he said. And Jane wondered at his calm.

He wanted her; she knew he did, at least as much as she wanted him. And, much as it pained her to admit it, she did want him. Lilith Townsend or no; last week or no; she *did* want him! But if he could play at nonchalance, so could she.

"I, ah, I want to thank you again for Venus. And for telling her what you did. That was very kind of you."

"Kindness didn't enter into it. A free man—or woman—is a better worker than a slave."

"If that's true, why do you keep slaves?"

"I don't. Not in the usual sense."

"You mean, they're all like Venus? When they work off their indebtedness, you free them?" He nodded. "Why?"

"I've already told you: If a man is serving himself, he's a better and more willing worker. If a slave knows that by serving *me* well, he can achieve that which he values above all else, he serves me well, indeed." Stopping, he pulled her within the curve of his arm. "But this is hardly a topic for a moonlight stroll."

Jane watched the untouched wine in her glass reflect the silver moonlight, then it sloshed around when she wrenched herself free of his arm. "Then, you don't really care about them at all. You use freedom as a goad, the way some men use the whip. And you use that, too, as it suits you!" she spat. "You're as bad as Squire Trent. Worse! You use people's dreams against them!" Hurling her glass aside, she turned back toward the house.

But before she had taken a step, the glass struck the brick border of what had once been a flower bed. That sound, the brittle tinkling of shattering crystal, brought her up short.

"Use their dream *against* them! I give them the opportunity to work *for* it, Johanna. Can't you see that?"

When Jane said nothing but continued to stare straight ahead, Damon muttered, "Idiotic female!" Then he smashed his glass against the bricks, too.

"Don't! Don't do that!" Jane shrieked, palms flattened over her ears. But the sound had already penetrated her mind, and echoed and reverberated there: a cacophonous din. Her face deathly pale, her eyes terror-filled, she turned, demanding, "Make it stop. Make it stop!"

Shocked, Damon stood his ground, staring at her, watching the naked terror on her face slowly dissipate.

"I'm—I'm sorry," she gasped at last, self-consciously lowering her hands.

"What frightened you?" he asked, venturing a cautious step nearer.

"I don't know. I don't know. It was . . . that sound. Breaking glass. That *sound* . . . I don't know!"

She stood rigid and trembling in his embrace, her mind spiraling in desperate confusion. When he led her toward a stone bench beneath the grape arbor and sat with her there, she slowly relaxed against him, letting his warmth drive the chill of her unnamed terror away.

"Has this happened before?"

"No. Never. Nothing like this!" She cuddled closer against him as if to ward off the memory.

"But you've heard glass break before," he reasoned. "Only last week Opal broke a crystal vase. Remember?"

"That wasn't the same." she said with a small shudder.

"How was it different?"

"I don't know."

Damn sighed. "Well, then, do you know *why* the sound frightened you?" Jane shook her head. "It must have reminded you of something," he prodded, hearing the impatience in his voice and regretting it.

Jane straightened and met his eye. "I don't know *how* the sound was different. I don't know *why* it frightened

me. I don't know *what* it reminded me of. I *don't know*!"
Standing, she started back toward the house.

Damon's hand shot out and caught her wrist.
"Johanna, wait! I'm only trying to understand what
happened."

"So am I," she said, refusing to look at him. "But I
don't. It's just like all the other times. I haven't been able
to understand them, either."

"What other times? I thought you said this hadn't
happened before."

"It didn't—not—not this. But sometimes, sometimes
it's as if I know things. Things I shouldn't."

"What sort of things?"

"Just—things," she said, trying to pull away.

"No. Tell me," he said, not letting her go. And when
she looked at him, he added a soft "please."

"They're—they're just little things," she said,
relenting and settling beside him again. "Like the rag
doll Mam made me for Christmas one year. As soon as I
saw that doll, somehow I knew it wasn't a very *nice* doll. I
knew how hard Mam had worked to make it for me, and
I loved her for that, but I knew, too, that I had had better
dolls; dolls with china hands and faces. Only . . . I never
had!

"And one year, at the fair at Four Corners, I saw a
bolt of blue silk. I had never seen silk before—How
could I have?—but I knew it was silk. And I knew how it
would feel under my fingers when I touched it." She
looked at him imploringly. "How could I have known
that?"

"Johanna . . ."

"And this afternoon, when I saw Venus, I thought
that her skin was the color of chocolate—hot chocolate
after the whipped cream has melted. But I couldn't know
that! I've never had hot chocolate! I couldn't have
known any of it!"

"Yes. Yes, you could. Of course, you could!"

"No! Don't you understand? China dolls and silk and chocolate . . . We had none of those on the farm!" With tears sparkling in her eyes, she turned her face away. "I'm mad, that's what it is. I'm going mad."

"Certainly, you are not," he said emphatically. "Everything you've mentioned, you had at Southwind. All that, and a collie pup, too." He watched her digest what he had said, then dash a tear from her cheek. "Do you remember?"

"I don't know. This—this place, Southwind, did it have . . . Was the house big? Very, very big, and built of red brick?"

"Yes!"

"And did it have . . . windows that opened like doors?"

"Yes. French windows, yes."

In a stunned, whispery, far-away voice she said, "I remember those. I remember they had lace curtains and . . . and I couldn't see out the other windows because they were too high, but I could look out through the glass doors." She stared at him suddenly. "Whose house was it? What was I doing there?"

Damon hesitated, choosing his words carefully. "The estate belonged to my mother's uncle."

"Then what was I doing there?"

"You, ah, cannot recall my great-uncle? His name was Chalmer Ralston."

Jane concentrated, but the man's face remained as unfamiliar as his name. "No. No more than I can recall the puppy. Why was I there?"

After another thoughtful hesitation, he said as if it explained everything, "Before he was my tenant, McPhee was foreman at Southwind."

But Jane knew, intuitively, that wasn't the whole answer. There was something he was keeping to himself: something important; something she ought to know. But fear, a gnawing, gripping fear, constricted her heart and kept her silent all the way back to the house.

Pemberton and Ives cut their stay short the next morning; Pemberton pleading urgent business. Ives making no excuse. Jane sensed that Damon was not sad to see them go. Mr. Jefferson spent his alotted three days at Raven's Oak. Having amended her first impression of that entertaining young gentleman, Jane was sorry to see him go. But she was sorrier still to say good-bye to Marianne and Robert the following day. It helped only a little to know that she and Marianne would exchange letters. Letters could not fill the quiet, empty house. And they could hardly chase the loneliness from her heart.

With a pang, Jane realized that was the problem. She was lonely. She had had little time to consider how very empty her life was. She had been too busy becoming educated and a lady, too awed and confused by her husband and her role as mistress here to spend time dwelling on her private needs. Even resumption of her lessons with Cullingford did nothing to fill the void Marianne's leave-taking had created. And often, while she struggled over the French vocabulary lists with which Cullingford had replaced the English ones, she found her mind wandering and her thoughts turning to Marianne's words: "Once you have a child, Johanna, you'll be much happier. You'll see." And she began to realize that having a child would, indeed, make her happy. A baby would fill her emptiness. It would take up her time. It would give her someone to love.

Damon, of course, was the fly in her ointment. If there was to be a child, he would have to cooperate. But, since that night in the garden, he had been more aloof than ever. He had not even bothered to keep up the pose he had started for the benefit of their guests, but had reinforced the wall between them just when it had seemed on the verge of toppling. Why that should be, Jane couldn't understand.

Damon understood—and wished he didn't! Jane's memory of Southwind might be tattered, but his was painfully whole, and he could not look at the fragile, beautiful girl he had taken as a wife without remembering the tragedy that had brought her to him. Her very presence in his house became, to Damon, a monument to Trevor's death. Had her brother, his dear cousin, lived, she would not be here now. There would have been no marriage contract; no compromise of Damon's honor! Had Trevor lived, all their lives would have been so different!

But even though Damon knew the churning, jumble of emotion he felt each time he looked at his wife would pass, it was there for the present, and he could do nothing but wait for time to heal the cruel wound memory had reopened.

Jane was less patient than he. It took nine months to have a baby. That was a long time to wait. There was no sense in making the wait longer.

"Damon? I've been thinking," she said across the drawing room one chilly evening late in November.

"Mmm?" he hummed absently, his attention on the book he was reading.

Jane didn't look up from her needlework. "I have more time now that you've decided I don't need dancing instruction anymore. I—I need something to fill it."

"Mmm."

"Did you hear me?"

"Uh-huh," he said, still not looking up.

"Damon!"

"What!" he barked, his eyes leaping to hers.

"I have a great deal of time on my hands and—"

"I know. I heard. What have you in mind doing with it?" Annoyance edged his every word.

Jane lowered her eyes to her stitchery. "This doesn't seem to be the right time to discuss it."

"What better time?" He snapped the book shut. "You have gained my undivided attention."

Meeting his eyes, Jane took the bull by the horns. "I want a baby."

Jane saw his look of stunned surprise before he dropped his eyes to the book in his lap and absently ruffled its pages. "You do, do you?"

"Yes."

He looked at her, then, long and hard, taking in the proud lift of her chin, the determined set of her mouth, the challenge in her cornflower blue eyes. There wasn't a trace of the hunger for him he wanted to see; not so much as a spark of desire. She was asking—Or was she demanding?—that he service her. Yes, that was exactly what it amounted to! He'd be damned and roasted in hell before he would let her use him that way!

"You're right," he said coolly, "this isn't the time to discuss it."

"When may we discuss it?"

Jane almost shivered under his cold stare. "When you can talk about wanting a child without making it sound like a contract for stud service."

The quietly spoken words lashed at her, leaving her shocked and wincing at the painful weals they raised across her conscience. He was right: She had made it sound that way. But what did he expect? Did he think it would ever be rapturous between them, the way it had been at first? But that was before she had understood it was required of her; before he had demanded her body as his due.

Watching him hurl the book aside and stand to leave, she cried, "That's what it is, isn't it? That's what our marriage is: a contract!"

Damon huffed disgustedly and stormed from the room, furious to find that he was questioning his wisdom in having looked a gift horse in the mouth—and refused it.

* * *

"It was my understanding, sir, that you had declined the invitation to the Williamsburg Assemblies this season."

Damon glowered at his valet. "Just pack!" When Simon dutifully went back to work, Damon grumbled, "A little socializing may do me a world of good."

Meticulously folding a dress coat and laying it away in the trunk, Simon said, "Forgive me, sir, but you do not appear to be in a humor for socializing."

"My humor will improve dramatically once I've put a few miles between myself and my wife."

"Indeed, sir, I *have* noticed that Madam has become morose of late."

"And are you implying that I am responsible for that?" Damon snapped defensively.

"Certainly not, sir. I only meant that I can appreciate your need for a bit of time away, sir. Madam's disposition being what it is. And I am sure, sir, you will rest better at night, even in a strange bed, without Madam's weeping to disturb you."

Damon glared at the man who had not raised his eyes from his chore, then began a restless pacing. Striding the length of the room like a caged bear, he muttered with his thoughts. "Damn! I've never seen the like of her!"

"If you are referring to Madam, sir, I quite agree. She is extraordinarily pretty. I thought that the moment I saw her, sir."

"That's not what I meant, and you know it." Damon growled, breaking stride to toss an annoyed glare at the man.

"Beg pardon, sir. Were you speaking, then, of Madam's astonishingly rapid adjustment to her situation? If so, I am quite impressed with that, too, sir. As I am by her tenderness and patience with Opal and with her efforts to please you, sir."

"Please me! P*lease* me? Are your eyes failing you, man? Haven't you seen me getting out of my own bed every morning for the past . . . God knows how long!"

"My eyesight is quite keen, sir. Thank you for inquiring." Damon muttered something unintelligible and resumed his pacing. "May I say, sir, it is most unfortunate Madam has not fulfilled your earlier expectations and proven to be a congenial partner in life?"

"You most certainly may!"

"Thank you, sir. And may I offer a word of encouragement?"

"If you must. If you can!"

"Oh, there are always encouraging words to be had, sir, no matter how dire one's circumstance. In time of strife, my mother was fond of saying, 'Patience. In time the grass becomes milk.'" Damon turned a puzzled frown on the man. "She was raised on a dairy farm, sir."

Damon returned to his pacing. "Sound advice, I'm sure. Unfortunately, patience doesn't seem to be the answer here."

"As you say, sir. This does seem to be more a case of the tree that is willing to break rather than to bend to the force of the gale, sir."

Damon leveled a challenging look at the man. "And which of us do you label the tree?"

"I would not presume to say, sir," Simon said, straightening and meeting Damon's eye with a look that left no doubt as to whom he considered to be the obstinate tree. "If there is nothing else, sir, I shall arrange for your luggage to be carried."

"Please do," Damon snarled. He watched the man walk to the door, angry at feeling the way Simon had always been able to make him feel: thoroughly chastised.

# 9

Jane pulled the woolen shawl more tightly about herself and welcomed the warmth of Damon's arm about her shoulders as they watched the carriage roll down the drive through a lacy curtain of snow.

"I wish they had waited to see how bad this storm is going to be before setting out in it," she said, raising a hand and smiling in response to the white hanky cousin Delia fluttered from the carriage window.

"You aren't trying to make me believe you're sorry to see them gone, are you?"

"Of course not! I simply don't want to get up my hopes that we've seen the last of Cousin Randolph, Lord Pomeroy, only to find him back with us this afternoon."

Damon laughed and guided her into the house. Leaving Simon to close the door behind them, he said as he hurried her toward the warmth of the drawing room fire, "I couldn't agree more. A week of that fop was seven days too many."

"It's a shame Mr. Cullingford isn't still here. I'm sure the two of them would have gotten along wonderfully well."

"What? Missing Cullingford, are you?" he teased.

Jane threw him a saucy smirk and he grinned. Then, with a shake of her head, she said, "I simply don't understand what Delia sees in Randolph. It must be some-thing. She seems happy."

"Ah, but appearances can be deceiving. Can't they?" Damon said, dropping his arm and stepping away.

Through hurt, angry eyes, Jane watched him squat on a heel and needlessly poke at the cheery fire. What had she expected? She ought to have known he would turn away, discard pretext, as soon as Delia and her groom were out of sight, just as he had when the house had emptied itself of guests after Christmas. She really should have expected this! Except, this time, *this* time she had forgotten that they were only pretending at happiness. Why hadn't he? Why couldn't he? If she, the injured party; the wronged wife; the woman he had betrayed and deserted last fall in favor of the company of his Williamsburg friends—male and female alike, she was sure—could be forgiving, why couldn't he!

Damon bellowed an oath and leapt to his feet, beating at the cascade of sparks that threatened to set his linsey-woolsey breeches afire.

"Are you burned?" she asked coolly, thinking that if he was, he deserved it.

"No. What has Marianne to say?"

Withdrawing the folded sheet of paper from the deep pocket of her skirt, Jane said, "I haven't read her letter yet. I'm almost afraid to. The baby was coming down with a cold the last she wrote. Winter is so terribly hard on babies."

"Would you rather I read it?"

Shaking her head, Jane softened the blob of sealing wax over a candle flame and unfolded the single sheet. "Oh, thank goodness. Lucinda's fine." She flashed Damon a relieved smile, then returned her eyes to the letter. "She asks how we're enjoying Delia's visit and . . ." Jane laughed. "She says, 'May not you please beg them extend their stay with you? Robert and I are not overly anxious for them to arrive.'"

"I can believe that!" Damon said heartily. "Go on."

"Ah . . . She says that Jonathan and Amelia stood as godparents at Lucinda's christening, and that they send us a hello. Who are Jonathan and Amelia?"

"Robert's brother and—"

"Pardon me, suh."

"—sister-in-law. For mercy's sake, Opal! Don't you know better than to interrupt?"

"I's sorry, suh, but it's important."

"What is important?"

"One o' de mares is foalin', suh."

"Which one?"

"I dunno, suh."

"Is there some trouble?"

"I 'spect so, suh. Joe say, 'Will Massah come?' "

"Very well. Tell Joe I'll be there shortly."

"He done gone back to de stables, suh."

"Then run out there and tell him."

Opal eyed her bare feet. "It's snowin', Mistah Seymour!"

"Then put on your shoes. Haven't I told you, time and again, that you are to wear shoes?"

"They hurt her feet, Damon," Jane interjected. "You bought them for her nearly a year ago. Children grow." She held his stare long enough to let him know she wasn't cowed by it, then shifted her eyes to Opal. "Run upstairs to Venus, Opal, and tell her to give you a pair of my slippers. Tell her I said so and that she is not to argue. Then go and do as Mr. Seymour told you. Do you understand?"

"Yes'um. I's to tell Venus to give me your slippers and no back talk, den I goes and tells Joe massah's comin'."

"Yes. Quickly, now."

"Yes'um!" Opal bolted from the room only to reappear in the doorway a few seconds later to drop a curtsy, before she disappeared again.

"She really does try, Damon. I wish you would be more patient with her."

"*Your* slippers?"

"Why not? She's big for her age. They'll fit her, I'm sure." He growled his disapproval. "If you disapprove of her wearing mine, why don't you buy her shoes that fit?"

"I <u>was</u> under the impression that the household was your responsibility!"

Jane bristled. She had long since made her peace with Oswald and, in so doing, had cut household expenses by more than fifteen percent. "Then why don't you leave it to me?" Damon's scowl grew blacker. But, since he was already staring daggers at her, and there were none at hand for him to throw, Jane decided to pursue her point. "If the house is my responsibility, why do you object to my opening the parlor in the guest wing?"

"Have I said I objected to that?"

"You don't have to *say* it. I don't understand why you're so upset! It isn't as if it cost much to redo the curtains. The fabric was only a few pounds, and Venus sewed them for nothing."

"It isn't the expense," he said, turning back to the fire.

"What is it, then?" When he said nothing, she went on persuasively, "It's such a pleasant room, Damon. And I thought, given the way we both feel about Cousin Randolph, that it would be nice if he and Delia had a place to spend some time separate from us." Still, Damon said nothing. "I like the room, too. It has a lovely view and such a . . . a friendly feel about it. It seemed a shame to let such a pleasant room go to waste. If you had wanted it kept shut, you should have told me."

"It never occurred to me that you would reopen it."

"You showed it to me when you gave me a tour of the house my first day here. Why did you do that if you didn't want the room used?''

"Why are you making an issue of it?'' he barked, rounding on her.

"I'm not. You are! You won't sit with me there in the evening. You look angry whenever you find me there, and you—''

His abrupt leave-taking and curt, over the shoulder, "I'm needed at the stables,'' struck Jane with the force of a slap.

From the doorway, Jane tried to see the upstairs parlor the way Damon must. As elsewhere in the house, the furnishings were expensive but not ostentatious: cherry wood tables; comfortably upholstered chairs; a small divan. The creamy white walls were hung with floral still lifes, and a serene landscape decorated the space over the mantel. The room never failed to have a soothing effect upon Jane.

She walked to the north window and, staring out at the snowy meadows and woodlands, worried aloud, "What does he find so objectionable?''

"Pardon me, madam?''

"Oh, ah, I was just wondering aloud,'' she said, tossing Simon a sheepish smile. But when he turned back to laying a fire, she asked with forced casualness the question Damon had twice evaded. "Why was this room kept closed, Simon?''

"Mr. Seymour had no need of it, madam.''

It was the obvious answer. Why didn't Jane think it the truthful one? "How long had it been closed before I reopened it?''

"Many years, madam.''

"Since Damon's mother died?'' she guessed. With more concentration than the simple task required, Simon lit the kindling. "It was her room, wasn't it? It—feels like a woman's room.''

"Indeed, madam. The late Mistress Seymour spent a

good deal of time here."

"And did my husband spend time here with her?"

"Considerable, madam."

"He was very close to her, then?"

Sorrowfully, the old servant said, "Yes, madam. They shared a great affection."

Jane sighed raggedly. So that was it. Damon saw her use of the room as an invasion of his memory of his mother. Why hadn't he just said so? "Leave that, Simon. I've changed my mind. I'll be in my sitting room."

"Yes, madam. Shall I light a fire there, for you?"

"No. I can manage that for myself, thank you." Simon cast her a reproving glance. "I'm quite capable, Simon."

"As am I, madam," he said indignantly. "And if you will forgive my pointing it out, madam, it is hardly proper for a lady to tend her own hearth."

"*Comme il faut*, Simon."

"Madam?"

"Were he still here—and thank heaven he's not—Mr. Cullingford would say, 'It is not *comme il faut*, madam, for a lady to soil her hands by engaging in servile activity.'"

Simon struggled against his smile; Jane's mimicry of the pompous little man was flawless. "Forgive me, madam, but he would be correct in saying so."

"Balderdash! I shall lay my own fire. But I promise not to tell anyone you didn't, if you promise not to tell anyone I did."

Simon lost the battle against his smile. "Yes, madam. May I see to anything else?"

Jane looked thoughtful. "Yes, as a matter of fact, you may. You may get yourself off to bed. I'll make a plaster for your back and send Eulalia up with it."

Startled, Simon protested, "Oh, but there is no need, madam. I shall feel quite fit once the weather clears."

"You shall feel fit before that, Simon. Now, off to bed."

"Oh, madam, I really must protest. There is dinner

yet to be served, and Mr. Seymour will require my services when he—''

"Pardon me, Simon. Eulalia is more than capable of serving dinner, thanks to your tutelage, and Mr. Seymour can manage without you for one evening. I'll hear no more excuses."

"Yes, madam." Worry added another furrow to those pain and age had already etched into his brow. In forty-two years of service, he had never retired before his master. At least, not without that gentleman's consent. But then, in forty-two years of service, he had never served a mistress quite like this one.

It was well past the dinner hour when, from where she sat sewing in their sitting room, Jane heard Damon bellow for Simon, then mutter an oath when he entered his room and found it empty.

"I sent him to bed."

"You what? Why?" he demanded, appearing in the doorway.

"His lumbago was bothering him again. How is your mare?"

"His lumbago always bothers him in the damp weather. He'll be fine in a day or two."

Jane's mouth firmed and she laid her embroidery aside. "And meanwhile, you expect him to suffer through, is that it?"

"He has a job to do. Yes, I expect him to 'suffer through.' "

"Well, I don't. He could barely walk for the pain. I sent him to bed with a plaster. How is your mare?"

"Dead."

Jane gasped. "Which one?"

"Sarah."

"And the foal?"

"A colt. He looks sturdy enough."

"That's a blessing. At least you didn't lose them

both. What happened?"

"She bled to death."

Jane swallowed thickly: Women bled to death giving birth, too. Beulah Gray had. Maybe she was lucky she wasn't with child. "She was one of your best mares, wasn't she?"

Damon nodded, but said, pragmatically, "She more than repaid my investment in her. She gave me Raven's Night, and her foals always fetched a good price at auction. She did what I expected of her."

Disappearing into his room, he left Jane smarting with his implication: His mares knew their duty to him better than his wife did. And they fulfilled his expectations, even unto death. How dare he be so arrogant! It wasn't all her fault. Gilyad's Sun preformed his duty, too!

Fuming, Damon began stripping off his blood-spattered jacket and blouse. Was there nothing that didn't remind him? Even his mares were throwing it in his face, with two foals in as many days! And that letter from Marianne was undoubtedly full of "sweet Lucinda" this and "darling little Lucinda" that! How he had hoped that with the birth of Marianne's child Johanna would swallow her pride and approach him. He had given her every opportunity; he had tried to make it easy for her. But, if anything, she had withdrawn from him further, busying herself with household affairs and even nosing into life at the quarters—as if he didn't treat his people well enough! And now that Delia and Randolph were gone, she would undoubtedly spend much of her time in "that" room.

"That room," he muttered, hurling his blouse after the jacket and onto the floor. "She has no right to it!"

But even before the words were out, reason forced him to conceed that he was wrong. Raven's Oak was her home, now. Jane could do what she wished with the house. She didn't know of the bittersweet memories that room held for him. She hadn't set out to hurt him by opening it.

But still, he couldn't bear seeing her there: sitting in Pamela's chair; sewing at Pamela's embroidery frame; filling the room with life and the scent of roses as Pamela would never do again.

Bending from the waist, he shoved the painful memories away and dashed a handful of water at his face. Its chill took his breath away. But not for long. After a moment's gasping and sputtering, he roared, "Damnation!" The nerve of her, dismissing his valet! If only she took her responsibility to him as seriously!

"What's wrong?"

"What's wrong?" he parroted, turning to face his wife. "If this water was any colder, it'd freeze!"

"I'm sorry," she said, her tone as cold as the water. "I had Venus heat it for you, but that was some time ago. I didn't realize you would be so late coming in. I'll have her bring you some from my room."

"Thank you," he said stonily. "And, if it isn't too much trouble, will you have the kitchen fix me a plate of whatever you had for dinner?"

"I haven't had dinner. I waited for you."

"Why? Weren't you hungry?"

"Not especially." With a growl and a gurgle, her stomach made a liar of her.

He almost smiled. "I'll shave, then join you."

"I'll wait for you downstairs."

"Why not up here, in your new little parlor?" It was a challenge.

"Because I've decided not to use that room anymore."

Jane left before he could question her, before he could guess—or force her to admit—that she had abandoned the room to please him . . . the ingrate!

February thawed into a blustery March. A pair of

ravens nested in their ancestral tree and set about the business of raising a raucous brood. Before March had blown itself out, the ellipse before the house was carpeted with daffodils. Damon's mares increased the size of his stable by four fillies and five colts. By mid-April, the meadows and woodlands were mantling themselves in emerald green, and even virgin mares needed no coaxing when Gilyad joined them in the pasture. Spring was in the air; in the blood. April was the month for new beginnings.

"Damon? Are you awake?"

"Mmm? What?" the groggy voice on the other side of the door groaned.

"I'm sorry I woke you," Jane said, hearing the forced brightness in her voice as she stepped into his room.

Damon elbowed himself up in bed and peered at her through the misty half-light. "What time is it?"

"Nearly dawn. It's going to be a beautiful day. See?"

When she flung back a curtain, he squinted against the glare of the flat white sky. "Yuh."

"Will you take me riding this morning?"

"Riding?" He smothered a yawn with his hand.

"Yes. I haven't been out on Eclipse, yet, and I'd like you with me the first time. He's so much more spirited than my mare."

"You can handle him. I wouldn't have given him to you otherwise."

"I'm—I'm sure you're right, but I really would feel better if you were with me. And—and I thought, it being such a beautiful day, that we might take a hamper along and—and have a picnic."

"A picnic," he said flatly.

"Yes. Wouldn't that be a nice change after being shut in the house all winter?" When he hesitated, eyeing her steadily, she said, "I don't usually ask favors of you, Damon. Might you grant me this one?"

He raked his fingers through his hair from brow to

crown. "I suppose so. I'll have to have a word with Grimes before we leave."

"Yes. Yes, of course. Thank you." As she left, she turned in the doorway to say with a faltering smile, "We'll have a wonderful time. You'll see."

"Is something troubling you?" Damon asked when they were well away from the house.

"Me? No. Why?"

"You seem—preoccupied."

"Do I?"

"Decidedly. Nervous, too."

"Oh, well, that's—that's only because it's my first time out on Eclipse. He's much taller than Misty." She tossed Damon a smile and, gathering her reins into a hand, stroked the gleaming, blue-black wither near her knee. "But he's beautiful. The finest birthday gift I've ever had. Thank you, again."

"You're welcome, again." He smiled. So did she. "What shall we sing?"

"Whatever you like," she said, confident that he couldn't confound her with a tune: Cullingford may have been obnoxious, but he had been thorough.

"All right. How about this: I know a man. He has a toad. A rare toad, a juggling toad. And he keeps it in the valley." He shot her a playful sidelong glance, and Jane laughingly joined in the chorus.

But they tired of singing before they reached the meadow. Bounded by woodland, it lay in a shallow valley scooped out eons earlier by a long-since vanished glacier and shaped in more recent times by the restless meanderings of Ravenswood Creek. Jane was well pleased with her decision to come here; it was as isolated a spot as could be found on Damon's grand estate. Only the brook, the song birds and the crooning breeze broke the stillness of the place.

Damon drew rein in the shade of the trees at the

meadow's verge. "I haven't been here in years," he said, more to himself than to her.

"It's very pretty. Peaceful."

"Yes." He eyed her suspiciously. "I wasn't aware you knew the place."

"Bundy showed it to me on one of our rides. We watered the horses at the creek," she said, sounding as innocent as she was. "There's an old beaver dam. Did you know that?"

"Yes. The last time I was here, that meadow was under six feet of water. We used to swim here as boys."

"Who's we?' "

He looked at her in quick surprise. "Some of my friends and I."

"Which friends? Have I met them?"

"No."

There was a considerable lot of finality in that single, simple word. With it he ended the discussion, slammed the door to his inner self in Jane's face, and turned the key in the lock. Something inside her rebelled. She wouldn't let him lock himself away from her. Not today!

"You've never spoken of your childhood, Damon. Who were your friends?"

"It doesn't matter."

She wanted to scream, "Yes, it does! I don't want you to be a stranger to me anymore!" But all she could do was follow his lead as he kicked his horse into a canter and set off across the meadow.

By the time she drew up behind him, he had already dismounted and was tying his horse to a sapling which sprouted through the jumble of rotting logs that had once been a beaver dam. Loudly, so as to be heard above the spring flood rushing over the weatherworn barricade, she called, "Will you help me down, please?" And when he had, she implored, "Why do you always do that?"

"Do what?"

"Shut me out. Why do you always shut me out? All I asked was to know something about you. I know so very little, Damon."

"You know me as the man I am, Johanna. The boy I was does not matter." Then he led her horse to the water to drink.

Jane bit her lip and dropped her gaze. She wouldn't beg. She wouldn't! And she wouldn't let him see how much he mattered to her. Most of all, she wouldn't let him see that.

"I only thought that if your friends still live close-by, and if they're married, I might meet their wives. I'm lonely, Damon. I don't know a soul here. With Mr. Cullingford gone and you busy with the estate, I've so much empty time to fill! I thought that if I only had a—"

"Child?" he interjected adroitly.

"A friend."

She saw pain fill his eyes before he lowered them and strode past her, toward the meadow, the horses in tow. He didn't stop until he reached the long, abandoned beaver lodge, now nothing more than a grassy hillock from which a few weathered sticks jutted at rakish angles. He tied the horses, then lifted the heavy, leather pouches that contained their lunch from behind his saddle. Depositing them atop the mound, he looked back at her.

From where she still stood, Jane watched him watching her. His expression was unreadable over the distance, but she knew that if ever it was to be, it must be now. If she didn't have the courage to do what she must, if she let this moment pass . . . Slowly, she walked toward him, stopping several yards away.

The sun was warm and the breeze balmy against her face. The brook gurgled and splashed behind her, and the meadow was alive with the scents and sounds and smells of spring. But she was aware of nothing but the amber depths of his eyes, and the painful, aching tightness around her heart. Suddenly, the words that had stuck in her throat floated free and she was amazed at the ease with which she spoke them.

"I love you, Damon. That's why I want to know about you. I want to know everything about you—all there is to know. And I—I want things between us to be again the way they were at first. That's why I asked you to bring me here today. I wanted us to be alone together. I thought, maybe, you can forgive me for being so—so proud and stubborn. I thought we might—you might —You did say once that whatever a man and wife chose to do together, and whenever they choose to do it, is right." Then she took off her jaunty little riding hat and the hair she had purposefully left unconfined tumbled in golden, sun-shimmering waves over her shoulders and down her back.

Damon stared, unable to believe his eyes, afraid to believe his ears.

"If I'm not going about this properly, I'm sorry. I've never been a temptress before. I really don't know what to do. I haven't been much of a wife, either. So, since today is our wedding anniversary, and I didn't know what to give you as a remembrance of the day, I thought I could give you my love and . . . me."

She waited breathlessly for his response, terrified that he would reject her. Or worse, laugh in her face.

He did neither. But the triumph he had thought to feel at this, his victory over her, failed to materialize. Instead, he felt small, humbled by her humility. His voice strained with emotion, he said, "I've nothing so fine as that to give you."

"You are fine, Damon. You are all I want."

Jane saw the glint of a tear in the corner of his eye before he enveloped her in his arms. Holding her tight against him, he buried his lips in her fragrant, sun-warmed hair. "I love you, Jane. I love you! I've been an arrogant, stubborn fool. Forgive me. Can you forgive me?"

Her heart soaring, Jane laughed and cried all at once. "I love you. I can forgive you anything. Anything!"

He held her off from him then, and smiled into her eyes. Smoothing the tears from her cheeks with his thumbs while he blinked back his own, he murmured, "My sweet, sweet Jane." A moment later, his lips met hers.

After so many months of famine, the need to feast at love's table, to devour every morsel of the banquet offered there, was irrepressible. The world was soon lost to the lovers in their all-consuming appetite for one another, their desperate urgency to sate and be sated.

They did not see the shadowy form in the woods at the meadow's edge. They did not hear the man's harsh, rasping breathing as he watched them at their feast. Or know the jealous fury that filled him when the woman cried out her husband's name—*his* name—when she found her ecstasy in the arms of the man who had usurped it.

It was dark when they arrived home. Flaring torches lined the drive, lighting their way to the door. An agitated Simon greeted them even before the waiting groom had caught the horses' reins.

"We were becoming concerned, sir," he said, his voice reflecting his worry.

"We made a day of it," Damon said, smiling at Jane as he lifted her down from the saddle. "Just as Mistress Seymour wanted." Setting Jane on her feet and encircling her with an arm, he led her into the house. "You ought to know better than to worry over me, Simon. I know my way home."

"Yes, sir. Quite, sir. But . . . if I may have a private word with you, sir?"

"Later, Simon." With Jane still snuggled against his side, Damon began to ascend the stairs. "We will take dinner upstairs this evening. Have it sent up in an hour or so. And don't disturb us in the meanwhile."

"Forgive me, sir, but it is most urgent that I speak with you now."

Damon pivoted on a step. "What's so urgent that it can't wait an hour?"

Simon's eyes darted to Jane, then quickly back to Damon. "Were it unimportant, sir, I would not insist."

Damon heaved an irritated sigh. "Very well. Wait for me in the study."

"Thank you, sir," Simon said, his relief as evident as his concern had been.

Seeing the man gone, Damon smiled apologetically at Jane. "I'll not be long, love." He kissed her softly, then straightened to ask with a playful glint in his eye, "Or have you had enough of me for one day?"

"I'll never have enough of you."

He grinned. "Just what I wanted to hear."

"And, suppose I'd had enough. What would you do then?" she teased.

"Change your mind!"

When he moved to kiss her again, Jane reluctantly turned her face away. "Simon's waiting."

"Let him wait."

"But if you see what he wants now, we'll have the rest of the night all to ourselves."

"We have the rest of our *lives* all to ourselves," he said, reaching for her lips again.

"All the more reason to give Simon his few minutes now," she said pragmatically. He scowled. "And while you're busy with Simon, I'll dismiss Venus for the night and . . ." Her hands slipped lightly over the fabric of his lapels to rest on his shoulders. Standing on tiptoe, she whispered something in his ear, then pulled back to smile a secret smile.

"Damn," he swore softly. "For a woman new to seduction, you are incredibly good at it!" He kissed her again, hard, before reluctantly releasing her.

Jane was flushed and giddy with happiness when she entered her room to find Venus laying out her evening attire.

"Oh, ma'am, you's safe!" the slave cried happily.

"Of course, I'm safe. Whatever could have happened to me?"

"I don't know, ma'am, but they wuz talking like something awful might've."

"Who was talking?" Jane asked, too preoccupied with her happiness to care what the woman's answer might be. Damon loved her! Nothing mattered but that. Pulling off her hat and shaking down her hair, Jane sighed blissfully and settled before her dressing table, letting Venus's chatter eddy in the background of her mind.

"Oswald and Simon. They's had their heads together, whispering and worrying, this whole afternoon. 'Course, they don't tell me nothing. Eulalia, she's the one talks to me. But she wuz too busy frettin' over Opal to . . . Lordy, ma'am! You's got a mess in your hair!"

"What did you say?"

"I say, you's got a mess o' grass and leaves all tangled up in your hair. Lordy, ma'am, did you fall off your horse?"

Jane blushed. "No. What was that you said about Opal?"

Putting down the brush in favor of the comb, Venus began working its ivory teeth through Jane's hair. "I say, Eulie wuz too busy frettin' over Opal to pay me mind today."

"Oh, dear. What's Opal done now?"

"That chile," Venus said with a wag of her head, "she done run off."

"Ran off!" Jane yelped, half turning in her chair and looking up at the woman.

"Yes'um. But that's all right, they found her. She's

fine now, ma'am."

"Thank goodness." Jane turned around again and, watching Venus's face in the mirror, asked, "Why did she run away?"

"Best as I can understand, ma'am, she left some door open that wuz s'posed to be closed, and she done run off to spare her hide a tannin'."

"What door?"

"That I don't know, ma'am. Even Milred wouldn't say. But I expect that's what put Oswald and Simon in such a dither."

"She ran off when it was discovered, sir. Ezra found her hiding in the potting shed."

His face ashen with shock, Damon said, "But you have not found *him*?"

"No, sir. In your absence, I took it upon myself to instruct Grimes to instigate a search. I did not think you would want anyone else involved, sir."

"No. What did he discover?"

"Nothing, sir. We have no idea in which direction he may have gone." Damon raked his hair with his fingers, then sank into the chair behind his desk. "May I bring you a brandy, sir?"

"No. Let me think." After a moment, he asked, "Did Grimes go to the lodge?"

"No, sir. He made discrete inquiry in Rendell and Reistertown. No one had seen him."

"What was he wearing? How was he dressed?"

"I laid out a black suit and dove waistcoat for him this morning, sir. I presume he is wearing them." Fondly, the old valet added, "He has always taken care with his appearance, sir."

"And he took no other clothing with him?"

"No, sir."

"You're certain?"

"Quite, sir."

Damon straightened in his chair and ran his lean fingers under the desk top. When the hidden latch released, a small panel above the kneehole opened and Damon withdrew two keys.

"Good heaven, sir, that never occurred to me!"

"Let's hope it didn't occur to him, either," Damon said, fitting the larger key into a locked drawer, then lifting out the strong box. It thumped as he set it on the blotter to apply the smaller key to its lock. After a quick but thorough inventory of the box's contents, Damon sighed. "It appears he is without funds. And afoot?"

"I—I presume so, sir. He did not request a mount from the stables. However, the horses had been turned out to pasture before he left, sir. It is quite possible he took one of them."

"No gentleman rides bareback. Not without attracting undue attention. That is something I should think he would want to avoid, at least until he is well clear of here."

"Then he cannot have gone far, sir."

"He's gone to Baltimore," Damon said quietly, conclusively. "To the bank. Or he will." After locking the box and replacing it in the drawer, he secreted the spare keys away again and stood. "I'll go there myself tonight. If I'm lucky, I'll reach Mr. Hamilton before he does."

"Yes, sir. I shall pack you a valise."

"Wait. What the devil was Opal doing up there in the first place? And where was Amos?"

"Eulalia thought to spare herself the trip upstairs with his breakfast tray, sir, and sent Opal with it instead. The child has been so much more tractable and responsible since Madam's arrival, sir, that Oswald saw no reason to object."

"And Amos?"

Simon cleared his throat uncomfortably. "He spent the night in the quarters, sir, and was late arriving at the house this morning."

"Damn!" Damon bellowed, slamming a clenched fist on the desk. "He knows how I feel about that! After the episode with Flygher, they all do! Those women are not harlots!"

"I do not think it was a case of . . . *that*, sir. Amos and Carolina have an understanding. She is carrying his child, sir."

Damon's outrage quieted. "I see."

"Might I ask, sir, what you intend telling Madam? I do not wish to contradict you, should she question me concerning your absence, sir."

Damon allowed himself a small smile. "Does she do that, Simon? Does she ask after me?"

"Yes, sir. Madam seems, if I may say so, quite fond of you, sir."

Damon's smile broadened. "Yes. I know." Then, turning away, he soberly answered the man's question. "I'll tell her I have urgent business in Baltimore. I see no reason for her to know more than that."

"But she is liable to hear something of what has happened, sir. The incident with Opal at the very least."

"I leave it to you, Simon, to see that she doesn't." He faced the man. "I'll pack for myself. See that Gilyad is saddled for me."


Jane smiled at the image the hand mirror threw back to her and gave the red satin bow in her hair a final, admiring pat. She had been saving it to wear on a special occasion, and what more special occasion could there be than the return of her husband to her bed? Laying the mirror next to the lighted candle on the bed-side, she thought of all the nights she had spent dreaming of this moment: of all the hours she had lain here, aching for him, knowing that he was too proud to come to her, and that she was too stubborn to go to him. But no more. That was all behind her now. She wouldn't think about it. She would think, instead, of all the nights ahead: of all the times when, as they had this afternoon, they would share not only their bodies, but their hearts.

Giving vent to an impatient little sigh, she plumped the pillows behind her back, swept her hair over her shoulders to demurely cover her breasts, then folded her hands in her lap and waited. And while she waited for him to come and give her new memories to treasure, she gave herself over to the vivid, fresh memories of their loving in the meadow. She heard him moving about in his room—the opening and closing of drawers; the ceramic clatter of his shaving mug—for some time before he finally appeared in her doorway. But when he did, her joyful smile faded into an awkward one.

"You're dressed to go out."

"I have business in Baltimore, love. I'm sorry."

"Now? You've business there now? At this hour?"

"I'm afraid so. Yes."

Disappointment, like some wild rabid creature, nipped at her heart with razor-sharp teeth. The pain brought tears to her eyes, and she turned her face away. "You haven't even had dinner."

She felt the bed give under his weight, and he reached out a hand to stroke her neck. "I've not had something I want very much more than dinner."

"Then, have that before you go," she begged him softly.

Resolutely, he shook his head. "There's no time, love. I must be off now."

"But it will take you hours to get to Baltimore," she snapped. "What sort of business can you transact in the middle of the night?" When he looked at her in annoyance but offered no answer, she changed her tactic. Kneeling before him and wrapping her arms lightly about her neck, she said, "And what if I won't let you go?"

In deadly earnest, he said, "You'll likely awaken

tomorrow to find yourself married to a pauper."

He saw shock register on her face, but then she held his solemn, worried eyes and said, "I wouldn't mind."

And he knew she meant it. "I would." He fingered the ribbon in her hair. "I want to give you everything your heart desires, Jane."

"You already have."

When they kissed, he knew she meant that, too.

From the window, Jane watched his horse canter off into the night and caught the quick, furtive darting of something—a fox, she supposed—beneath the trees in the ellipse before she let the lace curtain fall back into place. Then, staring glumly at her lonely bed, she listlessly pulled the festive ribbon from her hair.

She didn't know what had awakened her as she lay listening in the dark room, her senses alive with warning. An owl hooted nearby, and the sitting room clock chimed half past some hour, but there was no other sound, save that of her heart hammering in her ears. It must have been the owl, she decided, letting the breath she had unconsciously held escape in a rush of a sigh. Flopping onto her stomach, she hugged the pillow and, thinking of Damon, tried to recapture sleep. But the soft rustle of the straw beneath the carpet alarmed her again.

"Who's there? Venus?" A soft, manly chuckle was her answer. "Damon! Oh, Damon, you're home!" she cried ecstatically, rolling over to face him as he joined her in the bed. "What made you change your mind and come back?"

"You," he said in a harsh whisper.

"Will we be paupers in the morning?" she asked, not caring.

He said nothing, only swept the bedclothes from her. Her skin prickled with excitement and the touch of the cool night air. But when he lay down beside her, Jane wrinkled her nose: He reeked of rum. "I didn't know you liked rum. I've never seen you drink it."

His chuckled throatily and reached for her in the blackness. His hand found the curve of her hip, and he pushed her onto her back.

Running her hands up his cotton-clad arms to his shoulders, Jane said in surprise, "You didn't even take off your shirt."

But when she groped in the blackness for the buttons, thinking to remove it for him, he straddled her and caught her wrists, forcing her arms up and back until they were pinioned to the pillow on either side of her head. Braced on the arms that held her captive, he levered her legs apart with his and lowered himself between them, probing at her cruelly and bruising her tender flesh with the battering ram of his maleness.

Shocked, confused, and frightened, Jane arched her hips away. "Damon, don't. Please. You're hurting me!"

He paid her no mind but brutally took what she would gladly, eagerly have given, had he but asked.

Horror-stricken, Jane lay rigid and sobbing while the man who had taught her that love was a delight to be shared selfishly used her. And when he was sated, he left her abruptly, throwing himself from the bed with a cruel, jeering laugh that followed him toward his room.

For a long time she lay there, feeling betrayed and hurt and degraded, her sobs shaking the bed, her tears drenching the pillow as she tried to excuse his behavior. It was the rum, she told herself. The rum had made him act that way. But deep inside, she knew there could be no excusing what he had done. The words her heart had spoken only half a day before, "I love you. I can forgive you anything," now tasted bitter in her mouth.

"Morning, ma'am," Venus said, bustling into the room with Jane's cup of morning tea.

Jane ignored the offered cup and turned her tear-reddened eyes away.

"It ain't like you not to take your tea, ma'am. Are you feelin' poorly?"

"Just put it down and leave me alone," Jane snapped, snatching her robe from the foot of the bed and throwing it on as she stood.

"Yes'um." But Venus went only as far as the door, then turned troubled eyes on her mistress. "Don't you want me to help you dress, ma'am?"

"I want you to leave me alone!"

Venus stood her ground, torn between obedience and devotion. After a lengthy pause, she said quietly, "No'um." Shocked, Jane turned her tear-ravaged face on the woman. "They tells me not to worry you with what happened last night, ma'am. Not to tell you about the man that come in this house and tore up Massah's study. But you already knows about him, don't you, ma'am? He come up here to you," Venus said, tears sparking her eyes. "He done help hisself to more'n just Massah's liquor 'fore he left this house, didn't he, ma'am?"

Jane stared at the woman in mute horror. Then, for the space of a heartbeat, she felt a joyous surge of relief: It hadn't been Damon! But, if not Damon, then . . . "Oh, dear God," she whispered, trembling hands pressed to her mouth. "I thought he was Damon!"

It was well into the forenoon when the sound of a horse in the drive below roused Jane from her stupor and her bed. Through the lace of the curtain, she saw Simon greet his master. Then, with an air of urgency, both men disappeared into the house.

Her stomach churned sickeningly. What would she say to him? When he came to her tonight, he would know something was wrong. He would expect her to be eager for him. She couldn't be! The thought of being touched in that way again repulsed her. Yet, he would come, he would expect . . . And she could never tell him the truth. Never. He would despise her if he knew. For all that it made him a hypocrite—having once kept a mistress, himself—he despised loose women. And that was what she was now. She had broken her marriage vow. She had welcomed a strange man into her bed. She had *welcomed* him!

"What am I going to do, Venus?" she fairly groaned. "I can't face him. I can't face him after what I've done!"

"You didn't do nothin', ma'am," Venus said, laying aside her mending. "Most especially, you didn't do nothin' bad. That man, *he* the bad one. *You* didn't do nothin'!"

"But I did! I let him—" Unable to go on, Jane turned away.

"No'um, you didn't. He done *took* what he wanted from you. But Massah, he gonna make that man pay! He ain't gonna mind a couple o' bottles of his liquor being stole, but when he finds out that man come up here to you, he's gonna—"

"No! No! He must never know. Never!"

"But, ma'am, you gots to tell him, ma'am, so's he can make that man pay!"

"That man. *That* man!" Jane cried. "And just who was he, Venus? Does anyone know?"

"Not so as I heard 'em say, ma'am," the maid admitted miserably.

"Then what point is there in telling Damon anything! There is no one for him to pay back!" Jane willed herself to a semblance of composure. "Help me dress. Quickly. He'll know something's wrong if he finds me in my dressing gown so late in the day."

Silently, Venus did as she was told. But while she put the finishing touches on Jane's hair, she could hold her tongue no longer. Shattering the strained silence between them, she asked, "Can I say something, ma'am?"

"So long as you don't try to change my mind."

"No'um."

"What, then?"

Venus hesitated. "I knows it ain't my place to be trying to tell you how to think, ma'am. I knows that. But I been 'most the same place you is now, ma'am." Jane stared at the woman's reflection in mute horror as Venus quietly continued, "Not exactly the same, ma'am, 'cause I knowed who the man was. But still, I daren't say so to nobody. I had to carry the hurt of what he done to me around inside without letting on it was there, same as you, ma'am. And maybe, if you was to tell yourself what I told me, it help you some."

"What did you tell yourself, Venus?" Jane said in a barely audible whisper.

"It didn't seem right to me, ma'am, that I should worry on what happened when the man, he put it outta his mind as soon as it was done. So, I say to myself: 'He done hurt me. He done hurt me bad. But I ain't gonna let him go on hurting me by thinking on it. I ain't gonna let him hurt me no more!' Then I buries that hurt he done me in the deepest, blackest part of my mind, and when it start to rise up outta there, I made myself think hard on something else. After a time, ma'am, that got easier to do."

Their eyes met in the mirror then, and Jane raised a fair hand to the dark one near her shoulder. "Thank you, Venus."

And as their fingers entwined, each knew that a bond had been forged between them; they would never again be merely mistress and slave.

Damon inspected the shattered lock and ran a finger along a deep gouge in the liquor cabinet door. From behind him, Simon said quietly, "He applied the fire poker to excellent avantage, sir."

"So I see." Letting his eyes rove the room, he took in the evidence of the previous night's debacle. Although the chairs and tables Simon had reported as overturned had been righted, the breakage had been extensive: shattered vases; smashed alabaster busts of Homer and Plato; broken enameled hearth dogs; and torn paintings in their shattered frames. The desk and floor were still liberally stained with ink from the overturned well, and the draperies hung rakishly on their broken rods. "And none of you heard this?" he asked, incedulously.

"Our rooms are in the attic, sir," Simon defended rationally, but with apology in his tone.

"Johanna's room is not in the attic!"

"Madam heard nothing, sir. Venus has assured me."

"How much does Venus know?"

"Only that an intruder made off with some of your stock liquor and set your study topsy-turvy in an unsuccessful effort to discover valuables. It is what Mildred and the rest in the kitchen believe as well, sir. Oswald, of course, knows better. As I told you, sir, it was she who discovered him here, insensible from the rum, and immediately summoned me."

"And no one else saw him. You're certain?"

Simon nodded. "With the exception of Amos, who returned him to his room, no one, sir."

"He damaged no other rooms?"

"None, sir."

"Only mine. He destroyed only what was mine. Dear God, how he must despise me!" Damon said, more to himself than to the butler.

"He is not rational, sir. You must not hold him accountable for his actions."

Meeting the man's eyes steadily, Damon said with quiet conviction, "He can be as rational as you or I, Simon. Cannot you understand? *That* is what makes him the dangerous lunatic he is!" Turning away, he said, "I want him shackled."

"Oh, sir! You cannot!"

"What I cannot do, Simon, is run the risk of this happening again! I want him shackled. See to it. And tell

Amos I will speak with him this evening regarding the plans for the lodge we discussed last spring. I should never have postponed . . . Johanna."

"Am I intruding?"

"No, of course not." He saw her eyes dart past him and around the room. "Why don't we go into the drawing room and leave Simon to tidy things up."

"What happened?" she asked, feigning the ignorance she knew was expected of her.

"An intruder. It seems that he was trying to discover my strong box."

"Did he?"

"No. Shall we go?" Damon urged, cupping her elbow in a hand and turning her back out into the hall where he hesitated only long enough to say over his shoulder, "You *will* see to that other matter for me, won't you?" Then he hurried Jane away.

"An intruder, you said?" Jane asked, her trembling no sham.

"Yes. But he's long gone now, love. You've nothing to fear. I promise you, he won't be back."

Her heart in her throat, she asked, "He's been caught? Arrested?" Dear Heaven, what would she do if the man spoke out? Then everyone would know. Everyone!

"No."

Relieved of one fear, she was assailed by another. "Then how can you know he won't be back?"

"I'll give him no opportunity."

"But you aren't always here! Suppose he comes back while you're away, again? Suppose he comes upstairs looking for . . . for my jewels?"

Damon felt himself blanch. Turning her to him more roughly than he meant to, he demanded, "Did he? Did he last night?"

"No. No! But he . . ." Forcefully dragging herself back from the brink of the truth, Jane finished shakily.

"He might have. He might have! And the next time, he might—"

"There will be no next time, love. I promise you. I promise." And he gathered her to him and held her close. "You are the dearest thing in life to me, Jane. Do you think I would allow any harm to come to you?"

Enveloped in his arms, surrounded by his strength and warmth and the comfortably familiar and safe scent of him, it would have been so easy for her to sob out the truth. But she bit back the words that filled her mouth and refused to give way to tears; once loosed, there would be no stopping them.

"Here," he said, holding her away from him. "I brought you something."

"A gift?" she asked, forcing herself to return his smile.

"A gift."

And while he slipped a hand into his pocket, she asked, "Does this mean we aren't paupers?"

He chuckled. "As far from it as ever we were. Hold out your hand. No, no, the left one." Taking her hand in his, he slipped the oversized wedding ring from her finger and replaced it with a new one. "It has an inscription: 'To Jane, ever my love' and it is signed with my initials. Promise me you will never take it off."

Her eyes on the wide, gold band around her finger, she murmured, "I promise." Then, throwing her arms about him, she wept throatily against his chest. "Oh, Damon! I love you so!"

# 10

Jane pushed the untouched breakfast tray away and, gulping down a surge of nausea, fell back against her pillows. "Take it, Venus. I can't eat."

"You gots to eat something, ma'am. Just a sip of tea and a bit of . . . Oh, lordy, ma'am! Not on the bed!"

A napkin clasped to her mouth, Jane bolted for the basin in her dressing room. Venus was hot on her heels.

"Oh, ma'am," Venus crooned sympathetically, hugging Jane's shoulders as she wretched over the bowl.

"Where's Damon?" Jane gasped.

"'Don't you worry. He long gone about his business." Dipping a hand towel into the cool water in the pitcher, Venus dabbed at Jane's temples. "You can't keep this from him much longer, ma'am. He gots to know about it sometime."

With the nausea passed, Jane turned and headed back to bed.

"Why don't you just tells him, ma'am?" Venus persisted, rushing ahead of her mistress to smooth back the sheet and fluff the pillows. "He gonna be as proud as a rooster, knowing he got you with child."

"Did he, Venus?" Jane said, her voice stone cold. "Did *he* do that?"

"Don't you say that, ma'am. Don't you even think it! 'Course he did!"

"Don't tell me what to say and think! It's not your place!"

Hurt rampant in her eyes, Venus turned quickly away.

"Oh, Venus, I'm sorry. I'm sorry. I don't mean to take it out on you."

"No'um, you's right. Ain't my place to be telling you," she said, busily plumping a pillow. "I just can't hold my tongue when I sees you hurting, that's all. This ought to be a happy time for you and Massah. But that man, that wicked man, he done spoilt it! Don't seem fair this child come now when you can't be sure!"

"Hush, Venus!" Jane said in a desperate whisper. Then, dashing to the sitting room door, she flung it wide with the air of one expecting to catch an eavesdropper in the act. But the sitting room was empty and there was no sound from the room beyond. Turning back to the woman, she said in a low voice. "We must never speak of this again. Never! Do you understand?"

"Yes'um." But Venus broke her vow in the same breath. "But it got to be Massah's child, ma'am. You been with him every night since then. It *gots* to be his!"

Closing the door behind her and with a resolve she didn't know she had, Jane said, "Even if it isn't, Damon will *make* it his. He'll give it his name and he'll raise it and love it. And there won't be anyone to take that father's pride away from him. Not anyone! Not ever!"


"Is this where you want 'em, Mistress?"

"Yes. Oh, yes, that will be perfect. Thank you, Ezra."

The negro grounds keeper, one of Damon's freedmen, deposited the flat of marigolds at the edge of the garden path. "You sure has prettied up the place, ma'am. I don't recall it ever looking so nice," he said with an approving glance at the new garden.

"Why, thank you. That's a generous compliment, considering that it was you who did all the work. All I did was tell you what to put where."

The man grinned. "I can't take no credit, ma'am. Takes a good eye for color and the like to lay out a pretty garden. You's got that, ma'am. All I's got is a strong back."

Jane smiled up at the affable young man. He had a strong back, no question, and arms and chest to match. It was no wonder he had caught Venus's admiring eye. "What do you think about putting some cockscomb around the base of the sundial and more iris near the myrtle tree?"

"In amongst the forget-me-nots?" Jane nodded. "Oh, that'd be real nice, ma'am. Real nice!"

"Is it too late in the season to sow another bed with everlastings?"

"No, ma'am. If I shade 'em from the sun for a bit, they ought to come up all right."

"Oh, good. Will you put them in just along that path, where I'll be able to cut them easily?"

"Yes, ma'am."

"And asters. My cousin suggested that I might put in asters for color in the fall. Will they do well here?"

"Asters do well most anywheres, ma'am. Trouble is, we ain't never had 'em here so I don't have no seed."

"Mistress Drake sent me a packet from her own garden. I'll have Venus bring them out to you later." The man's reaction to Venus's name—and the prospect of spending time, however brief, in her company—was predictable. Cupid's arrows took no note of the color of a man's skin. "We'll put them over there, I think," Jane said, giving Ezra a moment to regain his wits, "as color against that hedge."

"Yes, ma'am. And by the time they's blooming, that oughtta be starting to look like a hedge, too."

Jane laughed. "I leave it to you to see that it does."

Still smiling, she turned away, inhaling deeply of the morning air.

A stroll never failed to dispel any lingering queasiness. She had no doubt that she would feel fine by supper, until teatime when the nausea would assail her again. She really couldn't keep it from Damon much longer. It was a wonder he hadn't noticed already. But then, he had been busy overseeing the clearing and planting of new acreage in wheat. He left the house early, each morning, often without awakening her. Thankfully, the afternoon sickness was not so bad as the morning, and Jane could usually quiet her stomach with a cup of peppermint tea.

Jane heaved a sigh and picked a faded lilac blossom from a bush as she passed. Thankful as she was that her husband left early, she did miss his waking her up. He did that so very nicely!

Suddenly throwing it down, she ground the blossom into the dirt of the path with her toe. Why couldn't she think of one without remembering the other! "Dear God," she beseeched silently, "why can't I forget? It's been weeks; months!"

Without conscious effort, her mind tallied two months, two weeks and four days. Or was it five days? She wouldn't try to figure it out. She would forget, let the days go uncounted and soon—please, God, soon— she would lose track of the weeks, then the months, then maybe . . . But over the hopeful reasonings of her head, her heart cried, *You'll never forget. There will be the child to remind you.*

Leaving the path, she bolted across the neatly scythed lawn bordering her garden, trying to out- distance her thoughts. Beyond the tended lawns, where the grass grew tall and wild and the dew soaked her shoes and dampened her skirt hem, she quickened her pace, running until her side ached and her throat was dry, until she had exorcised the ugliness from her mind.

It was only when she stopped, breathless, beside a waist-high stone wall that she realized how far she had come. Leaning heavily against the wall's smoothly rounded coping, she stared at the graves on the other side. Damon had brought her near here once, pointing out the spot with the bone-chilling explanation: "Our future resting place." But he had softened the remark with a smile, adding, "But not for a very long while yet, I trust."

Judging from the overgrown condition of the graves, Damon was not the only one on the estate to eschew the family plot. Apparently, even Ezra gave the place short shrift. Not that Jane blamed any of them. Cemeteries were not among her favorite places to be, either. But the condition of this one was appalling. Grasses, weeds, and even brambles grew in wild disarray, almost completely obscuring some of the smaller headstones and rambling up and over the taller ones. If flowers had once been cultivated on the graves, they had long since been smothered by weeds. How had Damon allowed this to happen? Where was his respect for the dead? He festooned his hallways with their likenesses, but let their final resting place fall to ruin. Such hypocrisy!

Pulling the iron gate open as far as its complaining, rusted hinges would allow, Jane gingerly squeezed through the narrow gap. Stepping to a headstone all but hidden by weeds, she brushed aside the lush tangle to reveal a child's grave. With a disgusted sigh, she raised her eyes to the tall, granite obelisk which dominated that section of the field and bore the deeply etched inscription:

Bertram Renwick Seymour
Beloved Husband and Father
Resting in Eternal Peace and with
The Sure and Certain Hope of the Resurrection

1688-1765

"Quite some poor example you set your son in the matter of proper respect, sir!" she said boldly. Then she dropped to her knees beside the grave of the half-brother who had not lived to know Damon.

Her gloves were grass-stained and filthy, and her skirt not much cleaner when she sat back on her haunches to eye her handiwork. Satisfied that she had done all she could without benefit of scythe, shears, and trowel, she set to work clearing the other markers in that row. Divesting the four remaining headstones of their burden of neglect—those of the first Mrs. Bertram Seymour and three more of her children—she then moved on to another row. There she cleared Damon's mother's grave; that of a sister who had died in infancy; and the grave of his brother, who had been about three when Damon was born, but who had died the following year.

Pulling off her ruined gloves and tossing them on a pile of weeds, Jane eyed the eight tombstones thoughtfully. It struck her as odd—sad, of course, but primarily odd—that having come from such apparently hardy, Seymour stock, only one of Bertram's seven children had survived to adulthood. Was there some inherent weakness in the family? Would *she* bury child after child here? Her heart surging with the first stirring of maternal love, Jane laid a protective hand over her still flat belly. But *this* child might not be a Seymour at all. There may be hope!

For an instant, her fledgling mother's heart soared. Then its burden of guilt sent it plummeting. Better to die and be Damon's child, than to live and be a . . . The ugly word, the word she had never even dared to think before, oozed with a vile hiss from the pit of her mind: bastard.

But it wouldn't be that, she argued within herself. It would be Damon's. He would make it his. And, no matter who the father, it would be hers. She would love it. If she expected to keep her own doubts from infecting Damon, she must love it! Surely, that would not be so hard. Surely, once it was born . . .

Thus preoccupied, Jane stood and walked to the grave which was set apart from the others, as if waiting for the space between to be filled. With its shroud of vegetation removed, the headstone revealed a girl's name surrounded by a dainty scrollwork of vines and flowers which was being lifted heavenward by a spread-winged angel.

Another lost daughter, Jane thought, dusting off her hands and standing to leave. She had turned away before the remainder of the stone's inscription touched her consciousness. Pivoting sharply on a heel, she read it again.

Pamela Merrick Seymour
Adored Wife
1743-1766

"Wife? Whose wife?" Jane puzzled aloud. Certainly not Damon's father's. He had had only two, and she had found the graves of both of them. And, just as surely, not Damon's. So whose?

Staring down at the marker, Jane decided the only possible explanation was that Damon had had a brother, and that Pamela had been *his* "Adored Wife." And she eyed the expectantly empty space between the young wife's grave and the others, which was, of course, the logical place for Pamela's husband to be. Why wasn't he there? He *must* be dead.

Perhaps he had died far from home, she thought, mulling the problem over as she paced absently toward the gate. That happened, sometimes. Back home in Virginia, Jack Kruger had gone off to fight the French and the Indians, and he had been buried where he fell. But, even so, his widow had put up a cenotaph: It was the loving thing to do. That was what Mamá and Papá had done, too, when Trevor's ship went down and his body was lost to the sea.

Jane stopped. Who was Trevor? And she had never in her life called anyone "Mamá" and "Papá!"

Her mind's eye was suddenly glutted with shifting impressions, like juxtaposed fragments of shattered dreams: A slender, mannish silhouette against the sun, a golden aura about its head. Smiling blue eyes, laughing dimples. Shuttered windows. Black ribbon tied 'round a gentleman's sleeve. A woman weeping.

And voices inside her head asked and answered: "Is she truly mine, Trevor? Is she truly mine?"

"All your own, sunshine. And she's a fine pup. What will you name her?"

Then, "Why is it dark, Mama? Why are you crying?"

"Trevor is gone."

"He'll be back, Mama, when he's done with school."

"No, my dear. He has gone to heaven to be with the angels."

Then Jane felt a pang of sorrow so sharp, it took her breath away. Close on its heels and with frightening vividness, she felt the suffocating closeness of a house drowning in mourning.

"Ma'am? Are you all right, ma'am? Mistress Seymour?"

"Wh—what? Oh. Oh, Bundy. I . . . I didn't see you there."

"No, ma'am. You were . . . off somewheres." Bundy swung easily out of his saddle. "Are you feeling all right?"

"Yes. Yes, of course," Jane said breathily, walking unsteadily toward the gate which Bundy yanked open another foot.

"I, ah, I wouldn't have intruded but that you got this

sorta queer look on your face all of a sudden. I thought you might be sick or something."

"No. I'm fine. Thank you," she said, regaining some of her composure and edging through the gate. But her thoughts were still focused inward. She had walked some way back toward the house before she realized that Bundy was pacing along beside her. It was all but impossible to rid her mind of the strange sense of other-worldliness she was still experiencing, so she absently asked, "How have you been, Bundy?"

"Just fine, ma'am. Just fine."

"I, ah, I understand the mares kept you busy this spring. Nine new foals, was it?"

"Yes, ma'am. And we bred eleven more."

Jane smiled wanly. "Then you'll be busy next spring, too, won't you?"

"Yes, ma'am, I expect so."

Conversation died, and Bundy cast desperately about for something, anything that would revive it. "How's that new gelding working out for you?"

"Wonderfully well."

"What was it you named him?"

"Eclipse."

"Eclipse. That's a fancy name. But then, he's a right fancy horse."

"Yes. Yes, he is."

An invisible barrier of silence walled them off from each other again. Still fighting to free herself from the disturbing workings of her mind, Jane didn't notice. And Bundy, for all that he wanted to batter it down, could find nothing sensible to say.

He had never had trouble talking to her before. But now she had changed. She was a bona fide lady now, more of a woman, too. Not that he was surprised by that. He had watched her change; he had strained for glimpses of her all through the fall and winter, when she had kept mostly to the house. He had done some pretty fancy stepping to catch sight of her in there! But that new glass door Seymour had put in the music room had helped. He had been able to see her playing her little piano a few times. And one night, when he thought he would die for want of a look at her, he had stood outside one long, dining room window, carefully keeping to the snowy shadows, and watched her take her supper. He had seen her smile down the table at the man at the other end, and had wished she were smiling at him. He had heard her laugh and had remembered that, last summer, she had laughed with him. But when she had rung her china bell to call the servants . . . that had put him in his place, right enough. He had gone back to his room over the stables feeling lower than when he had left it. And when he had dreamt of her that night, she had been laughing and ringing her little bell, while he had been dancing to her tune.

Bundy had tried to keep away from the house after that; he'd tried to get her out of his mind. But just about then, Mr. Seymour had seemed unable to do without him. Wanting his foremanly advice on this or that new scheme or improvement, the man had nearly worn Bundy's legs to nubs, summoning him up to the house for meetings. He had never walked into that rock-walled tomb of a house without a flurry in his stomach for knowing that she was there, too. His dreams turned fanciful after that; always on the theme of the valorous knight rescuing his fair damsel.

And then spring arrived, and she started going out more. He often saw her riding with Seymour, looking even more beautiful in the flesh than in his dreams.

Again, he had tried to stay clear of her. But, like iron to a lodestone, he was helplessly drawn to her.

Today she was lucky he had been around. No telling how long she might have stood there in the midday sun with that haunted look on her face. Damn Seymour!

What had he done to her? What had he done to send her stalking through the graveyard?

Staring at the reins in his hands, Bundy turned and tossed them over his horse's neck. "I guess I ought to be getting back to work. That is, if you'll be all right walking the rest of the way back by yourself?"

"I'll be fine, thank you, Bundy. I know you must be busy, and I don't want to keep you from anything important."

He wanted to say, "I'll never be so busy that I wouldn't take time to be with you." But he said only a quiet, "Yes, ma'am," and swung into the saddle.

"It's been good seeing you again, Bundy," Jane said, smiling and feeling more herself. "I'm sorry if I was rude. It's just that being out there . . ." She glanced back at the cemetery. "It was—unsettling."

"I reckon it would be. I'd sooner not know where I'll be planted." He smiled, too. But he was struck by how strange it was to be looking down at her from the back of a horse, yet to feel as though he was looking up. With a brusque, "Day to you, ma'am," and a tip of his hat, he wheeled his horse and cantered off.

"Goodness, Opal, you're undoing all the good you've done, waving the duster about like that," Jane chastised mildly, entering the house through the music room.

"Yes, ma'am," she said, continuing to flail the dust-laden feathers lackadaisically about.

"Opal!"

"Yes, ma'am?"

"Nevermind. Here. Take these flowers into the kitchen for me and tell Oswald they are for the dinner table."

"Yes, ma'am." Tucking the duster under an arm, Opal scuffed across the carpet and accepted the bouquet.

"Where are your shoes?"

"I takes 'em off."

"Do they hurt your feet?"

"No, ma'am."

"Have you soiled them?" Opal wagged her head and studied her mud-brown toes. "Then, why did you take them off?"

"You knows why, ma'am."

"And *you* know that Mr. Seymour expects you to wear shoes in the house."

Miserable, Opal murmured a barely audible, "Yes, ma'am."

Jane cupped the girl's chin in a hand and raised her face. "You like the feel of the carpet so well, do you?" The dark head in her hand nodded. "Shall we strike a bargain, Opal, you and I?" Another nod, this one more cautious. "Very well. I will agree to find you a bit of carpet all for your own, to put by your pallet. You can scuff in it to your heart's content, if—*if* mind you—you will agree to wear your shoes around the house. Do you understand the terms of our bargain?"

"Yes, ma'am."

"And do you promise to keep your part if I keep mine?"

"Oh, yes, ma'am!"

"Very well, then. It's agreed. Off you go with the flowers then, before they wilt."

"That was no bargain, that was bribery," Damon chuckled from just outside the garden door as the child scampered for the kitchen.

Startled, Jane spun on a heel. "What are you doing home so early? I thought you would be out all day."

"Well, that's a fine welcome if ever I heard one," he said, greeting her with a kiss. But he held her off from him quickly and wiped at her dusty nose with a fingertip. "Good heaven, what have you been up to?"

"Oh, ah, I was weeding," she said, hating the half-truth but not sure he would approve of the whole one.

"Weeding? Should a lady in your delicate condition be doing something so strenuous?"

Jane gaped at him and could find only enough voice to say, "How'd you know?"

Insouciantly cocking a brow, he parried, "How did you?" Then, he grinned. "When do we expect the blessed event, love?"

"Ah, January. Toward the end."

"Well," he said, his smile fading and holding her hands as lightly as if they were porcelain. He gave her a brief barely-there embrace, a peck on the cheek, and quickly released her again. Worry in his eyes, he said, "I've some matters to see to before supper. I'll join you at table."

Though she nodded and, by sheer force of will, kept her smile fixed, she found herself battling an awful fear: Did he know? Had he guessed? Did he have secret doubts of his own?

Later, she was "borrowing" Opal a small rug from the seldom used guest room in the family wing, with that fear still heavy on her heart, when Damon bellowed from his room across the hall, "I said no, Simon!"

"But it is inevitable that she know sooner or later, sir. And there is the question of," Simon cleared his throat brusquely, "the child's legitimacy; of the validity of your marriage."

"Don't you think I know that!"

Jane felt her heart stop. What were they talking about? What were they saying!

"It is not merely a question of being cognizant of the state of affairs, sir, but of taking remedial action."

"All in good time, Simon. The child will be christened Seymour, regardless of the legalities, and that will suffice," Damon growled. Then he chuckled humorlessly and added, "When one's family tree is rooted in bastardy, one small, rotten branch more or less hardly matters.''

Dazedly, Jane crossed the hall to numbly demand, ''What are you talking about? What's wrong with our marriage?''

The faces which snapped to hers, so disparate in every other way, were alike in their expression of horror. But Damon regained himself quickly and, just as quickly, covered the distance between them. ''Nothing that cannot, that will not be remedied, Jane, I promise you,'' he said, his eyes imploring. ''Trust me. Just love and trust me for a short time, my darling. That's all I ask.''

The look of betrayal in her eyes indicated that he was asking too much. But before he could stop her, she turned on a heel and dashed away.

Jane kept to her room throughout the sweltering afternoon. Damon tried to tell himself that it did not matter; soon, very soon, he would make things right. And, if she loved him enough, she would forgive him.

He was sitting at his desk and had reached that conclusion for the twentieth time in an hour, when Simon interrupted his master's thoughts.

''Pardon me, sir. The quarters just sent word; Carolina has given birth to a boy.''

''What name have they given him?'' he asked listlessly.

''They have left that to you, sir,'' Simon said, surprised.

''Amos is a freeman. Let him name his son.''

''Carolina is a slave, sir. Therefore, her issue is a slave. Amos respects your rightful authority in calling the child,'' the old man said, appalled at having to make such a salient point.

Damon sighed ponderously, and after some thought, said, ''Linus. I'll enter him in the chattel book as Linus.'' Simon nodded, but stood his ground before the desk. ''Is there something else?''

''Yes, sir. Mr. Grimes wishes to see you.''

"Concerning what?"

"He did not say, sir."

Damon heaved another ponderous sigh. "Send him in." Simon got the clear impression that the master had lost interest in his estate and resented the demands it placed upon him.

That opinion was not shared by Grimes, who saw his employer sit bolt upright and become keenly attentive when he launched into an explanation of the business that had brought him there.

". . . and it's all set anytime you say the word, sir," Grimes concluded.

"Gersham and Violet are already there?"

"Yes, sir. Ready and waiting. Everything's just as you wanted, sir."

"Good. Good!" Damon stood and turned away for a thoughtful moment. "Tonight," he said, turning back. "I want him moved tonight. Late. After the household is abed. Tell Amos."

"Yes, sir."

When Grimes was gone and he was alone, Damon said quietly, "It's the beginning of the end, my love. Tonight is the beginning of the end." Then he settled back in his chair and opened a special ledger to record the name, date of birth, and lineage of his new slave.

Damon listened to the sounds of the sultry, mid-summer night that reached him through the wide-flung windows of his room: the busy chirruping of crickets; the shrill peeping of tree frogs; the muted hooting of an owl. But they did nothing to soothe him. With every muscle taut, every nerve tight, he strained to hear the other sounds; the sounds that would tell him that Amos had removed his ward. That the man who—for nearly two years—had been imprisoned in the house where he was rightful master had been safely taken away.

He had not seen the man in all that time, and yet,

through the quirk of nature which bound them closer than ordinary brothers, he had seen his face every day. And he had constantly felt his brother's anger and hostility toward him, just as he had always felt—or sensed—the other's consciousness. Even at an early age, he had been bound to his brother by an indefinable, intuitive understanding. And, even at an early age, he had sensed a perverseness in him. But he had never suspected that such ugliness could come to that, that despicable perversity would infect his brother as an adult. He should have. He should have known, long before he did, that his brother was mad.

But it was not the obvious sort of insanity. He was not the raving, babbling idiot who, by his manner, warned others away. His was the quiet kind of madness; the sort of madness that could be hidden beneath a facade of normalcy. To look at him, one might never know.

But Pamela had known. She had always known. She had seen what *he* was afraid to see; had admitted what *he* was too proud, too loyal, to admit. And his blindness and pride and loyalty had killed her!

Damon's head fell to his chest, bowed by the weight of a guilt, hardly eased by the passage of five years. He groaned as he had done a thousand times before. "I'm sorry, Pam. I'm sorry."

It was the tapping on his door, at first quiet, then more insistent, that dragged him from his agonizing thoughts. Crossing the room in stockinged feet, he opened the door a crack and asked in a whisper, "What is it? Has something gone wrong?"

"Not wrong, sir, no," Simon said in a like tone. "But he insists that he will not go quietly unless you accompany him."

"What?"

"He is most firm in that, sir. He knows Madam is unaware of the goings-on tonight—indeed, that she is unaware of his very presence—and intimated that, if you wish her to remain so—''

''I will not submit to extortion!'' Damon hissed angrily. ''If he will not go quietly, then he will be bound, gagged, or rendered insensible, but he *will* be out of this house tonight!''

''Please, sir, for the sake of mercy, cannot you accede to his wishes in this? Cannot you allow him a modicum of respect and dignity? In his place, would not you desire the same?''

Damon was thoughtfully quiet for a time. ''Why? Why does he insist? What does he have up his sleeve?''

''I do not believe he is plotting chicanery, sir. It would be foolhardy. Grimes is armed. I believe, sir, he merely wishes to see you, for the final time.''

''Damnation, man! You make it sound as though he's going to his execution!''

Simon held Damon's eyes. ''I believe, sir, that is precisely what he thinks.''

Damon stiffened. ''You've told him, haven't you? You've told him he will be well cared for at the lodge?''

''It would ease his mind, sir, if you were to tell him.''

''If he doesn't believe you, Simon, he won't believe me.'' Damon paced a few agitated steps from the door. And he reconsidered. ''Oh, very well. Tell him . . . tell him I'll come.''

Lifting the latch from the inside, Jane swung the French window open as far as it would go. It was hot. Too hot to sleep. Almost too hot to move. Stepping out onto the path leading to her garden, she stopped and hauled her sweat-dampened nightdress up around her thighs. The night air felt like a warm, damp sponge against her skin.

''Not so much as a breath of a breeze,'' she complained aloud. But still, it was cooler here than upstairs, so she stood awhile, listening to the night and watching an oak tree filigree the moon. Then, reluctantly, she turned back into the house and headed for bed.

She had just started down the hallway toward her room when she heard the sound of heavy footsteps behind her. Wondering who else was up and about at this time of night, she turned to face the sound. The hallway was empty, but the concealed panel which gave access to the servants' stairs was ajar. The wavering, feeble light of a candle painted a golden wedge on the hall runner. Thinking that the servants must be having as hard a time sleeping as she was—it was undoubtedly even hotter in the attic than on the second floor—she had turned back to her own room when she heard the voices.

"I warn you, not a sound," the low voice that sounded like Damon's said.

"Lead on," another man said, in a hoarse dramatic whisper.

"You first," Damon said.

Jane heard a harsh, snort of laughter. Then a voice that sounded like Damon's but couldn't have been his, taunted, "Afraid you might take a tumble with me behind you?"

There was the sound of a scuffle and, over that, Simon's voice implored, "Please, sirs, please!"

Then the men and the light passed the landing, leaving her confused, and, inexplicably, very much afraid.

A sharp, stinging slap roused her from sleep with a start and a yelp.

"Rise and shine." Damon grinned from where he lounged against a footpost.

Rubbing her stinging buttocks, Jane shoved herself up against the headboard and glared at him.

He laughed. "You look mad enough to bite. It was only a love pat. I couldn't resist." His golden eyes raked her, taking in the expanse of naked flank her rumpled nightdress exposed, then sliding upward to her breasts. "Have I ever told you how much I appreciate your— ample charms?"

Hastily hauling up the sheet, Jane shielded herself against his lustful gaze. "I don't feel well, Damon," she said, marveling at the lie; for the first time in weeks of mornings, she felt perfectly fine.

His smile was more of a leer as he loosed the sash of his robe. "I've the cure for what ails you." Then he flung his gown wide, exposing himself to her eyes.

"Damon, please!" she gasped, shocked that he should speak and act so crudely.

"No need to beg, my dear. I'm only too happy to oblige." His eyes held a menacing glint as he pulled the sheet from her and flung it half off the bed.

Drawing her limbs into herself, Jane pulled away. "What's come over you? What are you doing?"

"Fairly obvious, isn't it?" he sneered, catching her ankles and pulling her toward him.

"Damon, no! Don't!"

But it was Venus's brusque tap on the door, not Jane's protests, that made him loose his grip on her and pull the front of his robe back into place. With an angry yank, he knotted the sash and snarled, "I trust, my sweet, you will be feeling marvelously well a bit later!"

Aghast but immeasurably relieved, Jane watched him disappear toward his room. But he didn't stay there long. No sooner had Venus been dispatched to bring up Jane's breakfast, than he was back. And in much less time than it took Venus to return with the tray, he had taken what he wanted from his wife.

He was gone all the rest of that day, not returning until dinner, and leaving again soon after. Shocked and angered at his brutish treatment, Jane didn't ask where he was going; she didn't care. But when he wasn't home at their customary bedtime and was still gone when the sitting room clock chimed twelve, she lay awake for hours, worrying. When he finally came home just before dawn, she stormed into his room to demand an explanation. A moment later, she regretted her action.

"Did you miss me?" he sneered.

"I—I was worried. You were gone all night, Damon!"

Wagging his head and clucking his tongue, he advanced to within arm's reach of her. "Have I neglected my poor, little wife?"

At the look on his face, the raw, naked lust in his eyes, Jane drew back from him. "What's come over you, Damon? What's come over you!"

Catching her wrist before she was out of reach, he chuckled nastily, "You're only just now beginning to know me, my dear. And I do think it's past time we became well and thoroughly acquainted."

He took her right there, on his bedroom floor, muffling her horrified screams by cramming a linen handkerchief into her mouth. Without mercy, he used her in ways even animals abhorred, until the sun was well over the horizon.

# 11

Jane stopped her nervous pacing to stare out the window. The trees in the ellipse were dark shadows against a darkening sky. Had it only been a week ago that she had risen early to watch the sun gild them while the birds sang their morning song? Had it only been a week ago that she had revelled in being alive? Had it really taken him so short a space of time to kill her soul?

"Everything's ready, ma'am," Venus said quietly, entering Jane's room. "Is you?"

"Yes." Even to her own ears her voice sounded hollow, devoid of life and emotion.

"I's ready, too."

Jane turned from the window. "What?"

"Take me with you, ma'am. You gonna needs somebody with you."

"I . . . Venus, I can't take you."

"Please, ma'am. Don't leave me here. He sell me soon's he figures out you ain't coming back. Don't leave me here to be sold, ma'am. Please, don't!"

Jane made her mouth smile. "Don't be silly, Venus. I'm only going across the bay to visit my cousins for a bit." But when Venus's black eyes emptied their burden of tears down her cocoa-colored cheeks, Jane knew the woman could tell she was lying. Grasping her hands tightly, she implored, "Venus, Venus please try to understand. I'd take you with me if I could. I don't want to leave you! But, I don't know how I'm going to live. Or where. Don't you see? How can I provide and care for you when I don't know how I'm to manage for myself?"

"We manage together, ma'am. You can't be alone. What you gonna do when that baby come if you be all alone?"

"I'll worry about that when the time comes," Jane said, lifting her gloves and reticule from the bed, unable to bear the look of pain in the slave's eyes.

"I guess I know'd that's what you'd say, ma'am, 'cause I fetched this from my room awhile ago. You keeps it with you always, ma'am. It keep you safe." Venus extended a closed fist.

"Oh, Venus, no. I can't take anything from you. You've little enough as it is."

"I wants for you to have this, ma'am," Venus said firmly. Then she lifted one of Jane's hands and deposited the small, ivory charm in her palm. "This juju done kept my gran'mammy safe through being taken by slavers and brung to this land. She done give it to me when I went with Miss Emily. It brought me safe through being sold—I s'pose it do that again—but you needs it more'n me, ma'am. You takes it."

"Oh, Venus, no. I—"

"You has to, ma'am." Venus dropped her hands and resolutely balled them into fists. "I done give it to you. The power of the juju already pass from me to you."

Jane looked at the creamy white rectangle carved with a coarse-featured face; a crude cameo. "Oh, Venus, maybe you and I were destined to make this journey together." Then, she reached into her reticule. "My grandmam passed this along to me," she said, laying the cameo brooch beside the juju in her palm. "We'll keep them together."

* * *

It was a long ride into Baltimore, and Jane spent every mile of it praying that Bundy, who had ridden ahead with the wagon and her luggage, had been able to hire her a boat. Everything depended on that. Everything! She had to be clear of Baltimore tonight. If Damon returned home early from his nightly debauch with Lilith Townsend and found her gone, there would be no time to wait for the morning mail packet. She had seen how relentless Damon was when something of his was stolen: He had ridden to Baltimore in the middle of the night in pursuit of a stolen necklace. How much more determined would he be to reclaim his so-called wife and the slave who had run away with her!

She was still praying when she drew the chaise up alongside Bundy and the wagon on the Baltimore dock. Even before she could ask the all-important question, he supplied the answer.

"I got you passage, ma'am. The boat ain't much, but Captain Howard's willing to take you across, and that's more than anybody else'll do this time of night."

With Venus close on her heels, Jane fell into step beside Bundy as he led her through the jumble of cargo toward the oyster boat that would carry her across the bay. "Like I said, it ain't much."

"It's a boat, Bundy, and that's what I asked you to hire." She looked up at him quickly. "Was the money I gave you enough?"

"More'n enough, ma'am. You got some coming back." He dropped the change into her palm and gave her a worried smile. "I hope you have a nice visit with your cousin."

"This isn't really a social call, Bundy. She's ill. I'm going to care for her baby while she's abed." The lie was a plausible enough one, Jane thought. Why didn't Bundy look convinced?

"Yuh. Well, I hope she's feeling better real soon." Then, turning away and cupping his hands to his mouth, he called toward the boat, "Captain Howard?"

Almost before she knew what had happened, Jane found herself standing at the stern of the sturdy little vessel, with Venus standing guard over the baggage, waving a solemn good-bye to Bundy. And she thought, as the dock fell away, of all that would go unfinished because she was leaving. Ezra would forget about the asters next year. Would he forget Venus, too? And the cemetery would be allowed to go to weeds again. Like as not, Oswald would go back to her spendthrift ways, and Opal would shuffle shoeless through the house. Simon would go without plasters for his aching, ancient back. The youngsters in the quarter would go without their sweets. And she would never again curl up on the window seat to read, or finish embroidering the canvas to cover the threadbare seat of Damon's desk chair. Or ride Eclipse. Or play the clavichord. Or laugh. Not ever, ever again would her heart be light enough to laugh.

The sky over the eastern shore was azure, streaked with saffron and peach when the oyster boat docked at the small, wooden pier. Wrapped in the sour-smelling woolen blanket she had accepted from the captain against the night's chill, Jane stood stiffly. She had spent the night on deck, declining the "hospitality" of the captain's bed when she learned that Venus would not be allowed to accompany her. Knowing men and their lustings as she now did, she far preferred an uncomfortable night huddled beside Venus in a corner of the stern to an even worse one spent elsewhere.

"Is we there, ma'am?" Venus asked, standing and trying to stamp the life back into a numb leg.

"We're docking, but this can't be Hook's Head. Marianne told me it was a sizable community. There's nothing here but that house and those out buildings." Looking across the ship, she called to the man who stood ready to toss the bowline to a man on the dock. "Where are we, Captain Howard?"

"Howard's Landin'," the man said gruffly, still angry at her refusal at his hospitality.

"Are we far from Hook's Head?"

"Near enough."

"And how near is that, please?"

"Ten miles."

"Ten . . . but you were hired to take me to Hook's Head!"

"I done you the favor of bringin' you 'cross the bay." He hurled the line and, while it was being made fast, walked aft to toss off the line there.

Furious, but knowing that arguing would do no good now, Jane said, "I'll need a wagon or a pony cart, then. Can you tell me where I might hire one?"

"I can rent you a wagon. Can't spare a driver, though. Of course, I might be of a mind to drive you myself if you, ah, make it worth my while. If you know what I mean."

Jane knew only too well! "I can drive a team. How much rental do you charge?"

"I got mules, not horses," he said significantly. "So, why don't you and me go up to the house and strike ourselves a little bargain?"

Jane stiffened and glared at the man. "I will drive myself. How much?"

Captain Howard's eyes narrowed to angry slits, and the man on the dock, who had overheard the exchange, quickly smothered a derisive laugh. "A shillin', English money. I don't trade Colony script. And that's *providin'* you have 'em back by tonight."

"Agreed." Howard held out his hand for payment. "I'll see the wagon and team first."

Howard spat over the side, narrowly missing the man on the dock. "I want it back by *tonight* you understand."

"Perfectly."

Eyeing Jane drolly, he hollered, "Hitch up for the

little lady, Will."

"I ain't no stable hand, Thom!" the man on the dock complained.

Howard's eyes slid to Venus. "Do like I tell you, and I'll see there's something in it for you."

Barely half an hour later, and with a crafty gleam in his eye, Thom Howard watched Jane drive off in his wagon.

"I didn't like the way them men look at us, ma'am," Venus said, casting a worried glance behind them.

"They can look at us any way and as much as they like, Venus. They'll not gain a thing by it. I'll have Cousin Robert see this wagon is returned, and we'll never lay eyes on them again."

"You ain't really meaning to go to Hook's Head, is you?"

"Certainly, I am."

"But, that's where you told Bundy we's going!"

"So?"

"So, what if Massah Seymour asks him where we is? He ain't gonna lie, ma'am. He tells him!"

"I'm sure he will. I'm counting on it. If I were Damon and I were looking for me, the last place I'd look is where I said I would be." She smiled at Venus with a surety she didn't feel and urged the mules into a faster plod.

But even that faster pace was slow, and they still had not reached the settlement by midmorning. "It can't be much further, Venus. He said only ten miles."

"Seems we come that far already. Do you s'pose he tol' you wrong, ma'am?"

"Why would he do that?"

"I don't know, ma'am. But this has been the longest ten miles I's ever gone!"

Jane had to agree. It seemed they had come twice that far. But as there were no milestones on the road and no familiar landmarks by which to gauge distance, she had to believe that they would come upon the thriving community of Hook's Head just around the next bend.

But when that bend had been rounded and left behind, she sawed back on the reins and stood on the brake to haul the team to a stop. "We must have taken a wrong turn."

"There ain't been no turns to take wrong, ma'am," Venus said from her side of the plank which served as the wagon's seat. "That man, he done sent you down the wrong road."

"Why would he do that?" Jane snapped in irritation. "He wants this wagon and team back by tonight. Surely, he has enough sense to know that he won't have them back unless we get to Hook's Head."

"Yes'um," Venus said glumly.

"Of course, if he doesn't get them back, he'll probably call out the constables and say that I stole them. Although, what he stands to gain by that is beyond me." Jane chewed her parched lip thoughtfully. Then, with a shout of "Hup!" and several sharp slaps on the reins on the broad, brown rumps before her, she said, "We'll go a little further. This road is too well-traveled to lead nowhere. We're bound to find a settlement soon. We'll get new directions there."

The sun was perched at its zenith, about to roll slowly toward the great bay on her right when Jane next sawed back on the reins and felt them bite through the thin cotton of her gloves and into her blistering palms. Despite the alternative, she had begun to regret her eagerness in proclaiming herself a mule driver!

"Is you fixin' to turn back, ma'am?"

"No. Listen."

"I don't hear nothing."

"Sssh!" Jane listened intently, her eyes scanning the sparsely wooded landscape to the left of the road. "There! There, did you hear those dogs?"

"No, ma'am. I didn't hear nothing but my stomach complainin'."

"Look! Look, there they are!" Excitedly, Jane pointed at the two lop-eared hounds that trotted into sight, tails high, noses to the ground. "And riders!"

Stuffing the reins into Venus's hands, Jane stood and waved an arm frantically overhead. The lady, who was dressed in a riding costume of royal purple with three plump, white feathers sprouting jauntily from her hat, glanced in Jane's direction, then averted her face with an arrogant lift of her chin. But the man who, in his brown coat, dove breeches and black tricorn, looked almost shabby by comparison, returned Jane's wave with a raise of his hand.

"Oh! He's seen us!" Jane cried, settling back onto the plank as gracefully as if it were a drawing room sofa. As she watched, the man spoke a word to the lady—who looked unmistakably annoyed—then, with a whistle for his dogs, jogged toward the wagon.

"Good afternoon," he said, touching a finger to the brim of his hat.

"Good afternoon, sir. I'm terribly sorry to have interrupted your ride."

"Think nothing of it. Down, Dan!" The dog which had braced its forepaws on the wagon hub and was snarling nastily up at Jane, dropped obediently to the ground where it sat, growling throatily. "He's not partial to ladies. How may I be of service?"

"Can you tell me, please, is this the road to Hook's Head?"

"Hook's Head? Aye, it's the right road." He smiled and his teeth gleamed white in his deeply tanned face. Pointing his quirt at the road behind them, he said, "Hook's Head is some fifteen miles that way."

"Fifteen miles back?"

"Aye. Or a bit more."

"Oh, lordy, ma'am!" Venus wailed.

Jane shot the woman a cowing glance, then smiled hopefully at the man who was giving the mules and wagon a thorough examination. "Is there somewhere up ahead, a town or an inn, where we might take a noon meal?"

"Dillard's Point is five or six miles further along. But as my home is nearer by, I would be honored if you would accept my hospitality."

"Thank you, no," Jane said, having had enough of strange men's offers of hospitality.

"It is no imposition, I assure you. We were just on our way home," he said, indicating the lady with a glance.

Jane hesitated. The presence of the gentleman's wife would assure propriety, but they still had to travel fifteen miles. "Thank you, no."

"As you will," the gentleman said, eyeing the wagon again. "Might I ask how you came by this wagon?"

"I hired it," Jane said, defensively.

"I thought as much. I'll wager Captain Howard gave you a fair price, too . . . on the condition that you return it to him by nightfall." At Jane's startled expression, he explained, "Thom Howard's shined many a traveler before you."

Jane swallowed thickly. "What does he gain by sending travelers on a wild goose chase?"

"Well now, in your case I'd say an extra day's rental of his wagon and team, the cost of a night's lodging and diet at Howard's Landing for you and your woman, there, and—" his eyes skimmed Jane's figure, "whatever else he can sweet-talk you out of overnight. My advice to you, Miss—" One black eyebrow arched expectantly as he waited for Jane to supply her name. When she didn't, he went easily on, "My advice, Miss, is for you to hightail back to Howard's Landing, pay him the extra day's rental, and make dust for Hook's Head. You might get there by dark if you don't dawdle on the way." He flashed another dazzling smile, raised a finger to his hat brim, then turned and, with the dogs loping at his side, trotted back to the lady who was impatiently awaiting his return.

Jane had never seen the sun set over water before. It was anticlimatic. No hiss or sizzle, no rising, writhing billows of steam accompanied the red-hot orb's descent into the bay. But it was a pretty sight—the prettiest she had seen in all of the long, hot, hungry day she had spent jolting over the dusty roads of Maryland's Eastern Shore. It was almost like a reward for having perserved. As if, she scoffed silently, she had any choice in that!

"There's blackberries in there, ma'am!" Venus called gaily, emerging from the woods where she had gone to answer nature's call. "If we can find something to put 'em in, I'll pick us some."

"We've no time for berrying, Venus. We have to get along before it's too dark to see the road."

"But you ain't had nothing to eat all day, ma'am, and you with child. Ain't good for you to go so long without eating."

"The Drakes' farm can't be more than a few miles ahead. I'll eat there. Besides," she added as Venus clambered back onto the seat, "I'm so hungry, I'm not hungry anymore. I really should have thought to bring along something for us to eat."

"You didn't know we'd take so long getting here, ma'am. And if you'd had 'em fix something to bring along, Eulalia would've spread the word you was going. Massah'd found out for sure. Lordy, but that woman do talk! They say as some folk gots eyes in the back of their head, well, I's here to tell you, Eulie gots a extra mouth back there!"

Jane smiled wanly and started the weary mules off down the road again. Venus continued to babble, giving a fine, if unconscious, imitation of Eulalia. "Once she gets to talking, she just keep going on like she's the only one knows anything worth knowing.

"Like all that business 'bout Mr. Renwick. She kept going on and on 'bout how *sad* all that was. How he was such a *fine* man and how—"

"Who?"

"Ma'am?"

"Who was Eulalia talking about?"

"Mr. Renwick, ma'am. That's *all* she done talk about the past few days. She been wailing and moaning, saying how his being sent off was all her fault and how, if she wasn't such a lazy nigger, Massah wouldn't have had to do that. And then she'd go on about—"

"*Who* is Mr. Renwick?"

"Why, he's the crazy man, ma'am. Don't you know 'bout him?" Jane wagged her head. "Oh, ma'am. I wouldn't have said nothing but that I thought you knowed."

"Well, I don't. Tell me."

"Well, I only knows what Eulie say, and there ain't no way of telling how *true* it all is. But she says Massah kept Mr. Renwick locked up, outta harm's way. And that he had him taken someplace one night last week. Even she don't know where. And if anybody else does, they ain't saying."

"What else did she say about him?"

"Only that he crazy. Bad crazy. He done kill his wife and his unborn baby with her. Bad crazy!"

Jane stared at the dark face now all but invisible beside her. "If he's a murderer, why wasn't he hanged?"

"On account of Massah done told everybody that Mr. Renwick's wife fell down the stairs and *that's* how she broke her neck."

"But, why? Why did Damon protect him?"

"He don't want his brother to get hanged, that's why! 'Sides, I don't s'pose gentry want that kind of talk going 'round; that one of their own's a crazy man and done killed his wife."

"This—this Renwick was—is—Damon's *brother*?"

"Yes'um. That's what Eulie say. And she been at Raven's Oak long enough to know."

Jane was quiet for a long time, staring at the road ahead, which was fast becoming as dark as her thoughts. "Was Renwick's wife named Pamela?"

"I don't know, ma'am. Eulie didn't say. But she say that he sure did love her. That's why it was so sad. They seem real happy, and Mr. Renwick, he was fair to bustin' he was that happy about the baby coming. Then, he just went crazy one night; up an' killed her. And when Massah found him with her body—'leaning over her like' was how Eulalia said it, and she saw all this part with her own eyes—Mr. Renwick lit out for Massah, screaming and crying, saying it was Massah who killed her. Then, he took off outta the house without no more than the clothes on his back. Crazy. All of sudden. Just like that. Nobody could hardly believe it, him being so fine and good before then." Venus wagged her head. "That sure must've been some night!"

"But, you just said that Damon had kept him . . . hidden away. How can that be, if he ran off?"

"He come back, ma'am. He was gone for years, and everybody thought he was dead. But then, he come back. That's when Massah locked him away. Eulalia say they all s'posed that was on account of Massah was planning to marry you, and he 'fraid Mr. Renwick might do you harm." Venus paused. "Eulie say that they all saw a change in Massah after he locked Mr. Renwick up; like he was a whole new man. And for the better, too. Changed his ways, she said: No more low women, no more drinking and gambling. And she say they all figure it was on account of you, ma'am. On account of he loved you." Jane looked sharply at the dark shape on the seat beside her, then quickly back to the road. "I seen that, too, ma'am. I seen he loves you. Why's you leaving when you loves him, too?"

"I don't love him."

"That ain't so, ma'am. I know it ain't."

"You know nothing, Venus!"

"I know you ain't ever gonna be happy without Massah. I know that."

"I'll be happier without him than I could ever be with him, now. And if you want to go on with me, Venus, you'll never mention him again!"

They said nothing more until they reached the neat, white two-story house that fit the description of the Drakes' house Jane had been given by a man in Hook's Head. But by then, Jane had reached some painfully simple conclusions: Insanity ran in the Seymour veins. Damon had gone as mad as his brother. She had been lucky to escape with her life.

"You want I should ask is this the right place, ma'am?" Venus asked meekly while the wagon rolled to a stop.

Jane only nodded, too tired and drained to find her voice. She hadn't realized until this moment, when the comfort and security of Marianne's home were so close at hand, how exhausted she was. Wearily, she watched Venus bang the iron knocker against its strike plate. If this wasn't the Drake house, she would ask for lodging here anyway; she didn't have the strength to go any further.

"Johanna!" It was Robert's voice, full of delight and surprise. "For pity's sake, why didn't you let us know you were coming? I'd have met your . . . boat. Good Lord! What are you doing in *that* thing? Where's your driver? Where's Damon!"

"I—I hired it. I'm the driver. And Damon's . . . He's home." Jane wanted to blurt out the newly discovered truth: He's mad. I can't live with him anymore. And she would have, had Robert been married to anyone else but Damon's adoring cousin. But as it was, she excused

lamely, "He's busy. He couldn't spare time for the trip.
But I wanted to see Lucinda—you and Marianne, too, of
course—so I came on my own. I hope you don't mind."

"Mind? Of course, we don't mind. We're delighted
you came." But in the faint light trickling through the
open door, she read disapproval on his face as he
helped her down from the wagon. Ushering her up
several wooden steps and into the house, he said gaily
enough, "Marianne's just putting the baby to bed. She'll
be down in a moment. You're just in time for some of
the tastiest roast chicken you'll ever eat!"

Once they were inside, though, he gave up all
pretense of unconcerned good humor. Eyeing her
severely, he noticed her sunburned face with its thick
powdering of dust and streaks of grime; the tendrils of
hair that straggled down from beneath her off-kilter
bonnet; her dirty, sweat-stained dress; and her filthy,
threadbare gloves. "You must have had quite a trip," he
said. "Forgive me, but I've seen you looking better."

Jane thought better of saying the same of him. No
stylishly cut coat and ruffled stock for him today; he
looked like any simple farmer in the loose fitting, full-
sleeved blouse that was open at the neck and tucked
into a pair of faded blue breeches that disappeared into
well-worn, ill-polished boots. His short, dark curls were
wind-tousled and tumbled about his ears and forehead,
while the longer part at his nape was bound with a
simple, leather thong. He was a far cry from the natty
gentleman she had come to call cousin.

"Well," Robert said with an awkward little grin.
"Why don't you make yourself comfortable in the
parlor?" He indicated a small room to the left of the hall.
"And you, ah, Venus, is it?"

"Yes'uh."

"You may come in and make yourself comfortable
on the bench by the door." Then, steering Jane into the

parlor, he lit a candle lamp. "I'll tell Mari you're here,"
he said, hurrying out.

Robert's appearance should have prepared Jane for
the simplicity of his home, but she was surprised to find
it so inelegantly furnished. The tables and chairs had
been locally crafted and lacked the fine carving and
delicately turned legs and finials of their more
expensive counterparts. Marianne had undoubtedly
made the chair cushions herself, and only one piece, the
divan, was upholstered. There wasn't a trace of gilt or
silver anywhere, but the lamp Robert had lighted had an
etched crystal chimney. It was the finest piece in the
room. Too tired to notice any more than that, Jane
settled into a rocking chair, not wanting to dirty the
divan.

"Good morning, sleepy head. Are you awake?"

"Hm? Oh. Oh, Marianne!" Jane shoved herself up in
the bed. Every muscle in her body complained at the
movement. "Oh, my! How did I get here?"

Marianne smiled. "Robert brought you up."

"I fell asleep in the chair, didn't I?" Jane said,
sheepishly.

"You were exhausted. Did you sleep well?"

"I must have. I don't remember a thing after sitting
down in that chair." Jane fingered her nightdress. "Did
you do this?"

"Venus and I. Well. I'll bring up your breakfast. You
must be famished."

"Oh, no, I'll come down! I won't have you waiting on
me."

"You'll do nothing of the kind. You'll stay right there
and rest if I have to tie you down! After the day you had
yesterday . . . Honestly, Johanna! Whatever possessed
you? Don't you realize what could have happened to
you, a woman traveling alone? You could have been set

upon by highway robbers. Or worse! Things aren't as civilized on *this* side of the bay!"

"It's not as civilized as you seem to think it is on the other side," Jane muttered.

"All the same, you're lucky you didn't run afoul of a rapscallion worse than Thom Howard!"

"How do you know about him?"

"Venus." Skirting Jane's trunks, which took up most of the room's floor space, she made her way to the window and opened the curtains. "She told us everything—except why you're here. She's very loyal to you, Johanna. She wouldn't say a word about why you left Damon."

"You shouldn't have asked her."

"I didn't. But Robert keeps putting himself in Damon's place, imagining how he must feel—how *he* would feel if I left him in the middle of the night without so much as a word.

"We're not trying to pry, Johanna, honestly. And if you tell me to be quiet, I won't say another word about it. But Rob and I love you both. If there's anything we can do to help set things right between you . . . If you'll tell me *why* you left, then maybe—"

"Be quiet, Marianne," Jane said softly.

But that evening Robert, who was not bound by Marianne's vow, could not be so easily silenced.

"Johanna, I realize that it must have been more than a petty tiff that made you leave your husband. But whatever it was will never be resolved with you on one side of the bay and Damon on the other. Now, will it?"

"Robert, please. I don't want to talk about it."

"So Mari told me at dinner. But I'm afraid, Johanna, that you owe us an explanation. You've involved us."

"I'm sorry. I shouldn't have. I should never have come here. You're Damon's family, not mine. You must feel as though you're giving succor to the enemy. But I—I didn't know where else to go."

"Certainly, we don't think you're the 'enemy,'" he said, sounding annoyed. Then, with a sigh, he sat on the bed near her feet and implored quietly, "Why did you feel the need to go anywhere at all?"

"I'll leave in the morning, Robert."

"Leave? You'll 'leave'? Not 'go home' or 'go back to Damon,' just leave?"

"Yes."

"Oh, for the love of . . . Johanna!"

"It's obvious that you don't want me here, so I'll go."

"It isn't that we don't want you. It's that we would like to see you back at Raven's Oak where you belong!"

"We can't always have what we like, Robert."

He held her eyes for a long moment, then wagged his head incredulously. "He was right. He told me you were stubborn, and he was right." Then he sighed and gave reason one more try. "How do you expect to resolve your differences with the bay between you?"

"I don't."

"All right. All right, fine. You don't. What about him? Have you considered that you are being unfair to him? Suppose he wants to apologize?"

"Believe me, Robert, he doesn't."

Throwing his hands in the air, he said, "I give up." But he didn't. "Can't I talk any sense at all into you?"

"I have *done* the sensible thing, Robert." When he turned disgustedly away, she said, "I understand that you're trying to help. I do! But what *you* must understand is that Damon and I aren't like you and Marianne. She would never leave you, any more than you would give her cause to go."

Robert was quiet for a time, then said, "So, if you're not going back to him, what are you going to do?"

"I don't know. But I would appreciate your not letting him know I'm here until I've figured that out."

Bundy worried as he hurried his horse down the

tree-shaded lane toward the house. It had been three days; suppose she had left? Or suppose she hadn't come here at all? Or, worse, suppose she had come but had been *taken* away? His heart hammered as loudly as his fist on the Drake's front door.

"There's a man to see you, Johanna. A Mr. Bundy," Marianne said, entering the kitchen where Jane was trying to spoon breakfast porridge into eight-month-old Lucinda.

"Bundy! What does he want?"

"To speak with you. If you don't want to see him, I told him I thought you might have gone walking. If you like, I can go back and—"

"No. No. I'll see him." Handing the baby to her mother, Jane wiped her fingers on her porridge-spotted apron.

"Who is he?"

"Damon's foreman."

"Ah-ha! Damon sent him, then. And with a letter of apology, no doubt." She smiled smugly. "I knew he wouldn't let this go on much longer."

Jane smiled weakly at Damon's adoring cousin. "Where is he?"

"In the parlor. Johanna?" Jane turned in the kitchen doorway. "You might look a bit happier. Whatever the quarrel between you, *you* seem to have won it!"

Jane forced a facade of brightness into her smile, then turned away down the hall.

"Good morning, Bundy," she said, her smile vanishing.

"Good morning."

"Did he send you?"

"No. I came on my own."

"Why?"

Bundy eyed the open door behind her and lowered his voice to a whisper. "You can't stay here. You've got to get away. I cut this out of the Baltimore paper yesterday. He's had bulletins printed saying pretty much the same thing.''

Jane took the small square of rag paper from fingers as unsteady as her own, and read:

## L50 REWARD

Stolen from the subscriber the twenty-eighth instant of July, a negro woman called Venus; about twenty-five years of age, five-feet-seven-inches tall, slim built, light of complexion. Will likely be in company of comely young woman posing as her mistress; seventeen years of age, five-feet-three-inches tall, blond hair, blue eyes. The above reward, and reasonable and proper charges, on delivery of said women to the subscriber or proper local authorites, will be paid.

Damon Seymour, Esq.

Raven's Oak; Baltimore County, Maryland. 30 July, 1771

All persons are forbidden to harbour or employ said negro, or to give shelter or aid to the aforesaid females, on penalty of law.

''Stolen! He says I stole her!''

''You left with a slave belonging to him. There's a lot of folks would see that as stealing.''

''But she came of her own free will!''

''Last I heard, slaves don't have a free will.''

It was a telling point. One that Jane had not considered.

''Not that it's Venus he wants back, you understand,'' Bundy said. ''But, seeing as a man can't very well advertise a runaway wife, he's done next best.''

Jane felt her knees turn to water; only sheer force of will kept them from buckling beneath her. "Thank you for coming to—to tell me, Bundy. I'm—I'm indebted to you."

Taking a step nearer, he laid a hand lightly on her arm. "I didn't just come to tell you. I came to get you away from here. Venus, too. I got a plan."

# 12

Jane sat beside Bundy on the seat of the Drakes' pony cart. Venus and the trunks were crowded in back, and Bundy's horse was tied on behind. Holding pretty little Lucinda on one hip, Marianne waved a gay good-bye from the doorstep. With a lackluster wave of her own, Jane looked back to the road ahead of them, wondering where it would lead and regretting the half-truth that had led Marianne to think her cousin was returning to Raven's Oak.

Venus thought that, too, although Jane did not feel as guilty about deceiving her. She would be told the truth soon enough, and it was best that she share Marianne's happy conviction until they were well away.

"I haven't told Venus, Bundy," Jane confessed quietly when they were on the road leading to Hook's Head.

"Why not?"

"She was so happy that we were going back. I couldn't bring myself to tell her. And I was afraid she might give things away."

"You'd best tell her now. If we run into trouble, she could say the wrong thing and give us away."

Jane sighed glumly and turned to look back at the woman. "Venus?"

Donna Gilmer

"Yes'um?" the maid said happily.

"Venus, we aren't going back to Raven's Oak. Don't say anything, just listen. Mr. Seymour has put a notice in the newspaper and had bulletins printed saying that I stole you and . . . just listen! He's offering a fifty pound reward to anyone who has us arrested and returned to him." Jane paused. "I have no intention of ever going back to Raven's Oak. You knew that when you asked to leave with me. But, if you've changed your mind, if you want to go back, Bundy will arrange for you to get there safely."

"There ain't nothin' there for me without you, ma'am," the woman said miserably.

"There's Ezra."

Venus wagged her head. "I goes back, I gets sold away. Ain't nothing there for me. But if we ain't going back, where are we going?"

"Bundy has a plan—a way for us to get to a northern colony where people aren't apt to have heard about us. But since every constable in Maryland and Virginia is going to be looking for us, he's going to say he's taking us back to Raven's Oak to claim the reward for himself. If anyone recognizes us and challenges him, that's what he'll tell them. Do you understand?"

"Yes'um."

"We're going to Hook's Head now, to leave this cart at the livery for Mr. Drake to pick up later, then—"

"I've been thinking about that," Bundy interrupted.

"Thinking about what?"

"All of us going into town. They read the Baltimore paper on this side of the bay, too, you know."

"So what if they do? If we're recognized and you tell them we're your prisoners, what difference will it make?"

"The difference between us having to take the packet back to Baltimore instead of choosing to take the one down to Dillard's Point, that's what."

"Then, what *are* we going to do?"

"I'll go in by myself, drop this cart and my horse off, and hire a wagon. We'll drive up to Papsqua Creek and take a boat south from there."

"Don't they read the Baltimore paper in . . . wherever you said?"

"Papsqua Creek. I'm sure they do. But nobody there saw you in a hired wagon asking directions to the Drake place a couple of nights back . . . just the time when your husband says his slave was stolen. Up in Papsqua Creek, they'll see Mr. and Mistress Albert Newell and Mistress Newell's maid."

"Albert Newell. Is that your name?"

Bundy nodded. "Sounds kinda queer, don't it? Even to me! I ain't heard anything but Bundy for so long. If somebody hollered, 'Hey, Albert!' I'd wonder who they were talking to." He laughed a little, and Jane smiled. "But, I guess I'd better get used to it. I guess you'd better, too, if we're going to fool anybody besides ourselves."

They exchanged uncomfortable glances; their gazes meeting, then dropping away. Jane said over her shoulder, "Did you hear, Venus? You'll have to call me Mistress Newell for a while."

"Yes'um. Can I ask something, ma'am?"

"Of course."

"If we's wanting to go north, why's we after a boat that's going south?"

It was Bundy who answered. "Because the fastest and safest way for us to get north is to go by ship. Ships sail to all over from Dillard's Point."

"But can't we take a ship from Baltimore or Annapolis?" Jane asked. "Why can't we go into Hook's Head as planned and, if we're recognized, take a packet across to Baltimore, then turn around and sail north from there?"

"Ain't no way we could get out of Baltimore without

being caught. They must be watching the docks there. Better we take the roundabout way through Papsqua Creek and book passage out of Dillard's Point."

"Passage!" Jane gasped, staring in horror at the man beside her. "Money. What are we going to do for money? I brought some of my jewelry with me, but until I can sell it—"

"Don't worry about money." Bundy threw her a confident if somewhat embarrassed smile. "I got my savings. It ain't a fortune, but it'll get us to New York and maybe a bit further if we're careful how we spend it."

Jane didn't smile. "I can't let you spend your life's savings on us, Bundy."

Grinning affably, he shrugged. "I don't see as you've got a whole lot of choice. We need money. I got it. You don't."

"Not now. But when I sell my jewelry, I'll repay every farthing you've spent. I promise!"

"Why don't we wait and see about that? We may be needing that jewelry money for something else."

"Every farthing, Bundy! I promise."

They were better than halfway to Hook's Head and had begun to relax and enjoy the drive when the sound of fast approaching hooves caused Jane to shoot Bundy a worried glance.

"We can't afford to get all roiled up every time we meet somebody on the road. We'll give ourselves away for sure if we don't act casual." But the easy smile on his face froze when he recognized the rider who rounded a bend in front of them. "We could've done just fine without running into him," he said, ruefully. "Just fine."

Jane's face went ashen under its smattering of freckles. "Maybe he hasn't seen the paper."

"Maybe not."

Thom Howard eyed the cart and its passengers appraisingly as he slowed his cantering horse to a trot. Well, well! This was his lucky day! Here he'd thought he'd have to track them down, and they were coming to meet him!

"Well, now," he said with a smile as he stopped his horse in the center of the narrow road, forcing Bundy to do the same. "Who have we here? Why, I do believe it's the little lady from Baltimore. And her slave woman with her. Why, glory be!" Jane felt Bundy tense on the seat beside her. "Out for a drive, are you? Tsk, tsk. I hate to spoil your good time, but you'll have to get outta that cart and come with me."

"I found 'em first. They're mine," Bundy said easily.

Howard looked at Bundy and fingered his chin. "You're the fella what hired me to bring 'em across, ain't you?" His eyes snapped to Jane. "Running off with your lover, are you? Now, that's touchin', that is." With another shift of his eyes, he ordered, "Drop the reins, boy-o."

"They're with me," Bundy countered quietly. "And they're gonna stay with me."

Howard slipped a hand into his coat and, with a flash of silver, produced a stout-handled, thick-bladed hunting knife. Turning his wrist this way and that, letting the dappled sunlight play along the evil-looking blade, he admired the knife for a moment, then flipped it neatly end over end and deftly caught it by the tip of the blade. "I once brought down a deer with this knife. Drop the reins, boy-o."

Bundy hesitated for a heartbeat of a second. "Look, Mr. Howard, we can make a deal here. I—"

"*Captain* Howard. And no, we can't. Drop them reins or I drop you."

Uncurling his fingers, Bundy let the reins fall.

"Get down from there."

To Jane's horror, Bundy meekly complied.

"Step aside."

Bundy wordlessly backed a pace away from the cart.

"Further back!"

Bundy couldn't move fast enough.

Howard cackled nastily. "Ain't made of very stern stuff, are you, boy-o?"

"They ain't worth losing my hide over."

Howard grunted his appreciation of the sage remark, but Jane glared at Bundy with such a look of furious loathing that he couldn't hold her eyes.

"You there, pick up the reins. I'm talking to you, Missy!" Jane turned her glare on Howard. "Pick up the reins."

"No."

"I said, pick 'em up!"

"And I said, no." Venus whimpered and Jane snapped, "Quiet, Venus! He'll not get tuppence from Damon if I'm dead."

"Well now, that's purely true," Howard said. "But then, I wasn't figurin' on handing you over to Seymour. That slave back o' you is worth considerable more on the auction block than a measly fifty pounds. So I was kinda thinkin' I'd make my money off her and keep you all to myself. Of course, if you'd rather die right here on this road, that's up to you. Now, you gonna pick up them reins or not?" Defiantly, Jane balled her hands into fists. "She's got more spunk than you have, boy-o." Howard laughed. Then, with a nudge of his heels, he urged his horse between Bundy and the cart, and leaned menacingly toward Jane.

It happened so fast, Jane couldn't believe her eyes. One minute, Howard was on his horse, knife in hand, reaching for her; the next, he was sprawled on his back in the dust with his throat cut.

"Grab his horse!" Bundy yelled, scrambling off the dead man.

Unthinkingly, Jane snatched at the dangling reins and calmed the rearing animal. When she looked back at Howard's body, Bundy was already dragging it by the ankles toward the trees.

A look of surprise lingered in the dead man's eyes and, above the gaping red wound, his mouth was open, as if to give expression to the cry he had had no time to utter. His head, on his tattered neck, twisted and rolled sickeningly. Fighting down the bile that rose in her throat, Jane looked quickly away. She heard Venus wretching behind her.

Within minutes, Bundy reappeared and carefully scuffed dirt over the blood and drag-marks Howard had left in the road. "Are you all right?" he asked, taking the horse's reins from Jane's trembling, white-knuckled hand.

"I think so."

"I'll tie his horse up out of sight of the road, then we'll be on our way again."

Jane stared at him. He had said it so matter-of-factly, as if he murdered men and tidied up the remains every day. "Doesn't it bother you? Killing him?"

"It wouldn't have bothered him to kill you."

Leading the horse, Bundy disappeared into the woods again. He returned even more quickly this time and, without a word, joined Jane on the seat and took up the reins. When they were rattling off down the road again, he said, "Just so you don't eat yourself up from the inside out wondering about it: Howard's not the first man I've killed."

Jane swallowed dryly. "I suspected that."

"I don't go around making a habit of it, you understand."

"I should hope not."

"Truth is, all the other killing I've done was—"

"All the other!"

Not looking at her, Bundy said easily, "Eight, nine years back, I killed my share of Frenchmen and Indians."

"You were in the army?" He nodded. "But, you must have been just a boy."

"I was older than you are now. Not by much, but I

was older." Glancing at her, he noted her surprise and
grinned. "I got a boyish face."

Jane found herself smiling back uncertainly.

Just up ahead, Jane could see the turn off, where the
road into Hook's Head met the one running south to
Dillard's Point and north to Papsqua Creek. They were
approaching the crossroads when they heard another
rider approaching. With fear rampant in her eyes, Jane
looked to Bundy.

"Don't worry. We got us some insurance this time."
And he pulled Thom Howard's knife out of his belt and
concealed it on the seat between his thighs, within easy
reach.

Like Thom Howard, this man also stopped them in
the middle of the road.

"Good day to you, madam," he said, touching a
finger to the brim of his hat as he had done a few
afternoons before. "I see you found your way safely to
Hook's Head . . . and into friendly company, as well, I
trust?" he added, eyeing Bundy suspiciously.

"Indeed, yes," Jane said, marveling that she had
found breath for the words. "Thanks be to you, sir."

The gentleman smiled. "It well may be with thanks to
me that you find your way safely away from it—Mistress
Seymour."

Jane's facade of a smile disappeared. "You mistake
me, sir."

"I think not," he said, sounding far too sure of
himself. "I heard that Damon had taken himself a
bride—a very young, very pretty bride. After seeing the
fliers he has circulated, I very much doubt that I am
mistaken."

"Doubt it or not, as it suits you," Bundy said with a
disarming smile as he casually draped a hand over a
thigh so that his fingers touched the knife's handle. "But
the fact of it is, this lady's my wife."

"Indeed. Then it would be of no interest to you at all

to know that I am master of a vessel bound for New York on the morrow's tide—and that I am no friend to Damon Seymour."

He pronounced Damon's name with such loathing that both Jane and Bundy found it hard to doubt him. They exchanged cautious glances, then Bundy said, "We've seen those bulletins, too. Seems there's a tidy profit to be had by the man lucky enough to return Seymour's property."

The gentleman sea captain shrugged. "Whether you, sir, trust me or not is of no matter. But for the sake of the lady . . ." His glance slewed to Jane's. "I warn you, Mistress, no one boards a vessel out of Maryland without having to walk under the nose of a constable or two." He let the import of his words sink in, then added, "My sloop is anchored in a cove just down the coast. I can have you and your maid—your 'husband,' too, if you like—in Dillard's Point by nightfall, aboard the *Lady Alice* under cover of darkness, and in New York before week's end. Consider it quickly, please. The tide is on the ebb, and I must put out within the hour."

Wheeling his horse, he rode back the way he had come.

"I don't trust him," Bundy said while the man was yet in sight. "We'll go on as we planned."

But when he lifted the reins, Jane stayed his hand with her own. "He was honest enough with me a few days ago. I should rather not discover for myself that he is also telling the truth about the constables."

# PART II

November, 1771 - October, 1772

# 1

" 'Tis not up to me, Anna, I want you to know that," the matronly woman said, pulling her shawl closer against the frosty night. "I'd keep you on if I could. You're as good a gal as we've had in the place but . . ." Her eyes dropped to the bulge which Jane's apron poorly concealed. "Mr. McComisky's a businessman and—the truth of 'tis—there's not many a man's going to tarry over an extra tankard of ale for a bit of a flirt with a barmaid what's in the same condition as the wife he left at home."

"I cannot help my 'condition,' Mistress McComisky," Jane said.

"Of course you can't, lamb."

"Then am I to be punished for it?"

"Oh, child! 'Tis his own best interests the mister has in mind, not hurting you. And 'tisn't as though you're being tossed out with the rubbish. After the babe's weaned, if you want to come back here, you'll be welcomed. In the meanwhile, you've that fine young husband to look after you."

"Bundy's out of work. I told you that last week." Mrs. McComisky's eyes fell, and Jane choked down her pride for the hundredth time since reaching New York to plead, "Please, if you could only talk to your husband

and convince him to let me stay on, just until Bundy finds work. I—"

"His mind's set, Anna. And he's already found a new girl. She starts tomorrow. God bless you, lamb." Turning in the kitchen doorway, the woman was quickly inside, leaving Jane standing in the dark back alley, staring at a closed door.

Jane wasn't surprised by her dismissal. For weeks, as her pregnancy slowly became more apparent, fewer extra pennies had been tossed onto her bar tray; fewer hands had slipped under her skirt; fewer lewd suggestions and lustful glances had come her way as she went stoically but cheerfully about her chores. Mr. McComisky was right: Men wanted a pretty face with a figure to match it serving them their ale.

And Jane wouldn't miss the job. She had hated working in the tavern! But, awful as it had been, it had paid well enough for her to save a bit for the midwife she would need in another dozen weeks or so. But now, with both herself and Bundy out of work, she supposed those meager savings would have to be put to more immediate use.

Heaving a sigh, Jane pulled her woolen shawl up over her head. Holding the shawl close under her chin with one hand, she fingered the hilt of the stiletto tucked into the waistband of her apron with the other. She had never had cause to use the knife that Bundy insisted she carry, and she wasn't sure she could if she had to, but it was comforting to know it was there. A lady was wise to have protection at hand in a place like this.

Like other seaports, New York was largely a city of vagrants. There were sailors looking for berths on ships; newly arrived settlers looking for work; fugitives from almost any country one could name looking for anonymity. And preying on them and the citizenry alike were rapscallions and ne'er-do-wells the like of which made long-dead Thom Howard look a saint.

a wife, the prettiest, dearest little wife a man could have. I told him her name is Anna. He said we're welcome to the room."

Grasping at straws, she had argued, "But my name isn't Anna and I'm not your wife."

"To me you're Anna," he had said. "In my dreams you've always been Anna. And in my dreams you're my wife, too." He had leaned toward her, then, to peer earnestly into her eyes. "Why do you think I came away with you? Do you think I'd have left Raven's Oak and the finest job I'm ever likely to see if not for you? Don't you know I would've spent my life there, waiting for a look at you, hoping for a minute alone with you, loving you more than any man has ever loved you; more than any man ever will? How can you not know that, Anna?"

Even now, Jane could feel the longing that had coursed across the room to her. She had felt that same warm pulse in the air between them dozens of times since that night. She had felt him stroking her with his eyes.

But, in all the nights since then, even though they had taken the room behind the harness shop and slept there together—she in the bed, he in a blanket roll on the floor—he had never touched her as she knew he longed to do. Despite the fact that her heart and her conscience would not allow her to do otherwise, she often felt guilty in denying him her bed. And, when he had left the room one night, not returning until nearly dawn, she had hated herself for having driven him into the arms of a harlot when it would have been such a simple thing to welcome him into hers.

And yet, he neither blamed nor resented her, a fact which only made her feel worse. As had his reaction to the news that she was with child.

Though she knew that the prospect of having another mouth to feed must have worried him, he had smiled and said, "We'll christen it Newell, as if it was mine. I'll love it, Anna. It'll be as much a part of you as any child of mine would be."

He had taken to working most of the night after that, making or mending nearly as much harness as he did by day. Mr. Drummond, being a fair man, had rewarded his efforts with an increase in pay, which Bundy had cheerfully spent on the shiny apple or plump fish which he proudly presented to Jane almost every noon. "You're eatin' barely enough for one, yet you're feedin' two. This here's for the baby," he had said more than once. Watching him work so hard for her had made Jane's guilt redouble.

Thus she'd been driven to find work. There were precious few jobs a woman could fill, and Jane was ill-qualified for most of them. But she could cook and bake, and New York had taverns and coffeehouses aplenty. Unfortunately, most of them had no need of a cook. But at the *Soaring Gull* the McComiskies had welcomed her with open arms—mistaking her for an applicant for the newly vacated position of barmaid.

"I won't have it, Anna!" Bundy had ranted. "It's beneath you. I'll not have you workin' at anything at all, *least of all* traipsing through a taproom and being leered at by every drunken sot in the place! And how long do you suppose you can work? You're with child, Anna!"

"I'll work as long as I'm able."

"I'll not have you work at all!"

"That's not for you to say."

He had said nothing more about it, but he had purchased the stiletto, and had met her every evening to see her safely home. She had hoped, in time, he would be proud of her for helping to set them on their feet. But he showed no sign of that. And, even now, he would not take her wages in his hand but shunned them, as if they were ill-gotten gains.

Then, as if matters were not already bad enough, last week the world had collapsed about their ears. Mr.

Drummond had suddenly died. Within days, the old man's nephew had taken over the shop and thrown them out, bag and baggage, and without Bundy's last week's pay. It was then that Jane had looked into Bundy's face and seen a broken man. After venting his spleen on Drummond's nephew, he had dragged her at breakneck speed to the cheapest inn he could find. He'd rented them a shabby room, then spent precious money on a three gill flagon of rum.

That night, for the first time since she had started working, he had not met her afterwards. It seemed to be becoming a habit, now. She supposed that tonight, like every other since Fate had frowned upon him, she would walk into the squalid cubbyhole that passed for their room to find Bundy cuddling an empty flagon to his chest like a suckling babe.

She was mulling over Bundy's destructive self-pity when she became aware of the wagon and team pacing her along the deserted street. Her heart fluttered nervously, as she tightened her grip on the knife, kept her head down, and hurried on.

"Can I offer you a ride, ma'am?"

Jane broke into an awkward jog.

"Hey!" the driver yelled. "Hey! For cripe's sake, Anna, it's me!"

Jane turned and found she was unable to believe her eyes. "What in the . . . Where in the . . . How did you come by it?"

Bundy leapt down to stand on the cobbles beside her. "I won it." He gave her a gentle boost up to the seat, then climbed up himself.

"Won it?"

"You ain't gonna like this, Anna, and I want you to know that if I hadn't had a few drinks in me, I wouldn't have done it. But, seeing's we didn't have much to lose, and seeing's I've always been lucky at cards, I threw into the pot of a game of jack-draw down at the tavern."

"You were gambling?"

"I only figured to play a hand or two. But those cards," he chuckled, "those cards just kept jumping into my hand—all the right ones! I couldn't hardly believe it, Anna! It was like—like there was an angel sittin' on my shoulder, telling me when to hold and when to draw. I tell you, Anna, I couldn't hardly believe it!"

"God does not send His angels to help a fool at gambling."

"Well, there was somethin' helpin' me. Call it God or call it the devil, I never before in my life won like I did tonight! Git hup there, mules!" When the wagon was clattering over the cobbles, he added, "And this here wagon and team ain't all I won, neither."

"What else? Money?"

"A goodly bit of that, yuh. But something even better." He beamed at her, his eyes sparkling in the cold moonlight. "We got us a farm, Anna. You and me and the baby, we got us a farm!" Jane stared at him. "Ain't you gonna say nothin'?"

"You'll have to give it back."

"Give it . . . What's the matter with you, Anna? Are you moonstruck? We got us a farm! Farming's what I know. It's what you know! Whatta ya mean, give it back?"

"I mean, you cannot take another man's farm, Bundy. It isn't right."

"I didn't *take* nothin'. I won it, fair and square, in an honest game of jack-draw at the New Amsterdam. I got a paper in my pocket, signed by witnesses, that says that very same thing."

"I don't care what your paper says. It isn't right to take a man's livelihood in payment for a debt at cards!"

Bundy looked away, his jaw firm. "I told you, I didn't take nothin'. He threw it away. And if it'll make you feel any better for knowing it, it wasn't his livelihood. He was gentry. Probably has a half-dozen more just like it. It's a tenant farm."

"And what of the tenants? What will become of them?"

"They'll have to get off. It's ours, now."

"You'd evict them? Throw them off land they're working as if it were their own? Bundy, how can you be so—"

His face snapped back to hers. "We were evicted, thrown out of our place, left with nothin'. We've found ourselves another place. They'll have to do the same."

"How can they when you have their wagon and team!"

"This ain't theirs. I won this off another fella. And don't ask me what he'll do without it, 'cause I can't rightly say and don't much care!" Miserably, Jane looked down at her pale-knuckled hands and Bundy, in a voice rife with hurt, said, "I thought you'd be happy, Anna."

If only she could share his enthusiasm without this cutting sense of guilt . . . and dread.


"Are you certain this is the right place?" Jane asked three mornings later as Bundy drew the wagon up before two ramshackle huts.

"Fella back in New Haven said it was three miles out. That there's the three mile marker," Bundy said glumly.

"Where are the tenants?"

"Tenants! Holy Moses, Anna, there ain't no tenants. Don't you understand?"

"No."

"The fella in that card game was a sharper."

"I still don't understand."

"I was took, Anna! Bamboozled! Hoodwinked!" He let his disillusioned eyes roam to the shack that no amount of imagination could make resemble a barn, then over the rocky, weed-strewn ground surrounding it.

"This ain't no farm. Never was. That land's never seen a plow. Just look at it, will you? There ain't a square foot that ain't sproutin' a boulder!" He huffed in disgust. "I'd have to be twice the fool I already am to try to make a go of land like this. There ain't even a well. Probably 'cause there ain't no water!"

"Wells can be dug, Bundy."

He gaped at her. "You ain't sayin' you want to stay here?"

"Where else have we to go?" Bundy looked miserably away and Jane, after a thoughtful silence, asked, "It's yours, isn't it? Your land, legal and proper?"

"I reckon. But that don't change what it is."

Jane shook her head. "You're not seeing what it is, Bundy. It's a *place*, Bundy! It's the only place we have!"

He looked at her slowly, then scoffed. "And what are you thinkin' I should do with it? Start a rock quarry?"

She smirked at him in annoyance. "First, you might tear down those shanties and build us a proper house—there looks to be enough lumber for that twixt the two of them. And then, Albert Newell, we might set out to build ourselves some kind of future!"

# 2

The house Bundy laboriously built from the scrap lumber proved to be something quite fine—a snug, two-room lean-to with the long, single slope of its roof facing north, as his new neighbors told him it should. But the future he set out to make for them there looked bleaker than the leaden, January sky.

From the gathering room window, Jane watched snowflakes spiral down, flipping end over end, softening the harsh landscape around her, making her remember . . . Damon. Laughing. Tossing back his head and squinting at the sky to catch snowflakes on his tongue. Damon, throwing his cloak about her, holding her safe and warm, protected from the storm. Damon, hunkering down to tend the fire while winter swirled against the windowpanes.

She remembered Damon: the strength and gentleness of him, the flickering flame of desire in his amber eyes, the patient tenderness of his lovemaking.

No! Not always patient. Or tender.

Other memories came then, unbidden and unwelcome. But she had no strength to ward them off. They filled her mind's eye with ugly images of the lust-filled beast who had wounded her in body and spirit as no loving man would ever do. The softness that, for a moment, had been in her heart turned again to stone.

"Hulloooo!" Bundy hooted from the larder where he was stomping snow off his boots.

Dashing tears from her eyes, Jane heaved herself from one of the two backless benches which flanked a trestle table and provided the only seating, and pressed her balled fists into the small of her back to ease its ache. "Did you shoot something?" When a brace of rabbits was proudly thrust through the doorway connecting gathering room and larder, she cried, "Rabbit stew! Your favorite."

"I field dressed 'em for you," he said, plopping the half-frozen carcasses on the larder table as Jane waddled into the room. "Do you want me to skin 'em?"

"No. You'd best get out of those wet clothes. Did you see any deer?"

"A few tracks is all. I was lucky to get the rabbits 'fore my flint got wet." He disappeared into the gathering room. "I gotta find steady work, Anna. I still owe Mr. Spence on the musket; I'm runnin' low on shot, and I ain't got the money for molds and lead to make more. Powder don't come for free, neither, *and* we're runnin' low on foodstuffs."

Jane felt a stab of guilt: She shouldn't have mentioned the shortage of cornmeal and peas.

"What about that job as groom across the river?"

"I'd have to live over there, and you know I can't do that!" he snapped bitterly.

Another stiletto-sharp stab of guilt: If he hadn't come away with her, if she hadn't insisted that they settle here . . . Jane rested her palms on the table and stared down into the glazed, dead eye of one rabbit, her own eyes glazed with tears. Then, picking up the cleaver, she whacked off its head and paws, reached for the fleshing knife, and set about skinning it with a vengeance. It wasn't until he rested his hands lightly on her shoulders that she realized Bundy was back in the room.

"I didn't mean to say it like that, Anna. You know there's no place I'd rather be than here with you."

"For all the good it does you!" Her tears fell on the matted rabbit fur. "I owe you so much, Bundy. And how am I repaying you? By keeping you tied to me when there's no reason for you to be!"

"I'm where I want to be, Anna."

She wagged her head. "I'm a chain about your neck. I'm weighing you down!"

His fingers gripped her arms, and he turned her to him. "Don't you think that. I'm where I *want* to be. I'm with you." He cupped her face in his cold, rough palms and wiped at her tears with calloused thumbs. "It's just that I love you, and I want to be so much better for you. I want to give you things—pretties and niceties. I don't want you to have to live like this. You deserve better than what I'm givin' you, Anna!"

"So do you. You deserve a wife."

"You *are* my wife—in all ways but one. And I'm coming to see that the ways you are a wife to me are more important than the way you're not. My life wouldn't be nothin' without you, Anna. Nothin' at all."

By nightfall the gentle snow had blown into a blizzard. And when Jane lifted the heavy bar and opened the front door the next morning, a small mountain of snow tumbled in at her feet.

"Oh, Bundy, I've never seen such snow! It must be two feet deep! And by the look of the sky, there's more still to come." Shoving the door closed, Jane turned to find Bundy pulling on his threadbare coat. She remembered that he had planned to chop wood for a neighbor in exchange for supplies this morning. "You're not going out?"

" 'Course I'm going!"

Jane watched as he snatched the yellow and green striped muffler she had knitted him and draped it over his head, tossing the ends loosely about his neck.

"You'll have to tie it more snugly than that!" she said, irritated for no good reason. While she flipped the fringed ends over each other and tied a snug knot under his chin, she nagged, "And don't forget your mittens. It's colder than cold out there, so keep them on! Don't think you fool me, Albert Newell. I've seen how you take them off outside, then put them back on just before you come in. You'll lose your fingers to frostbite that way, sure as you're born!"

"Criminy sakes, Anna! What set you off?" He smiled. "You're soundin' more like a wife every minute!"

With that, he kissed her soundly on the mouth, clapped his shabby, tricornered hat over the clownishly striped scarf, and marched into the larder. Just before the outside door banged shut behind him, Jane heard him call, "A man can't keep a grip on his axe with mittens on!"

The fishbelly-white sky began lowering toward noon. By dusk, when Bundy, aching in every muscle, started his long walk home, there were four inches of fresh snow on the ground.

It was dark as pitch when he got there, and he almost missed the cottage because there was no candle in the window to guide him. Trudging through the drifts, he wondered if Anna still had her dander up because he couldn't chop wood in mittens. As he approached the door, he thought how good it would feel to wiggle his near-frozen toes—and fingers—before the fire. But the gathering room was as dark as the night, and very nearly as cold.

Had she gone visiting? Impossible! She hadn't gone farther than the well these past two weeks: walking was too hard for her. Groping his way to the table, he lit the candle atop it.

"Oh, Bundy! I'm so glad you're home!"

He pivoted sharply, nearly dousing the candle in his

hand. The cot that served as her bed was still bathed in chill shadow, but he knew without seeing her that she was there. When, an instant later, Jane panted throatily, then groaned through clenched teeth, the hand holding the candle developed a tremor.

"Oh, God," Bundy heard himself breathe. Then he said in a voice that sounded strange and distant to his ears, "I'll light you a fire, then I'll run for the midwife."

He would remember Jane's answer to his dying day. "No! Don't leave me! There's no time!"

In an agony of indecision, Bundy stood poised to run. He could no more ignore the frightened appeal from the bed than he could his utter ignorance of the process of childbirth.

"I'll be no more use to you than a tick to a dog, Anna. A midwife is the one you need with you now."

"I—need—you!" she cried and groaned at once, groping toward him with a desperate hand.

Telling himself how wrong she was, he nevertheless met her reach and felt her fingers curl around his.

As the night wore on, the world might have come to an end outside the little lean-to cottage. And yet, neither the woman who strained to push the life within her into a life of its own nor the man who instinctively cupped his hands to receive it would have noticed. Neither of them noticed, either, the tears of joy that wet their cheeks when Bundy crowed, "It's a boy, darlin'! It's our son!"

"Ethan," she said, reaching down to stroke one pale cheek and to finger the wet, auburn curls on his head.

But the name she had chosen seemed ill-suited. Ethan meant strong; this little fellow looked far from that. But he looked enough like his father to make Jane's heart wrench.

"Ethan Newell. Ethan *Albert* Newell. That sounds fine!" Bundy said, his eyes on the baby he was tenderly wiping clean.

A minute passed. Then part of another.

"Bundy. He ought to be crying."

Concern etched deeply into his brow. "I'll cut the cord. Maybe that'll set him off."

"Do it. Quickly!" Jane said in a torment of anxiety. "Why doesn't he cry? He's supposed to cry right off!" Oh, God. Please, God! "Wrap him up warm, Bundy. Pinch his toes. Do something! Do *something*!"

But though Bundy tried what she suggested, along with some ideas of his own, the little chest never heaved as it should. The piercing, sweet wail of new life never came. And, as the warmth of her body left him, Jane cuddled her silent infant against the breast he would never suckle. Rocking gently, she began to sing a lullaby.

"Anna, don't. He can't hear you."

But, with the little head cupped in a palm and pressed against her breast, Jane unhurriedly finished the song. "I always planned to sing that to him," she said, stroking the cool, downy head. "I wanted to do it just once. Just once." Then, for the first time since he had placed the blanket-swaddled bundle in her arms, Jane looked up from it. With her cheeks wet with tears, she said, "I don't even know the color of his eyes."

A sob wrenched free of Bundy's constricted throat. Sitting beside her, he pulled her close; the cause of their sorrow sandwiched warmly between them.

It wasn't until Bundy spread the sorrowful word and neighbor women began arriving with falsely smiling faces and willing, helpful hands that Jane suffered the truest torment of her grief. Without exception, they spoke encouragingly of the future, of the other babies she would bear, and Jane was forced to keep her torturous secret: There could be no other babies; she was not a wife.

# 3

Bundy's eyes followed Jane as she went about the cottage, chasing cobwebs from cracks and corners. The loss of her baby had changed her. She was distant, quieter than he'd ever known her to be. Most of the time, she acted as though he wasn't there.

What was the matter with her? Couldn't she see it was for the best? Didn't she know that if the boy had lived, looking more like his father every day, he would have been a wedge between them, driving them apart? Didn't she understand that by dying the child had freed her from Damon Seymour, cleared the way for her to start a brand new life?

Morosely, Bundy dipped his pewter noggin into the kettle of simmering cider liberally laced with rum. Jane caught the movement from the corner of her eye and cringed. She felt like a fly caught in one of the webs she was knocking down, a helpless, hapless victim, waiting for the spider to pounce, hoping that, just this once, it would go against its nature and set her free.

But she had no illusions concerning the nature of spiders. Or men. Eighteen years of living and her mockery of a marriage had rid her of those. She knew what was on Bundy's mind, especially when he had had too much rummed cider. He lay awake longer each night and rose a little earlier each morning to stand beside her cot, lusting after her. Sometime soon, he would pounce. And she, caught in the double-stranded web of dependency and gratitude he had woven about her, would be powerless to turn him away.

"I'm going out," she said, standing the twig broom in the corner.

"Where? Where are y' goin?"

"I've an errand in town. Stir the stew now and then, will you? Otherwise, it will scorch."

"I'm sicka stew, Anna!" Bundy roared, standing and kicking the pot, spilling half its contents into the fire. The acrid smell of burning meat and vegetables filled the cottage. "And I'm sick of a whole lot more, too!"

In a trice Jane was across the room and standing before him. "Well, I'm sick of this!" Putting her thin-soled shoes against the hot metal, she dumped what was left of his brew onto what was left of the fire.

She was out of the cottage before he could gather his bestotted wits, but she didn't stop trembling until she was some way down the road. Dear Lord, how long could they go on this way? If only he could find work—or make some for himself.

"Afternoon, Mistress Newell. Fine day we're havin'," the man on horseback said as he passed.

"Good afternoon, Mr. Jenkins. Yes, it is."

But Jane had not noticed the fineness of the day; her difficulties with Bundy, coupled with the doleful errand which had brought her out, blinded her to all else.

Slipping a hand into the pocket of her worn, brown serge dress, Jane fingered the letter. She ought to have written it weeks ago. Venus knew when the baby was expected; she would be worrying. But it had been so hard to pen the words!

"Oh, Venus, I wish you were here!" she whispered.

But wishes were for fairy tales. She would never see Venus again. She had known it, deep in her heart, when they had said their teary good-bye on board Captain Merrick's ship.

Oh! There had been so many good-byes in her life! First Trevor, then . . . Mamá. Papá.

Stopping in the middle of the road, she let the memories come; she watched them flicker through her mind in kaleidoscopic flashes of fire and fear. She saw again, through her child's eyes, the sun fallen from the sky; trapped inside her house; trying to get out. It pushed at the windows, sending a thousand—a thousand-thousand—tinkling, glittering shards of glass scattering into the night as its fiery fingers groped up, up, up toward the smoky stars. And over the shattering roar of it, above the shouts and cries of frantic men, she heard, loud in her ears, her own childish screams: "Mamá! Papá!"

Jane felt no shock of surprise at the truth so unexpectedly revealed to her. It was something she had always known; something which, like a flower preserved between the pages of a book, she had tucked away long ago and only now rediscovered: She was Johanna Ralston, heiress of Southwind, her father's Virginia plantation. Mam had been her nursemaid—had saved her life that long ago night—and she had gone to live with the McPhees after the fire had destroyed Southwind. But . . .

Why had they never told her the truth? She was Johanna Ralston, yet she had married as Johanna McPhee; had signed Parson Dye's paper that way. Surely that rendered her marriage invalid? Why hadn't they told her! Why hadn't Damon? Why had he forced them both to live an immoral lie? And, if he loved her, how could he have allowed the lie to go on so long?

Jane shied away from the answer to that last question, but it was there, in her mind, before she could stop it. He had not loved her. Not ever. Not at all. He had married her for the sake of his honor—and for

Southwind. How naive she was ever to have thought she meant anything more to him!

But she had thought it. With all the intensity and surety of the love she felt for him, she had believed he loved her.

*Fool! You believed what he wanted you to believe. He never meant a word of it!*

But even as the thought filled her head, her heart told her it was a lie. He *had* loved her. It was madness that had turned his love away.

The cottage's interior was swathed in dusky shadow when Jane returned home, but the single, south-facing window admitted enough light for her to see that Bundy was still where she had left him.

"What kept you so long?"

"I—lost track of time," she said, choosing a simple explanation. "If you'll start the fire, I'll see to supper."

"Forget supper. We gotta talk."

Something in his tone made Jane's scalp prickle. "We can talk later," she said, hurrying toward the larder.

In three quick steps, he barred her way. "No. Now. We gotta settle things between us, Anna. I can't go on wantin' you and not havin' you. And you can't go on being afraid to so much as look at me for fear you'll set me at you. We gotta talk now."

But when they sat facing each other across the narrow, trestle table with the dancing candle flame between them animating their shadows on the walls, it took Bundy some time to find a way to begin. At last, he said quietly, "I love you, Anna."

"I know."

"You don't feel much of anything for me, though, do you?"

"I—I feel a great deal for you. It's just that—"

"You don't love me," he said flatly.

"I wish I did, Bundy. For your sake, I wish I could."

"Why can't you?"

Jane looked down at the table. Ignoring the inner voice that cried, *You're weak! I can't love a man who's weak*, she said, "Love isn't something we make happen, Bundy. It either comes or it doesn't, all on its own."

"So that's how you come to love Seymour, is it? As if by magic?"

Jane looked up quickly. "I don't love him. Not—not anymore."

"That ain't how it sounds to me," he scoffed. "You talk in your sleep, Anna. You say his name—moan it soft-like, the way a woman does when a man's makin' love to her, when she's makin' love back."

"That isn't so! I don't love him. I could never love him again!"

Bundy wagged his head. "You ain't foolin' nobody but yourself, Anna. If it's what you want, if it'll make you happy, I'll take you back to him."

"No!" she cried, jumping up from her bench. "I don't want to go back. I don't ever, ever want to go back!"

"Then what do you want?" he demanded, standing so quickly that he overturned the bench. Seeing that she had no answer, he said, "Then I'll tell you what I want. I want you for my wife—for my *true* wife, Anna!"

"But—but you said it was enough just being with me. You said the rest didn't matter."

"That was before the baby. It's different now. Things have changed. You've changed! It can't be the way it was no more, Anna. I can't go on pretendin' to the world we're married, then act like a brother to you when we're alone! Whatta you think I am, a stick o' wood?"

"And what do you think I am, some immoral little trollop who'll lie with a man just because he wants her to?"

"If that's what I thought, I'd have bedded you at the start, and that would of been the end of it!" He stared her down, then asked, "Do you intend stayin' married to him, or don't you?"

"Wh—what?"

"Don't tell me you ain't never heard of divorce."

"He would never divorce me. He's too proud. He could never publicly admit—"

"I ain't talkin' about him divorcing you. He's got a mistress, Anna. Had her for years and everybody knows it. You can get a Writ of Divorcement without hardly tryin'."

So, she thought dispassionately, Bundy knew about Lilith Townsend, too.

"He ain't worthy of you, Anna. He ain't worth one particle of that sweet, pure love of yours!

"Why do you s'pose the neighbors stayed clear of him? Why do you think not one of their wives or daughters came to call on you? It's because everybody clear to Reistertown on the one side and Baltimore on the other knew about Damon Seymour! You know what he is for yourself, Anna. You found out the last few days you were there!" A look of sheer hatred filled his face. "I wanted to kill him for what he was doin' to you. If you hadn't left when you did, so me help me God, I would've done it!"

"He—he wasn't himself that last week. He wasn't always like that."

"He was more himself then than he'd been for more'n two years!" Bundy said. "I grant, it did appear as he'd changed when he started tendin' to business and quit his gamblin' and carousin'. And his bootin' Flygher off the place after what the two of 'em had been to each other, that did come as a surprise. But a skunk can't change its stripe, Anna. We all knew he'd turn on you one day." Hurrying around the table, he gripped her shoulders more roughly than he intended and implored, "Why can't you see him for what he is? Why'd you leave him if he was so fine? Why didn't you just excuse him to yourself like you're tryin' to do to me!"

Jane said nothing, the answer was too damning.

"Listen to me, Anna," he said, the touch of his hands as they stroked her arms echoing the sudden softening of his voice. "Listen to me and believe what I'm tellin' you. I've been trying to spare you the sin of adultery, Anna. That's why I ain't touched you. But the . . ." His voice broke. "But the hell waitin' for us if we give into the devil's temptation can't be worse than the hell we're livin' in! I'll marry you, Anna. You know I will! Just as soon as you're free of him, we'll—"

"I'll never be free of him!" she cried, lurching away, then turning on him. "God help us both, Bundy, you were right. I love him!"

"After what he done to you, you can stand there and say that?"

"He can't help being the way he is, any more than I can help loving him for the way he was!"

"What he was, what he is . . . It's all the same, Anna! I told you, he never changed for more'n the blink of an eye!"

"Maybe that's so, but it doesn't change how I feel."

"What will?"

"I don't know. Maybe nothing. Maybe time."

"You've had time, Anna. Close to a year of it. I can't give you more." Jane heard herself swallow thickly. "I ask you again: Do you want to go back to 'im?"

"I can't. I can't go back."

"Then, if you're gonna stay, you gotta be my wife."

"How—how can you ask that of me, knowing I don't love you?"

"I love you. I need you."

He took a step toward her. She took two back.

"It would be wrong, Bundy."

"Nobody'd know. Everybody thinks we're married."

"We'd know!"

"Divorce him then, and we'll make it right!"

"I can't divorce him!"

Bundy stared at her and felt tears drying on his cheeks. He hadn't shed a tear since he was a small child. "You're saying we'll never, ever, have nothin' more than what we've got now?"

His pale, tortured face blurred before her eyes. But it wasn't until he brushed roughly past her and the larder door banged shut in his wake that she buried her face in her hands and cried as she hadn't since her baby died.

That night he carried his pallet and blanket outside, and slept under the stars, far from the cottage where he couldn't hear her weeping and she wouldn't hear his. Before it was light, he crept into the larder and took the musket, powder horn, and what was left of the shot.

Jane reached the outside larder door in time to see his shadowy form disappearing into the murky, predawn grayness. There was something in the purposefulness of his stride, in the set of his shoulders, that told her he wasn't just out for a morning's hunting, that kept her from calling him back.

# 4

She never once blamed him for going: for leaving her to face the neighbors' questions without answers; to scratch a kitchen garden out of the rocky soil and plant and tend and harvest it herself; to chop her own firewood and split her own kindling. But, while she forgave him his going, she could not forgive the trouble he had left her.

To be sure, he had left her plenty: her self-respect; a sturdy home; the deed to forty acres of land; two mules and a fine wagon. But he had also left her deeply in debt, and he had not left her the means to get out of it.

When word got around that Albert Newell was gone—and apparently wasn't coming back—his creditors began appearing at Three Mile Farm. The first to show up was Mr. Spence, who wondered if he mightn't have his musket back. In lieu of the gun, he took what money Bundy owed him on it. Then the wheelwright arrived with a bill for repairs he had made on the wagon. He was accompanied by a surly-looking fellow by the name of Grogan, who waved a promissory note for two pounds under Jane's nose: the amount of the credit he had extended to Bundy at his tavern. Jane paid each man a portion of what was owed him and dreaded the day when they would reappear for the balance. Then there was the man whose name Jane didn't catch but who claimed that Bundy owed him "a sum of money" for losing to him at cards. He said he would "be pleased to make other than financial arrangements" with her for the discharge of Bundy's debt. When he tried to do that—forcibly—Jane cut his arm with the stiletto she had taken to carrying in an apron pocket after meeting the churlish Mr. Grogan.

And though they didn't press their claims, Jane knew that Bundy owed sums to many of their neighbors for goods they had given him with the understanding that Bundy would pay for them when he was able. Clearly, Bundy would never be able. And unless she found the means to replenish the contents of the empty candle box which, by late summer, was also an empty cash box, neither would Jane.

Seeing only one solution to her problem, she went in search of their nearest neighbor, Isaac Lowe. She found the stocky, middle-aged farmer splitting firewood in his yard.

"Mornin', Anna." He sent the axe whistling down, then stooped to toss the resultant oak logs onto a pile off to one side. "Maggie's over to Crockers'."

"I didn't come to see Maggie. I came to talk to you."

"What about?" He stood another log on end.

"Buying my mules."

The axe thunked into the log and stayed there. "Your mules?"

"Yes, the ones I keep stabled at Thom Bent's. Are you interested?"

He stared at her for a moment, opened his mouth to speak, then clamped it shut again.

"They're good strong animals, Isaac. You admired them last fall, so I thought to give you first offer on them."

He jimmied the axe loose and sent it smashing down again. "It appears as you ain't heard."

"Heard what?"

He stood a piece of maple where the oak had been and rested the axe on a broad shoulder. "Do you know what glanders is?"

Jane felt a tightening in her chest. "Yes."

"Well—" The maple split neatly in two. "They had it."

"Had it?" she echoed weakly. "They had to be—destroyed?"

"A-yuh. T'other day. Thom's mare, too." He glanced at her stricken face. "I thought Thom woulda told you by now."

Blinking back tears, Jane raised her face to the cloud-streaked, September sky and compressed her lips to still their trembling. She listened to the fall of the axe and the raw sound of splintering wood for a few minutes, then asked, "I don't suppose you'd like to buy my wagon? It has a new whippletree."

"Got no need of another wagon, Anna."

"Can you put me on to someone who might?"

Isaac chewed his lip for a thoughtful moment. "Nope."

"What about one of the liveries in town? Do you think I might be able to sell it there?"

"Couldn't do no harm askin'. But don't go to Hardin. Sayer's more fair-minded."

She nodded, but Isaac didn't see her; he had turned his back to stack his wood. "Say hello to Maggie for me, will you?"

"A-yuh." Still without looking at her, he offered as she turned to go, "If you like, you can tell him to see me about it. I'll dicker you a fair price."

Jane smiled. "I'll do that. And thank you, Isaac."

Mr. Sayer paid a pretty penny for Jane's wagon—and for the harness which Jane had forgotten she had, but which Isaac shrewdly threw in to sweeten the deal. The next morning, even though the sky promised rain, Jane hiked the three miles into New Haven with her purse heavy but her heart indescribably light.

Her first stop was the wheelwright's shop where, with an only slightly smug smile, she paid the surprised man the balance of what was owed him and Mr. Grogan's share besides, wisely requesting a receipt for both amounts. Next, feeling that she owed herself something of a treat after more than a year of self-denial, she bought a small tin of tea and a bar of lavender-scented soap, even though the exorbitant price of the former made her cringe. Then, having nowhere in particular to go and no set time to be there, she made her way against the rising wind and toward the harbor, draping her plain woolen shawl over her head as she went.

There was nostalgia in the movement: Damon had once draped a hood about her face and smiled approvingly at the results. Would he smile if he could see her today?

Forcefully, she pushed the thought away. But she could not shutter her mind against the handsome, smiling face with its warm, amber eyes. As it hadn't for a very long time, her heart swelled with love and longing for the man she had at first reluctantly, later gladly called husband. But even as she watched it, the vision in her mind's eye contorted and changed. The smile became a leer; the eyes turned cold. Memories of their last days together ricocheted through her mind, wounding her heart.

How could it be? she agonized. How could he have changed so much, so quickly? But, she reminded herself, if what Bundy had said was true, then Damon had scarcely changed at all. He had started as an evil man, softened for a while, then returned to his evil ways. Full circle.

She smiled sadly. She had come full circle, too. From a dirt farm, to riches and luxury—and the lady she had pretended for a little time to be—and back again.

It did not occur to her that either her circle was incomplete or that she was on her second trip around it, because her memories of Southwind were still fragmented and unpleasant. When she thought of her beginning, she did not think of it there. The farm on Moss Creek had begun her dizzying spin through life, and Three Mile Farm marked the end of it. She would make a life there—the rest of her life—by herself, for herself. She would buy geese and fatten them for market, and maybe she would invest in a cow or a goat, so as to have milk and cheese. Then a chicken or two for eggs, and then . . . And what would she do then? Live alone for the rest of her days? Share her joys and her disappointments with no one? Would she watch her friends raise their children, become grandparents, grow old and die while she, like the ancient widow down the road, doddered on, renting a lean-to room off the gathering room to young people who could fetch and carry for her in her dotage?

It was a sobering and altogether unappealing future. But, what else could she do? She was bound heart, spirit and soul by the vows she had exchanged and the love she had too briefly shared with a man she ought rightfully to hate. There could never be a husband to warm her bed, or children to warm her heart. Never.

Hating herself for the maudlin, self-pitying turn her thoughts were taking, Jane raised her eyes to the harbor, to the ships which strained at their anchor chains as they rode the cresting swells; their bows pointed seaward, into the eye of the wind. She thought how bravely they faced the coming storm, just as they must have faced other storms in other places to which they had been taken without wanting to go. They were tossed and blown by the winds of Fate, and steered by the hands of men, even as she had been.

She stood at the seawall for a long while, watching

them, thinking without being aware of her thoughts until the wind-driven rain forced her eyes away. She had a long walk home. She had better start back.

No. Why should she? She would not melt for being wet. And there was no one waiting for her. No one to fix supper for. No one to account to. No one to care whether she went home or not. No one. No one at all.

But though she stayed there a bit longer, watching with downcast eyes as the rain pockmarked the sea, she could not recapture the mindlessness which reality had driven away. Dispiritedly, she started for home.

But an inspired thought struck her as she trudged along the muddying road: She would send for Venus! Yes! Why not? There was nothing to prevent her doing so, and everything to recommend it. From a purely practical standpoint, Venus was an accomplished seamstress. She could take in sewing while Jane raised her geese and, between the two of them, they could do very nicely, indeed! And on a personal level . . . Sending for Venus was the solution to everything!

She would write the letter this very afternoon and, with luck, she would have her answer—maybe even Venus herself—within a month! Of course, she would have to fix up the cottage a bit—put curtains on the window, at the least. And she would need another cot, and a good heavy quilt.

"Oh, Venus! It will be so good to have you here!" Jane laughed aloud, feeling happier than she had in what seemed like forever and very nearly skipping the last few yards to her front door.

Lost in her excitement, Jane didn't notice the thick rectangle of rag paper wedged between the door and its frame until it fell with a soggy thump at her feet. Picking it up, she stared at it numbly. It was obviously a letter, although the inked address was nothing more than a watery blur. The only person who could be writing to her was . . .

# 5

Jane dropped the handful of pea pods—the season's last—into the basket of her apron and dashed the tears from her cheeks before looking toward the wagon that had pulled off the road and stopped.

Isaac Lowe caught the quick movement of hand to cheek and wagged his head. Why she spent so many tears on that idler of a husband who had deserted her, neither he nor anyone else could figure. She ought to be feeling lucky to be shed of the man!

"Mornin', Anna."

"Morning, Isaac."

"Harvestin', eh?"

"Yes."

"Fine lookin' pumpkins, those. They're fetchin' a good price this year."

"So I'm told."

Isaac nodded and fiddled with the reins in his hands.

"Is there something, Isaac?"

"A-yuh. A-yuh, as a matter of fact there is. I, ah, I overheard a fella back in town askin' directions to your place. He can't be more'n a minute or two behind me. I, ah, I thought if, maybe, he isn't somebody you want to see, I might, ah, visit with you for a spell."

Jane felt her stomach flutter. "What did he look like?"

"Seafarin' man, by the cut of his coat."

Jane smiled. "Did he have a negro woman with him?"

"Not that I saw. Somebody you know, then?"

"Yes. Yes. Thank you, Isaac. Thank you for stopping by. My best to Maggie."

Jane had barely enough time to wash her hands and splash cool water on her face before she heard a horse in the yard. Quickly swinging a kettle of water over the fire to heat for tea, she hurried to the door, tucking wayward locks of hair into the thick knot at the back of her head as she went. Fighting down her rising excitement, she took a composing breath—as Cullingford had taught her to do—and smoothed her apron before opening the door.

"Captain Merrick. How delightful to see you again," she said, her eyes darting past the man to the hackney horse he had tethered to a tree limb. With sinking heart, she realized he had come alone.

"Mistress Seymour," he said, doffing his hat. "May I say you are looking well?"

"Thank you, sir." Jane forced her disappointed eyes to his suntanned face. "Please, won't you come in?"

Seated at the crude table, Merrick watched her prepare the tea; admired the drape of skirt over shapely hips; the full, ripe breasts that strained at the cotton of her dress when she raised her hands to the pewter mugs on the mantel shelf. She was a fine-looking woman. No wonder Newell had killed for her.

Quickly shifting his eyes to the view beyond the gingham-curtained window, he said as she set the kettle and mugs on the table, "New England's pretty in the autumn—the color of the leaves."

"Yes. Yes, it is." She ladled tea into his mug. "Forgive me, Captain, for being so direct, but I was expecting Venus to be with you."

His eyes returned to the window. "She was unable to accompany me."

"She—she is not unwell, I trust," Jane said, breathily.

"At our parting, she was quite well."

"Then, why—"

"Please, mistress, do sit down. I have not come on a happy errand."

Easing herself onto the opposite bench, Jane asked quietly, "Have you come to tell me about Damon, then? That he is dead?"

Merrick stared at her pallid cheeks and tear-sparked eyes. "Aye. I did not expect you would know."

"I had a letter. From Bundy." She looked at the hands she clasped in her lap. "I assume he was hanged?"

"Over a month ago."

Jane nodded stiffly. "His, ah, his letter was vague. Can you tell me how he . . . What happened?"

"Your husband was shot while riding with a companion. She identified Newell as the assailant, and he was apprehended."

"She?"

"A Miss Townsend."

Though he thought Jane could get no paler, she blanched. "Go on."

"There is little more to recount. Damon died of his wound. Newell was hanged."

"Because of me," she whispered, closing her eyes against her tears. "It would not have happened but for me."

Merrick looked at her for a long, silent minute. As he watched, a tear slid down her cheek. It had occurred to him, of course, that she and Newell might have plotted Damon's murder together, but he was surprised to hear her as much as say so. At last, he said, "Newell vowed with his dying breath that he had no knowledge of your whereabouts; that you had parted company in New York. You are held completely innocent of the murder."

It took a moment for the veiled accusation to register in Jane's guilt-befogged brain. But when it did she looked at him sharply. "Do you hold me to be otherwise, sir?"

"I think you sent your lover on an errand, and when he did not return, you assumed the worst," he said easily.

Jane stood, a small, trembling pillar of indignation. She was tempted to show him the letter; to let him see for himself that Bundy had acted alone. She was tempted to scream that Bundy had never been her lover; to protest her innocence in *all* things; to label him a liar and his thoughts and accusations obscene!

She had drawn breath to do so when Merrick said, "I do not fault you, madam. Or your Mr. Newell. He had the courage to do what other men only wished to do."

"Less courageous men like yourself, Captain?"

Merrick smiled at the insult. "I prefer to consider myself prudent, rather than cowardly; I have a wife and four children to think of. However, I'll not deny that the world is a finer place for want of Damon Seymour."

"Why do you hate him? What did he do to you!"

"He deprived me of a sister, madam. And you of a sister-in-law," he said, standing. Then, seeing the confusion on her face, he added, "It does not surprise me that you know nothing of Pamela. Damon was not nearly so forthright—nor so innocent of murder—as you appear to be."

Sister-in-law? Pamela? she thought dazedly. Of course. Pamela Merrick Seymour; Beloved Wife. Renwick's beloved wife!

"No. No, it was Renwick who killed her. Damon protected him. He told everyone it was an accident."

"He was protecting himself! Renwick had no wish to see Pamela dead. He loved her."

"But he was mad; insane!"

"No, madam. It was you, not Pamela, who married the madman. Renwick never was, nor is he now, insane," Merrick said with perfect conviction. "You may count yourself fortunate that Damon allowed you to live long enough to become his widow. You are heir to a sizable fortune."

Jane gaped at him. Damon's widow? She was hardly that, never having legally been his wife! But even if she were . . .

"No," she said, turning and pacing a few shaky steps away.

"I beg your pardon?"

"I want no part of the estate."

"But you are entitled to—"

"I don't want it!" she cried, rounding on him. "I want nothing, ever, to do with Raven's Oak!"

"You would be decidedly more comfortable there than here," he said, his tone deprecating.

"I am comfortable enough, thank you, and will be even more so once Venus joins me. When may I expect her?"

It was Merrick's turn to pace away. Staring blindly out the window, he said, "You may not."

"But you promised that she should rejoin me whenever I sent for her. And as you say she is well—"

"As, I assure you, she was at our parting."

Jane felt a horrible stab of understanding. "You sold her," she accused in a horrified whisper. "You sold her! She had a mortal fear of being sold, I told you that! You gave me your word of honor that you would not—"

"I have not dishonored my word to you, madam!" Merrick said, clearly affronted. "She is not sold, but returned to her rightful owner."

"Her 'rightful owner' is dead!"

"Quite so. She belongs to the estate of which you say you want no part." He faced her. "Or she did, when I left Maryland."

"What do you mean?"

"It is only reasonable to expect—since you deserted his brother—that Renwick will contest your claim to Damon's estate. He may already have done so and succeeded. I cannot know what has transpired in my absence. But I do know that Damon left considerable debts. If Renwick has acquired the estate, he has also acquired its debts. It is likely that he will be forced to liquidate some valuable assets to make good on them."

His implication was clear enough. Jane felt her blood run cold, then suffuse with the heat of anger. "Then you as good as sold her! You gave her over to be sold!" she shrieked, unaware that she had crossed the room to him until he caught her wrist and stopped the slap she had aimed at his face.

"If you are as passionate in the throes of love as you are in anger," he said, drawing her close with the arm that was suddenly about her waist, " 'tis no wonder Newell killed for you. Were I not a married man, I might be tempted to test the extent of your passion for myself." He let her go and Jane, for once shocked beyond words, backed hastily away. "Should you change your mind about returning to Maryland, I sail on the afternoon tide."

"Never!" Jane spat as his blue-coated back disappeared through the door.

She heard him laugh, then call as he mounted his horse. "A bitter word to swallow when one has to take it back!"

Jane stood like a pillar of stone before him, the deck of the *Lady Alice* rolling gently beneath her feet. Meeting his eyes with a proud lift of her chin, she said, "I've come to take it back."

"Have you, indeed?" Merrick made no effort to contain his smug smile.

"Will you accept this in payment of my passage?"

He looked at the long-treasured cameo brooch she displayed on an open palm. "I am not a jeweler, madam."

Jane swallowed dryly. "I shall pay you in cash, then. How much?"

"I daresay, more than you have."

"I have more than you think. How much?"

Merrick smiled his handsome, white-toothed smile, then called over his shoulder, "Mr. Grant! Show the lady to my cabin."

"We have not agreed on the fare, Captain," Jane said, standing her ground.

"Your passage has been paid."

"Paid by whom?"

"A friend."

"What friend?" she demanded as he turned away.

"Prepare to weigh anchor!" he cried, then he shot her a glance over his shoulder and said before he strode away, "An anonymous friend."

# PART III

November, 1772

# 1

For what must be the dozenth time since she had settled into the hackney coach she had hired in Baltimore, Jane counted the money out into her lap. No matter how often she counted it, the total was always the same; never enough.

How much had Damon paid for Venus? One hundred thirty pounds? She hadn't even half that! But she had the deed to Three Mile Farm—that ought to be worth *something*—and the cameo brooch.

She supposed she ought to have had the brooch appraised, but she hadn't wanted to spend the time for that. The Rendell Auction couldn't be more than a few days off. If Renwick was going to sell Venus, he would most likely do it there. If he hadn't sold her already.

Sending a silent prayer heavenward, she cinched the drawstrings of her reticle tight against the loss of so much as a penny, and looked out the carriage window. She caught a glimpse of gray stonework and slate roof tiles before a thick stand of scrub oak and sumac obscured the house from sight. With her heart leaping in her breast, she closed her eyes and imagined the next view she would have of Raven's Oak.

It was early afternoon. The downstairs windows would be shaded by the trees in the ellipse but those of the upper floors would wink at her in the sunshine. The peonies along the front of the house would be long past their bloom, but off to the right, if it had been tended, her garden would be vibrant with the gold and magenta of chrysanthemums and asters. If she looked to the left, she would catch a glimpse of the stables before they disappeared behind the house, but the miles of post and rail fence crisscrossing the pastureland and marking off the boundaries of the paddocks would be visible even from the front door.

And, opening her eyes when she felt the carriage turn into the drive, that was exactly what she saw. But she had forgotten to picture the profusion of black-eyed Susans which grew wild, tall and lanky, at the fringes of the scythed lawns and along the paddock fences. She had forgotten, too, how massive and imposing, and how somber, Raven's Oak was. But, try as she might, she could not forget her last, stealthy leave-taking of the place . . . and the dozens of happy homecomings, with Damon at her side, that had gone before it.

While she stood at the edge of the neatly swept walk which led to the front door, waiting for the coachman to hand down her portmanteau, Jane's eyes leapt of their own volition to the stone-walled cemetery on a distant knoll. And even while one part of her ached for knowing it, another part was glad that Damon was there. Then, with the coach rattling off down the drive and her pathetically light traveling bag in hand, she advanced on the door.

The door swung open an instant before she reached it; Simon's timing was as perfect as ever. His eyesight seemed to be failing, though, for he squinted at her myopically for several moments before his ancient face registered recognition.

"Madam? Madam, it is you!" He grinned so broadly that Jane thought his parchmentlike skin must surely crack. "Please, do come in!"

The foyer looked the way she remembered it, but it felt colder, emptier, without Damon at her side. Half fearfully, half eagerly, she raised her eyes to the wall at the head of the stairs and sought out his likeness there. His father was still the last man in line.

"Please, allow me, madam," Simon said, taking the bag from her hand. "Might I be the first to welcome you home?"

Jane tore her eyes from the sacrilegious wall. "Thank you, Simon, but I—I shan't be staying."

The old retainer's face fell. "Not staying, madam?"

"I've come on a matter of business. If you will be so good as to tell Mr. Seymour I am here?"

"Mr. Seymour is not at home, madam."

Jane was surprised by the intensity of the relief she felt. Despite her urgent need to see the man, she dreaded her meeting with Damon's lunatic brother. Let Captain Merrick defend Renwick's sanity if he would, she put more stock in what Venus had told her. Who knew the true goings-on in a house better than servants?

"When do you expect him?"

"He did not say, madam. May I extend his hospitality in his absence?"

"Thank you."

Looking every bit as relieved and pleased as he sounded, he said, "The southeast guest room has been prepared for you, madam. If you will follow me?"

"Prepared for me? Do you mean he expects me?"

"He has—entertained the hope of your arrival, madam."

But when Simon turned and moved toward the stairs to show her up, Jane stood her ground and asked with her heart in her throat, "Is Venus here?"

"I regret that she is not, madam. However, I shall send the housemaid up to—"

"Where is she!"

Startled by the desperation in her question, Simon

turned to look back at her. "In Rendell, madam."

Jane gulped reflexively. "And Mr. Seymour? Is he ir Rendell, too?"

"I believe he was, earlier in the day."

Where Jane found voice to ask the terrible question she did not know, but she heard herself gasp weakly, "Is this auction day?"

"No, madam."

"Oh, thank goodness! I've not come too late!"

Clearly perplexed, Simon asked, "You've come to attend the auction, madam?"

"No. No, I hope never to see it again!" Then she hurried past the befuddled old man and began her ascent of the stairs.

But midway up the broad, straight flight, her steps slowed and, when she reached the top, she stopped to stare at the picture-hung wall. "Why is Damon's portrait not here?"

"It has been stored away, madam," Simon said, laboriously continuing his climb.

"But it should be there!"

"Mr. Seymour does not believe so, madam."

Jane rounded on the man. "By what right does he make such a judgment?"

"By right of being the master here, madam. This way, if you will?" Simon said, reaching the landing and turning toward the guest wing.

Jane was astonished at how "prepared" her room had been. A bowlful of fresh flowers sat atop the chest of drawers, and a smaller bouquet of asters brightened a windowsill. The chiffonier had come from her room in the master suite as had the pierglass, the washstand with its monogrammed towels, and the dressing table. Crossing the room to the dressing table, she picked up the heavy jewel case. "Why is this here?"

"Mr. Seymour wished it placed here with your other articles, madam."

"They are no longer mine. This, most especially! Please, take it away."

"I am sorry, madam, but I was instructed to place it here."

"And I am instructing you to remove it."

Jane saw Simon's inner turmoil reflected in his eyes, but he reluctantly accepted the case. "Will you take tea, madam?"

"Will Mr. Seymour be joining me?"

"I do not know, madam."

"Is it not his habit to return home at teatime as it was his brother's?"

"I was not told when to expect him, madam."

"I see." Jane fingered the coarse, green drugget of her skirt: It was hardly the stuff of which tea gowns were made! But then, this wasn't a social call. "Yes, thank you, I believe I will have tea."

"Very good, madam. Shall I send the housemaid up to assist you in dressing?"

"That won't be necessary, Simon." She flashed him an embarrassed little smile. "The truth of it is, I—I neglected to pack a tea gown. I'm afraid this dress will have to suffice."

"If I may take the liberty of suggesting that Madam may care to wear one of her other gowns?"

"Other gowns?"

"Yes, madam. Those which you—left behind."

Jane made no effort to conceal her surprise. "He kept them?"

"Yes, madam. In anticipation of your return. I am certain Master Renwick will be delighted should you care to wear them."

Jane's impulse was to reject the suggestion out of hand: She had no desire to see the gowns, to brook the bittersweet memories of Damon they would surely evoke. Still, they were hers, and there was no denying that deep in her woman's soul she yearned to wear something finer than scratchy drugget and threadbare serge!

Steeling herself against her feelings—she would not be maudlin; she would not remember the last time she had worn each gown and what she and Damon had done on that occasion—she followed Simon toward the master suite. But when they had passed the head of the staircase and entered the short hall to its left, she stopped abruptly.

"What stairs are these?"

"They lead to the ballroom, madam."

"They weren't here before."

"They had been walled-off, madam."

"Why?"

"The room was not in use," Simon said, mentally kicking himself for his inability to contrive a more plausible excuse. His wits were failing faster than his eyesight! Unfortunately, his eyes were still keen enough to see the suspicion on young Madam's face, and so, truthfully and the consequences be hanged, he said, "Master Renwick's wife fell down these stairs to her death. It was his wish that they be removed from sight."

Jane felt her stomach tighten uncomfortably. "Why, then, have they been reopened?"

"It has been a number of years since the incident, madam, and the ballroom is again in use."

"Was she . . . Do you believe her death was an accident?"

"It was not proven to have been otherwise, madam."

"Nevertheless, there are those who believe it was not."

"So I understand."

He continued along the hall and Jane, her eyes lingering on the treacherous stairs, slowly followed.

Her former bedchamber felt as familiar as it looked strange: The arrangement of its furnishings was the

same, but the once creamy white walls were now
painted blue. The color's coolness was warmed by the
butter-yellow coverlet on the bed and touches of the
same hue in the rich window draperies and bed curtains.

"It's been redone. And very prettily."

Simon looked at the woman whose eyes and hair
had inspired the room's colors. "I am certain Mr.
Seymour will be delighted that you approve, madam."

Jane looked at him quickly. "Surely, Simon, my
approval or disapproval is of no matter to Mr.
Seymour." But something in the cataract-clouded
depths of Simon's eyes told her she was wrong.

"I believe," Simon began as he made his way toward
the twin armoirs, "that you will find most of your gowns
still here, madam. However, I regret to say, Master
Damon disposed of a few." His stomach churned at the
remembered sight of the tawdry little strumpet Damon
had lustily entertained for most of a week, strutting
about in the gowns young Madam had worn with such
grace.

Jane instantly missed the green silk with the gold
lace inserts and immodest neckline; the topaz taffeta with
the cream-colored lace overskirt; the lilac and blue satin,
which she had never much liked, anyway.

"Did he dispose of some of my day dresses, too?"

"I believe not, madam." The tart's taste had run to
the more elegant and showy evening attire, Simon
miserably remembered as he opened the other armoir
for Jane's inspection.

Forgetting her promise to herself, Jane fingered the
yellow dimity of the dress she had worn to her first and
only Rendell Auction. That had been a bittersweet day!
But she would relive even the worst of it if she could.
Lovingly touching the Kendal green riding habit she had
worn on the occasion of their first anniversary, she
thought she would do anything, endure anything—even
the worst of Damon's madness—to relive that special

day.

Dropping her hand, she firmed her resolve and, with scarcely a glance at it, lifted a less nostalgic dress from its hook. "This one, I think."

With the rose-colored silk draped over an arm, Jane had turned to go when the open door to the adjoining sitting room caught her eye. She stared at it. It had been beyond that door that she had last seen him; last suffered abuse at his once-loving hands. But there were happy memories there, too. There were the figurines on the mantel, caught forever in the graceful if improbable movements of a dance. On a rainy, spring afternoon, she and Damon had laughed until their sides ached at their comically futile attempts to mimic the posturing, porcelain couple. And there was the music box he had given her—just because he loved her—that played "Oaks and Willows." They had danced to it more than once. And there were the books Damon had ordered for her from London, each with its frontispiece embossed "Ex Libris" and inscribed with her name.

And it was there, in that room, that he had promised to give her the world: Paris, London, Geneva, Rome. They would see all of it together, he had said. Together they would make the world their own. The world: Without love, without Damon as he had used to be, it was such a desolate place!

But maybe—maybe it needn't be quite so comfortless. If she had a token, a tiny remembrance of his love, something to touch when she needed to feel close to him, when she hungered to remember the happy times . . .

"Simon? Do you think Mr. Seymour would mind if—if I had the music box?" she asked breathily, her eyes still on the door. But when the awful thought struck her, she looked at the man. "It is still here, isn't it?"

"Indeed, madam, yes. I am certain certain Master Renwick will be most pleased for you to have it."

Jane entered the room on eager feet, her eyes searching out the small, delicately carved rosewood box. They had scarcely found it, on the table between the chairs before the hearth, when she felt her gaze drawn upward to the imposing portrait above the mantel.

She thought her heart would stop, strangled by the tight knot of emotion that gripped it when she met the deep-set, golden eyes that looked benignly into hers. But Damon's coat was claret, not green, and his well-fitted buff breeches disappeared below the knee into a pair of riding boots. In his hand he held a riding crop, not his father's walking stick, and behind him, where there had been nothing but a darkly muted landscape before, the paddocks of Raven's Oak teemed with the progeny of Gilyad's Sun.

"It's a new portrait," she said.

"Yes, madam."

"Then, the other has been stored away?" she whispered, unable to tear her eyes from the canvas. It was so like him! If the other had been a masterpiece, then this one was alive with inspiration.

"No, madam. There was only the one of Master Damon. This is a portrait of Master Renwick."

Jane gaped at him in shocked silence for a time, then said, "Twins? They were twins?"

"Yes, madam."

Staring up at the portrait again, she said in a voice laden with stunned disbelief, "They were so very alike!"

"Alike in appearance only, madam," Simon quietly disagreed. "As I've no doubt you will soon come to know, Master Renwick was always the finer of the two."

Turning on him angrily, she cried in defense of the man she loved, "Not always, Simon! Not always!"

Though his eyes denied the statement, Simon wordlessly bowed to her opinion.

* * *

Jane turned an almost wistful eye on the shabby drugget dress which she had folded and placed across the foot of the bed. Her old dress buttoned in front, while the tea gown . . . Gyrating like an inept contortionist, she renewed her struggle with the laces at her back and wondered for the umpteenth time what was keeping the housemaid Simon had promised to send. But when a quiet knock at last sounded on the door, she did not hear it for the rustling of silk.

"I's come to help you with your dressin', ma'am," the woman said, poking her head into the room.

"Venus! Oh, Venus, you're truly here!"

"Yes'um. And so's you!" the beaming woman said, meeting Jane's outstretched hands.

Jane laughed and pulled Venus into a warm embrace. "I've missed you so!" But she quickly held her off again. "Let me look at you. You look wonderful. Beautiful!"

Venus laughed through her tears. "Lordy, ma'am, I ain't never been called that. But you—you's even prettier than I remembered! Oh, ma'am, I's so glad you's come!"

"I came the very day I heard what had happened. How could I not, knowing how you fear being sold?" Jane squeezed the dark-skinned hands which were again gripping hers. "You needn't ever fear that again, Venus. I've come to take you with me."

Venus's smile faltered. "Take me with you, ma'am?"

"Yes! You know that Mr. Seymour intends selling you, surely? Why shouldn't he sell you to me?"

Venus stared miserably at the floor.

"What is it? Don't you—don't you want to come with me?"

"It ain't that, ma'am. Oh, ma'am, it ain't that!"

"What is it, then?"

"Massah Seymour . . . He ain't gonna let me go."

"Well, certainly he won't just let you go; you're far

too valuable for that. But I have some money and the deed to—'' The anguish in Venus's eyes shocked Jane to silence.

''Massah Seymour, he ain't gonna sell me, ma'am. Not to you; not to nobody. He gonna keep me here, to serve the new mistress.''

Jane felt the bottom fall out of her stomach. ''Has he married, then?''

''No'um. Not as yet. But that's why he fetched me back here, ma'am, on account of he be expectin' to.''

''Well . . . Well, he'll simply have to find someone else to serve his wife. Won't he?'' she said, even while a voice somewhere inside her agonized, ''Dear God, mayhap I have come too late!''

When she went down to tea, Jane was surprised to find the drawing room precisely as she had left it. Her embroidery frame was still positioned beside her favorite chair, as if only an hour had passed since she had put aside her needle. Her likeness still smiled down from above the mantelpiece. But it was only that, a likeness. She felt no kinship with the painfully young, ingenuous girl who had once called herself mistress here.

Staring up at the portrait, she felt a surge of indignation. How dare Renwick deny Damon his rightful place among his predecessors, yet do honor to her? He was pretentious, surely!

Or was it pretentiousness? Did he hate Damon? Was that why he had barred his likeness from the balcony gallery? What if Renwick was neither mad nor a murderer, but had been made the scapegoat of his brother. What if Damon had made Renwick prisoner in his own home? Then Renwick had every right to hate him.

But hadn't Venus said that Renwick had left the house the night his wife died? If so, why had he not gone to the authorities and exposed Damon as a murderer?

Was that because there was no proof of murder? Because Pamela's death had looked like an accident? And why, after having left it, had he returned to Raven's Oak? To avenge his wife?

There were too many unanswerable questions. And what did any of them matter now, anyway? She would leave them behind with Raven's Oak. She would conduct her business with Damon's brother, then be gone as quickly as she had come!


"Where is she now?"

"In the withdrawing room, sir, taking tea." Simon added a dollop of cream to Renwick's coffee, then handed the cup across the desk.

"Has she asked after me?"

"She inquired, upon arriving, as to whether or not you were in, and a bit later as to whether or not you would join her for tea, sir."

"Then she is anxious to meet me," Renwick said, smiling. "She found her room comfortable?"

"I believe so, sir, yes."

"Good. Tell the others that she is not to be treated as a guest in this house but as the mistress."

Simon cleared his throat brusquely. "Yes, sir."

"Does that trouble you, Simon?" Renwick fairly challenged.

"Not I, sir."

"Who then?"

"I fear, sir, it may trouble madam herself. I do not believe she wishes to be considered mistress here."

"Why do you say so?"

Simon looked uncharacteristically nervous. "When I made so bold as to welcome her home, sir, Madam stated that she does not intend to stay."

"That's ridiculous! You must have misunderstood her."

"That is, of course, possible, sir," Simon said with more than a touch of skepticism.

"Why has she come, then?"

"She said, sir, that she is here on a matter of business. Judging by her luggage, sir, she does not anticipate a lengthy stay."

"Damn!" Renwick said, slamming the desk with a fist. "Damn, but I'll not have her quickly gone!" He stood, then paced absently to a window. "Inform the stables: Eclipse is to be at her disposal, but no carriage is to be readied without instruction from me—personally."

"As you say, sir."

"What else has she said?"

"She was—chagrined, sir, upon finding the jewel case in her room. She refused to accept it on the grounds that it was no longer hers."

Renwick's brow furrowed thoughtfully. "Did she, indeed? What else?"

"She requested the rosewood music box, sir. As something of a keepsake, I believe."

Renwick looked considerably more pleased with that bit of news. He smiled. "You gave it to her, of course?"

"Yes, sir."

"Go on."

"She expressed considerable displeasure upon finding that Master Damon's portrait has not been hung, sir."

"Well, well," he said, reaching for his untouched coffee. With the cup poised halfway to his mouth, he asked, "Has she seen my portrait?"

"Yes, sir."

"Excellent. Impatient though I am to see her, I'll not have her suffer unpleasant surprise when I do." He took a sip of coffee. "Tell her . . . Tell her I look forward with pleasure to her company over dinner."

# 2

From where he stood, watching the quiet sunset from a drawing room window, Renwick heard Jane's light step on the stair and the silken rustle of her gown. He heard, too, her quiet intake of breath when she caught her first sight of him—a flesh and blood ghost.

As prepared as Jane thought she was, when she saw him standing there—lounging against the window frame, the curtain caught back in a hand—she felt her knees go weak. And when he turned to her, when Damon smiled at her in Renwick's guise, the blood drained from her head in a giddying rush.

"Forgive me," he said. "I have startled you."

Although she gave it all the strength she had, Jane's voice sounded weak and very small when she said, "Please, do not apologize. The fault is mine not yours. Your likeness to your brother is—astonishing."

"But only superficial. I beg you, bear that in mind." The warm, golden eyes she had thought never to see again smiled into hers. "May I say, madam, that your portrait fails to do your beauty justice?"

"You are too kind, sir," she said by rote. She could not have thought to say it; there was no room for parlor courtesies in a head so full of thoughts of him. Had his eyes really been so bold? So honest? Had she not noticed the few silver strands in his hair, or hadn't they been there before? And the faint creases in his once-smooth brow . . . Had worry put them there? Or madness? No. There was no madness in these eyes, the eyes of her lover.

"Not at all, madam, I assure you. Your husband was a most fortunate man."

"Madam," had he called her? "Your husband," had he said? Dear Heaven, where had her thoughts been leading her! Horrified by her heart's treachery, Jane looked quickly away.

Wordlessly, she accepted his invitation to a seat and did not decline the wine he offered. Like it or not, she felt in need of something to steady her nerves. She'd had too many shocks in too few days.

"I was given to believe," he said, having watched her quaff half her wine in the time it had taken him to fill his glass, "that you did not care for wine."

"As a rule, I don't. Much." Nervously, she took a daintier sip.

He refilled her glass, then, reclaiming his own, he took the chair opposite hers. Settling comfortably back in it, he crossed his legs at the knee—right over left—just as Damon had always done when taking his ease. And Jane, as she watched him, thought again how very like Damon he was; not only in the ways the portrait had led her to expect, but in his manner and his carriage, in the measure of his speech—in everything, *everything*, he was so very like him!

Suddenly realizing that she was staring, Jane averted her eyes. "I was surprised to find this still here," she said, indicating the embroidery frame and glad for having something to say.

"I believe you will find that everything that was yours is still here," he said, smiling softly.

"Even certain things which oughtn't to be," she said, raising her eyes to her portrait. "I should think, sir, as

you do not see fit to display Damon's portrait, that you
would remove mine."

"Your potrait belongs there, madam, as mistress of
this house."

"I am no longer mistress here." She met his eyes. "I
must insist you take it down."

He looked at her smugly. "If you are no longer
mistress, by what right do you make demands of the
master?"

Jane's first thought was to argue that it was *her*
portrait and she had a right to say where it hung—or if it
hung anywhere at all. But she pushed that argument
aside in favor of a better one. "I should think, sir, you
would much prefer to see your own wife's portrait
there."

She saw a spark of surprise brighten his eyes before
he said, easily, "Pamela and I were married but a short
time. Her portrait was not painted. Therefore, until such
time as there is a new mistress at Raven's Oak, your
portrait will remain where it is."

"If I understand Venus correctly, that may not be so
long awhile."

He smiled. "I trust not. However, that matter is
entirely in the lady's hands. Will you have more wine?"

"Thank you, no."

"Excuse me. I believe I will." The mantel clock
began chiming as he unstoppered the decanter. Over
the tinkling chime-bells and the splash of wine into his
glass, he said, "I ought to have had Simon tell you that
dinner will be a bit late this evening, but the truth of it is,
I had quite forgotten I was expecting guests."

"Oh? Then, I'll excuse myself. I shouldn't want to
intrude."

"No, no, please," Renwick said quickly when she
stood to go. "I should be delighted to have you meet
my friends. And you would be doing me a service in
staying. You see, they will be in company with their

wives and . . ." He paused, as if to measure his words. "As the lady who claims my heart was not at hand to accept my invitation, you could, if you will, spare me the ill-ease of being the odd man out."

Jane thought to make some polite excuse, but she heard herself accepting the invitation and felt herself returning his smile.

Renwick had barely retaken his seat when the noise of a carriage announced the arrival of the first of his guests.

"That will be the Rykers. They invariably arrive early," he said with an indulgent smile. But that smile quickly grew awkward. "Might I ask another favor of you?" She nodded. "So far as my friends are concerned, I left Raven's Oak immediately after Pamela's death and did not return to it until after Damon's. Might I ask that you not correct their misconception?"

Jane looked deep into the clear, hazel eyes that surely had never been those of a madman and promised her silence with a nod.

The Rykers were eventually followed by the Wheatons, who arrived just on time, and the Palmers, who arrived late, thereby delaying supper an extra ten minutes which was just enough time to allow Jane to finish her second glass of wine. Then, feeling slightly giddy from the claret and flushed with pleasure at the warm acceptance of Renwick's friends—Oh, if only she had met Peggy Wheaton years ago!—Jane accepted Renwick's arm in to supper.

The seating arrangement at the table was informal, and each couple was left to choose its own place, which resulted in the Rykers and the Palmers sitting opposite the Wheatons, Renwick and Jane. The dining room soon echoed with a *joie de vivre* that it had sorely lacked when Damon had been the unsociable master here, and Jane looked at the man to her right with newly opened eyes. How different he was from Damon, after all! Quite unexpectedly, she found herself envying the absent lady who claimed Renwick's heart, and the happy future she would surely have at his side.

Banishing the unwelcome thought, she raised her glass in a silent toast to the future—however lonely—that would be hers.

"Might I offer a word to the wise?" Renwick whispered as she set her glass down. "As you are unused to wine, moderation is advisable."

"Oh?" she asked with an owlish blink.

"Yes." He chuckled. Then he turned his attention to Simon, who whispered something in his ear. He did not at once share the message, but waited until dessert had been cleared before announcing, "The musicians have arrived. What say you: Shall we gentlemen dispense with our brandy and you ladies with your gossip and join them directly?"

"Oh, yes! Let's do!" Peggy Wheaton cried. Then she leaned across her husband to Jane. "I simply adore dancing! And the best of it is, *here* we needn't empty the parlor of furnishings to do it!"

"Ah-ha!" Renwick said, standing to hold Jane's chair. "You have just confirmed what I have long suspected, Peg: You would have married me solely for my ballroom, had I asked you."

"I am not so fond of dancing as all that." Peggy said, pretending indignation. But she smiled to add, "Of course, you never asked me."

"Lucky thing, that, too." her husband George put in, "else she would have, and where might I be now?"

"Why, you'd have wed Grace Little, of course!" John Palmer laughed from across the table.

"Ahhh! I mightn't have fared so badly at that!"

"Oh! Bite your tongues, the two of you!" Peggy yelped, playfully whacking her husband's shoulder with her fan.

Everyone laughed.

When Peggy tucked an arm companionably through hers as they trooped toward the ballroom, Jane asked, "Is Grace Little another of your friends?"

"Good gracious, no!" Peggy cried. "Oh, I see. You don't know about her. Well, Grace was an early bloomer, you might say. She had the eyes of every boy in Baltimore County popping before she was twelve —and had popped the buttons on the breeches of most of them by the time she was fourteen! It was scandalous the way she carried on! And when Damon cast her aside in favor of Lilith Town—Oh, my. I've spoken dreadfully out of turn, haven't I?" Peggy said, blushing scarlet.

"Nonsense," Jane said, but her smile was forced. "I am well aware that Damon had an eye for the ladies. Lilith Townsend in particular."

"Is that why—Forgive me for asking, but there's been so much speculation. Is that why you left him?"

"No."

"Oh. Well, whatever the reason, none of us has ever blamed you. We all knew Damon, too, you realize."

Jane bristled at the woman's well-intentioned condolence and the slander of Damon it implied. Loyally, she defended, "Every man has some virtue, and few are without vice."

Peggy looked at Jane oddly. "I am sure you are right. Although, I confess, so far as Damon was concerned, none of us could see beyond the vices. He and Renwick always were as different as night and day."

"They do not seem so very different to me."

"But that is because you've only just met Renwick. And you never saw them together." Over her shoulder, she glanced at her host. "Why, every girl Renwick had ever smiled upon thought to die of a broken heart when he married Pamela Merrick. We thought her the luckiest girl in the world!"

"Not quite so lucky as that," Jane said as they began their climb of the ballroom stairs and she found herself wondering upon which tread the unlucky bride had tripped. Or if she had tripped at all.

Taking her point, Peggy said nothing more and Jane, feeling sure that her enjoyment of the evening had ended, wordlessly finished her ascent of the stairs.

The ballroom bore little resemblance to the dusty, shrouded room she had happened upon some two years before. In the soft candlelight, the parquet flooring glowed like satin, and the once dustily swathed windows stood open to the cool evening air. An army of gilded and upholstered chairs, freed from their dust covers, flanked the landscape-papered, mirror-hung walls and led Jane's eyes the length of the room. The door at its far end stood invitingly open now, exposing a comfortable room where weary dancers could refresh themselves with punch and cakes. Even at a glance, Jane could see that there was nothing to hint at its other, ignoble use. But still, she knew. And, watching him smilingly greet the musicians, she marveled that Renwick could put the past so well and completely behind him. To be able to climb those stairs again; to look upon that room, his prison . . . What a strong, commendable man he was!

"Ladies and gentlemen," one of the musicians called, his violin at the ready. "If you will take your places for the allemande?"

"Oh, I do so love dancing!" Peggy chirruped before she hurried off to join George.

"I'm certain I've forgotten the steps," Jane said apologetically when Renwick presented himself and his arm.

"Just as certainly, you shall recall them," he said, smiling and leading her onto the floor.

Amazingly enough, Jane found that her feet fitted themselves to the sprightly tune as neatly as her hands fitted her partner's. And with much less thought.

With each effortless turn under his arm, with each

light, guiding touch of his hand, she was transported
backward in time to the happy hour when Damon had
taught her this dance and the next one, and the breathless jigs and stately minuets that followed. For a time,
for so long as the music and the laughter lasted, she
forgot the months and the heartaches that had intervened since last she had been happy: truly, deeply
happy! And as she danced with this man, who was so
very like him, she danced with wings on her heart.

But when, wiping the sheen of perspiration from his
brow, the violinist announced, "Pray, take your places
for the *Oaks and Willows!*" Jane's heart drew up inside her.
More keenly than ever, she now felt the loss of the
happiness that had once been hers.

"Forgive me. I cannot," she said when Renwick
expectantly offered his hand.

"You know it, surely. And it is the last dance of the
evening."

"Please, I cannot!"

So he danced it with Peggy and got no complaint
from footsore George.

Watching him, hearing the music played as it ought
to be played—a harmony of flute and strings—Jane knew
how wrong she had been to come here. She had known
that being in this house again would awaken the dead
past. But she had not thought memories such as these
would rise to haunt her. She had not expected to yearn
for the past. She had come steeled against remembering
the pain and the hurt and the ugliness that had driven
her away. She had not girded her heart to do battle
against this other. How could she have? She had not
expected to find Damon still here, incarnate in his
brother. She had not expected to look upon the one and
see both! She had never thought that her eyes could
deceive her heart, or that her heart could give rise to
such treacherous thoughts. For, watching him bid his
guests a good night, she caught herself wondering if she

might not recapture with Renwick the happiness she had thought forever lost.

"Did you have a pleasant evening?" he asked, turning to her as Simon closed the door behind the Rykers.

Jane forced herself to smile. "Yes, thank you. But, since the evening was as long as it was pleasant, I shall bid you a good night."

Renwick scowled, just as Damon used to when he was annoyed with her. "I beg you, madam, not to end the evening so quickly. Mayn't I impose upon you for a bit of conversation?"

Everything inside her told Jane to say no—to put an end to the evening and her turmoil now! But there was the business she had come to transact . . .

The music room, like the drawing room, was exactly as Jane had left it: Not so much as the sheet of music on the clavichord had been changed. It seemed the only changes in the house had been made in the master suite—and the household staff.

When the new maid had deposited the decanter and glasses Renwick had dispatched her to fetch and had curtsied her way out, Jane said, "I have not seen Mistress Oswald, or any of those who served here while I was . . . before. Are they no longer here?"

"No. Damon surrendered Eulalia, and Opal with her, in payment for a gambling debt soon after you left. Mistress Oswald quit his employ shortly thereafter. As did Mildred."

"But Eulalia had earned her freedom!" Jane said, sounding as shocked as she looked.

"A point Damon chose to overlook."

"But—but he was always so fair-minded concerning his slaves."

"I beg to differ." Renwick said tightly. "Damon used people as and when it suited him. Fairness was never his virtue."

"He was not that sort of man in my experience!"
"Was he not?"

The accusing question hung heavily between them.
The damning answer hung even heavier in her heart:
Damon had lied to her; deceived her; brutalized her in
unspeakable ways. Yes, he had used her as and when it
suited him. When she accepted the glass of claret
Renwick offered, her hand trembled.

"Do you still enjoy an early ride?" he asked. She
looked at him in surprise. "I often saw you riding
out—with Mr. Newell."

With tight-lipped brevity, Jane responded to the
question—or was it an accusation?—she saw in his eyes.
"I did not send him to murder Damon. I had no idea that
was what he intended."

"I confess, I am relieved to know that." He turned
away. "But I cannot help wondering . . . Had you known
his intention, would you have prevented him?"

She wanted to run: from him; from the suddenly
suffocating closeness of the airy room; from the answer
screaming through her mind. But she stood her ground
and, through sheer force of will, made herself confess
aloud that which she had not admitted even in her
thoughts. "No."

She saw Renwick's green-coated back stiffen and
thought he would round on her; accuse her even as she
now accused herself. Instead, he asked with abject
sorrow, "Did you hate him so much?"

"I did not hate him at all," she said, her voice steady
despite the proximity of tears.

"But you left him for Newell."

"My leaving had nothing to do with Bundy."

"You lived with the man in New York! He admitted
as much to me!" Renwick roared, rounding on her now
as she had expected he would do before.

Inadvertently, Jane took a small backward step. She
had grown used to Bundy's more quiet anger. She had

forgotten how Damon could bellow. She had forgotten, too, how anger brightened his eyes and . . .

*He is not Damon!* she forcefully reminded herself. *I owe this man nothing, for all that he treats me like an errant wife!*

"That, sir, is no concern of yours." She set her wine atop the clavichord. "I bid you a good night."

"Wait! Please! You are right. The past is of no matter now."

"My relationship, or the lack of one, to Mr. Newell, is of no matter to you, sir. But what is past matters greatly!" she corrected from the doorway. "Had I not left Raven's Oak, and had Bundy not followed me, Damon would still be alive and you, sir, would still be locked away!"

After a brief hesitation, Renwick covered his heart with a hand and made her a mocking bow. "It appears, then, madam, that I am forever in your debt."

Jane stiffened. "It is not your gratitude I want, sir."

"Ah," Renwick sighed, straightening. "Which brings us, I suspect, to the reason for your return: Your 'matter of business.' I do not discuss business so late in the day. Might I suggest we take up the matter in the morning?"

"It was my desire to conclude my business today and make an early start in the morning."

"I regret, madam, that we do not always manage to achieve that which we desire," he said, his eyes reflecting the softness of his voice. "I bid you a comfortable night." He turned away and took several steps toward the open French window before he suddenly turned back, a thoughtful look on his face. "Have you never asked yourself why it was that so long as I was in this house, Damon was kind and gentle with you?"

The question startled her.

"And have you never wondered," he hurried on, "why it was not until I was gone from Raven's Oak that you felt the need to leave it, too? You and my brother were alone in this house for but the space of a week. I beg you to consider that, madam. Carefully. You may well find that my debt of gratitude to you can be repaid in kind." Then he disappeared out into the night.

Jane stared incredulously after him. His questions were ludicrous! How could his presence in the house—or out of it—have changed a thing? He had been locked away the entire time! And as for owing him gratitude . . . Jane felt a sudden chill. For all his apparent sanity, Renwick Seymour was most certainly mad!

"Ma'am? It's time you's up, ma'am. Massah Seymour, he's waitin' on you."

"Hm?"

"Massah Seymour, ma'am, he's waitin' on you." Venus repeated as she sent the window curtains scurrying along their rod. "The horses, they's already out front, ma'am."

"Horses?" Jane echoed groggily.

"Yes'um. Massah Seymour, he say you's goin' ridin', ma'am."

Riding? When had she said she would go riding?

"I done fetched one o' your ridin' costumes, ma'am. The green one you always liked so well." She filled the porcelain basin from the ewer she had carried upstairs with her. "And Massah—Lordy, ma'am, if he don't look like a *genuwine* ghost wearin' that ridin' coat! I ain't never seen two men look so much the same!"

Jane sat bolt upright. "He's wearing one of Damon's coats?"

"Yes'um. The nankeen one with the brown cotton velvet lapels and cuffs. He sure do look fine, ma'am! Just like Massah Damon! Why, if you didn't know the difference in 'em, you'd never tell it from lookin' at—"

"Dear Heaven! What is he trying to do?"

"Ma'am?"

Throwing off the covers, Jane erupted from the bed.

"Where are my things?"

But when Venus presented the too-memorable Kendal green riding habit, Jane brushed it angrily aside then stormed across the room to yank open her portmanteau. "Where are my dresses?"

"Ma'am?"

"My dresses! What have you done with them?"

"I sent 'em to be laundered, ma'am."

"Oh, for the love of . . . Fetch me something else, then. Something suitable for traveling. And tell Simon I want a carriage. We're leaving, Venus!"

"Leavin', ma'am? But—but Massah Seymour say you done changed your mind 'bout that last night. He say you's stayin', ma'am."

"He what!"

"That what he say, ma'am. That you done change your mind, and you be stayin'."

"Dear Lord, he's mad as a hatter!" Jane muttered, then she said more loudly, "Do I seem to have changed my mind, Venus?"

"No'um."

"Then do as I told you."

Venus was back again almost before she had gone. "Is this all right, ma'am?" she asked, displaying the royal blue corded cotton dress in her hands.

"That's fine. How soon before the carriage is ready?" Jane demanded, tying a garter ribbon.

Venus's face fell. "I's sorry, ma'am, but Mr. Simon, when I say you be wantin' a carriage, he say—he say there ain't to be no carriages readied 'less Massah hisself say so."

Jane felt a prickle of fear. "Then—then go to the stables and tell them *he* sent you!"

But the answer was still the same, and Jane's fear grew. With an hysterical tremor in her voice she said, "He can't keep me here against my will. He can't!"

Twenty minutes later, in the front hall, she said the

same thing to Simon.

"I am certain that is not his intention, madam," the old butler said, shocked by the fear he saw on her face.

"Then tell him to let me leave. Tell him to let me go!"

"I regret, madam, that you must take that up with him yourself."

Jane stared at the man. "How can you be a party to this? He's mad! Can't you see that? He's—"

"No, madam, I assure you—"

"I'll not be his victim as I was Damon's! I won't!"

Simon's ancient heart wrenched as it hadn't since that long-ago morning when he had found her gone—and discovered the reason for her going. But he said, "I assure you, madam, if only you will hear him out—"

As she bolted past him and out the front door, Simon couldn't be sure if she had actually said it or if only her eyes had screamed, "No!"

Jane was startled to see the two horses and their groom waiting in the drive as she rushed from the house. Willing herself to a semblance of calm and her feet to a slower pace, she said, "I will be riding alone. You may return Gilyad to the stables."

"Yes, ma'am." And making a step of his interlaced hands, he boosted Jane into the saddle.

Without so much as a backward glance, Jane kicked the black gelding into a canter and headed for Reistertown. She would take the post coach to Annapolis, she frantically extemporized, and once there—once there she would hire a lawyer. Yes. She would hire a lawyer to deal with mad Renwick! She would never see Renwick or Raven's Oak again. This time, she truly was leaving it behind forever!

"Bring back that horse!" Renwick bellowed, running after the groom.

"I'm sorry, sir. The lady said—"

Snatching the reins from the man and vaulting into the saddle, Renwick took off at a hell-for-leather gallop.

Seeing the direction he was taking, the groom ran after him, impotently waving his arms and shouting, "Mr. Seymour! Mr. Seymour! The lady, she went the other way!"

# 3

Renwick gave up the pretense of eating and pushed his supper plate away. He had spent all day on the Baltimore docks, certain that if she meant to cross the bay she would embark there. It had never occurred to him that she might take a coach from Reistertown! He had lost her. Lost her!

Bracing his elbows on the table, Renwick buried his face in his hands. How could he live the rest of a lifetime without her?

Simon paused in his clearing of the table to offer consolingly, "I am certain, sir, that once Madam comes to understand the situation—"

"Once she comes to understand?" Renwick parroted sarcastically, shoving himself back from the table so strongly that the china rattled and Simon grabbed for a listing candlelabrum. "She's gone, Simon! Who is there to explain it to her?"

"Perhaps, Captain Merrick, sir? He did fetch her back for you."

"Knowing him to be a friend of mine, she'll not confide in him again!" Renwick scoffed, striding from the room.

He had barely gained the front hall when Simon called after him, "Sir! Mr. Prine asks a word with you."

"Not now!"

"Excuse me, sir, but I do think you ought to speak with him," Simon persisted, doddering after him. "Madam's horse has been returned, sir."

Renwick stopped to fish a coin out of his pocket. Flipping it toward Simon, he said, "Give this to the stableman who returned him, and tell Prine the matter has been taken care of."

Ignoring the coin—which he had not seen until it bounced off his chest—Simon stood his ground and called sharply, "Master Renwick!"

Renwick stopped, a foot on the bottom stair. Simon hadn't spoken to him like that for better than fifteen years!

"I do believe, sir, you ought to speak with him. He seems most distressed."

"Distressed about what?" Renwick asked, feeling like a scolded schoolboy.

"The return of Madam's horse, sir. May I show him into the study?"

"If you feel you must!"

"Very good, sir."

The moment Renwick saw Josiah Prine, his stable foreman, he knew that Simon had been right to insist: The normally composed, articulate man was a stammering bundle of nerves.

"I'm—I'm sorry to intrude on your evening, sir. I wouldn't have if—if this weren't of some importance."

"What's happened?"

"It's regarding the lady, sir. A lad brought her horse in. Found him grazing his father's oat field 'bout six miles t'other side of Rendell. It—it doesn't appear as the lady reached Reistertown, sir." Prine saw his own fear reflected in Renwick's eyes and hastened to give what reasurance he could. "It doesn't look like the animal went down, sir. There's not a mark on him. If he did throw her, he didn't go down atop her."

"She's not been found?"

"Not so far as the boy knows, she hasn't, sir. He says his father and some his hands were out looking for her when he left. I had him wait. If you want, he can show you where they're searching."

But by the time the boy had done that, the light was beginning to fade. Renwick's hope dimmed with it as he spoke with the boy's father.

"I'm sorry, Mr. Seymour, but there seems no point in continuing to search. It'll be dark as coffee in another quarter hour. Then, too, we might be looking for something that's not to be found." The man eyed his twelve-year-old son, then lowered his voice, to add, "A woman riding alone; no sign that the horse went down; some men being what they are . . . You take my meaning, I'm sure."

Renwick did and wished he didn't. It was the one ugly possibility he had not allowed himself to consider. Shifting in his saddle, he surveyed the darkening countryside. "How far have you looked?"

"Clear to the crossroads." He hesitated, doing some quick calculations in his head, then said, "You're welcome to my hospitality for the night. That is, if your men don't mind doubling up with mine. I've a shed that'll serve for your negroes. You could save some time getting a start in the morning."

Renwick's consideration was less than brief. After politely declining the man's generous offer and thanking him for his help, he turned to his men as the others rode home to their beds.

"There is no telling how far the horse may have strayed. We'll separate. Grimes, you and Jonah search between here and the mill. Prine, take Amos with you and work your way back along the north side of the road. Ezra and I will follow the creek. We'll meet at Auction Meadow. If we've not found her by then, we'll return to Raven's Oak for torches and more men."

* * *

Jane shivered and raised her eyes to the colorless sky. It would be dark soon. Already a star twinkled through the interlaced branches overhead.

"Star light, star bright, first star I see this night, I wish I may, I wish I might . . . find something that looks familiar!" And, as she had done half a hundred times before, she turned in a slow circle, trying to get her bearings.

"So much for wishing on stars!" she muttered, hoisting her skirts and doggedly resuming her trek in the direction of Reistertown—she hoped.

It was the fall that had befuddled her. She ought to have given herself time to gather her wits instead of setting out immediately afterward. But her only thought—if she had had a thought left in her head after the jolt she had taken—was to try to regain her horse. But in searching for him, she had gotten herself so hopelessly turned around that even when the fog in her mind had finally cleared she had no idea where she was.

At first she had taken consolation in the thought that Eclipse must certainly be found and that someone would find her, too. But after a day spent wandering over miles and miles of Maryland and with darkness making the woods seem to close in around her, consolation no longer came easily. Darker thoughts possessed her now.

Suppose Eclipse hadn't been found. Or suppose that he had been discovered by someone who cared more for his good fortune in finding so fine a horse than he cared for the fate of its rider. In either case, no one would come looking for her. Those at Raven's Oak certainly wouldn't miss her! The awful truth was that when neither she nor the horse returned, Renwick would simply conclude that she had taken the coach from Reistertown and had stabled the horse there. He probably wouldn't bother to send anyone to fetch Eclipse back until tomorrow!

Footsore, tired, hungry, and with the woods grown so dark that she could not see the ground at her feet, Jane sat on the fallen log that had tripped her and cried.

Auction Meadow was ablaze with torchlight when Enoch Slater joined the men assembling there.

"Mr. Slater," Renwick said, turning his horse to meet the man's advance and offering his hand, "Thank you for coming."

Slater shunned the handshake. "No need to thank me, Seymour. I'm doing you no favor. 'Tis purely that I loathe to think of the pretty little thing your brother's wife was, laying out there with her neck broken. Seymour women have a weakness in that body part, don't they?"

He sneered as he waited for the barb to strike home. But Renwick didn't so much as blink, and it was Slater who looked uncomfortably away.

With a jerk of his head, he indicated the two riders who had followed him. "Where'bouts you want us to look?"

"The woodlands between your place Tidwell's. I'll be on the far side of the creek, making my way upstream. Send word to me if you find her."

With a mocking tip of his hat, Slater jerked his horse around and set a pace so brisk that the slave who carried his torch was forced to run.

"What the man lacks in decency," George Wheaton said from Renwick's side, "he more than makes up in gall! Pray God we find her well and quickly." Then, with a hopeful smile for his friend, he, too, rode off.

When the last of the searchers had dispersed, Renwick said to Ezra, who would accompany him, "We'll cross at Eaton's Ford."

"Yes, suh." Then, eyeing the sky, he said, "This ain't no night to be lost in. Them clouds is gonna dark the moon. Even wit' these torches, suh, we could pass wit'in arms reach of her and never know it."

The freeman's thoughts having come too near to echoing his own, Renwick wordlessly turned his horse toward Ravenswood Creek and into the chill, easterly wind that smelled of rain.

The first raindrops percolated through the dense foliage overhead before they had gone a mile. By the time they had gone five, the cold downpour had all but extinguished their torches and was streaming from the triple-spouts of their tricornered hats.

"Ezra! We'll wait out the storm at the lodge!" Renwick yelled over the downpour and the rush of the creek.

Squinting against the rain and the smoke of his dampened firebrand, Ezra shouted back, "Don't bother me to keep lookin', suh! If little Ma'am be out in this rain, don't bother me to be!"

"And how will we find her without torches?" Renwick's fear and frustration put an angry edge on the words. "We've no choice but to wait it out!"

Jane shivered and wriggled deeper into the straw. It was a godsend, this haymow! Even if she was still lost and wet and cold and hungry, she was out of the rain and off her feet. Now, she had hope again! In the morning, when she could see farther than the tip of her nose, she would find the farmer to whom the mow belonged and ask him to take her home—much as she dreaded the thought of returning to Raven's Oak! But where else could she go, looking like something the cat had dragged in?

Home? Had she really thought of Raven's Oak as *home*? A mental slip, she decided, piling more straw over herself. She wasn't thinking very clearly just now. She was in no state to think, clearly or otherwise, about anything at all. Except how nice it would be to have a blanket and a bed. And how delicious such a humble thing as a bowl of hot oatmeal would taste. And her feet—she tried to wriggle the toes, imprisoned in cold, shrinking leather and winced at the effort. Oh, how wonderful it would feel to give her feet a soak in Epsom salt!

How far had she walked? How could she have become so utterly, so miserably lost? Did she, truly, dare go back to Raven's Oak? Where else *could* she go?

But before she even began to formulate answers, she was asleep.

"Stable the horses, Ezra, then come inside," Renwick said, dismounting.

Taking Gilyad's reins, Ezra spoke his hopeful thoughts. "I'm sure little Ma'am's found a dry place, too, suh. Maybe she even safe back at Raven's Oak, by now."

"Maybe so," Renwick said, his tone anything but hopeful, and his heart heavier than his sodden clothing.

But as Ezra led the horses away, Renwick made no move to enter the place that would provide protection from the storm; the place that had been his prison.

He had vowed never to set foot here again. A vow made long before the night, well over a year ago, that Damon had turned the tables on him and had reasserted himself as master of Raven's Oak. The lodge held uglier memories than that for Renwick. It had too often been the site of Damon's debaucheries, the scene of many a cruel and carnal act. From his teen years, when he had first understood that his brother and such fellows as Damon had called "friends" came here for sport other than hunting, the place had been abhorrent to him!

Why he had not equally abhorred his brother was a question he had never asked himself; one which he did not ask now as he fumbled at the wet masonry near the door, counting the stones by feel in the darkness until he located the loose one which concealed the spare key. He had somehow understood that Damon was not to be held accountable for his actions, although it had taken him years—too many years—to name the demon that drove him to his vile deeds. Even then, he had not despised his brother. One could despise madness, but not its hapless victim.

And Edan Merrick had never understood that, Renwick thought, fitting the key to the lock and shouldering open the heavy, warped door. Edan had laid the blame for Pamela's death squarely on Damon's head; he had made no distinction between the madness and the man. But even if he had, his blame would still have been misplaced. A healthy portion of it rightly belonged to the man who had taken Pamela to live in the house with a madman!

Angrily, Renwick fumbled with the tinderbox on the table just inside the door and lit the candle he also found there. Dear God, he agonized, would he never forgive himself!

Taking up the candle, he lit the torch on the far side of the door. Even in his agitated state, he was struck by the cold austerity of the lodge's cavernous meeting hall. His grandfather had seen fit to pattern the lodge after a medieval castle—though its exterior lacked a true castle's turrets and battlements—complete with wall-blackening torches, unbanistered stone stairways, and a lack of creature comforts which would surely have made even a medieval lord cringe. But, as he had years earlier, Renwick again concluded that it had been well designed for its intended purpose: a bivouac from which bloody forays against wild beasts were made. A lack of amenities brought out the beast in man himself, the primitive, primal urges more civilized surroundings tempered. Hadn't it done so in Damon?

Furious with himself for the path his thoughts again seemed bent on taking, Renwick crossed the expansive, high-ceilinged room to start a fire in the fireplace that was taller than he was and deep and broad enough to roast an entire stag. He had partaken of just such a hunter's feast many times in the days before he had come to hate this place. He had even joined in a few times since then, out of deference to his father's wish that both his sons join him on the hunts he enjoyed so well.

Hunting had been his father's passion. But there had been no bloodlust in his father, no excitement in the killing itself. It had been the camaraderie of friends, the sport of the chase, the skill of the stalk, that had sparked his father's eye. And his own. It had been the killing that had sparked Damon's—the gun in his hand or in someone else's. It was on a hunt that Renwick had first sensed his brother's madness.

He had spoken to no one of his fear of Damon. As a child, he had been unable to put a name to the malicious glint in his brother's eyes; as a youth, he had lacked the courage to name it; as an adult, he had rationalized it away. After all, he had told himself, Damon was not the first man to revel in the power, in the supremacy over life and death, that was innate in making a kill. But there had come a time when he should have spoken out. When the brutally violated body of an itinerant tinker's daughter had been found not far from here . . . He had known in his heart and soul that Damon was responsible. He had known it, yet . . .

Damnation! Renwick seethed, furiously throwing too large a log atop the kindling and smothering the fire's first flames. Why was he recalling all this now? Damon was dead! Why had the past not died with him?

Because, came the quiet, unbidden answer, it touches you even now.

It was true. His present and Damon's past were inextricably entwined. He would not be here now, were it otherwise. He would be home, in a warm bed: Pamela's bed. But for Damon's madness, she would still be his wife; he would be living an empty life with her, thinking it was full. He would never have known true happiness or a love so deep that it was etched upon his very soul. But for Damon's madness, he would never have found Jane—and he would never have lost her.

Renwick was instantly on his feet, pacing and praying; offering his soul to the devil in one mental breath and vowing unwavering fealty to God in the next if only Jane could be his again; not caring which of them answered. And not knowing which to credit—or blame—when Ezra elbowed his way through the door with Jane's limp body in his arms.

"Dear God, is she . . . ?" Renwick stopped short of the terrifying word and sandwiched one of Jane's small, pale, cold hands between his warm ones.

"No, suh. No, suh!" Ezra promised, grinning ear to ear. "I found her in the hay mow, not fifty yards from the lodge. She fine, suh. Just tuckered out, is all. Can't hardly keep her eyes open long enough to blink 'em, suh!"

Renwick allowed himself to smile. "I'll take her. Light the way upstairs."

Jane heard muted voices; she felt the strong arms about her exchanged for other, familiar arms, arms that had carried her often. Once—once so very long ago, now—they had carried her upstairs just as they were now, and Damon had teased as he went, "Tempt me with come-hither glances, will you? I shall make love to you, madam, until you beg for mercy!" And she had laughingly promised, "Then you shall be at it some while, sir. I shall never beg for mercy! Only for more!" He had kissed her then and whispered of his love—just as he was doing now. And then, just as now, she had cuddled more closely against his chest and buried her face in his neck to murmur, "I love you so!"

But before—before Damon had laid her on a soft, feather bed not a straw pallet on the floor. And before . . . Who was he talking to? They had been alone before.

Struggling to lift the leaden weights of her eyelids, Jane was rewarded with a fleeting glimpse of his face. "Damon?"

"I'm here, love. I'm here."

And, miracle of miracles, he was! He was here, holding her; kissing her; stroking her hair, her face; promising that he would never let her go.

"Oh, Damon. Damon," she wept, "I've missed you so!"

"And I you, sweeting. And I you!"

And when he stripped her wet clothing from her and quickly shed his own, she welcomed him to her with a cry of rapture and gave herself over to a lovemaking that was the sweetest she had ever known.

# 4

It had only been a dream. It had merely seemed real because she'd wanted it so much, Jane told herself the next morning. But if a dream was all she could have of him, then she would have it to the fullest! So she tried to cling to sleep, knowing that when she woke, harsh reality must force the dream to fade. But the floor was hard beneath the pallet, and the pillow . . . Where was it?

It was her search for the ill-stuffed pillow which awakened her fully, making her aware of her nakedness—and other things.

Renwick was in the main hall, down on bended knee on the huge hearth, when she found him. And as she watched him from the top of the stairs, her first thought, the one which had driven her from bed despite her swollen, blistered feet, was to take him to task for what he had done. But other thoughts held sway. Hadn't she been his willing victim? Had she resisted him? Had she, even for a moment, so much as thought to? Dear heaven, she couldn't face him!

He sensed her watching him, felt the irresistible pull of her gaze as he had always felt it. He was iron to her lodestone; it would ever be so. But when he turned to smile up at her, he found her hurriedly limping away.

"Jane? Stay there, love. I'll carry you down."

He saw her stop and brace a hand against the wall. But as he jogged up the stairs to her, she rounded on him, wearing such a look of furious loathing that it stopped him in midstride.

"Save yourself the trouble, sir, of pretending to be who you are not! I am fully possessed of my faculties, now. I'll not mistake you twice!" His jaw dropped in stunned surprise and she took advantage of his stupefaction to defame him as roundly as her innocent vocabulary allowed. Taking great satisfaction from the look of pained understanding that flooded his eyes as she ranted on, Jane finally concluded her tirade with, "No honorable man would have taken advantage of me as you did! You knew I thought you were Damon!"

"Yes," he said tightly, "I thought you knew I was Damon."

Jane stared at him. That wasn't what she had said at all. It most certainly wasn't what she had meant! But when she tried to say so, he cut her off.

"Look at me, Jane! Look at my eyes! You found the difference between us there before. You said the eyes in Damon's portrait were cold. What you saw in them was madness. Do you see that in mine, or are these the eyes of the man you knew as Damon?"

He saw the anger and defiance drain out of her. The firm set of her mouth soften as she grappled with a truth that was too impossible for her to grasp. And he stood patiently a few steps below her, steadily holding the eyes that bored into his.

"You are," she whispered incredulously. "You're Damon!"

He wagged his head in slow denial. "I am the man you *called* Damon; the man who took you to wife; who came to love you more than he has ever loved—"

"No."

"It's true, Jane. The proof is there, inscribed inside

your ring: To Jane, ever my love—and my initials. Mine,
Jane, not his!"

She had no need to look at the ring; the truth was
written in his glowing, amber eyes. But she shrank from
it, even as she shrank from him. Because if he was
Damon—the man she had called Damon—then he was
also the man whose savage madness had driven her
away!

Renwick saw fear replace disbelief in her eyes and
knew—Dear God, how he wished he didn't!—what had
put it there. Suddenly, he was afraid, too: He had
convinced her too well!

"You don't understand, Jane. You don't—"

"I do!" she cried, backing away as he finished his
climb of the stairs. "You lied to me, used me, deceived
me! You—you made a slattern of me with your mockery
of a marriage!"

He stopped, stunned by the naked terror he saw in
her tearing eyes. "I lied to you, yes. About many things.
For that, God knows, I am sorry! But I love you, Jane. I
have never lied to you about that!"

"I don't believe you!"

"I believed you," he countered quietly, his hurt plain
on his face. "Was your love a lie? Were you playing out
a charade in my arms last night?"

Jane groped behind her, seeking the support of the
wall. "You defiled my love—and me—the last week I was
the woman you called your wife!"

"That was not me, Jane. That was Damon!"

"You were Damon!"

"Not then! Not that week! I was here—here—as much
his prisoner as he had ever been mine, and so frantic
with worry for you that even Simon thought I was mad!"
He paused, then implored, "How could you not have
known? How could you have thought that I would—"

"Because I knew nothing! You never allowed me to
know! You kept everything from me. Everything! Why?

Why!"

Her anguish tore at him. She had every right to demand to know his reasons for having done what he had. Every right! But what had seemed so rational, so justifiable before, seemed insufferably arrogant and selfish now. Still, she deserved to know, to hear him do penance for his well-intentioned sins against her.

"It was the only thing I could do, Jane—to put myself in Damon's place. There was the marriage contract, my father's honor to uphold, and I could not—"

"What of *my* honor! Did it never occur to you that in honoring your father you were dishonoring me!"

"I was protecting you! You saw what Damon was. Would you really rather have suffered death at his hands than dishonor at mine? I could never have lived with myself had I turned you over to him!"

"But you could live with lying to me," she accused. "You, who always spoke so highly of honor! Why didn't you tell me what you'd done? Why did you let the lie go on so long?"

He wagged his head, guilt and self-condemnation showing in his eyes. "At first, I saw no reason to tell you. It was enough that I had accomplished what I had set out to do by marrying you. And later . . . later, after I came to love you, I was afraid to tell you. I feared I would lose you; that you would hate me for having deceived you, for having forced you into a sham of a marriage. But I *did* intend to tell you, Jane! I never meant for you to pay the price of my cowardice!"

"When?" she demanded. "When would you have told me? After our bastard son was born?" Had she slapped him, he could not have looked more pained. "How could you do that to our son!"

She saw his Adam's apple bob under his linen stock before he asked with breathy anticipation, "Have we a son, Jane?"

The question startled her. She had forgotten that he

did not, that he could not, know. "He—was stillborn."

Renwick looked stunned for a moment, then, blinking quickly, he turned his face away. "I, ah—I thought you might have left him in someone's care. Foolish of me not to have considered . . ." He broke off and it was a moment before, his voice husky with emotion, he said, "I'm sorry. It must have been an ordeal for you."

His pain at their loss revived Jane's own, and she felt hot tears on her cheeks. "Yes. He was all I had left of you."

Renwick faced her, his eyes shining with unshed tears. "We will have other sons, Jane. And daughters—flaxen haired daughters with cornflower blue eyes."

But when he moved to draw her into an embrace, she reeled unsteadily away. "No. Don't!"

"I love you, Jane!"

"You said you loved me before."

"And you believed me, then. And last night. Why cannot you believe me now?"

With tears still pouring down her cheeks, Jane wordlessly shook her head.

The landau, which Ezra had been dispatched to send back, looked every bit as ostentatious and out of place before the hunting lodge as it had in the McPhee farmyard. And, just as she had on that other day, Jane found herself hustled inside.

"Go, Eb," Renwick said to the man at his back, though his eyes were on Jane.

There were no gawking wedding guests, no teary farewells today, but Jane felt a heart-wrenching sadness all the same. Swallowing thickly, she asked, "Do you remember what you told me as we left the farm on our—our so-called wedding day?"

"No," he said tightly.

"You told me not to look back; to look ahead." In a voice barely loud enough to be heard over the clatter o the carriage, she added, "I think it only fair to tell you, find that easier said than done."

The pain she saw on his face nipped at her heart like some wild, rabid thing and she could not hold his eyes

The drive to Raven's Oak seemed interminable, anc Jane was shocked to realize how far she had walked anc how lost she had been. But she kept her astonishment tc herself and her eyes on the scenery. She could see the ballroom windows winking in the midday sun before Renwick broke the tense silence between them.

"Newell was hanged, you know."

She looked at him sharply. "I know."

"Then, 'tis pointless for you to—to harbor any love for him."

"I don't. I never loved him."

"You left with him. You lived with him."

"Not as his wife!" she cried, hating her defensiveness.

Renwick looked understandably surprised. "Why did you stay with him, then?"

"He stayed with me," she said, adding pointedly, "for a time."

"Do you feel a misplaced sense of loyalty to him, then?"

"I feel nothing but pity for the man! Why are you harping on Bundy!"

"I'm trying to understand you! You love me, Jane, you cannot deny that!"

"I don't deny it," she said around the lump that was suddenly in her throat.

"Then why cannot you believe I love you?"

"I believe that."

He gaped. "What is it, then?" Jane looked at her hands and said nothing. "Is it—is it that you cannot forgive me?"

"I forgive you. Of course, I do."

"Then, what is it! What is wrong!"

She forced herself to meet his frantic, pleading eyes. "I love you. I believe you love me. I forgive you. What I cannot find it in my heart to do is—trust you!"


"You be wantin' the rose scent, won't you, ma'am?" Venus asked, thumping the empty bucket down beside the full hip bath. She turned her beaming smile on Jane. "Massah Seymour, he always did like the rose scent best."

"No."

"But, you told me yourself he like the rose best."

"You're confusing them, Venus. It was the other Mr. Seymour who liked the rose."

The slave's expression was knowing. "They's twin brothers, ma'am. Seems as they both like the same."

Jane stared at the woman, then quietly accused, "You know, don't you? Who else knows?"

"Mos' everybody, ma'am."

"How? Who told them?"

"Don't nobody need tellin', ma'am. They's all been wonderin' who was where and who was who ever since Massah Renwick came back from wherever it was he went after Miss Pamela died.

"Then, when you left, ma'am, that's when they started to figure that somehow the two Massah's got turned 'round again. But when Massah Renwick got free o' that huntin' lodge and lit right out lookin' for you, they all knowed for sure that he had been playin' at bein' Massah Damon, 'cause if Massah Renwick was the one who was locked up *all* the time you were here, he wouldn't o' had no business wit' you at all. He'd o' come straight back here, fixin' to get even wit' Massah Damon for puttin' him away like that." Venus paused for breath. "Leastways, that's how Carolina say they figured it."

"Carolina! Is that where you got all this—gossip?

From the slave quarters?"

Venus's expression was grave. "They know down
there, ma'am. They know the difference 'tween the two
massahs better than anybody. Exceptin' you, ma'am."
When Jane miserably turned her face away, Venus con-
soled, "Lordy, ma'am, ain't no shame to you in it. You
was fooled same as everybody else—for a time. But
now . . . You ain't still thinkin' to leave, is you, ma'am?"

It had been a statement, not a question, and Jane
glared at Venus angrily. "Whether I am or not, whether I
go or stay, is no one's concern but my own!"

"And Massah's," Venus murmured.

"No!" Jane threw herself from the bed and instantly
wished she hadn't, her blistered feet burned hot as
embers when they hit the floor. "He has nothing to say
in this! It is my decision and mine alone!"

Venus lowered her eyes. "He don't want you to go,
ma'am. Nobody does. Mos' 'specially me. You goes,
ma'am, and Massah ain't gonna have no more need o'
me, and that's a fact."

The astuteness of the observation brought Jane up
short.

Renwick was entering the mare's death in the ledger
where such events had been recorded since his grandfather's day when the grief assailed him anew. Flipping
back through the ledger's yellowing pages, he
recognized, in fading ink, his grandfather's and his
father's fine hands. How neatly all had been entered
here. Page upon page of equine family trees; records of
sales and purchases; matings and foalings and deaths.
How orderly it all was. How orderly, too, the passing of
pen from father to son, father to son. Where was the son
whose hand would take the pen from his?

He swiped at a watering eye with a knuckle, then put
the ledger away. He wanted to put his grief away with it,

but it hung about his heart like a drape of mourning even after he had turned his mind to other things.

"May I speak with you, please?"

Renwick's head snapped up.

"If you're very busy," Jane said quickly, "it's nothing that cannot wait."

"No, no. An order to my London agents," he said with a negligent gesture at the list of personal and household items on the blotter before him. 'Please, come in."

But as he returned his quill to its holder and stood, he regretted the invitation. If her downcast eyes and grim expression were indicative of what she had come to say, he would have done better to have put her off.

"Ought you, ah, to be up and about?" he asked, eyeing her bandaged and slippered feet.

"I'm much better, thank you." Her eyes darted quickly from his. "You've changed things."

"A bit."

"I always thought that table would look nicer where it is than in that corner."

"Why didn't you say so?"

She shrugged. "It was your study. I thought the arrangement suited."

"It suits me better as it is, than as it was," he said, thinking how ridiculous it was for them to be discussing furiture arrangements when there was so much more to be said. But he was in no hurry to change the subject. "Have you visited your upstairs parlor?"

"N—no."

"I thought you might like to use it, so I had it opened for you."

"Thank you, but—"

"I was never angry with you for opening the room, Jane," he interrupted, not wanting to hear her say she would not be staying long enough to use it. "It was more that I . . . It had been Pamela's little parlor. I couldn't be there without feeling—guilty."

"Guilty?" She had expected him to say almost anything but that!

"I have always held myself partially responsible for her death. She was terrified of Damon. I should never have brought her here. Then, too, I . . . Deceiving you never set well with me, Jane."

She dropped her eyes. She could hear his love and remorse, but she couldn't bear to see it. Instead, she looked to the chairs which, as they had always been, were arranged before the hearth. "Might we sit?"

When they were seated, she said, "I have just had a conversation with Venus and—I've come to ask you to keep a promise you made."

"What promise is that?"

"When you bought Venus, you told her that if she served me well and long enough, you would grant her her freedom. It has been two years since then, so I thought that you might—"

"For the love of heaven, Johanna!" he cried, leaping to his feet. "At a time like this, your concern is for a slave?"

"She wishes to stay here, to be with Ezra, which she cannot do unless you free her."

"Or unless you stay."

Jane stared at him, appalled. "Would you use my regard for her to keep me here?"

He shrugged.

"Why should she be forced to pay the price of your arrogance!"

"Why should she pay the price of your stubbornness is more the question. Listen to yourself! You're putting her happiness above your own!"

"She has a right to happiness!"

"So have we all! And, say what you will, you will never find yours far from mine."

It was a telling point, one which Jane had neither the strength nor the will to argue. "I have calculated—after deducting her two years service—that forty-four pounds will more than recompense your investment in her. I am prepared to make up that difference. In cash."

Renwick looked at her long and hard, then a smug smile curved his lips. "It is my understanding—no, my sure and certain knowledge—that for a period of some fourteen months she was not in your service at all, but in that of Mistress Merrick."

"She served Mistress Merrick at my behest."

"Nevertheless, she was not serving you."

Jane felt a plummeting sensation in the pit of her stomach. He was demanding the equivalent of another year's wage! She had only fifty-eight pounds and change. How much was the brooch worth? Not enough, surely! But, if she gave him the deed to the farm, where would she go? How would she live?

Seeing the desperate dartings of her eyes as Jane performed her frantic mental calculations, Renwick asked quietly, "Does she mean so much more to you than I do, Jane?"

"I will not see her sold again. Not on my account!"

Dispiritedly, Renwick turned away. "Free her yourself, then. She is yours. As is everything that was owned by or purchased in the name of Damon Seymour."

Jane gaped at his back. "What are you saying?"

"I thought Merrick must have told you: Damon died intestate. As his widow, you have full dower right to his estate."

"I can't be his widow. I was never his wife!"

Renwick smiled dryly. "Ah, but a court of law has determined otherwise. Both the Certificate of Marriage and the Reconveyance of Title for Southwind—which you signed as Johanna McPhee—were held to be legal and binding when their validity was challenged."

"Challenged by whom? You?"

He shook his head. "One of your Ralston relations. He had long hungered after Southwind. He is the reason we sent you to be raised by the McPhees. The man was not above chicanery to get what he wanted. Fortunately for you, he failed abysmally. Every inch and acre of Raven's Oak, and all that goes with it, is yours. Southwind as well, of course."

Over the space of perhaps a minute, he watched the mask of shock and surprise she wore eroded away by a look of disillusioned betrayal.

"I don't want it. Any of it," she said in a barely audible whisper. "But you do, don't you? You want it all."

Slowly, he walked back to her. "If I must choose between losing Raven's Oak and losing you . . ." He raised a hand as if to touch her face but let it fall heavily back to his side well short of its mark. "But then, that isn't my choice to make, is it?"

The turmoil in his eyes was almost more than Jane could bear to see, but she forced herself not to look away. "You may have it—everything but Venus. I'll sign whatever papers." She stood, then, and made her way to the door where she turned and said with a miserable attempt at a smile, "You needn't have gone to such trouble, you know—pretending to love me. You could have had it for no effort at all."

"I pretended to nothing, Jane!" he cried, "Didn't you hear a word I said this morning?"

"It's what you didn't say! It's what you kept from me!" she accused. "I'll not be used again. Take your precious estate. I don't want anything more to do with it—or with you!"

When she spun away, before she could bolt down the hall, Renwick caught her arm and turned her roughly back to him. "What *do* you want, then? What do *you* want?" His eyes bored into hers, searing her soul, but she could not look away. "For once, Jane, consider only yourself! You have Raven's Oak, Southwind—a fortune, even after Damon's debts are paid! You have more than most people ever dream of having! But what is it you *want*?"

He felt the fight go out of her, felt the softness return to the taut-muscled arms that had strained against him; he felt the hands that had pressed against his chest in a vain effort at escape lie still and gentle there.

*I want to be with you, always!* her heart cried. *I want to laugh and to cry and to share with you. I want your children; I want to give you mine. I want to feel you near me, surrounding me, a part of me; I want to soar as one with you to the place where your love first took me and where I've never been with anyone but you. I want . . .*

"You," she sobbed, pulling free of his gentle grip. "I want only you! But how will I ever, truly know why you want me!"

"If you can look into my eyes and not see the answer there, nothing I can say or do will convince you of it."

From an upper window, Jane watched Ebenezer enclose the landau against the first drops of rain, then set about strapping the luggage at the carriage's rear.

"Where's you goin', ma'am?" Venus asked from behind her.

"To Southwind. Renwick said the house has been restored. I should like to see it."

"Will you be stayin' there long?"

"I don't know." Jane turned from the window and said with a smile, "But I doubt you'll miss me overly much, what with Ezra to occupy your time."

The blush tinged Venus's face with dusky rose but her eyes filled with tears. "I can't thank you enough, ma'am. I can't thank you enough!"

Jane laughed. "You've already thanked me *more* than enough!"

"Ain't no way I can do that, ma'am," Venus

disagreed, laughing and crying at once.

Jane hugged the woman to her. "Oh, Venus, I do so hope you'll be happy!"

"I hope the same for you, ma'am."

A knock on the door interrupted the embrace, and Jane called, "Come in."

It was Robert Drake who shyly poked his head into the room. "Everything's ready, Johanna."

"Good. So am I." She smoothed invisible wrinkles from her skirt. "Where is he?"

"He's waiting. In the drawing room." She nodded and nervously touched a hand to her hair. "You're sure about this, Johanna? It's not too late to change your mind."

"I've never been more certain of anything, Robert," she promised, crossing the room to him. "Shall we?"

With a courtly bow, Robert offered his arm. Fifteen minutes later, he offered the first toast:

"To the newlyweds, Renwick and Johanna: May the love which unites you endure throughout eternity!"

While the answering round of "Here, here!" echoed through the crowded drawing room, Jane raised her joyfully tearing eyes to Renwick's and knew that it would.

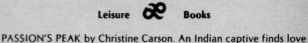